THE CASE OF THE DEADLY BUTTER CHICKEN

The Case of the
Deadly Butter Chicken

From the Files of Vish Puri,
India's Most Private Investigator

TARQUIN HALL

McClelland & Stewart

Library and Archives Canada Cataloguing in Publication

Hall, Tarquin
The case of the deadly butter chicken : Vish Puri, most private investigator / Tarquin Hall.

ISBN 978-0-7710-3829-7

I. Title.

PR6108.A544C37 2012   823'.92   C2012-903429-0

We acknowledge the financial support of the Government of Canada through the Canada Book Fund and that of the Government of Ontario through the Ontario Media Development Corporation's Ontario Book Initiative. We further acknowledge the support of the Canada Council for the Arts and the Ontario Arts Council for our publishing program.

Typeset in Garamond Three by Palimpsest Book Production Limited
Printed and bound in the United States of America

McClelland & Stewart,
a division of Random House of Canada Limited
One Toronto Street
Suite 300
Toronto, Ontario
M5C 2V6

www.mcclelland.com

1   2   3   4   5   16   15   14   13   12

For Ax and the childhood we spent together

· ONE ·

Stripped down to his undergarments and tweed Sandown cap, Vish Puri stepped on to his wife's old set of bathroom weighing scales. He watched with apprehension as the needle jerked violently to the right and settled on 91 kilos.

'By God,' the detective muttered to himself. 'One extra kilo is there. She is going to kill me – certainly if not totally.'

He tried lifting one foot off the pressure pad and shifted his weight to see if it made a difference. It didn't.

'Well, nothing for it,' he said with a sigh, stepping back on to the floor.

Puri checked that the bedroom door was locked, picked up the scales and turned them over. He removed the bottom panel, exposing the crude mechanism inside. Then he squeezed the pressure pad between his knees. When the needle reached 90, he jammed a wooden peg into one of the cogs.

The scales could now register only one weight: 90 kilos.

'Hearties congratulations Mr Puri, *saar*!' he told himself

with a smile after double-checking his handiwork. 'Diet is coming along most splendidly.'

Still the detective knew that he'd bought himself a week or two at the most. Eventually all the lapses of the past fortnight would catch up with him – for lapses read numerous chicken frankies; five or six kathi rolls (he had been on a stakeout; what else was he supposed to eat?) and a significant portion of the Gymkhana Club Sunday brunch buffet (the Pinky Pinky pudding had been irresistible).

He was going to have to lose at least a token amount of weight – enough to keep Rumpi and that bloody Dr Mohan off his back.

Fortunately, he believed he had found the answer to his prayers: diet pills. According to a flyer that had been stuffed under the windscreen wiper of his car, these promised 'miraculous and exceptional results!'

Puri fished out the flyer from his trouser pocket and read it again just to check that his eyes hadn't deceived him. 'Tired of being a big *motu*, but want to enjoy your *gulab jamuns?*' he read. 'ZeroCal is the answer! It contains a special fibre that absorbs fat molecules and converts them into a form the human system doesn't absorb. So now you can carry on getting your *just desserts*!'

Puri chuckled to himself. 'Just desserts,' he said. 'Very good.'

He stuffed the flyer back into his trouser pocket as footsteps sounded on the top of the stairs. They were accompanied by his wife's voice: 'Chubby? Are you ready? We had better get a move on, no? There are bound to be traffic snarls.'

The detective went to the door and opened it.

'What have you been doing in here?' asked Rumpi as she entered the room. 'Don't tell me you were listening in on the servants again with one of your bugs. You know I don't like it when you do that, Chubby.'

'Just I was weighing myself, actually.'

'And?'

Puri stepped gingerly back on to the scales, one foot at a time. They gave a creak, but the peg held.

'Hmm. Ninety kilos,' she read. 'So you've lost . . . three quarters of one kilo. It's something at least. But so far I don't *see* any improvement.'

She looked her husband up and down, scrutinising his stomach, which bulged out beneath his cotton undershirt like a lumpy pillow.

'You still look . . . well, if anything I would say you've got a little *larger*, Chubby.'

'Must be your eyesight, my dear.'

'There's nothing wrong with my *eyesight*, I can assure you,' said Rumpi, her voice thick with suspicion. 'I just hope you're keeping off those chicken frankies,' she continued with a sigh. 'It's for your own good, Chubby. Remember what happened to Rajiv Uncle.'

Ah, poor old Rajiv Uncle. Last month, he'd suffered a massive heart attack while at the wheel of his Mahindra Scorpio and taken out four feet of the central barricade of the Noida Expressway. The fact that he'd been fifty-four, only a couple of years older than Puri, had not been lost on Rumpi or his three daughters. Mummy had seen fit to comment on it as well – along with his three sisters-in-law, numerous aunties, and even a cheeky

3

nephew or two. Indeed, given the great Indian family system in which everyone knows everyone else's business and everyone exercises the right to involve themselves and comment upon everyone else's affairs, the detective had recently found himself on the receiving end of a good deal of health-related advice. Most irritating of all had been the impromptu lecture from his seventeen-year-old niece, whose opinions on most things in life were informed by India's edition of *Cosmo* magazine.

Age still trumped youth even in today's changing middle-class society, so he had been able to tell her to put a sock in it. But over his wife, he enjoyed no such advantage.

'Yes, my dear,' he replied with a prodigious yawn. 'Now I had better get changed. You're right. It is getting late. And I would be making one stop along the way.'

'Please don't tell me you're working, Chubby – not today of all days.'

'Ten minutes is required, only,' he assured her.

Puri escaped into the bathroom to attend to his handlebar moustache, which was looking limp after the rigorous shampoo and conditioning he'd given it earlier. First, he groomed it with a special comb with fine metal teeth. Then he applied some Wacky Tacky wax, which he heated with a hairdryer so it became soft and pliable. And finally, he shaped it into a symmetrical handlebar, curling the ends.

'Pukka!'

He returned to the bedroom to find his wife sitting at her dresser, putting on her earrings. Her long, straight hair hung down her back over the blouse of her lustrous black and gold Benarasi sari.

Puri went and stood behind her, placed his hands on her elegant shoulders and smiled.

'Beautiful as the first day we met. More beautiful, in fact,' he said.

Rumpi smiled back at him in the mirror. 'Still quite the charmer, aren't you?' she said.

'Once a charmer always charming,' cooed the detective, and bent down and kissed the top of her head.

A thick January fog had engulfed Delhi and its unstoppable suburbs overnight. And when the Puris set off for south Delhi at midday – some eight hours before the murder – mist still veiled the imposing glass and steel buildings along the Delhi–Gurgaon Expressway. Bereft of the sunshine usually gleaming off their futuristic facades, the beacons of the new India suddenly looked pale and subdued.

It was still bitingly cold as well. Not freezing, it had to be said, but the short winter always found the vast majority of the capital's inhabitants woefully ill prepared. With no means to heat classrooms, the city's schools had been closed for the past week. 'Load shedding' led to frequent blackouts. And the morning newspapers brought daily reports of a dozen or so deaths amongst the countless thousands living in Delhi's makeshift *jugghis*.

The languid figures Puri spotted through the fogged-up windows of his Ambassador, layered in chunky cotton sweaters, reminded him of Victorian polar explorers in the days before brightly coloured, mass-produced puffer jackets and fleeces. He spotted security guards standing outside the gates of a call centre huddled around an electric cooking ring, chins tucked on chests like disobedient boys sent to the naughty corner. Further on, a gang of labourers breaking rocks in a ditch wore scarves wrapped over the tops of their heads and under their chins, lending them a strangely effeminate look despite the arduous nature of their task.

Puri and Rumpi had spent yesterday afternoon volunteering at a local charity, distributing blankets to the city's poor. Many of those they'd encountered had been visibly malnourished, making them especially vulnerable to the cold. The experience had served as a sharp reminder that for all the growth in the economy, for all the fanfare about dazzling GDP figures and IT this and that, there was still so much need and want. Upon returning home last night, Puri had felt moved to write a new letter to the most honourable editor of *The Times of India*, pointing out that it was the duty of the 'proper authorities' to make improvements and the responsibility of 'ordinary citizens' to hold them accountable.

'With so much of change coming to modern society, it is of the upmost importance and necessity, also, that we continue to uphold the role of *dharma*,' he'd written. 'Dharma has been the underlying concept of our civilisation over so many of millennia. Let us not forget the meaning of the word itself. This most cherished and honoured of words comes to us from the root *dhr* meaning "to hold, to bear, to carry". For both Chanakya, founder of the Maurya Empire, and our great Emperor Ashoka, it meant "law, virtue, ethics and truth". Let us abide by these most honourable of principles, and with them firmly set in our minds, let us remember our collected responsibility to others and one another also.'

His message was evidently lost on the city's drivers. Despite the poor visibility, cars and trucks sped up behind the Ambassador flashing their headlights and honking their horns, and wove through slower-moving traffic like getaway vehicles fleeing bank robberies. Cocky hatchbacks, their side mirrors folded inward, squeezed between other vehicles, making three lanes out of two. The occasional, rusting three-wheeler suddenly came into view, puttering along in the fast lane. And sports cars rocketed past, vanishing instantaneously into the fog. Puri kept bracing himself, anticipating a screech of brakes and the boom of a high-speed impact, but they never came. Could this lack of carnage be attributed to divine providence, he wondered? Or had Indian drivers developed the heightened reflexes of demolition derby drivers given that they faced similar conditions?

Certainly the police played no part in keeping the traffic moving safely. Puri didn't spot a single patrol car along the entire route.

There weren't any hazard signs in place, either. And so it was with a sigh of relief that he greeted the exit sign for South Delhi and the Ambassador was delivered safely down the off-ramp.

A broad carriageway carried the car past the gated communities of the super-elite, where the tops of luxury villas peeked over high walls ringed by security cameras. They passed a series of identical concrete 'overbridges', which held aloft the city's new flyovers, and soon reached the AIIMS spaghetti junction. The detective found it impossible to pass the installation art steel 'sprouts' growing from the embankment without making some disparaging comment, and today was no exception. 'If that is art then my name is Charlie with a capital C!' he said, becoming all the more vocal when Rumpi said that she quite liked them.

She and Puri were still arguing, albeit it good-naturedly, when the car turned into Laxmi Bai Nagar.

'Number four oblique B, H Block, Lane C, off Avenue B.' He read the address from a text message he'd been sent on his phone. 'Behind all-day milk stall.'

Handbrake, his driver, acknowledged these instructions with a 'Yes, Boss' and promptly pulled over to ask for directions.

'*Aaall daay milk staall kahan hai?*' he asked an autorickshaw driver.

'What is this case you're working on, Chubby?' asked Rumpi as they waited.

She rarely enquired about Puri's work (and he in turn usually only told her about an investigation once it was over). However, on this occasion, she felt she had the right to know. It was a big day for her family, after all.

'You remember Satya Pal Bhalla?' he replied.

'That tabla player?'

'No, other one – moustache fellow.'

'Oh God, don't tell me,' she moaned.

Puri gave a knowing nod. 'Absolutely, my dear. A total weirdo, we can say. But he called this morning, only, in quite a panic. Seems he got looted.'

This was an oversimplification. But the detective had no intention of providing Rumpi with the details. The whole thing would sound ridiculous and she would insist on driving directly to their destination, the Kotla cricket stadium, where her nephew, Rohan, was due to play in one of the opening matches of the new, multibillion-dollar cricket tournament, the ICT.

To the detective, however, the case was as tantalising as a *jalebi* to a fly. He'd had to handle a lot of run-of-the-mill work in the past month or so – a slew of bog-standard matrimonial investigations, a mundane credit card fraud, several death verifications for insurance companies.

Worst of all, he'd found himself helping that bloody Queenie Mehta of Golf Links prove that her upstairs tenant was eating non-vegetarian food when the lease strictly forbade the consumption of meat on the premises. It didn't help matters that from the start Puri had sympathised with the 'offender'; nor that the investigation itself had been especially unchallenging. True, the tenant in question had been careful not to place any incriminating evidence in his garbage, disposing of the bones from his illicit meals outside his home. But after one of Most Private Investigators' operatives had followed him to the butcher's and covertly videoed him buying a kilo of mutton, the case had been brought to a speedy conclusion.

Was it any wonder that the attempt to cut off Satya Pal Bhalla's moustache, the longest in the world, had every cell in his detective brain tingling with anticipation?

Who would have done such a thing? A rival for his title? Someone with a grudge? Anything was possible in Delhi these days, Puri reminded himself. With the city's population growing exponentially, corruption endemic, and the elite amassing fabulous wealth as well as adopting

Western tastes and lifestyles, Indian crime was taking on ever-new facets.

Just look at the story on the front page of today's paper. Six months ago, if the report was to be believed, an Indian hacker had accessed America's Pentagon computer system and downloaded dozens of top-secret files related to security in South Asia.

A commentator in the same paper likened these times to the myth of Neelkanth, when the demons churned the ocean in search of *Amrita*, the nectar of immortality. What they created instead was poison, which had to be consumed by the god Shiva.

From this legend came the Hindi saying: '*Amrut pane se pehle Vish pinna padta hai*.' Roughly translated it means, 'You can't have the sweet without the sour.'

Three wrong turns, a couple of U-turns and two more stops-to-ask-directions later, Handbrake pulled up outside the address. Puri's prospective client, Bhalla, lived in a three-storey government-housing complex for *babus* and their families. There were dozens of such blocks in south Delhi, most of them built in the 1950s and '60s. Architecturally uninspiring, painted in the same government-issue off-pink, and only distinguishable from one another by the letters and numbers stencilled on their facades, they had become some of the most desirable addresses in the capital. H Block was set amongst neem trees and small communal gardens known as 'parks', where children played in the sunshine that was now breaking through the fog.

Puri made his way up the bare concrete staircase to the second floor. The sound of hissing pressure cookers came from inside one of the other apartments. A smell of roasting cumin and fried mustard oil filled the air.

Outside the door to 4/B, he found several pairs of shoes lying in a jumble. He unlaced his and placed them to one side. The bell brought an elderly servant woman bearing a pair of rubber chappals.

The detective was standing on the landing trying to get his stockinged toes between the toe rings when Raju Pillai stepped out of the apartment.

'Thank the God you've come, Mr Puri,' he said. 'I'm at my wits' end!'

As was fitting for the Director General and Honorary Secretary of the Moustache Organisation of Punjab (MOP), Pillai sported a thick, black walrus with bushy mutton-chops. He pulled the door shut behind him.

'Satya-ji's in such a state, I tell you,' he said, keeping his voice down and giving a quick glance backwards as if someone might overhear. 'Thought I'd come over to see what I could do for him.'

'Very good of you,' intoned Puri.

'I thought it better we have a private conference before you get the facts from the horse's mouth.'

'Must have been quite a shock, losing half his moustache and all,' said the detective, who was still struggling with the chappals.

'Can you imagine, Mr Puri? Thirty years plus he's been nurturing and grooming it. Cared for every last whisker. That level of dedication and commitment is seen only rarely these days. And then *phoof*! Half of it vanished into thin air! From right under his nose, no less. I tell you, Mr Puri, India has lost one of its greatest treasures. The

Taj Mahal of moustaches! Something of which *all* Indians could feel proud.'

'On phone, Satya-ji said it was removed in the wee hours,' said Puri. 'He was sleeping or what?'

'Seems so, Mr Puri. Must have been drugged somehow.'

'He said also one security guard got hold of the thief but he escaped.'

'Exactly. The guard spotted a gentleman climbing up the side of the balcony in dead of night. Thus he alerted the police, but they failed to arrive. So he took it upon himself to investigate. Quite a fearless fellow, it seems. He caught the intruder in the act and gave chase. Seems a struggle took place. Thus the removed portion of the moustache was recovered.'

Puri finally managed to get the chappals on, more or less, his heels protruding over the backs.

'He is present – this security guard?' he asked.

'The police inspector, one Surinder Thakur, got hold of him for questioning.'

'He was able to make positive ID – the security guard, that is?'

'Not that I'm aware.'

The detective took out his notebook and wrote down Thakur's name before asking: 'The removed section of the moustache is where exactly?'

'Thakur has taken it for evidence. Against all our protestations, I should say.'

'He offered any theory to what all happened?'

'Frankly speaking, Mr Puri, I don't believe he's taking the case seriously. Seemed to find the whole thing amusing for some reason!'

'Our Dilli police are not performing their duties in a professional manner,' said the detective with a solemn shake of the head. 'You've any theory yourself as to the identity of the guilty person? Could be a rival moustache grower, no?'

'Not a member of MOP, that is for sure!' said Pillai, bristling. 'Our members are *all* respectable gentlemen. From well-to-do families, I should add. You yourself are a member, Mr Puri.'

'Yes, but surely—' ventured the detective.

'Each and every member is aware of the supreme effort and sacrifice required to grow an award-winning moustache,' continued Pillai. 'Never have I seen one hint of jealousy aimed at Satya-ji. Everyone is proud of his accomplishment. You recall the reception after he returned from US last year? One and all gave him a hero's welcome.'

Puri gave a knowing nod, loath to admit that he hadn't attended the special dinner that had been held to honour Satya Pal Bhalla. The truth was he attended few MOP functions if he could help it. He'd become a member to do his bit for promoting the growth of moustaches amongst Indian youths (it was, after all, sad and shocking to see how many young Punjabi men were not 'sporting' these days), and to indulge in a bit of socialising and networking with like-minded individuals. But over the years the organisation had been hijacked by a competitive group of individuals. All they talked about was, well, moustaches. And Rumpi, for once, refused to attend any more of their functions.

'I can't listen to the debate about wax versus gel ever again,' she'd protested after the 2007 annual dinner, her last.

Satya Pal Bhalla was the worst offender. A Grade II bureaucrat employed in the Central Secretariat Stenographers' Service, he was one of a breed of Indians who were desperate to stand out from a crowd 1.2 billion strong and therefore dedicated their lives to extreme pursuits. The ultimate prize for such types was an entry in the best-selling *Limca Book of Records*.

Growing his thirteen-foot-long leviathan had brought Bhalla fame and kudos. Indeed, no one stepping into his living room could fail to be impressed by the collection of photographs on the walls, of Ballah posing with the great and the good.

While Pillai went to fetch the victim from his bedroom, Puri circled the room admiring the photos. Mother Teresa; ace batsman Sachin Tendulkar; the father of India's nuclear bomb, Dr Abdul Kalam; Bollywood legend Amitabh Bachchan . . . Bhalla had met them all.

His moustache had also brought him promotional work. By the window hung some framed print advertisements in which he had appeared. One for SHIFT clothes detergent depicted him standing with his moustache stretched out in both directions. Brightly coloured shirts and underwear hung from it. A DEEP CLEAN YOU'LL WANT TO SHOW OFF, read the slogan.

But now it seemed Bhalla's career was over and the man himself looked bereft. His moustache's left tendril had been completely shorn off, leaving the right section still curled around his cheek like a Danish pastry.

'Heartfelt condolences, sir,' said Puri as he entered the room. 'What you must be feeling I cannot imagine.'

'Is no one safe in their own house?' asked Bhalla, as if

the detective was somehow responsible for the break-in. 'Look at me! Look at what is left! I'm a freak!' He tugged at the bare section of his upper lip, his eyes burning with anger. 'I want him caught, Puri! Do you hear? I want him to pay! We all know who did this and I want you to get him! Whatever it takes!'

The detective raised a calming hand. 'Who is it you believe was the culprit exactly, sir?' he asked.

'Ragi of course!' Bhalla's anger flared. 'He's been after my number one status for years! Finally he's found a way to get me out of the way!'

It was true that Gopal Ragi was now, by default, the Moustache Raja of India. It was also true that he and Bhalla hated one another.

'Recently that bastard accused me of wearing hair extensions!' he continued. 'I told him, "Go to hell!" And he threatened me! You know what he said? That if he was *me*, he would watch his back! *And* his moustache, also! His exact words!'

'There were witnesses, sir – to his threat?'

'So many!'

'You can provide names, is it?'

'Everyone knows he threatened me, Puri! Ask anyone.'

Pillai now spoke up, reiterating in an equitable manner that he could not bring himself to believe that a fellow MOP member could be responsible for such a horrific act. But he was shouted down.

'What does he know?' bawled Bhalla with a smirk. 'Nothing! I'm telling you. It was that bastard for sure.'

'The truth will come out in the wash,' said Puri. 'But first I must know what all happened here.'

'All I can tell you is this,' said Bhalla in an irritated monotone. 'After eating my *khana* last night, I felt ill and went to bed early. This morning I woke later than usual. Must have been nine. The maid was waiting by my bed. She was the one who broke the news and informed me the police were waiting. I went directly into the bathroom and looked in the mirror and . . . and well, you have seen this . . . this *massacre*. What that bloody bastard has done to me!'

'You said you felt ill, is it? What is it you ate exactly?'

'*Channa bhatura.*'

'You like it *mirchi* is it, sir?'

'Hotter the better.'

'Who else shares the house?'

'Myself and the maid.'

'No family?'

Bhalla raised his hands and dropped them on to the arms of his chair, clearly frustrated at the line of questioning. 'What has that got to do with anything?' he demanded. Puri's placid, enquiring gaze elicited an answer.

'My wife's no more. A boy comes during the day to clean and do shopping and so forth. He's a new one. Useless.'

'He's present, also?'

'Didn't come today. Inspector Thakur's visiting his home. It's far – two hours at least.'

'He comes every day back and forth is it?'

'Look, I don't give two damns about his travel arrangements. What I care about is Ragi's whereabouts last night.'

'I understand your frustration, sir,' responded Puri. 'Nonetheless facts are required. So tell me: this channa batura . . . the maid prepared it, is it?'

'Yes,' was the laconic reply.

'Any is left over?'

'It got finished off.'

'What time you ate exactly?'

'Eight-thirty.'

'You always eat at this hour, sir?'

'Always.'

'She ate also – the maid that is?'

'Must be.'

Next, the detective examined what was left of the moustache, scrutinising the shorn section of the upper lip. The hairs were cropped close to the skin. It was a meticulous job.

'Expertly done, one can say. Any implements were left behind – scissors and so forth?'

'Nothing was found.'

A honk of the Ambassador's horn reminded him that Rumpi was waiting. He checked his watch. Fifteen minutes had passed. He would have to make his search of the crime scene a quick one and return later if necessary.

He made his way to the bedroom, the chappals cutting into the middle portion of the bottom of his feet so that he was forced to tiptoe. On the bed sheet, the detective found a few shavings, indicating that the work had indeed been carried out while Bhalla lay asleep. There was also some shaving foam residue on the side table, as well as a watermark in the shape of a razor.

But why not cut off both parts with scissors and be

done? Puri wondered. Surely the spiteful thing to do would have been to cut both ends off and leave them lying on the floor – a matter of a couple of minutes' work.

'Why so thorough a job?' he said out loud.

'What was that you said?' Pillai, who was lingering in the doorway, asked.

But the detective ignored the question.

'Tell me one thing,' he said. 'The security guard saw this moustache thief climb inside over the balcony, is it?'

'Came banging on the door from what I understand,' answered Pillai.

'Thus our visitor got panicked and ran away. He went over the balcony again?'

'I believe so. That was when the security guard fellow gave chase.'

Puri headed into the kitchen. The maid, an elderly servant woman, was standing at the counter making *paneer*. She looked scared, but the detective read nothing into this. Servants were often shoddily treated and always fell under suspicion as soon as anything went wrong in a household. Was it any wonder they feared authority?

He began by asking her if it was true she'd eaten any of the same food.

'Yes, sahib,' she answered timidly in Hindi.

'You felt drowsy?'

'Yes, sahib.'

'How much did you eat?'

'A small portion.'

'Where did you sleep last night?'

'The same place I always do. Here on the kitchen floor.'

'On a bedroll?'

'A sheet of newspaper.'

Puri managed to disguise his disgust at the manner in which this woman was forced to live.

'Did anyone else enter the kitchen in the past twenty-four hours?' he asked.

'One man came yesterday. To check the gas canister registration.' She added hurriedly: 'He showed me his identification. He was from the MCD.'

'He was alone in the kitchen?'

'The phone rang after he came. I went to answer it. So I—'

'Who was calling?' interrupted Puri.

'A sales wallah. From the phone company.'

'The channa was sitting on the stove?'

'Yes, sahib.'

'Would you recognise this gas canister wallah?'

She looked down at the floor. 'My eyesight is not good, sahib.'

Puri asked her whether she'd been woken in the middle of the night by the security guard banging on the door and she confirmed that this was indeed what had happened. He thanked her and made his way to the apartment's back door. It led on to a small balcony. There were scuff marks on the top of the wall and down the side of the building.

He returned to the living room. The Ambassador's horn sounded again.

'Vish Puri will take the case,' announced the detective with a bow that was intended to convey humbleness. 'Seems we are dealing with a cunning individual. He entered the premises yesterday afternoon only. Then and there, he added some knockout drug to your channa. So much chilli was present that you did not notice the taste.'

His fee, Puri went on to explain, would be 4,000 rupees per day, plus expenses.

'So much?' exclaimed Bhalla, wide-eyed.

'One week I'll require in advance. Cash, banker's draft or electronic transfer, only.'

'Show me results first, Puri, then only I'll make payment,' insisted Bhalla.

The detective gave a truculent shake of his head. 'Rest assured, sir, Vish Puri never fails. In my long and distinguished career, no mystery till date has gone unresolved or unsolved.'

'Two thousand per day, three days maximum,' suggested Bhalla.

'Price is final, no negotiation.'

Puri tiptoed towards the door. As he reached for the handle, Bhalla relented. 'Just get me Gopal Ragi!' he said. 'All right you win.'

'First class,' replied the detective. 'I would be sending my man later to pick up payment.'

He returned to the Ambassador to find Rumpi fuming.

'You've been twenty minutes, Chubby!'

'Hearties apologies, my dear,' answered Puri. 'The case is more complicated than I imagined. A most *hairy* set of circumstances we can say.'

• TWO •

The roar of fifty thousand fans greeted the Puris as they found their seats in the VIP section reserved for the 'near or dear' of ICT players. Delhi Cowboys captain Gopal Shastri had just hit a six, smacking the ball deep into the west stand, and the home crowd had gone wild. Throughout the hallowed Feroz Shah Kotla Stadium, built on the site of the capital of the fourteenth-century Delhi Sultanate, air horns blasted over the sharp beat of *dhol* drums, and the team's Hindi–English anthem was bellowed out: '*Khel Front Foot Pe!*'

Even Rumpi's father, Brigadier Mattu, who'd dressed in a tie and blazer for the occasion (he was also wearing a brown monkey cap that framed the centre of his face and lent him the look of a gentleman bank robber), was up on his feet waving the team's colours.

'Seems we're off to a first-rate start, sir,' said the detective as he sat down in the seat next to his father-in-law.

'Three fours off the first over alone, Puri!' replied Mattu. 'Good to see our boys on the offensive.'

The Brigadier – slight and grey-haired with an inquisitive face – slowly re-took his seat. Then, with a sharp pencil and meticulous hand, he updated his scorecard. It was resting on a thick sudoku volume; a bookmark indicated that he'd completed at least half of the brain-teasers. 'Most probably did them over his cornflakes,' the detective thought to himself. Mattu had a registered IQ of 137 and was a former code breaker, after all. He spoke seven languages fluently, including Mandarin and Tani, which he'd learned while stationed near the Chinese border in the contested Indian state of Arunachal Pradesh. He was a topper at bridge, the Gymkhana Club champion no less. And he was a walking encyclopaedia of cricket.

'Our team's weakness is with the bowling,' he told Puri. 'We're unlikely to see much swing in the ball today. Let's just hope Maharoof's in good form. He's certainly got a supportive crowd behind him.'

The stadium was indeed heaving – every seat was occupied, some by more than one fan. Children sat bunched atop walls and concrete overhangs, legs dangling through railings. All the aisles and steps were jammed with eager faces.

When the Cowboys' captain hit another six, the whole place erupted in cheers and Bollywood songs – a feverish carnival of flags and banners and impromptu dancing. STUNNER! flashed across the stadium's giant screens, quickly followed by advertisements for mobile phone networks, fast food chains and popular skin-whitening creams – all this to the bone-shaking decibel level of Queen: 'WE WILL, WE WILL ROCK YOU!'

'Very good, young man!' called out Rumpi's mother, who was sitting to the right of the Brigadier, patting her hands together in delight. 'Very good!'

Down on the boundary, they could see India's latest cultural import from the West, American cheerleaders in little pleated skirts and tight halter tops, performing acrobatics with their sparkly pompoms and favouring the crowd with flashes of their cleavage and knickers.

'Give us a D . . . E . . . L . . . H . . . I! GO COWBOYS!'

The reaction from the almost exclusively male – and by the looks of it totally *tulli* – fans down in the bleachers was no less frenzied than it had been for Shastri's stunning shot. Like lewd punters at a strip club, they ogled the *goris'* ample proportions and howled and wolf-whistled.

Thank the God Rumpi's mother, who was hard of hearing, couldn't make out the Punjabi obscenities being shouted, Puri thought.

'Do you know, *beta*, I used to be able to do that?' the detective overheard her telling Rumpi as the girls performed a series of cartwheels. 'I was junior gymnastics champion. But I didn't wear uniforms like those. Must be very practical I suppose.'

Practical was not a word Puri had come across in the reams of newsprint that had been dedicated to the cheerleader controversy in the Indian press over the past few days. 'Vulgar', 'obscene' and, perhaps most damning of all, 'un-Indian' had been the reaction from not only the religious right, but the liberal, self-appointed guardians of India's secular democracy as well.

'All the organisers are doing by making scantily clad white women dance in front of huge crowds is to stoke the base, voyeuristic and sexual insecurities of the Indian male,' historian and cricket aficionado Ramachandra Guha had been quoted as saying in the *Hindustan Times*.

Puri could not have agreed more. 'Why we are taking worst characteristics of Western world, I ask you?' he had written to the honourable editor of *The Times of India* last week. 'This is most certainly *not* cricket.'

But as Puri well knew, the presence of the cheerleaders, who were on loan from major American football teams like the Washington Redskins, was in keeping with the new, highly commercial face of cricket. India had, in the words of one commentator, 'masala-ed' the sport of its former colonial masters. Pristine whites and tepid bitter and understated British 'I say!' applause had been subverted by garish uniforms blazing with advertising and raucous bhangra dancing.

The sport's new Twenty-Twenty format was electrifying – fast paced and, at three hours long, tailor-made for TV. In India alone, the audience numbered in the tens of millions. Bollywood stars and billionaire tycoons ranked amongst the owners. And along with the deities of Indian cricket, the cream of Australia, South Africa and the West Indies had signed up.

Perhaps most extraordinary of all, however, was the participation of eleven Pakistani players. The Kolkata Colts had bought Kamran Khan, the twenty-three-year-old fast-paced bowler, for the duration of the annual month-long tournament.

It was Khan who now claimed the Delhi captain's wicket.

Approaching from the Willingdon Pavilion end, he delivered a devastating yorker, clean bowling Shastri's off stump and sending the bails flying. 'SHAME!' flashed up on the screens as the crowd emitted a harsh sigh of disappointment. The American cheerleaders, for whom cricket was clearly a total mystery, launched into another series of cancan high kicks and the loss of Delhi's star batsman was soon forgotten amidst the male fans' leering and caterwauling.

'Twenty-two off fourteen balls,' said the Brigadier as he updated his scorecard. 'I believe our boy is up next.'

Soon, cheers greeted Rumpi's nephew Rohan as he stepped out on to the field, bat in hand. The entire Mattu clan rose to their feet, beaming with pride. Rohan was being touted as one of the country's new hopefuls. At just eighteen, he'd captained the Indian Juniors and, last month, been called up to the national squad for a friendly against New Zealand. Batting at number ten, he'd scored an impressive thirty-three not out.

'Just look at him out there – so handsome and confident,' said Rumpi, eyes brimming with tears. 'I feel so proud.'

Puri felt caught up in the moment as well. 'Little blighter's come a long way from knocking balls through my window,' he said with a smile.

Rohan gave the pitch a thorough inspection, positioned himself in front of his stumps and, having made a considered survey of the field, readied himself for the first delivery.

Kamrah Khan shone one side of the ball on the crotch of his trousers as he sized up the Delhi boy. His delivery began as a mere trot, a series of short, light steps. Then his long legs began to eat up the distance like a panther. His arms wound round in a fluid, graceful movement, and as he planted his right foot millimetres short of the crease, his six-foot frame arched back like a giant bow. The ball left his hand at a staggering 84 miles an hour, bounced short and shot upwards at a 45 degree angle.

Rohan anticipated its trajectory and ducked as the ball whistled past his helmet. BOUNCER! appeared on the giant screens and a collective Boo carried through the stadium.

'Isn't that illegal?' asked Rumpi, who knew little more about cricket than the cheerleaders.

'No, no, perfectly legal,' answered her father. 'Invented by the British to thwart their old foes the Australians. Khan's just trying to put the frighteners on him.'

'But it's dangerous!' exclaimed Rumpi. 'Rohan could get hurt!'

The Brigadier chuckled. 'Not to worry. He can take care of himself.'

Puri felt his heart racing as the Pakistani bowler made his second approach. This delivery was even faster, 89 miles per hour, and the length was perfect. Rohan misjudged the bounce. The ball deflected off the edge of his bat and was caught at gully.

'Howzat!' screamed the delirious Kolkata players.

The umpire's arm shot up, signalling a no ball. Khan had overstepped the crease. A sigh of relief passed through the stands.

'That's Khan's second no ball today,' commented Brigadier Mattu as he updated his scorecard. 'And he's bowled one wide as well. Not his best form.'

The next four balls saw Rohan score a total of six runs. He appeared to be finding his form. But as Khan prepared to deliver the last ball of the over, a commotion broke out on the boundary. The cheerleaders were screaming and pointing at something along the boundary. A moment later, they scattered in all directions. A few clambered over the barrier and into the stands. The rest sprinted across the field towards the clubhouse.

At first the reaction amongst the crowd was a kind of bewildered amusement. But when the players started to run, too, everyone strained forward to try to get a glimpse of whatever it was that had invaded the field.

A mangy pye-dog soon came into view – barking, snarling, frothy saliva dripping from its mouth. Like a wounded bull in an arena, it trotted around the field for a couple of minutes before stopping in the middle of the field, its long, grey tongue hanging out.

Puri could see the animal in close-up on the giant screen now and could hear its painful whimpers courtesy of the miniature microphones hidden in the stumps.

'Must have rabies, I suppose,' said the Brigadier with nonchalance.

An announcement came over the public address stating that play would resume shortly while down down on the field, entertainment of a different nature began. Two groundskeepers set out from the East Hill gate with a length of netting stretched between them. They looked nervous, unsure of themselves. As they approached the dog, it took a few steps towards them, snapping and snarling. This was enough to cause the duo to turn on their heels and run, both getting their feet tangled in the net and falling over.

Another few minutes passed in which the dog's condition appeared to worsen. It started swaying from side to side. Blood ran from its nose. Then, three tubby *jawans* ventured out on to the field, brandishing their archaic bolt action Lee Enfield rifles. The dog didn't notice their advance; by now its head was hung low and it was trembling, as if in the grip of a fever.

The police wallahs advanced, two slower than the first, until they were approximately thirty feet from the animal. They stopped, raised their rifles. Took aim.

A hush fell over the stadium.

A volley of shots rang out.

Smoke drifted across the field.

It cleared to reveal the pye-dog still standing, oblivious to its near execution.

'Try it with your eyes open next time!' shouted a wag in Hindi amidst hoots of derision.

Visibly embarrassed, the jawans took aim again. But before they could get off a second round, the dog keeled over, lifeless.

'I think we got it,' one of the jawans was heard to say over the microphones.

The groundskeepers soon appeared again, this time with a wooden barrow, and the dog was unceremoniously tossed on to it.

Five minutes later, the players and the cheerleaders returned to the field. Rohan faced the next ball and sent it crashing over the boundary.

• THREE •

Puri's mother had opted to watch the match at home and join the family for the dinner afterwards. She was waiting in the lobby of the Delhi Durbar Hotel.

In her yellow and green Punjabi pantsuit, she looked out of place amidst all the mirrors, marble and glamorous 'page three' types in their sequined dresses. Still, Mummy-ji had found a sympathetic (or perhaps patient) ear in the form of the young assistant manager who was standing attentively before the gilded divan upon which she was perched.

'Aaah, finally, he's come, na,' she said as Puri approached. 'This is my second son – the investigator one I was telling you about.'

'Honour to meet you,' said the assistant manager.

'Just Rajneesh here was telling that the Maharani of Alwar would be coming to stay soon,' continued Mummy-ji with a glint of excitement in her eye. 'She's the one with the famous Golkonda Diamond, na? It's going on exhibition in coming days.'

'Wonderful news, Mummy-ji,' said Puri as he bent down to touch her feet, his girth stopping him short.

'Now come. Rumpi and the rest went ahead to the banquet hall.'

The assistant manager wished them both a good evening and withdrew.

Puri offered his hand to his mother, but she insisted on standing up unaided. 'That Rajneesh has got a sweetheart, na,' she said as they made their way through the busy lobby, past shops selling western designer brands. 'That pretty Bengali girl over there. The hospitality desk one. Just they were making eyes back and forth. But his parents are marrying him off to another one.'

The detective could not have been less interested in the marriage prospects of the hotel's assistant manager. He had, however, long ago mastered the art of appearing to be listening to his mother's trivial observations when his mind was engaged with more important matters. Besides, after the Delhi Cowboys' win and Rohan's impressive innings, he was in good humour.

'You watched the match, is it?' he asked.

'Load shedding was there,' she sighed. 'We caught ten minutes, only. Soon after that dog episode, the TV was going off. But what a thing to happen, na! How that pooch came to get there? That is the question!'

'Never mind the dog, Mummy-ji,' sighed the detective. 'What about Rohan's innings?'

'That I caught on my portable.'

'Your phone?' asked Puri.

'Why so surprised? FM is available these days, na.'

It was not unusual for Mummy to be more up to date with technical matters than her son and this irked him.

'A wonderful performance by Rohan, no?' he said, trying to cover up his ignorance.

'So impressive it was, Chubby. Nineteen was his total, na?'

'A most respectable nineteen, one can say.'

'Agreed.'

They found the banquet hall where the after-match reception and dinner were being held packed with guests, paparazzi and waiters bearing trays of wine, hard liquor and hors d'oeuvres. Puri recognised tycoons, cabinet ministers, top bureaucrats, lobbyists, socialites and celebrities from the worlds of cricket, film and fashion.

Over by the bar stood India's playboy Booze Baron in earnest conversation with the Cabinet Secretary said to be the most powerful man in the country. Neetika Sahini, who handled 'public relations' for India's biggest corporate houses, was huddled with A. Daaku, the telecoms minister, and Dwarka Butt, reporter and part owner of *Action News!* Next to the grand piano stood the Bharati Brothers and Sandeep Talwar, member of parliament for Indore. Popularly known as 'Sahib', he was currently Minister of Public Affairs, Food and Distribution and was said to have interests in sugar cane, pharmaceuticals, real estate and schools. He was also the president of the powerful Indian Cricket Board (ICB).

If ever there was proof of how power in India still lay in the hands of a relatively small, incestuous elite, it was here, the detective reflected. The old cabal of dynastic politics and family-run business houses retained their grip on most aspects of Indian life – and that included the world of cricket. But such a sobering observation was hardly in keeping with the spirit of the day – and certainly not the festive mood of the Mattus, who had gathered at the far end of the banquet hall.

By now, Rohan had arrived and was looking faintly embarrassed by his family's very public display of admiration. This didn't stop Puri giving the young man a big, congratulatory hug.

'Oi, Cheeky!' he bawled, Cheeky being his nephew's nickname. 'So proud of you, beta! That sixer! What a shot! I tell you the whole stadium went wild!'

'Even I went wild!' chimed in Rumpi's mother.

Rohan's smile was gracious. 'Actually, I would not be here in this place if it was not for you and Auntie – all that support and encouragement you have given me over the years,' he said.

'Not at all, beta,' said Puri. 'You've worked so hard, actually, you deserve.'

'I mean it, Uncle. I'll always be in your debt.'

'Nonsense, *yaar*! How there can be debt where family is concerned? Now let us have a toast, no?'

Everyone helped themselves to drinks provided by a passing waiter.

'To many more of those sixers, yaar!' announced Puri.

The clink of their glasses coincided with a burst of camera flashes.

'Oh my God look, it's *him*. It's Sanjay!' squealed Rohan's teenage sister, Mini, pointing to the main door.

She meant Sanjay Sala, Bollywood action hero turned cheesy romcom star, and the Delhi Cowboys' 'brand ambassador'. Behind him and his wife, Bubbles, came the young, charismatic chairman of the ICT, Nilesh Jani, and finally, the man of the match, Kamran Khan.

Spotting the young Pakistani bowler, Rohan shouted out, 'Kam! Kam!' and crossed the banquet hall to greet him. 'Over here!'

Puri and the Mattus watched, astonished, as the two exchanged hugs and backslaps, and then turned and headed towards them.

The detective found himself first in line to be introduced. As the young bowler offered him his hand, Puri hesitated. He'd never met a Pakistani in the flesh before and suddenly found himself at a loss as to how to react. His instincts told him Khan was one of the enemy, but good manners dictated that he greet him as he would any other guest.

Manners held sway and he reached out and received Khan's firm grip.

'Honour to meet you, sir,' said the bowler politely in English, towering over the detective.

'Welcome to India,' Puri heard himself reply.

Rohan's father and grandfather were introduced, both greeting the Pakistani in a respectful yet reserved fashion. Rumpi and her mother both raised their hands, palms pressed together, and said a pensive '*Namaste.*' Mini blushed and squealed, 'Hi!'

Only Mummy failed to greet the bowler. She just stood there, staring, disbelief writ large across her face. Khan didn't seem to notice. He looked nervous himself, his eyes moving around the room, searching.

'So how you two know each other?' Puri asked the young cricketers, breaking the awkward silence that followed his mother's uncharacteristic behaviour.

'Kamran and I used to play against one another in the

33

juniors,' offered Rohan. 'We've had some epic battles, the two of us.'

'Absolutely,' said Khan.

Everyone nodded. Mummy was still staring. Rohan said hurriedly, 'Kamran's from Rawalpindi. Isn't your family from there, Uncle? I mean originally.' The question was addressed to Puri.

'Well . . . um, long time back, only,' he replied.

'You were born there, sir?' asked Khan.

'Um, well, not exactly. I'm Delhi born, actually . . .' He cleared his throat. 'My parents came in '47, only.'

'I'd be delighted if you would come and visit Pakistan one day. It would be my honour to receive you as my guest,' said Khan.

'That would be wonderful, no, Uncle?' responded Rohan. 'We could go together!'

The detective fidgeted with his wedding ring. 'Let us see,' he said.

'We say insh'allah,' said Khan.

'Insh'allah – that means if Allah wills,' interpreted Rohan with unwavering enthusiasm. But this drew weak smiles from the rest of the family and he added quickly: 'Bet you could do with a drink, Kam, right? Must be thirsty.'

'Absolutely,' replied the Pakistani, sounding relieved. 'And I should find my father. If you'll excuse me.'

'Pleasure,' 'Nice to meet you,' and 'Best of luck,' murmured the Mattus as they watched the tall bowler follow Rohan through the throng of guests towards the bar.

The family said nothing for a moment, lost in their

own thoughts. And then Rumpi's mother broke the silence: 'Such a pleasant young man,' she said. 'And very handsome, also. Is he married?' She made it sound as if she might be interested.

'Didn't I read in one of those magazines that he's very much attached to Noor Sultana?' asked Rumpi.

'They were going to marry but it got called off,' said Rohan. 'His father didn't approve, she being a film star.'

Mummy had gone and sat down on a chair away from the rest of the family. Puri went to check on her.

'Everything is all right?' he asked.

She didn't answer.

'He tried again, placing a hand on her shoulder. 'Mummy-ji, something wrong?'

She looked up at him with sad, troubled eyes and asked in a faint voice, 'What is that, Chubby?'

'Look as if you've seen a ghost.'

She blinked as if waking from a dream. 'Just my mind was doing wandering.'

'Anything is wrong?'

'No, no, fine actually. Just one glass of *pani* is required.'

The family was sitting down to eat – Rumpi had brought a plate of salad and a token chicken breast from the buffet for her husband – when a waiter approached.

'There's one Vish Puri present?' he asked.

'Present and correct,' replied the detective.

'A phone call for you, sir. You would need to take it in the lobby.'

'Who exactly?'

'Mr Gurbachan Singh Oberoi.'

'Who?' asked Rumpi.

'A client,' answered Puri. 'I left word that I would be here, only.'

'Why doesn't he ring you on your portable?'

'I'm not having the foggiest, my dear,' said the detective as he stood up from the table. 'Must be important.'

The waiter led the way across the banquet hall until they were out of sight of the Mattu table. Puri slipped him a 100-rupee note and thanked him. He then made straight for the buffet, brazenly cutting into the queue. Halfway along the long table, which groaned with all kinds of delicious delights, he found one of his favourite dishes, butter chicken, and ladled out a large helping. Having also helped himself to two pieces of warm Peshawari *naan*, the detective stole out through the French windows on to the terrace.

Finding it deserted, Puri sat down at a table hidden in the shadows, tucked a napkin into the top of his safari suit and dug into his illicit meal.

He was in the process of lapping up all the delicious orange sauce, and reflecting on how it was some of the best butter chicken he'd eaten in a while, when the French windows opened and an elderly, gruff-looking gentleman stepped out. Puri judged him to be in his seventies and, given the flaccid face, flared nostrils and pockmarked cheeks, unmistakably Punjabi. In fact, he looked a lot like one of his uncles, the detective reflected – especially in that pinstriped three-piece suit, a style that only gentlemen of a certain generation could get away with wearing these days.

The man stopped roughly six feet from where Puri sat unnoticed, reached into his trouser pocket and took out a round little tin. He twisted off the top, extracted a pinch of a green substance and put it in his mouth.

Puri recognised it as *naswar*, dipping tobacco. That made him Pakistani. Could this be Kamran Khan's father? He was certainly the right height.

A low whistle came from the lawn beyond the terrace. It caught the Pakistani's attention. He looked, searched, spotted a male figure coming out of the darkness, and hurried down the steps.

Halfway across the lawn, he was met by the other man – short and bald was as much as Puri could make out by the light cast from the hotel. They greeted one another with a handshake, their voices but a murmur.

Another door opened further down the terrace and a third man stepped out, his face masked by the darkness.

Puri's attention was drawn back to the lawn. The bald man – 'Full Moon' the detective had decided to call him – was taking something out of his jacket. It looked like an envelope. He handed it to the Pakistani, who slipped it inside his jacket.

They talked for a while longer and then went their separate ways, Full Moon heading off across the lawn and the Pakistani returning to the terrace into the banquet hall.

As soon as the doors closed behind him, the Third Man hurried down the steps. Puri pushed himself up out of his chair followed after him as fast as he could manage – which was not very fast at all, given the shortness of his left leg not to mention all the butter chicken in his belly. Out of breath, his brow moist with sweat, he reached the hotel car park in time to see Full Moon pull away in a chauffeur-driven Mercedes Benz.

Of the Third Man there was no sign.

When he returned inside, Puri spotted the elderly Pakistani seated at the large, round VVIP table in the centre of the banquet hall.

'That is Kamran Khan's father, is it?' Puri asked Rohan when he got back to the Mattu table, pointing him out.

'You don't miss much, Uncle, do you?' responded his nephew.

'I did not get to be India's number one detective for nothing, beta,' said Puri immodestly. 'What is his name, exactly?'

'Faheem Khan.'

'You've met him, is it?'

'A few times over the years, Uncle. Why? Anything the matter?'

'Tell me: what sort of man he is?'

'Very tough, Uncle. He pushes Kamran hard. Too hard, actually. I've seen him slap him around before.'

'Somewhat old to be Kamran's father, no?'

'He took a young wife. His fourth, I believe.'

'He's in business or what?'

'I believe he's retired, Uncle. The family used to own a lot of land, but he lost it all.'

Puri kept a close eye on Faheem Khan throughout the rest of the meal. The thought of a Pakistani engaging in some kind of nefarious activity on Indian soil was not a matter he could ignore.

But Rumpi soon grew impatient with him. 'What *has*

got into you and Mummy?' she asked. 'Both of you have been staring at God knows who or what. Anyone would imagine you were star-struck!'

The detective couldn't help but glance over at the VVIP table again. Kamran Khan was not in his seat. Faheem Khan, having finished his food, was now washing his hands in a finger bowl.

Puri noticed him massaging his throat as if it was sore.

Rumpi lost all her patience. 'Chubby, really! What's so interesting? Tell me,' she scolded.

'Something suspicious is going on, actually,' answered the detective.

'What nonsense! What could possibly be going on here?'

Her words were punctuated by the crash of crockery. Half the room turned and stared. There were a few cheers. A jovial round of applause. Over at the centre table, however, no one was smiling. Faheem Khan had knocked his plate to the floor and was trying to loosen his tie and collar. He grabbed a glass of water and glugged it down, spilling half the contents on his shirt. Then he stood up, gasping for air, his eyes bulging. Foamy, orange saliva started to trickle out of the corners of his mouth.

Puri was up out of his chair now, heading across the banquet hall.

'Security! Stand back!' he shouted, pushing past the other guests. 'Any doctor is present?'

He reached the stricken man as he collapsed on to the floor, taking half the tablecloth and most of the plates and glasses with him. Bubbles, the actress, let out a protracted theatrical scream.

A doctor came forward and knelt down next to Faheem Khan. He lifted the back of his head. 'We must try to keep his air passages open,' he said.

But blood had started to trickle out of the Pakistani's nostrils. Puri could see that he was fading fast. With some difficulty, he crouched down by the stricken man's side.

'Who did this to you?' he asked. 'Who poisoned you?'

Faheem Khan tried to respond, but his mouth was full of saliva and the words came out slurred and incomprehensible. He gripped the doctor's arm, arching his back. A last anguished breath escaped through his gritted teeth with an eerie whistle.

His body slumped on to the floor, and his eyes fixed on the crystal chandelier above.

'I'm afraid we've lost him,' said the doctor.

A shocked murmur carried through the banquet hall. A few seconds later, Kamran Khan burst through the ring of guests and hotel staff gathered around the body.

'What happened?' he demanded, aghast.

Puri looked up.

'Unfortunately, your father is dead,' he said.

• FOUR •

'DEATH BY BUTTER CHICKEN.'
Puri's eyes lingered on the banner headline on the front page of the newspaper before proceeding to the article below.

> The mysterious murder of Pakistani national Faheem Khan, 76, father of international cricketer and Delhi Cowboys star bowler, Kamran Khan, yesterday evening at a posh dinner in the Delhi Durbar Hotel, in plain sight of numerous shocked cricket and Bollywood celebrities, has been attributed to deadly poisoning of a suspicious nature, police sources said.

'A very strong dose of aconite was somehow secreted into the victim's butter chicken and thus he experienced an uncomfortable death within minutes,' Delhi's Chief of Police was then quoted as saying.

'Aconite', the article added, 'is a deadly poison which the Minaro people of Ladakh use on their arrows for hunting purposes.'

Puri smacked the page with the back of his hand in anger.

'Ty-pi-cal!' he bellowed. 'What is relevance of deadly poison arrows to the case, I ask you?'

The detective's patient and loyal secretary, Elizabeth Rani, recognised this as a rhetorical question but answered nonetheless.

'That I could not say, sir.'

By now she had been standing in front of Puri's desk in his Khan Market office for more than five minutes, waiting for an opportunity to tell him about the important phone call she'd received. No opportunity had yet presented itself – or rather her employer was completely absorbed in his own thoughts and strangely oblivious to the presence of others. This was typical of him at the beginning of a big case when so many questions loomed in his mind and none of the pieces fitted together. Impossible was the most appropriate word she could think of to describe his temperament.

'Proper name of aconite is *Aconitum*, actually,' fumed Puri, who was still talking to the newspaper. 'It is a herb, only. Most common. The roots of certain species are deadly. *Aconitum ferox* for example – a favourite of the Bengali poisoner Rathin Dey.'

'Someone you apprehended, sir?'

'Not at all,' he answered as if to himself, eyes still fixed on the newspaper. 'Dey lived in Mughal times, only. He is most famous for poisoning Emperor Aurangzeb's taxman.'

Puri read on.

The article stated that two lakh rupees had been found

inside Faheem Khan's suit pocket. Preparations were under way to return his body to Pakistan. Kamran Khan had been interviewed by the police and cleared to leave the country.

The rest of the report was riddled with inaccuracies.

'The police quickly cordoned off the hotel and ensured all guests remained inside the banquet hall,' read Puri out loud in a contemptuous voice. 'What nonsense! These VVIPS and VIPs – *netas*, page three types, everyone – they refused to stay and left forthwith!'

There was more. Dippy, the Bollywood starlet and girlfriend of Rocky Schroff, could not have witnessed Faheem Khan's 'last desperate breath' as she had fainted at least a minute before the victim expired. And it had been a certain *jasoos* by the name of Vish Puri whose foresight had prevented the waiters from clearing away Faheem Khan's broken plate.

The detective would willingly have done a great deal more of the police department's work for them, too, had it not been for that total charlie the Delhi Police Chief who'd arrived on the scene forty-five minutes after the murder and taken charge.

'What are *you* doing here?' he'd demanded when he'd spotted Puri, making no effort to disguise his abhorrence. '*I* am taking personal control of this investigation. Your *services* are not required! I'm sure there must be some errant groom you should be chasing! Now go!'

Puri had done so with aplomb. 'Leave donkeys to their pastures,' he'd mumbled to Rumpi as they'd left the banquet hall. But privately he'd been livid.

He still was.

And, naturally, he was itching to investigate the murder. The Chief's involvement was an extra hunk of grist to the detective's ego mill.

There was just one problem. Puri didn't have a client. And Most Private Investigators Ltd couldn't afford to take on such a time-consuming and inevitably expensive case without someone footing the bill. The agency was starting to face stiffer competition in the market. 'Every Tom, Dick and Harry – not to mention all the Rajus and Viveks – are getting into security and investigation agencies,' as Puri had put it recently.

Inflation was also starting to bite with the cost of living for the Delhi middle classes fast approaching that of suburban America. The Indian state shamelessly failed to provide the most basic of services, which meant that health care, decent schools, security, and a constant supply of water and electricity had to be paid for privately. The rates of taxation had gone through the roof. And then there was baksheesh.

Hardly a week went by without Puri having to fork out to some official or other. Renewing his driver's licence had recently cost him 500 rupees. Buying a backup gas canister for the kitchen – another 200 rupees. And a few days ago, an official representing the dreaded Municipal Corporation of Delhi (the body that was supposed to provide civic services to most of the city and was corrupt to its core) had stopped by Khan Market to demand his regular payment for turning a blind eye to the fact that the rooms rented by Most Private Investigators as offices were only authorised to be used for residential purposes.

Puri had paid him off; he'd had no choice. If he'd defied

him the official would have returned with his lackeys and a couple of jawans and 'sealed' the property. They'd done just that recently to poor Mohit, the dry cleaner. He was now operating his business out of a van parked in front of his premises while he looked for an alternative place to rent.

'What to do, Madam Rani?' asked the detective with a sigh. He finally looked up from his newspaper, thereby properly acknowledging his secretary's presence. 'The most sensational of murders falls directly and most conveniently straight into my lap and I am powerless to do further investigation,' he said.

She opened her mouth to tell him about the message when there came a knock on the door. It was Bhajwati, the cleaner. '*Safai kar doon?*' she asked, greeting him with a timid namaste.

Elizabeth Rani let her in and she started to clean the floor with a wet rag, crouched down on her haunches and moving sideways back and forth across the room like a crab.

'You asked her why she was absent last two days?' Puri asked his secretary in English.

'Yes, sir. She said her boy intervened to stop a fight and got bashed up. Then *his* friends went and bashed up the ones who bashed him up. Then the mother of the first group came with the police and demanded Bhajwati's boy be arrested. She had to pay 3,000 rupees to get rid of them.'

Three thousand rupees was the amount Bhajwati was paid each month to clean the offices of Most Private Investigators. It was one of five jobs she held.

'I tell you honestly and truthfully, Madam Rani, sometimes I wonder if there is any justice left in India,' said

Puri, shaking his head. 'Vast majority of the population are so vulnerable, actually. Their rights are violated each and every day.'

'Thankfully there are people like your good self working for truth and justice,' said Madam Rani.

Such naked veneration might have embarrassed many an employer, but not Puri.

'So kind of you, Madam Rani,' he said. 'Now, what all I can do for you?'

'You received an urgent call from a Britisher, Mr James Scott,' she answered.

'Jaams Scott! When he called, exactly?' Puri rose half out of his chair and sat down again.

'Fifteen minutes back—'

'Why you didn't tell me, Madam Rani?' Puri's tone was urgent, not accusatory. 'Scott is former Deputy Commissioner Metropolitan Police, London!'

'Yes, sir, I—'

'I worked with him few years back.'

'Yes, sir, I—'

'The Case of the Naked Jain, you remember?'

Elizabeth Rani just nodded.

'Former Deputy Commissioner Scott came begging to me for assistance. His case was dead in the water, we can say. Also, he was a fish out of water, working in India for the first time. Fortunately I was able to clear up the matter single-handedly. But, frankly speaking, Madam Rani, the working relationship – between Scott and my good self, that is – was not always smooth sailing. When all is said and done, these *Angrezi* types believe they know better. A lack of trust is there, actually.'

Puri leaned back in his chair, linking his hands behind his head.

'Nowadays Scott is heading this International Cricket Federation anti-corruption unit,' he said, sounding hopeful. 'Must be he needs my help once again. Well, very good.'

'Actually, sir, he resigned that post last week,' stated Elizabeth Rani.

The detective's face showed startled dismay. 'Certain, Madam Rani?'

'Yes, sir,' she said, handing him a press release printed off the ICF website.

Puri read the first couple of lines and then said, 'So what's his game exactly?'

'He requested an urgent meeting right away.'

'He's here in Delhi, is it?'

'Yes, sir. Staying at the Maharajah.'

Puri was thoughtfully silent for a moment. 'I cannot meet him there,' he said. 'It would raise eyebrows – and suspicions, also.

'Yes, sir.'

'The Gymkhana Club is out of the question, also.'

He leaned back in his executive swivel chair and looked over at the portraits hanging on the wall of his father, Om Chander Puri, and his long-dead guru, the patron saint of Indian detectives, Chanakya.

'Madam Rani, we will need to do a Number Three Pickup,' he said. 'Get Randy Singh at International Backside on line.'

James Scott – half-sleeve shirt, farmer's tan, ruddy complexion, semi-permanent frown – stepped out of the main doors of the Maharajah Hotel at exactly twelve-fifteen and asked the doorman to call him a taxi. The order was passed on to a subordinate, and then another, who in turn shouted the command into a microphone, his words booming from an amplifier installed at the taxi stand on the road beyond the hotel wall.

'*Ek taxi! Ek taxi! Jaldi karo!*'

Soon, a black-and-yellow Ambassador with lopsided suspension and the words 'Power Brake' painted on the bonnet chugged up to the door. Behind the wheel sat a Sikh wearing thick glasses and a pink turban. His beard was wrapped in a chin net.

'I need to go to . . .' Scott referred to a piece of paper in his hand. 'Jaan taar maan taar,' he said in an affected Peter Sellers accent.

The driver repeated the words back to himself, as if trying to make sense of baby babble, and then exclaimed with a triumphant grin, 'Jantar Mantar! Jantar Mantar. Very beauty place! No problem, good gentle man!' Holding the taxi's back door open, he added, 'My city your city.'

After haggling over the price and agreeing to abide by the ruling of the taxi's archaic meter, they set off through the hotel's gates.

'Which country, please?' asked the driver as he honked his way through Delhi's gridlock.

'UK,' answered Scott. He looked out the window, hoping his aloofness would make it clear that he wasn't interested in conversation.

'United Kingdom of Eng-land! Very good beauty countree! Ton-i Blaar. Manchestar Unite!'

Scott gave a weak smile.

'Personally my home Paanjab! Patiala! Very famous and beauty city also!'

The taxi turned into the inner circle of Connaught Place – 'See fine architecture built by Britisher people, kind gentle man!' – with its pillared arcades. Out on the pavements, vendors were hawking bright Rajasthani cushion covers and *bhel puri*. Tourists sat on cane stools getting intricate henna designs painted on their hands. Smoke rose from barrows where sweet potatoes smouldered in hot charcoal.

'You want nice Indian handicraft? Kashmiri shawl?'

'No, thank you.'

'Tasty chicken tikka?'

'Just drive the taxi, will you?'

'As you like, sir.'

Twenty minutes later, after a prolonged journey to India Gate and back, the Ambassador reached its destination.

'Do waiting, good gentle man?' asked the driver. 'I'm parking. You give missed call, OK?'

Scott declined his offer, paid the fare and, with the words 'pleased to make friendship' ringing in his ears, hurried through the entrance to the park.

To Scott's eyes, Jantar Mantar, the eighteenth-century astronomical observatory built by Maharajah Jai Singh II of Jaipur, looked like a cross between Escher's impossible cityscapes and a skate park. He passed orange-stained staircases that led nowhere, a large heart-shaped structure that curled in on itself, and a couple of enormous, empty bowls.

Following the instructions that had been pushed

under the door of his hotel room, he carried on straight through the park. An autorickshaw with a likeness of a curled sandal painted on the hood was waiting on the other side. No sooner had the Englishman clambered on to the back seat, hunched down so as to keep his head from hitting the low ceiling, than the three-wheeler's engine putt-putted into life and the vehicle jerked into action.

The driver zigzagged through the frenetic traffic with the dexterity of a hare until they reached Sundar Nagar market. He stopped in front of a small commercial unit that housed an ATM machine and indicated that this was their destination. An OUT OF ORDER sign hung from the handle of the glass door and this caused the Britisher to hesitate. 'There must be some mistake,' he grumbled. But then, a security guard opened it for him. Cautiously, and with a pronounced frown, the ex-Scotland Yard man stepped forward and proceeded inside.

For an ATM booth, it was spacious and plush, furnished with laminated wood panelling on the walls, red carpeting, a small coffee table stocked with bank deposit forms, and two leather armchairs. On one of these, a man sat reading a newspaper.

'Good to meet you again, former Deputy Commissioner,' said Puri as he put aside the broadsheet and stood to greet his guest.

'Christ alive, Vish!' exclaimed Scott. 'Was all that necessary? All the driving around and switching vehicles, I mean?'

'Undoubtedly! You were followed, actually,' answered Puri.

'Who says? Not that taxi driver – surely! Don't tell me that lunatic's one of yours!'

'One of my best,' answered the detective, looking a little hurt.

Scott ran a hand through his thinning hair. 'Right. Well. Sorry. He just went on a bit. About chicken tikka and shawls and God knows what else. Did he lose whoever it was?'

'Naturally.'

'Any idea who it was?'

'Another private investigator. I know the fellow. An idiot person.'

'He's probably working with the Indian Cricket Board. They'll be nervous I'm here. Want to know what I'm up to.' Scott glanced around him as if he'd just noticed the setting in which he found himself. 'Do you mind explaining why we're meeting here?' he asked.

'I often make use of this place, former Deputy Commissioner. The location is central. It is private and most comfortable – air conditioning is there. Lovely it is in summertime.'

'What if someone comes along and wants to withdraw some cash?'

'Jagdish, the security guard, will make certain we don't face interruption.'

Puri invited Scott to take a seat.

'India hasn't changed one bit, has it?' observed the Britisher as he occupied one of the armchairs. 'It's still like *Kim*. Great Game, disguises, cleft sticks – all that stuff.'

'Some changes are there,' said Puri. 'For one thing we have Angrezi liquor these days.' He produced a bottle of Johnnie Walker from beneath the table. 'As I recall, you were not at all keen on our Indian whisky, isn't it?'

'Let's just say it's an acquired taste,' said Scott.

Puri mixed them each a glass of whisky and soda and they toasted one another's health.

'So all is well with you, former Deputy Commissioner?' asked Puri.

'Please just call me James, Vish.'

'Absolutely, Sir Jaams. And tell me, how is the lovely Mrs Scott?'

Scott shifted uneasily in his seat. 'Um . . . well, fine I suppose,' he said, looking faintly embarrassed. 'I mean . . . we got divorced. She . . . she's married to another man now, you see.'

'Is it?' responded Puri, placing his drink on the table. 'Sir, I don't know what to say.'

Scott gave a shrug. 'Worse things can happen,' he said, staring down into his glass, missing Puri's wide-eyed reaction. 'Now, look,' he continued. 'I understand you were there at the Durbar last night when Faheem Khan was murdered.'

It took Puri a moment to recover from the revelation about the divorce. He had never met Mrs Scott to whom Scott had been married for thirty-odd years, but he had always asked after her. It felt as if he'd lost a friend.

'Right, yes, correct,' said the detective, trying to collect his thoughts. 'It happened there before my eyes.'

'Have the locals got it right? He was poisoned with aconite?'

'That I could not say, sir. The laboratory report has not come into my possession. But it was poison. No doubt about it at all.'

'Any idea how it got into the curry he was eating?'

'Butter chicken,' corrected the detective.

'Sorry?'

'It's a Delhi dish popular all over these days – one of my personal favourites, actually. The Durbar version is really wonderful. Creamy and delicious. I myself was eating some last night minutes before the victim succumbed.'

'There was a buffet, I understand.'

'Correct. But waiters served those at the centre VVIP table. Faheem Khan was seated there himself, only.'

'So given that you suffered no ill effects and presumably no one else did either, we can safely say that only Faheem Khan's plate was poisoned,' concluded Scott.

The detective indicated his concurrence with a nod.

'Think the son did it?' The Britisher's tone was breezy, but it suggested an inherent cynicism.

'Fact is any number of persons present could have done the needful,' answered Puri.

'You mean poisoned his food?'

'It was lying untouched on the table for some time.'

'He left the table?'

'Ten minutes exactly,' answered the detective, keeping his knowledge of the Faheem Khan/Full Moon rendezvous to himself for the time being.

'But surely if the aconite was added to his food at the table, someone would have noticed.'

'Sir, has been my experience over these many years having investigated so many of cases that often people such things go unnoticed. Especially with so many of people getting up and down from their chairs like yoyos.'

Puri sipped his Scotch. It wasn't as good as Indian whisky, he reflected. But then Britishers enjoyed bland things. Like toad in the hole and depressing poetry about damp valleys and all. Such a strange people: highly civilised in many ways, yet with no fire burning in their bellies. Still, there was something gratifying about helping them out when they turned up in Delhi. Despite their inherent conceit, their fundamental belief in the superiority of Western civilisation, they were always out of their depth here in India – trying to operate in a world that was impenetrable to them. 'Welcome to the real world!' he often felt like saying to them. 'Welcome to India!' And yet somehow Puri always found himself adopting a subservient manner when dealing with the British. India was free and independent, had been for more than sixty years now, but he couldn't help trying to impress upon them that he, too, was civilised. 'Sir, I take it your visit here is not a coincidence,' he said. 'Evidently you left London last night only and in something of a hurry, isn't it?'

Puri had concluded as much from the fact that Scott had shaven with a plastic razor – no doubt supplied by his airline or hotel. There were no less than six nicks to his face and neck. He was also wearing odd socks.

'I see you're as sharp as ever, Vish,' said the Britisher looking somewhat uncomfortable with the fact that his appearance was so easily interpreted. 'Yes, as it happens, I left London as soon as I heard the news. I had about five minutes to get my things from home. As for what I'm doing here, I'll come to that in a minute. I'm sure you heard that I resigned from the ICF.'

'Yes, sir, after seven months in the job, only,' replied the detective who gave no indication that he had only come by this information earlier today.

'It was eight. But that's hardly the point. It was a mistake to take the job. The ICF has no teeth and I found myself in an untenable position. I'm working for another organisation now, but I'll come to that in a minute. Firstly, I need to fill you in on what I got up to at the ICF. Obviously I do so in the strictest confidence.'

'Confidentiality is my watchword, sir,' said the detective.

'Yes, I know, Vish. You're a good man – which is why I'm here. We've had our differences in the past with regard to procedure. I'm thinking of the Jain fraud case, of course. But I want you to know that I've always had the highest regard for your abilities.'

Puri took this as a compliment despite the patronising undertone.

'I saw it as my job at the ICF to get to grips with the illegal betting business here on the subcontinent,' began Scott. 'It's a vast enterprise as you know, worth billions of dollars a year, with bookies in every town and city from here to Peshawar and Colombo. The Syndicate, as it's often called, is run by the individual known as Aga – the underworld kingpin, who's believed by most intelligence agencies, including the CIA and your Indian RAW, to reside in Pakistan under the protection of that country's intelligence agency, the ISI.

'Aga has his fingers in a lot of other pies as well – gunrunning, terrorism, prostitution, you name it. But no one has ever satisfactorily identified how he runs the Syndicate. Are all the bookies in India, Pakistan and beyond part of the same outfit, as the conventional wisdom holds? Do they all pay Aga a remittance for operating in their given zones? Frankly, there are a lot of unanswered questions.'

Scott went on to explain that in his view the only way to get to grips with Aga's organisation was first to identify the bookies working for him. And the only way to do that was to ascertain which players were on the take.

'Number one on my list was young Kamran Khan,' continued the Britisher. 'There are times when his bowling's erratic. He's about the best fast pacer I've ever seen – up there with Curtly Ambrose, I'd say. He'll bowl two or three flawless overs and then suddenly a wide or a no ball. At times he'll also offer up an easy delivery as well – a four on a platter. It's a similar story with his batting.'

Outside the ATM, a woman had stepped up to the door and was berating Jagdish, wanting to know why the cash machine wasn't working. The guard held his ground, insisting that the repairs would take at least an hour, until, cursing, she stormed off.

'Please continue, sir,' said Puri. 'Coast is clear.'

'Are you sure, Vish? It doesn't seem right somehow – us sitting here.'

'This is India, sir,' said Puri with a flick of his hand.

'Right, well, if you say so.' He took a glug of his Scotch before continuing. 'So as I was saying . . . at first, I made progress. By cross-referencing the names of attendees of international matches around the world – the UK, Dubai, Australia – with airline and hotel records, I identified a number of individuals who've stayed in hotels occupied by the teams. Two of these individuals were Indian nationals. The first was a certain Mohib Alam from here in Delhi. The second was from Mumbai, Vikas Sengar, whom everyone knew as "The Spade".'

Puri smiled broadly.

'Did I say something funny?' asked Scott.

'Apologies, sir. But if we are talking about the same individual – and I believe he is familiar to me – he was known as "Fawda". Means he had buckteeth sticking out.'

'Oh. Right. Well now that you come to mention it, he *did* have buckteeth – very prominent ones, in fact. Funny. I just imagined the nickname had to do with something sinister – like digging graves . . . Now where was I?'

'You had identified two individuals, sir.'

'Right. So I kept an eye on Messrs Alam and Sengar. Discreet surveillance. And where should they both turn up during the World Cup last year? Faheem Khan's hotel room in Hyde Park.'

'They came together, sir?'

'Separately.'

Another swift swig of whisky and the Britisher continued: 'A few weeks later – June of last year – Sengar was *supposedly* found hanging from a ceiling fan in his luxury pad in Mumbai. The investigating officer said it was suicide, but I have my doubts.'

'Such as?'

'He didn't leave a note, he'd just eaten a large meal and there was a good deal of cocaine and alcohol in his system. He was also a big lad – about 220 pounds. I don't believe any ceiling fan could have taken that weight.' Scott paused for a beat. 'When it came to finding out more about these two individuals here in India – I was after financial records, phone taps, that sort of thing – I got stonewalled. No one would lift a finger to help. I certainly couldn't count on the ICF's India investigator who was supposed to be working for me.'

Puri asked for his name.

'A former senior police inspector called Johri Mal,' answered Scott, at which the detective let out a hollow chuckle.

'A total scoundrel. Could not organise a game of bingo in a bingo hall.'

'Yes, well, naturally I made an official complaint, but my boss, the ICF President, told me not to "rock the boat". Worse, he said he saw no grounds for any further investigation of Mohib Alam or Vikas Sengar.' Scott drained his glass again and wiped his mouth with the back of his hand. 'The fact is, Vish – and I don't need to tell you this – when it comes to cricket, Britain might be the home of the sport, but this is where all the money is being made. The ICB has grown – very quickly, mind – into the richest cricket board in the world. The Indian Cricket League Tournament alone is worth billions. That makes the Indians very powerful. And they're starting to flex their muscles. The ICB has started laying down the law when it comes to scheduling of international series, appointing umpires, taking on advertisers—'

'And naturally ICB is totally corrupt,' interrupted Puri.

'I didn't say that,' said Scott.

'Sir, you did not need to. The ICB is unlike any other cricket board in the entire world, actually. Its members are not appointed by any higher body like a sports minister and such. It is a private syndicate. Like a kind of mafia, we can say. Members are elected by other members, only. Thus no accountability is there. Many of these individuals are total *goondas*. Take the current president, Sandeep Talwar, who, by the way, was seated at the table along with the victim. He is a crook. Of the highest order. Most probably he's in league with the bookies, who are providing so much of black money during elections. So he will not want any Indian bookie unmasked, that is for sure, and he will make sure that charlie Johri Mal does not do any singing for his supper.'

The two men drank in silence for a minute.

'You said you were working for another organisation, sir?' asked Puri.

'It's relatively new, Vish, so you wouldn't have heard of it. We don't even have an office yet. But we're calling our campaign Clean Up Cricket.'

'We, sir?'

'Retired players, umpires, coaches, senior commentators – all concerned individuals. Concerned that all this over-commercialisation and the illegal betting industry are ruining the great game of cricket. We want to see it cleaned up – something the ICF is failing to do and in our view will carry on failing to do.'

'And you want my help, is it?'

'We'd like to hire you to investigate this murder. Find out who did it.'

'That will not be at all easy, sir. We are talking about a can of worms. Many cans in fact. And it will be dangerous, also.'

Puri was thinking of his counterparts who had delved into Aga's affairs. Pakistani detective B.K. Laghari, for example, who had turned up in a sports bag at the Gadani Ship Breaking Yard near Karachi. And the head of Mumbai's Detection Unit . . . hit by a suburban train at Andheri, an accident according to the official report, despite the lengths of rope found tied around his arms and legs.

'Look, Vish, we'll understand if you don't want to take us up on our offer,' said Scott. 'But Clean Up Cricket has got deep pockets.'

'Where the money is coming from exactly?'

Scott put up his hands in a defensive posture. 'Look, I'm not going to lie to you,' he said. 'We're being financed by two of Europe's biggest betting companies.'

'No doubt they'd dearly love to get their hands on the Indian market,' observed Puri.

'Is there anything wrong with that? The only way to clean up cricket is to legalise betting on the subcontinent.'

'True. And match fixing hurts the legal betting business in Europe and elsewhere, no? Keeps the punters in Britain away from the betting shops if they believe the game has gone for a toss.'

'There's that as well,' conceded Scott. 'But I'm not in this for the betting industry – and that goes for my fellow members as well. We just want to see the game cleaned up.'

Puri replenished their glasses for a third time. Scott watched him, waiting for a response.

'I would be having certain terms,' said the detective. 'Naturally a contract should be there – signed, sealed and delivered. But also –' He faltered. 'Well, the thing is, sir, well, you see –'

'You want a free reign, Vish – want to handle things your way.'

'Exactly, sir. Not to say of course that your advice would not be invaluable –'

Scott held up a hand. 'I got it: no back seat driving,' he said. 'Just provide me with updates now and again, some indication of how you're getting along and I'll keep out your hair. So do we have a deal?'

Puri's face showed marked relief. 'Undoubtedly,' he said.

They shook on it and Scott stood to leave. He was due to fly back to London in a few hours.

'One other thing I wanted to mention,' he said. 'In case you run into difficulties getting a visa to Pakistan, my colleagues and I will sort it out for you.'

'Pakistan?' asked Puri, his voice suddenly weak.

'I assume you'll want to travel there. Surely the Indians aren't going to be able to keep Kamran Khan here? He's going to want to return home with his father's body.' Until now the thought of going to Pakistan had not even occurred to Puri. It was the one country in the world that he had vowed never to set foot in. He hated the place with every ounce of his body.

'Well, yes . . . I . . . naturally, why not?' he stuttered.

'Good,' said Scott. 'You can reach me on my BlackBerry night and day. The line's scrambled.'

Puri saw his client to the door and watched him climb into the waiting auto. He then exited through a door in the back of the booth. The taxi he'd hired from Randy Singh at International Backside was still parked in the lane that ran behind the shops.

On the front seat lay a fake beard, a chin net and an unravelled pink turban.

• FIVE •

Tubelight had been asked to track down all manner of unusual items in his time – everything from a runaway *nautch* girl to a eunuch's disembodied head. When Mahatma Gandhi's glasses were stolen from the National Gandhi Museum, it was Puri's senior operative who traced them to the den of a so-called *super chor* known as Ruby. Tubelight had also been instrumental in recovering his friend Hazrat Ali's kidney after he was abducted and operated on by organ dealers.

But locating a dead pye-dog? In the middle of Delhi?

'You'd have better luck finding a virgin on GB Road, Boss,' he told Puri on the phone about an hour after the ATM meeting with Scott.

There were tens of thousands of stray, flea-bitten mutts living on the streets of India's capital and every day dozens succumbed to disease or were mowed down by the city's angry traffic, Tubelight pointed out.

'Few years back it would have been totally impossible,' replied Puri. 'Now at least we're in with a chance.'

The detective was referring to the demise of Delhi's

traditional, eco-friendly, cost-free and thoroughly efficient canine clean-up service.

Namely, its vultures.

These magnificent birds, which had always been a feature of the capital – circling on the heat eddies in the skies overhead or perched up high in the branches of diseased trees – had been accidentally killed off in the past few years after feeding on the carcasses of cattle treated with a banned but still widely available veterinary drug.

Dog disposal was now the detail of the Municipal Corporation of Delhi's street cleaners, who were supposed to cart the carcasses off to landfills but often dumped them in more convenient locations like drains and ditches or 'jungles', as the wooded areas of Delhi were known.

'I'll get on to it, Boss,' said Tubelight. 'But what has this dog got to do with the case?'

The canine in question was, of course, the one that had made such a scene at Kotla Stadium yesterday afternoon.

'I suspect the pooch died from the same poison that was used to kill Faheem Khan,' answered the detective. 'We need it for post-mortem. Find out if the grounds wallahs saw anything out of the ordinary – someone feeding it, perhaps? Could be they can identify the murderer.'

'What if the police are looking for the dog as well?'

Puri guffawed. 'Don't do tension, yaar! The Chief could not tell his backside from a hole in the ground.'

* * *

Tubelight hung up and continued eating his lunch. Before him, laid out on the grass in a semicircle, sat the three round, stainless steel sections of his tiffin box. The first contained a few rotis, the second some *aloo subzi*, and the third cucumber raita seasoned with roasted cumin. The food had been prepared by his wife in the early hours of this morning, and he had carried the container with him in his autorickshaw while fulfilling his first assignment of the day, namely picking up and dropping off Puri's new client, the pink-faced Angrezi police wallah.

As he tore off a piece of the flat bread and scooped up a lump of potato with his right hand, he felt the sun's rays break through the winter haze. He had almost forgotten what its warmth felt like; the cold had penetrated into the very marrow of his bones.

His home, a small rented apartment in a typical, shoddily constructed building with no insulation, was like a fridge at this time of year (an oven for the other eight months). The two heaters he owned required electricity and with all the neighbours hooking on to the overhead lines illegally (the new scam was to draw electricity from overhead lines using TV antennas and step-up transformers), the colony's junction boxes kept overloading and tripping.

He closed his eyes and turned his face to the sun. The heat spread through him like an isotope, warming the blood in his veins. The other men and women – paint-splattered decorators, sweepers, a clutch of office workers – eating their lunch amidst beds of poppies and sweet peas, reacted in the same way, stretching and yawning as if emerging from hibernation.

Tubelight finished his food, lit a *beedi* and lay back on the grass. For a few minutes, he almost forgot about the latest task he had been assigned by Boss — and the fact that he was in the middle of New Delhi's Mathew Chowk roundabout at the junction of the Akbar Road and Tees January Marg. About fifty feet across and set with flower beds and neem trees, it was one of the few truly beautiful places in the city where anyone of any background was free to sit without fear of being moved on. Sometimes, between jobs, he even came here to take a nap, impervious to the honking traffic.

But today he couldn't afford that luxury; not if he was going to find the dead dog. Tugging on the last of his beedi, he sat up and packed his tiffin, stacking one container upon the other and locking it with the metal arm that held the whole thing together.

Before returning to his autorickshaw, which was parked next to his friend's *paan* and cigarette stand on Tees January Marg, he picked up a marigold blossom lying on the grass and tucked it behind his ear.

Tubelight was barred from entering the Kotla Stadium by the security guards on duty. He turned instead to the *dhaba* near the gate on Bahadur Shah Zafar Road and there, he struck up a conversation with the owner.

'Yes, I recognised that dog, *bhai*,' said the dhaba wallah, a large, greasy-faced man who was busy doing four things at once — taking orders from new customers who all expected to be served simultaneously; frying baturas in a wok; counting change; and scratching his groin.

'Sometimes I used to give it scraps,' he continued while garnishing a tobacco plate of channa with chopped chillis and coriander. 'It was always friendly, but then it went crazy.'

'Any idea why?' asked Tubelight.

'I didn't say the dog was my best friend! How should I know?'

'Did you see anyone else feeding it?'

More customers arrived; more change was begrudgingly handed over from a container of grubby notes and coins; a big steel pot with a blackened underside was given a stir.

Puri's operative repeated his question and in reply got an irritated, 'Haaa? Why the interest in some dog, bhai?'

Tubelight produced a fake police ID. 'I'm working undercover,' he said, flashing it conspiratorially. 'We suspect terrorists of using dogs to spread disease.'

The man looked unmoved, his apathy born of a lifetime spent on Delhi's brutal streets.

'Look, I was busy that day,' he answered. 'There were big crowds. Think I can watch everything that goes on? There are lots of dogs hanging around. Why don't you bother someone else? Like those two over there.' He gestured to two groundsmen crouched on the pavement eating their lunch. They were the ones who'd taken the dog off the cricket pitch.

'Oi, you two! What happened to that dog? The one that went crazy?' the dhaba wallah shouted.

'We dumped it over there,' one of them replied.

He indicated a ditch next to some big sewer pipes

waiting to be laid. Tubelight went and investigated but there was no trace of the dog.

'The Kala Bandar must have eaten it,' concluded the other groundsman.

The Kala Bandar, literally 'monkey man', was a kind of Indian Big Foot who was said to prowl the streets of Delhi. Dozens of people claimed to have been attacked by him; many more witnesses had described his nocturnal activities: bounding down streets, jumping ten feet over cars, scaling walls. The police were taking the issue seriously and had issued a likeness, plastering wanted posters on to walls and lamp posts across the city. They showed a creature covered in black hair with razor-sharp claws and a monkey face. His only apparel was a motorcycle helmet.

'He doesn't eat dogs,' bawled the dhaba wallah. 'So you shouldn't worry!'

'Chippkali ke jhaant ke paseene!' swore the groundsman. *Sweat of a lizard's pubic hair!*

The dhaba wallah's helper, who was about ten years old and was standing on a stool pouring small glasses of *chai* the colour of mud, spoke up. 'I just remembered something!' he announced.

'The name of your father?' quipped the dhaba wallah.

'No bhai! Two men came and took that dog away!' he said. 'They wore masks and gloves. There was something written on the side of their Tempo.'

'You're talking about that dog?' chimed in one of the stadium security guards, overhearing the conversation.

'You saw the men who took it?' asked Tubelight.

'Maybe. Who wants to know?'

The fake police ID was produced again, but the security guard said he still couldn't quite remember the details. It took a 50-rupee note to refresh his memory.

'They were from Rabies Control,' he said.

Tubelight drove as fast as his autorickshaw could travel (top speed 31 miles per hour) north to Timarpur Marg. But he was too late. A blood sample had been taken from the dog, and according to the *chowkidar* on the gate, the usual rag picker charged with disposing of animal carcasses had taken it away. He'd done so on a bicycle cart a couple of hours ago.

'What's the rag picker's name?'

'How should I know?'

'Where does he come from?'

'Get lost.'

It was then that Tubelight noticed an oily trail leading out of the gate and down the road. The route taken by the rag picker's cart? He decided to follow it. A mile on, he found himself in front of a concrete dumpster where cows grazed on a mound of garbage. Here, another rag picker confirmed that he was on the right track and pointed him in the direction of the Bhalswa jugghi.

Tubelight continued north, past dense, suffocating townships of bare concrete blocks. And soon, above the otherwise flat terrain, he spotted the mountain. The air turned foul, a toxic stench catching in the back of his throat as the massif loomed larger. He could make out a road cut into its side, a dump truck heading towards the flat-top summit. A black cloud of birds wheeled overhead like a portent of doom. There were figures picking their way along the escarpment – women, the reds and pinks of their saris bright against a crumbling, unstable terrain the grey of nuclear ash.

The English word for the place was 'landfill' but this was a misnomer, Tubelight reflected as he turned off the highway on to a rough track. An open 'drain', or sewer, with garbage-strewn banks led to a tangle of tumbledown shacks blackened by dirt and pollution. He stopped to ask a *kabari* wallah if a rag picker with a dead dog had passed that way. By a miracle the man knew his name: Raju. Finding this Raju, however, didn't prove easy. The area's geography was defined, indeed as most of Delhi is by the majority of its inhabitants, by landmarks and narratives.

'Turn down the lane where the old blind man sits,' Tubelight was told.

When he came across the blind man (who, fortunately, was where he was supposed to be), a woman hanging wet clothes on a barbed-wire fence pointed in the direction of a communications tower jutting up above the tin roofs. 'Beneath that you will see the place where the men have been digging these past days and where another died when he fell off his ladder.'

Eventually, he found the rag picker's shack, built against the exterior wall of a crematorium. Tubelight saw him crouched amidst a pile of gutted computers. His wife sat nearby, baby cradled in one arm, stirring a big metal basin sloshing with a soup of nitric acid and circuit boards. A teenage son panned for bits of copper, gold and lead.

'I sold it,' said Raju when asked about the dog.

For a small fee, he agreed to take Tubelight to the buyer and led the way deeper into the jugghi. They passed more rag pickers bundling and weighing recyclable refuse – cardboard, newspapers, tin cans, bags of plastic bottle caps – until they reached a compound surrounded by a brick wall. The smell was different here: the stench of death hung in the air, and for the first time, Puri's operative felt the urge to retch.

Stepping into the compound he spotted a couple of men lowering a bloated dog carcass into an oil drum of boiling liquid. Another dog lay nearby, equally bloated. Raju the rag picker recognised it as the one he'd brought from Rabies Control.

Fifty rupees, a little more than the price the animal's bones would fetch from the agro fertiliser industry, gave Tubelight possession of the dog, and ten more went to procure a large piece of dirty plastic sheeting to wrap it in.

Once the stinking carcass had been loaded into the back of the auto, Tubelight handed Raju thirty rupees. He took the payment without a word and set off back through the slum.

Not once had the rag picker queried why someone would want the animal. Everything had a value in Delhi. Even a dead dog.

· SIX ·

While Tubelight was ingratiating himself with the dhaba wallah and the coolies outside Kotla Stadium, Puri returned to the Delhi Durbar Hotel. He found the banquet hall cordoned off and three jawans guarding the main doors. That is to say they were sitting around, drinking tea and talking idly amongst themselves – three vocations at which jawans the length and breadth of India could justifiably claim to excel.

Through the banquet hall's open doors, the detective could see two forensics officers in white jumpsuits examining the round dining table where Faheem Khan had met his fate. He dearly wanted to slip inside and find out if they had come across a delivery device for the poison. Getting past the jawans would not present too much difficulty. But doing so would risk his involvement in the case becoming known.

Besides, the detective had other means. Half an hour ago, he'd spoken to his friend and occasional collaborator Inspector Jagat Prakash Singh, who'd agreed to meet him in the evening and let him know what the official investigation had discovered. Assuming, of course, that the Chief had discovered anything aside from his own shadow.

For now, Puri would settle for a copy of last night's dinner seating plan and went in search of the resourceful young waiter who'd sprung him from the Mattu table last night. Gunny was his name, and the detective found him in the Sea of Tranquillity, the hotel's Thai restaurant.

'What can I do for, sir, this time?' he asked in a conspiratorial manner, making it clear that he was willing to be of assistance in any way he could.

'I'm not here to eat,' said Puri, who sat down at one of the tables nonetheless. 'Some information is required.'

He went on to explain what he needed.

'Not a problem, sir,' was Gunny's response. 'I've one copy of the seating plan in my locker. It's got Sanjay Sala's autograph on the back. So it is worth one thousand at least.'

'Understood.'

Gunny eyed his manager who was standing over by the entrance to the restaurant.

'Sir, it would be best if you ordered something. Perhaps a drink.'

'Bring one bottle water – room temperature.'

Gunny returned with a bottle of mineral water and presented it as if it was a fine bottle of wine. The detective gave a connoisseur's nod and the waiter poured him a glass. He also slipped the seating plan on to the table before heading off to attend to some other customers.

Puri took out his notebook and began to write down the guests' names, adding the odd annotation of his own.

Left of Faheem Khan clockwise:
Satish Bhatia, 'Call Centre King'.
Jasmeet Bhatia, elderly mother of Satish Bhatia.

Sandeep Talwar – politician, President of the Indian Cricket Board, crook.

Mrs Harnam Talwar, elderly wife of above.

Nilesh Jani – ICT Chairman.

Mrs 'Mini' Jani – page three type, twenty-something.

Neetika Sahini – 'public relations' power broker.

J.K. Shrivastav – PM's cabinet secretary.

Mrs Shrivastav.

Sanjay Sala, Bollywood 'actor'.

Mrs Sanjay Sala – known as 'Bubbles'.

Kamran Khan – son of murder victim.

Ram Dogra – industrialist, known as the 'Prince of Polyester'.

Mrs Megha Dogra, elderly wife of above.

Gunjan Bhangu – construction.

Mrs Anita Bhangu, elderly wife of above, sat on right side of Faheem Khan, victim.

Gunny returned as Puri finished copying the list. 'Tell me. You were serving that table, is it?' asked the detective.

'Yes, sir. Filling glasses and all.'

'Everyone was seated exactly and according to the plan?'

'Yes, sir. Name cards were provided.'

'Some guests were getting up and down, no? Like the murdered gentleman. He left the hall for some time before eating.'

'Yes, sir. He left for ten minutes.'

'Anyone sat in his seat meanwhile?'

'No, sir.'

'Sure?'

'His food was sitting there getting cold and I was wondering should I cover it.'

The waiter was obviously telling the truth, yet Puri was certain he would never share anything incriminating about the guests. Not consciously, at least. They were powerful people and he was but an *aam aadmi*.

'Anyone else approached the table – while Mr Khan's food was sitting idle?' asked Puri.

'By then all the other guests had taken their seats and were eating. The photographers had been sent away.'

Puri paid for the water and then took two one-thousand-rupees note from his wallet.

'Anything further you wish to tell me?' he asked, fingering the bill.

Gunny glanced nervously round the restaurant to ensure his manager wasn't watching. 'One thing, sir,' he said, keeping his voice down. 'That model, Dippy: she lost one earring during dinner. Said it was worth two lakhs. She was crying and all.'

'It was found?'

'One of the cleaners picked it up on the emergency stairs, handed it in.'

'Emergency stairs? How it got there?'

Gunny gave a shrug. 'No idea, sir. They're at the back of the hotel.'

Puri left the notes under his napkin.

His next stop was Defence Colony, C Block, home of his parents-in-law.

Theirs was a large detached house, three floors in all, built in the early 1970s with the intention of leaving an equal portion to each of their children. The architectural antithesis of the Taj Mahal, the Mattu residence, with its chunky bungalows and concrete slab window awnings, looked as if it had been designed by the same architect as Hitler's bunker.

Every effort had been made to soften its harsh appearance. Lovingly tended flower beds ran along the outside wall, and the old peelu tree that burst out of the pavement shrouded half the facade with its umbrella canopy. Beyond the wrought-iron gates, marigolds and snapdragons in little terracotta pots lined the marble forecourt; and rosewood planter's chairs graced the edge of a small lawn.

The bell summoned the Christian maidservant, Alice, to the front door, and Puri greeted her, as he always did, with the words, 'Namaste! How is Wonderland?' This elicited a shy giggle (as it always did) and Puri stepped inside.

The living room had changed little from the first time he had visited the house in 1981. The rattan couch and armchairs remained in the same position around the Rajasthani cart-style coffee table. The British railway station clock up on the wall was still keeping good time, despite being a replica. The collection of curios the Mattus had picked up on their travels in various parts of India (an Assamese Japi hat; a pair of clay ornamental horses from Gorakhpur) and the two holidays they had taken to Europe (Eiffel Tower and Swiss cowbell) remained on the sideboard along with the family photos. Everything wore a faded look, like an old sepia print. But then – by God! – it had been some twenty-five years or more.

Puri had been in his mid-twenties at the time – pencil thin and somewhat nervous. He and his parents had sat in a row on the couch, and Brigadier – then Captain – Mattu and his wife had sat directly opposite them. Although the two mothers had met on three occasions in the weeks preceding the meeting and laid their plans, they were careful to let their husbands take the lead.

Formal introductions were made, tea and savoury biscuits were served, and the prospective groom's credentials and prospects were discussed. Mattu addressed him as 'young man', wanting to know details about his army career and where he saw himself in ten years. Puri answered confidently, explaining that he had recently been recruited into army intelligence and saw it as a lifetime career.

This was a truthful answer. It had never been Puri's ambition to become a jasoos, private detectives being little thought of in Indian society (down there with midwives). It was the Shimla Affair that changed all that, forcing him to resign in the early 1980s.

However, Puri did tell a lie that day – 'Yes, sir. Absolutely, sir. No doubt about it at all, sir,' he'd stated when asked whether he was ready to marry.

And then Meena walked into the room.

She was wearing a simple cotton sari and a string of fragrant jasmine in her hair.

Puri was rendered completely inarticulate.

Two months later, they were married.

The detective returned to the present, pausing by the sideboard to pick up the framed, black and white photograph taken of him and Rumpi on their wedding day. They were seated in front of the holy fire – he in a three-piece suit and a *sehra*. Through the curtain of flowers that hung in front of his face, you could make out his young moustache and thin features. Rumpi's eyes were cast down, a silk *chunni* draped over her head and a large nose ring chain encircling her right cheek. They both looked apprehensive; quite miserable, in fact.

Funny. That had been one of the happiest days of his life. He'd loved Rumpi from the first. Proof that arranged marriages made for the strongest unions – for individuals and their extended families.

He put the frame back and knocked on Brigadier Mattu's study door.

'Enter!'

Being a creature of habit and given that it was now exactly six o'clock, the Brigadier sat behind his desk sipping a cup of packaged tomato soup and listening to the news headlines in English on All India Radio.

'Come, young man,' he said with a welcoming smile, motioning Puri into a cane armchair.

The lady announcer, her dulcet voice a reminder of the more civilised days before the advent of hysterical 24-hour TV news presentation, spoke calmly about a massacre of police recruits by Maoist rebels in Chhattisgarh State. A politician from Uttar Pradesh had been accused of rape and of trying to cover up his crime, she went on to explain. And in the ICT league, the Hyderabad Hyenas had beaten the Bangalore Bears.

'Those are the headlines. And now we continue with our Hindi drama *Life Gulmohar Style*. In today's episode, Aruna and Chanchal have a chat about marriage and expectations of life after marriage. Why is it that some women seem to think that marriage is the ultimate aim of life?'

Brigadier Mattu looked as if he might like to carry on

listening but reached over and turned off his radio nonetheless. 'How is Mummy?' he asked. 'She's not well, I'm told.'

'Some fever is there, actually,' replied Puri, who'd only come to know she was ill an hour or two ago. 'The doctor has given medicine and she's taking rest. I'll be paying her a visit later, only.'

'Must have been the shock of last night,' commented Brigadier Mattu.

'Must be,' agreed Puri. 'It's not every day one sees a murder right before one's very eyes. And at her age—'

'At any age,' interrupted Brigadier Mattu, who was only three years younger than Mummy. 'Believe me when I tell you, Puri, I did not sleep one single wink last night.'

The Brigadier sipped his soup. A smidgen of tomato soup clung to his grey moustache.

'Sir, there is something I would want you to look at,' said the detective, coming straight to the point.

'What are you mixed up in this time?' asked Brigadier Mattu with a mischievous twinkle in his eye.

'I've been asked to put the murder of this Pakistani fellow under the scanner,' said Puri. 'Seems he and his son are in the dock for match fixing.'

He reached into an outer pocket of his safari suit and took out one of the sealable sandwich bags that he always kept about him, mostly for collecting and preserving evidence at crime scenes. They also came in useful for storing emergency samosas.

This one contained a crumpled piece of paper.

He handed it to the Brigadier and explained how he'd 'found' it in Faheem Khan's pocket.

'This is evidence stolen from the scene of a crime,' pointed out his father-in-law, looking alarmed.

'Not stolen, exactly, sir,' replied the detective. '*Liberated* is more like it.'

Mattu cocked an eyebrow in his direction.

'Sir, let me assure you the paper was sticking out of his pocket,' insisted Puri. 'What is more, such evidence would be one hundred per cent wasted on our Chief of Police. Doubtless, he would imagine those numbers written there were Faheem Khan's suit measurements. Probably start rounding up all Delhi tailors.'

But Brigadier Mattu wasn't listening; he was already studying the piece of paper.

Written on it was a series of numbers:

12, 11, 6
15, 9, 12
22, 14, 7

'Perhaps they correspond to overs and balls?' he wondered out loud.

'That would certainly make sense, sir,' replied Puri. 'The suspicion is there that Khan has been bowling no balls and wides and offering up easy deliveries. Thus a bookie can place bets on individual balls and overs and make a fortune. They call it spot betting.'

The Brigadier opened his desk drawer. 'I have the scorecard here,' he said. 'Let's see if the numbers correspond.'

He ran his fingers over the rows of meticulously recorded figures. 'Khan's first no ball came in the fourth over. Second delivery. Does that correspond with the number on the paper you stole?' he asked.

It did not.

He got the same negative result when he tried to match Kamran Khan's first wide ball.

'Perhaps they've reversed the numbers, balls then overs,' he suggested next.

Again the numbers didn't correspond.

'Could be these are instructions for the next match,' said Puri. 'Delhi is playing again day after.'

'In which case, we must watch the match carefully. Meantime I will keep trying different permutations.' The Brigadier's gaze remained fixed on the numbers.

'Most kind of you, sir,' said Puri.

He made his way out of the study, not entirely convinced that his father-in-law had noticed him leave.

En route to the Gymkhana Club, Puri made a quick stop at his usual chemist. He found six customers crowded around the counter, all of them simultaneously reeling off long lists of drugs with names that all ended in 'nox' or 'ozil'. Behind the counter, eight shop assistants fetched and carried their orders from shelves stocked to the ceiling with hundreds of white cartons containing every conceivable type of drug – a testament to the cavalier manner in which medicine was prescribed and eagerly guzzled down in India.

Mr Joti, the chief pharmacist, was sitting in his usual place behind the till. Puri elbowed his way past the other customers to reach him.

'Someone has overdosed again, sir?' asked Mr Joti, who

had helped the detective with medical-related expertise in the past.

'Nothing like that, actually. My wife is after me to get my weight down.' Puri showed him the ZeroCal flyer. 'You've this product?' he asked.

Mr Joti immediately called out to nobody in particular, 'One box ZeroCal!'

A carton was placed on the counter by one of the shop assistants. It was already open. There were about twenty blister strips inside.

'How many pieces you want?' asked the pharmacist.

'Four only,' replied the detective.

Four strips were promptly extracted and slipped into a little brown paper bag.

'Take one with every meal, sir,' instructed Mr Joti. 'Anything else?'

'*Buss.*'

There was a party being held at the Gymkhana Club, the diamond wedding anniversary of a Parsi couple called Mr and Mrs Gaariwala. Delhi's elite were arriving in their chauffeur-driven sedans. The dress code was 'sober', a word that had come to mean tasteful in a country that increasingly delighted in bling. The women wore heavy silk saris and expensive but discreet jewellery; the men blazers and cravats. There was an air of self-satisfied urbanity about them.

Puri spotted the club secretary, Colonel P.V.S. Gill (Retd.), and his harridan of a wife standing under the portico in front of the main entrance and ordered Handbrake to drive on.

'Go round back!' he shouted in English as he ducked down in his seat.

Gill had been on at him to run background checks on some of the latest applicants for club membership and Puri couldn't spare the time. As for that terrible woman, she had been gunning for him again recently. This time it was his Sandown that was at issue: hats and caps, according to Mrs Colonel P.V.S. Gill (Retd.), were not to be worn inside the Gym. One evening last month, she'd ordered the detective to remove his offending headgear, and when he'd refused, a disciplinary committee had been assembled. The spirit of the code of conduct laid down by the 'Founding Fathers' was being violated, the old crow had claimed. But Puri had argued — successfully for now — that she was talking 'total nonsense only'. Members were at liberty to wear turbans or topis. Why couldn't he don a cap?

Only a naïve fool would have considered the war won, however. Mrs Colonel P.V.S. Gill (Retd.) was like a Rottweiler. Her long-suffering husband had the teeth marks to prove it.

Puri took the back way into the club and reached the terrace bar without incident. 'Hearties apologies, Inspector sahib!' said Puri as he joined Inspector Jagat Prakash Singh, who had already claimed them a table.

They ordered a couple of Patiala pegs.

'So you mind telling me what all the Chief has been up to?' asked the detective as he settled into a comfortable armchair.

Singh looked uneasy. He leaned forward. 'Sir, if he knew I was sitting here with you discussing his case he'd have my badge.'

'Who is going to tell him, Inspector? Not you. Not I. And the barman is a mute. So why worry?'

'And what if I share some piece of evidence with you to which only he's privy, some salient detail, and it helps you solve the case? What then? He'll know it was me for sure.'

'Put it this way, Inspector sahib: no one is aware it was I who solved the tantric fraud case. Correct?' Puri didn't like to bring up past cases in which he had anonymously assisted Singh, but sometimes it was necessary to remind the inspector of what the detective called their 'mutual back scratching' arrangement. 'Point is,' continued the detective, 'many of the witnesses present were VVIPs and all. Such types won't speak with yours truly.'

Singh stared down into his glass. 'I printed off copies of the interviews and statements,' he said with a quiet reluctance. 'They're in the bag under the table.'

'Most kind of you, Inspector sahib.'

'Chief's taken statements from everyone who sat at the victim's table,' added the inspector.

'He's interviewed each and every one of them personally?'

'Some statements were submitted in written form – from the likes of the cabinet secretary, obviously. As for the Bollywood types, Chief talked to them by phone. All very cosy.'

'And the hotel staff?'

'They've been Bhatt's remit.'

Inspector Ravindra Bhatt was the Chief's lackey.

'One of the waiters is a charge-sheeter. Credit card fraud.'

'He's charging him, is it?'

'I would not be surprised,' replied Singh, who had nothing but contempt for his fellow officer.

Puri asked about Kamran Khan and was told he'd accompanied his father's body back to Pakistan in the afternoon.

'After he gave his statement, he was cleared to leave the country.'

The detective gave him a look of despair.

'You think he was involved?' asked Singh.

'Till date every person in that room is a suspect – even my dear Mummy-ji. So how can the son of the victim be allowed to leave the country, I ask you?'

'It's not that straightforward, sir. There's politics involved here – pressure from Islamabad.'

'Is there by God? Pressure from Islamabad? Then *challo*, never mind! No matter Pakistan is a terrorist-supporting state, occupying half Kashmir, wreaking havoc with Afghanistan, sharing nuclear secrets with likes of North Korea. Main thing is we should keep them happy. No boats should be rocked.'

'Sir, you've no argument with me. The fault lies with our politicians.' Singh drained his drink. 'Now if you'll excuse me, I should be getting home.'

Puri could see he was upset. 'Apologies, Inspector sahib!' he said. 'Didn't mean to get hot under the collar and all. Stay for another, haa. Have something to eat at least. I ordered one plate chilli cheese toast.'

'Didn't you tell me just last week that you had been put on a diet, sir?' asked Singh.

'Thank you for reminding me, Inspector sahib,' answered Puri, taking out the medicine he'd purchased earlier. 'Just I am planning to start it now, in fact.'

• SEVEN •

Mummy needed a cover story. And a suitable travelling companion. Someone with whom she could make the journey to the holy city of Haridwar, where she planned to continue her own investigation of the murder of Faheem Khan without raising the suspicion of her three sons. Someone who wasn't suspicious by nature and could be easily distracted.

Only one name fit the bill: Ritu Bawar, better known to everyone as Ritu Auntie.

Not the best traveller in the world, it had to be said – what with her bad hips, strict dietary requirements and highly superstitious nature. But she of all people had time on her hands. Her husband was no more (clogged arteries), her eldest son had emigrated (UAE) and her second son had someone else to cook for him (married off). She passed her days gossiping on the phone and from the balcony of her apartment, playing *teen patti* at the Punjabi Bagh Club, and badgering her young daughter-in-law for a grandson.

Still, persuading Ritu Auntie to travel so far was going to take some doing. Recently she'd baulked at going after dark to the Ananya Festival at Purana Qila – and that was only a few miles away.

Mummy sat in her bedroom in her house in Punjabi Bagh, where she lived with her eldest son, Bhupinder, mulling over the best strategy. Her thoughts were interrupted by a knock at the door.

'Mummy-ji? All OK?'

It was Jassu, her daughter-in-law. Mummy quickly hid the train timetable she'd been studying and her notes from the calls she'd made that afternoon to various friends and contacts in Delhi, Mumbai and Amritsar.

'Much better thank you, beta,' she said as she opened the door. 'Fever has totally vanished.'

'You should still take rest, Mummy-ji,' said Jassu. 'Must have been a terrible shock – seeing what you saw last night and all. I can't imagine. Bhuppie and I have been so worried! And you've hardly eaten all day. Only a little curd for lunch, no? I made *khichri*. You'll take some?'

'Some hunger is there. I'll be joining you shortly, na. Just I'll take bath. Ten minutes only is required.'

Jassu headed back downstairs to the kitchen and Mummy closed the door.

Her daughter-in-law was right about one thing: the events at the Delhi Durbar Hotel had indeed come as a shock. A bigger shock than anyone could possibly know. Mummy had hardly slept last night, tossing and turning on her thin cotton mattress well into the early hours. The image of Faheem Khan's last moments – arms flailing, froth oozing from his mouth, his taut, terror-stricken expression – had played in a loop over and over again in her mind. She had experienced terrible flashbacks from the past as well. Painful memories she thought she had buried deep down for ever.

Finally, at around three o'clock, she'd woken from her tortured half-sleep with a cry and sat up in bed, tears rolling down her face. Jassu came running into the room to check on her, but Mummy sent her daughter-in-law back to bed. 'Just some bad dream was there, na.'

Rather than going back to sleep herself, however, she bundled herself in a chunky cardigan and sat down on the floor in front of the puja shrine and marigold-draped photograph of her late husband, Om Chander Puri, that occupied the centre section of her dressing table. She lit a few *diyas* and an incense stick and engrossed herself in the Gita.

An hour or so passed before Mummy found her mind calm and at peace, and began to meditate on her dilemma.

She was probably the only person in the world in a position to unravel this murder. Should she act upon what she knew? Surely it was too much of a coincidence that she should find herself at the scene of his murder after all these years.

Mummy did not believe in coincidences. Everything was connected in this life. Everything.

But what would her involvement achieve – assuming, that is, she could identify the killer? What was the point in dredging up the past?

At five-thirty, before the rest of the household had risen, Mummy tiptoed downstairs, slipped on her tennis shoes, and with her shawl wrapped tight around her shoulders and a woolly hat pulled down over her head, stepped out into the cold, misty dawn.

For an hour, she followed the pathway that circled the neighbourhood's tatty communal garden. Round and round she went, head bent in contemplation, the arguments for and against going back and forth in her head, until she came to a decision – a compromise of sorts. She would try to establish the identity of the murderer. Her natural curiosity demanded no less of her. And once she'd solved the mystery and confronted the individual in question, looked that person directly in the eye, then and only then would she make a decision as to whether to inform the police.

This meant that, for now at least, what she knew would have to remain a secret. Not even Chubby could be told. This was her case to solve. It had been from the start.

Besides, when it came to detective work, the great Vishwas Puri never listened to his Mummy-ji. What was it he had told her when he had found out she was dabbling in a bit of harmless matrimonial investigation for some of the neighbours? 'Detectives are not mummies?' Haa!

Let him make his own way – that is, assuming that he was investigating the murder. 'Eleven people will choose eleven routes.' That was the old saying – one of her aunt's, in fact.

Mummy had returned to the house at around six-thirty in the morning with a temperature. Unfortunately Jassu noticed and sent for that total duffer, Dr Mohan. He lost no time in prescribing a course of antibiotics and a sedative and confined her to her bed.

Mummy pretended to take the pills (in fact she flushed them down the toilet, opting instead for ground sunflower seed with honey) and slept a natural sleep until lunchtime.

She awoke feeling much better and started making her calls, the first being to her friend new Rajneesh, the assistant manager at the Durbar Hotel.

By early evening, Mummy had reached the conclusion that a trip to the holy city of Haridwar on the Ganges – to consult with the Pandas, the Brahmin genealogical record keepers – was vital to establish the identity of the murderer.

There was a Shatabdi express train leaving at six-thirty tomorrow morning from New Delhi station. Mummy already had a reservation for two but still needed an excuse for taking Ritu Auntie along.

Fortunately, the solution came to her while she was taking her bucket bath.

'So stupid of me!' she cursed. 'Why I didn't think of it before, na?'

Once dried and dressed, Mummy picked up her port-able and found her friend's number among the hundreds stored in her electronic address book.

'Ritu? Yes, yes, quite all right. Now listen.'

But Ritu Auntie was upset: Mummy hadn't returned any of her calls in the past twenty-odd hours. She wanted to know every grisly detail about the murder. And then she wanted to know all about the page three types who'd attended the dinner – what they'd worn, how they'd behaved . . .'

Only after Ritu Auntie's appetite for celebrity

tittle-tattle had been fully sated was Mummy able to spin
her web.

'Never mind all that, na,' she said. 'Something urgent
is there. Last night, only, I was having one dream. So
strange it was. Concerning yourself. And your dear late
husband. His ashes are still lying with you, na?'

• EIGHT •

Puri's mobile phone rang shortly after six the following morning.

'Chubby? Bhuppi this side. You're awake? Listen, yaar!'

It was his elder brother, sounding grumpy. Mummy's room was empty. She and Ritu Auntie had taken off together for Haridwar, he said.

The detective had been up until two in the morning reading all the witness statements and interviews provided by Inspector Singh. In the process, he'd downed a quarter of a bottle of Royal Challenge. This had not mixed well with the ZeroCal tablets and he had a pounding headache. It took him what felt like an age to register what he'd just been told. When the information finally reached the relevant synapses, he rolled over on to his back and groaned, 'By God.'

In the light cast by the digital clock, he could see that the heavy Indian quilt on Rumpi's single bed was turned back and it was empty. No doubt she'd risen at five, her normal hour, and was down in the kitchen drinking her morning glass of lemon water mixed with *kala namak*.

'Mummy discussed her plans with you, is it?' croaked the detective.

'Course not, yaar. I'd have given you SMS.'

'So how you came to know she's going to Haridwar?'

'I'm no detective but I can read. She left a voucher on the kitchen table.' By 'voucher' he meant a note.

'What time they departed exactly?' he asked.

'Five-thirty – must have been. Says they've gone to scatter Jagdish Uncle's ashes in Ganga.'

'Why so sudden, haa? No prior notice?'

'My question exactly.'

'You reached her?'

'Few minutes back. The train was already on the way. Lots of disturbance on line. Mummy claims they planned to go long time back.'

The detective let out a half-exasperated, half-resigned sigh followed by, 'What to do, Bhuppi?'

'Think we should order them home? I'm worried about Mummy.'

'Her health was much improved by the time I came last night, no? Fever over, buss.'

'She should rest, yaar.'

Bhupinder went on to describe how Mummy had again cried out in her sleep and how Jassu had found her sitting up in bed in tears.

'Sorry to hear that, Bhuppi, but it's to be expected,' said the detective. 'She was witness to a brutal murder, after all. During my long and distinguished career I've seen such a reaction many times over. Doubtless some fresh air will do her no end of good.' He paused. 'For peace of mind, I would ask a fellow in Haridwar to keep an eye or two on her. Make sure Mummy-ji and that Ritu Auntie stay out of trouble.'

'He'd better be *bilkul* number one, Chubby. So strong-headed she is.'

'Just look on bright side,' said Puri. 'You'll be having R and R over next few days, no? Why not enjoy? For every cloud there is silvery lining.'

The detective lay in bed, loath to get up from beneath the cosy covers, staring up at the damp marks on the ceiling left by last year's monsoon. There was something else bothering him apart from his headache – a 'brain itch' – and it had to do with Mummy.

Her reaction to Kamran Khan had been totally out of character. At the time, Puri had put her behaviour down to a natural animosity towards Pakistanis, one he felt keenly himself. Pakistan had long been India's enemy, after all. The two countries had fought three wars, four if you included the Kargil conflict of 1999. And although Mummy had never talked about her experiences during Partition and the murder of her brother, Anil (he'd always imagined that she was suffering from a kind of selective amnesia, and had long ago learned not to pry into her past), Puri knew that she'd been forced to flee from her childhood home and, along with millions of others, embark on a frightening, arduous journey to Delhi.

It occurred to him now, however, that there might be some connection between his mother and the Khans. She had grown up in Rawalpindi, after all, their home. He would ask her about it when she returned from Haridwar.

Puri also made a mental note to find out if any of the suspects had past connections with Pakistan. It was possible that the motive for the murder had nothing to do with cricket or match fixing.

His brain itch suitably scratched, he sat up in bed and reached for the cup of bed tea that had been brought by one of the servants. While he sipped the contents, he reflected on the events of the past couple of days – the clues he'd collected, the unanswered questions, the steps he now planned to take in order to move the investigation forward.

The interviews and witness statements supplied by Inspector Singh had made a few things clear – at least to Puri.

Firstly, the food had been poisoned *after* it had been put on the victim's plate. Faheem Khan's neighbours had all eaten butter chicken from the same serving dish and none of them had died or shown symptoms of having ingested poison. As for the waiter who'd served the food, he was a shy young man with no previous record.

Next, all the interviews corroborated the fact that from the time the food was served to the time Faheem Khan died, no other guests sitting elsewhere in the banquet hall approached the table. Therefore it was safe to conclude that one of the individuals seated at the centre table was the murderer.

What else? Ram Dogra, the 'Prince of Polyester', had knocked over his wine glass while Faheem Khan had been absent from the table. And the actress, Dippy, who'd been seated at another table, had left the banquet hall fifteen minutes before Faheem Khan died.

There was one further important detail that Puri had gleaned. All the suspects had attended a drinks function at a private residence the night before. Arriving for his first visit to India, Faheem Khan had gone there straight from the airport.

As for the dog that had invaded the Kotla pitch, it didn't even get a mention in the Chief's interviews. As Puri had anticipated, he'd not made the connection between the pooch's death and the murder. But assuming the mutt had been poisoned with *Aconitum luridum* (and Puri would know for sure later today, Tubelight having dropped the carcass off at Dr Pathak's laboratory last night), then the following conclusions could be made:

Number one, the murderer had attended both the match *and* the dinner. That more or less ruled out any of the waiters or hotel staff as suspects.

Two, the murderer had either accidentally dropped or disposed of some of the poison at the stadium and the dog had gobbled it up, or he or she had given it to the dog deliberately to test the effectiveness of the dosage.

If the latter proved to be true – and Puri thought it the most likely scenario – then it meant the murder had not been the work of the Delhi underworld. A hail of bullets was more their style.

The case that former Deputy Commissioner Scott was investigating – the killing of the alleged Mumbai bookie Vikas Sengar, aka 'Fawda' – was similarly unusual. Such goonda types usually ended up getting gunned down by *supari* killers, who weren't exactly known for using the subtle approach. Either that or they were 'encountered' by the police – in other words executed in a raid to save the trouble of a trial and/or to cover up links with the local constabulary.

Last night, Puri had called one of his sources in Mumbai, a female crime reporter on a local newspaper. In her Mumbaiya pidgin jumbled with Indian English slang, she'd told him that Sengar had died from eating poisoned biryani.

'Fawda *Bhaiyya* was *game bajaana suumdi* style,' she'd said.

Puri interpreted this to mean that Fawda, the bookie, who hailed originally from north India, was bumped off, but in a subtle fashion.

'Someone made it look like a suicide?' he tried to clarify in Hindi.

'Ji, Uncle,' she replied. 'He was *dedu foot* so couldn't reach the *punkah*. Plus, he was totally *fultoo* and doing *balle balle* with his *biscuit*.'

Translation: 'He was a short man so he couldn't have reached the ceiling fan with the rope with which he is alleged to have hanged himself. Also, he was extremely drunk and there's every reason to believe that he was "making happiness" with his mistress before he was killed.'

It confirmed everything Scott had said.

'The biscuit was questioned?' asked Puri.

'She told some *blo bachhan* [bullshit] story. That *mama* [police officer] is a *khaali pili* [one who scratches his balls]. His boss is even worse – *dedh dimaage* [one with half-brains]. The investigation was a *chuna* [cover-up].'

Vedika had no idea who had been behind the killing – '*Haila*! [God knows], Uncle' – but agreed that it hadn't been the underworld. As for Fawda, she described him as a Johnniewalker (heavy drinker).

There was no doubt in Vedika's mind that he had been one of Aga's chief Mumbai bookies.

'*Keeda* [insect],' she added.

Breakfast that morning consisted of a bowl of pomegranate seeds – sheer torture given the sight of the crisp aloo parantha being prepared on the stove by Rumpi for herself. Puri sat at one end of the kitchen table as Monica the maidservant chopped fresh *methi* leaves in preparation for lunch, and Sweetu the houseboy perched on a bamboo stool in the corner, polishing the detective's black orthopaedic shoes.

Malika, the other maidservant, had called to say that she wouldn't be coming to work today. Her youngest son, one of four, was sick with a high temperature, headaches, aching limbs. It sounded like *chikungunya*.

'Her husband's back at home,' Rumpi told Puri.

Subtext: Malika's layabout, good-for-nothing husband had lost yet another job and was sitting around drinking Double Dog whisky while watching saucy item numbers on Bollywood video channels.

'Malika's asked for salary advance,' added Rumpi.

Subtext: she didn't have enough to pay the doctor.

Puri sighed and reached for his wallet. 'I tell you if she was not like a daughter to me . . .' he said as he fished out 200 rupees and laid the notes on the table. He considered this a gift; his staff's health care costs were his responsibility given that the government failed to provide for them. 'That bloody bastard requires a good thrashing, I tell you,' he grumbled, referring to Malika's husband.

Rumpi placed a cup of sweet milky chai on the table in front of him and sat down with her parantha. Then began the daily round-up of family news and domestic issues.

Their grandson Rohit's hair-shaving Mundan ceremony was to be held the following Monday, Rumpi reminded him. And Radhika, their youngest daughter, had called yesterday from Pune, where she was studying, to discuss travel plans for Holi.

'She'll be reverting home?'

'Of course, Chubby. What are you thinking? Jaiya and Lalita are coming also.'

'Wonderful! All our girls at home together. Holi's when exactly?'

The festival fell on the last full moon in the month of Phalguna in the Hindu calendar and so it was on a different date in late February or early March every year.

'I told you twice already,' scolded Rumpi. 'It's in ten days.'

'Apologies, my dear, my mind is getting overload.'

By a quarter to seven, Puri was on the expressway heading back into south Delhi. It wasn't long before he received his first phone call of the day from Satya Pal Bhalla demanding an update on the moustache case.

'I've been trying to reach you!' he said without so much as a good-morning.

The detective had no intention of telling him that he had taken on the murder investigation. Thinking fast, he opted for the one excuse no Indian could ever argue with. 'One family wedding was there,' he said. 'My *chacha's* granddaughter.'

Puri had lost count of the number of times this particular niece had been married over the years.

'Listen!' insisted Bhalla. 'Gopal Ragi declared himself owner of the longest moustache in India – on national television! Didn't have the common courtesy to wait even twenty-four hours out of respect for my loss! I saw him smiling. Celebrating, Puri-ji! *Saala kutta!* What are you doing about it?'

Puri assured him that he was well on top of the case, gave his usual 'no stone will go unturned' assurance and hung up.

'Son of an ox!' he cursed, wishing he hadn't taken on the moustache case. The Khan murder deserved his full attention and this bloody Bhalla was going to be calling every hour on the hour.

Oh how he hated impatient, pushy clients! They had no appreciation for the special talents required for detective work. Worst were the ones who read that bloody Agatha Christie. They imagined that because some old memsahib in an Angrezi village with a population of a dozen – mostly Christian priests and old duffers and the like – could solve a murder over a cup of Earl Grey, the same could be done in India. India with its 1,600-plus languages; myriad ancient religions; castes, sub-castes and tribes; five-and-a-half-thousand-year-old culture – not to mention a billion-plus population and cities expanding before your very eyes.

But there was no turning back. Vish Puri, Most

Private Investigator, winner of one international and six national awards, and the only Indian PI ever to be featured on the cover of *India Today* magazine, had given his word.

In fact he was on his way now to start his enquiries.

It was shortly after seven when he reached H Block, Laxmi Bai Nagar, and found the nightwatchman who'd tackled the intruder into Bhalla's apartment.

'Illiterate Bihari village type' was how Puri summed him up in his mind. He was thin and swaddled in a dirty shawl but stood up straight and looked the detective in the eye.

'*Namashkar*,' said Puri, greeting him.

'Namashkar, sahib!'

'What's your name?' the detective asked in Hindi.

'Dalchand.'

'I want to ask you some questions. About the attempted robbery the other night.'

'I did nothing wrong, sahib! I was only doing my duty!'

Realising that the police had probably given him a hard time, Puri tried to put him at ease. 'I'm working for Bhalla sahib to catch the thief,' he explained.

Dalchand's smile revealed a crooked row of paan-stained teeth. 'I'll help in any way I can to catch that son of a bitch,' he said beaming.

Puri took out a pack of Gold Flakes that he had anticipated might come in handy. He offered one to the guard, who readily accepted the cigarette and lit up.

'I was on my rounds when I saw a figure climbing up the balcony,' he began, the smoke spilling from his mouth indistinguishable from his breath in the chilled morning air. 'I rang the police but they never came. So I went up the stairs and started banging on the front door. After a couple of minutes the maid answered. I ran inside and the man fled. He went to the balcony again and started to climb down.'

'What did you do?'

'Went after him of course, sahib!' Dalchand said this with pride. 'When I reached the ground I ran very fast. I'm good at running! I cut him off before he reached the gate and tackled him.'

Puri asked about the thief's size.

'He was big, much bigger than me, over six feet tall! He was strong, also. I managed to get my teeth into his ankle. He cried out and let go of his bag – the one in which he was carrying some of Bhalla sahib's moustache. I grabbed it and ran.'

'He pursued you?'

'I got up that tree over there – I am good at getting up trees! He shouted at me, told me to give him back his bag. Promised to make me rich.'

How much had he been offered?

'Twenty thousand, sahib!'

The detective whistled.

'A fortune, I know! But I refused. I spat at him. I told him he deserved to hang. He cursed me and swore vengeance. Called me a son of a whore, son of a pig, sister f—'

'What happened next?' interrupted Puri.

'Another watchman came running with a flashlight and he ran away.'

'You chased after him?'

'Of course, sahib! We didn't give up. But he had a scooty.'

'You saw the number plate?'

Dalchand averted his eyes, embarrassed. 'Sorry, sahib, I'm not good with letters and numbers. There was some writing – a goose and two snakes curled around themselves.'

Puri took out his notebook and wrote '2 8 8'. 'Like this?' he asked.

'Exactly, sahib! Those three came at the end.'

'What make was the scooty?'

'Hero Honda. Red colour.'

'What language did he speak?'

'When he cursed it was in Punjabi.'

'You speak Punjabi?'

'Since coming to Delhi I've become very familiar with Punjabi insults. I hear them often.'

'You said you bit him. Did you draw blood?'

'Yes, sahib!' Again this was said with pride. 'The man was limping as he ran.'

Puri made a note of this. Dalchand looked pleased with himself.

'Anything else you can tell me about him?'

'Did I tell you he was very strong, sahib? He had the strength of five men and yet I managed him.'

'Aren't you worried he'll come back?'

'Let him come, sahib!'

The local police station was nearby. In a cold, sparsely furnished office, Puri found Inspector Surinder Thakur huddled behind his desk, a small glass of chai cupped in his hand.

'You're wasting your time, sir,' he said after Puri had explained the purpose of his visit. 'I'll be making two arrests later this morning.'

'*Accha?*'

'There's only one man who stands to gain from putting Bhalla sahib out of the picture. And I have all the evidence I need to charge him and his accomplice.'

'Gopal Ragi?'

'He's been after Bhalla sahib's crown for years. Recently he accused him of cheating and threatened him *and* his moustache.'

'That is by no means enough to prove his involvement,' pointed out the detective.

Thakur was smugness personified. 'I've come to know that Ragi has a Punjabi driver, one Sunil Singh, a charge-sheeter,' he said. 'He matches the description of the thief given by the nightwatchman – six foot tall, very strong.'

Puri still looked unconvinced.

'*And* this individual walks with a limp,' said Thakur, cracking a wry smile.

'Is it?' said Puri, eyebrows raised.

'Like I told you, sir, case is in the bag. All that is required now is a confession.'

'Still one question is there, Inspector,' said Puri. 'Assuming Ragi instructed his driver to do the needful, why he didn't cut the moustache to ribbons? Vandalise it, so to speak. Why he tried to carefully remove the moustache?'

'I believe he wanted a trophy, sir. These people are obsessed with moustaches. I've come to know that Ragi and Bhalla and one hundred or so others belong to a kind of moustache club. These people actually get together and talk about their moustaches! Can you imagine?'

Puri managed a strained smile. 'It is a way of being sociable, no? Such like-minded people have a good deal to talk about.'

'They're all like-minded, that's for sure, sir!' exclaimed Thakur.

'Yes . . . well, seems I have taken plenty of your time,' stuttered the detective. 'Best of luck to you, Inspector.'

He left the station hoping Thakur was right. Puri had very little to go on, after all. In a city of 16 million he was after a tall, limping Punjabi who drove a scooty with a number plate that ended in a goose and two snakes.

· NINE ·

Puri rendezvoused with Tubelight at eight-thirty later that morning at Shyam Sweets in Chawri Bazaar, Old Delhi. They both ordered plates of *bedmi aloo*, stood at one of the elevated tables and got straight down to business.

The operative had traced Full Moon's Mercedes Benz from the Delhi Durbar Hotel. It was owned by a certain Mohib Alam.

'Bingo!' exclaimed Puri.

'Know him, Boss?' asked Tubelight in Hindi.

'Our Angrezi client has been doing investigation of his match-fixing affairs. Mohib Alam – I am calling him "Full Moon" – met with our most esteemed Pakistani victim, Faheem Khan, in London last year only.'

'This one's into everything, Boss.'

'Let me guess. Builder? Marble? Runs medical colleges on the side? Who's his godfather?'

'Sandeep Talwar – recently appointed President of the Indian Cricket Board.'

Puri clapped his hands together with glee. 'And very much present at the dinner! Dots are beginning to connect!' he said.

Their breakfast order arrived: drowned in each of the servings of steaming potato curry was a whole red chilli. As if that wasn't enough spice, the stuffed bedmis came with a dollop of green chutney.

Both men dug in, eating with their hands and talking with their mouths full.

'Full Moon's got a farmhouse in Chattarpur,' said Tubelight. 'You should see this place, Boss. The Mughals never knew such luxury.'

'Give me round-the-clock surveillance,' ordered the detective in English, a trickle of curry running down his chin. 'Phone tapping, home tapping, car tapping. Garbage analysis, also. I want to see the dark side of Full Moon.'

The joke was lost on the operative, whose English was rudimentary. 'Right, Boss,' he said. 'One other thing: he's having a *satta* party tomorrow. During the Goa Beachers–Mumbai Bears match.'

'Pukka?'

'The tent wallah told me.'

Puri gave Tubelight a mischievous look to indicate what he was thinking.

'Tight security, Boss. Invitation only,' Tubelight warned.

'We'll manage, no?' said the detective with a flick of his hand. 'Always remember, yaar: will-and-way, will-and-way.'

Their salty lassis were brought to the table, straws protruding from both glasses. Puri sucked on his as he passed a piece of paper across the table: a list of the guests who'd sat at the centre table during the dinner. He had already scratched out six names. These were:

Nilesh Jani, Chairman of the ICT, and his socialite

wife, Mini, who were the only guests who hadn't risen from the table during the meal (this having been corroborated by the hotel staff and all the other witnesses).

Sanjay Sala, the actor, and his wife, Bubbles, who hadn't left the stands once during the match at the Kotla Stadium and therefore could not have deliberately or inadvertently poisoned the dog.

And J.K. Shrivastav, the cabinet secretary, and his wife, who had only attended the dinner.

'That leaves ten total,' said Puri. 'Give me background checking on each and every one of them – top to bottom, inside out, no stone unturned.' Background checking meant dirt, rumour, word on the street.

The operative cast his eye over the list, tilted his head to one side and said, 'Bilkul.'

'Also, should any of these individuals have any connection with Pakistan, past or present, I would want to be knowing,' added Puri.

'No problem, Boss.'

Shyam Sweets were open to the narrow, dirty street, which was getting busier by the minute. Bedraggled labourers pushed handcarts piled high with every kind of merchandise – fans, engine parts, great packages swathed in muslin cloth. A bicycle rickshaw appeared with a teetering mountain of hose pipes balanced on its passenger seat. Motorised three wheelers weaved past honking like irritated geese. A wandering holy man in patched garb held up a steel tin soliciting donations.

'You suspect Kamran Khan?' asked Tubelight, pointing out his name on the list.

'His father was doing match fixing – no doubt about

it at all. For that Kamran Khan would most definitely be involved. Who knows what all went on between them? There is no honour amongst goondas after all. It has come to my attention also his father stood in the way of his marrying one Noor Sultana.'

At the mention of the actress's name, Tubelight puffed out his cheeks and blew out the air like a wolf baying at the moon.

'Beautiful, haa?' asked the detective, who'd never seen an image of her.

By way of a response Tubelight started to sing from a 1960s Bollywood hit made famous by singer Asha Bhosle: 'Man has prayed to me; The angels have bowed their heads to me.'

This drew smiles from the customers standing nearby: 'Under my veil there is such a beauty; Lifting it you will be mesmerised!' one of them chimed in, prompting smiles all round.

'Kamran Khan had motive for sure,' said Puri as everyone returned to their business.

'But he's in Pak,' said Tubelight.

'That indeed presents something of a problem,' said Puri, who was still hoping that he could avoid travelling to Rawalpindi to interview him.

His operative started cleaning between his teeth with a toothpick. 'My money's on Full Moon's godfather, Sandeep Talwar,' he said. 'Remember few years back his son ran over two Jats, killed them? Witnesses vanished. I tell you, Boss, his mother mated with a jackal.'

Puri gave a loud, dismissive tut. 'I've told you before, no? Leave stargazing to stargazers. Now tell me: where is Flush exactly? He's reverted or what?'

The young electronics and computers whizz had gone to visit his family in his 'native place'.

'In that hole he calls home,' answered Tubelight. 'Eating Domino's and reading adventures of Savita Bhabhi . . .'

Puri looked up from his food and frowned; he considered pornography to be immoral, even in the land of the Kama Sutra.

'. . . I meant Spider-Man,' added Tubelight, hastily. 'Reading Spider-Man comics.'

'I'll give him call,' murmured the detective. 'We would be needing him.'

After they'd finished their food, Puri phoned Satya Pal Bhalla and broke the news that the arrest of his nemesis, Gopal Ragi, was imminent.

'Excellent work, Puri!'

The detective tried to explain that it was Inspector Thakur's decision, but to no avail.

'I knew it was that bastard,' he kept saying. 'Let him rot!'

Next, Puri rang Elizabeth Rani and explained that he needed the goose and two snakes licence plate traced.

'Only a partial number, sir? That will be difficult,' she said.

'I'm quite aware, Madam Rani. Please just do the needful.'

From Chawri Bazaar, Puri set off on a fool's errand: trying to question some of Delhi's most powerful and wealthy individuals. The likelihood was that few of them would deign to see him. And there was a good chance that he'd be reported for harassment and arrested on some trumped-up charge. At the very least, it wouldn't be long before the Chief and the murderer would know of his involvement in the case.

Yet as an outsider, this was often how he was forced to work. He took pride in calling his approach 'jugaad investigation', 'jugaad' being a useful Hindi term that meant 'to improvise'. To the detective, as to many an Indian, it was a fine concept, the idea that they could make do with anything and come up with a solution.

His first stop was the Lutyens bungalow on Janpath in British-built New Delhi where the politician Sandeep Talwar and his family resided. It was the detective's understanding that the MP for Ghaziabad and President of the Indian Cricket Board was usually to be found at this hour sitting on his veranda consulting with his astrologer.

Handbrake pulled up outside the main gate, where three Special Protection Group soldiers stood guard. Puri sent in his card. It drew out an obsequious minion in a *kurta* and sleeveless Nehru jacket.

'You've an appointment?'

Puri explained that he was investigating the murder of Faheem Khan and was eager to know from Sir and Madam whether they had seen anything at the dinner that might assist in the successful identification of the murderer.

'Saheb has engagements all day.'

'Perhaps Madam could spare five minutes?'

That was out of the question. As the patron of a number of charities, she couldn't possibly spare the time.

The minion turned and headed back in through the gate.

One of the soldiers gave a flick of his hand as he might have done to a fly.

'Out for a duck,' said the detective.

*　　*　　*

NOIDA, the New Okhla Industrial Development Authority, Delhi's sprawling eastern suburb, lay across the giant sewer where the sacred Yamuna River once flowed. A pristine eight-lane highway, better known as the Flyway, swept past the colossal, Disneyfied Akshardham Temple complex to a cityscape of luxury tower blocks and shopping malls wreathed in the ubiquitous golden arches.

Satish Bhatia's company, Outsourcing Consultants, was housed in a glass tower off Knowledge Boulevard. The foyer was all shiny marble, leather furniture and giant canvases splattered in colourful paint. A row of clocks above the reception displayed the time in seven cities.

'You would be having an appointment, sir?'

In this instance, Puri was able to answer in the affirmative; he had called ahead and Satish Bhatia, the Call Centre King, had agreed to give him ten minutes of his time.

'Please follow me, sir.'

A security guard led the detective to a glass elevator activated by an electronic pass. Puri glided up the side of a towering atrium, past open-plan floors where rows of young Indians wearing headsets stared into computer screens. He'd visited many a call centre before and always found them surreal places – filled with people with names like Palaniyappan Kurukulasuriya passing themselves off as Robert or Steve and selling car insurance to people in Newcastle.

A young secretary was waiting for the detective on the top floor. She led him down a long, impersonal corridor that led to Bhatia's office. A double door opened on to a large room furnished with a conference table, a treadmill positioned in front of a wall-mounted plasma screen and a seating area with a glass coffee table.

The Call Centre King was standing behind his desk, looking out over the panoramic view of NOIDA beyond. He was talking on the phone; to California, according to the secretary.

Puri couldn't make heads or tails of what he overheard. What the hell was 'dynamic content'? And how could a computer eat cookies? But he was fluent in body language and as he waited, he was able to gain a good measure of the forty-seven-year-old. Bhatia was the embodiment of the Indian IT nerd, right down to the glasses and the oversized collar in which his thin neck looked like a straw protruding from a bottle. His concave stomach, not much wider than the span of a man's hands, suggested a vegetarian diet; while the *kalava* around his right wrist spoke of religious belief.

Two other things evidently mattered to the Call Centre King: recognition – framed covers of prestigious business magazines featuring his profile were prominently displayed around the office; and family, in particular his mother. Hers was the largest portrait of all on the wall, even dwarfing the image of Bhatia's young wife.

'So you're a real private detective, Mr Puri?' he asked as soon as he put down the phone.

His accent was Americanised – like one of those voices in TV advertisements that tried to make toilet cleaner sound exciting. Puri was reminded that Bhatia had spent a considerable amount of time outside India – in Silicon Valley, mostly.

'Most Private Investigators at your service,' said Puri,

producing a copy of his card and handing it to the young man.

'So you go after bad guys? Like bank robbers and kidnappers?'

'All sorts, sir. Murderers, also.'

'Wow, you know, I grew up reading detective stories. Couldn't get enough of them. Feluda was my favourite. I used to lie in bed reading his adventures under the covers with a torch.'

'Feluda is fiction whereas I am fact,' said Puri rather drily.

'Right. So I'm told you're looking into this Khan business. Any ideas who did it?'

'That is a work in progress, shall we say.'

'Am I a suspect? I was sitting right next to the victim.'

'Putting it bluntly, sir: yes, you are on the list.'

Bhatia put up both arms in a playful gesture. 'I did it, Mr Puri!' he announced, with impish, crinkled eyes. 'You got me! Take me away!'

The detective's mouth twitched into a smile. 'Sorry to disappoint, sir, but I've not the power, actually. You would have to make a full confession to the police.'

'You can't make a citizen's arrest?'

'In India there is no such thing, sir.'

'Then I guess I'm off the hook. Phew!'

'Not quite, Sir. Few questions are there.'

'Do you mind telling me who you're working for?'

'That I cannot say.'

'Wow, mysterious! You're a dark horse, Mr Puri. But it kind of makes it hard to know whom I'm talking to here. How do I know this conversation is going to stay confidential?'

'Sir, confidentiality is my watchword. Furthermore I'm a member of the World Federation of Detectives and winner of the Super Sleuth Award. I am more than certain you searched my name on your wifee prior to my arrival also.'

Wifee was how Puri referred to the Web.

'Well, a man in my position has to be careful,' said Bhatia. 'So what is it you want to know? Did I see anything suspicious? Like the guy who spiked Khan's butter chicken? I'm afraid not.'

Puri decided to use the scatter approach – random questions, see if he could catch him off guard. 'You've ever been to Pakistan, sir?' he asked.

'Pakistan?' Bhatia frowned. 'No, Mr Puri, I can't say I have.'

'You've contact with any Pakistanis?'

'*Contact?*' He let the word hang and made a face. 'I've some Pakistani friends, if that's what you mean. In the US, mostly. I guess that makes me a traitor, right?'

'I would not say that, sir.'

'No, but it doesn't sit comfortably with you, does it, Mr Puri? Pakistan's the enemy, right?'

'Isn't it, sir?'

'Not from where I'm sitting. Know what I see when I look at Pakistan? Potential. We have a lot of what they need and vice versa. It's time for some détente, Mr Puri, time to bury the hatchet. I tell you, the best remedy to all this hostility is trade. We should open up our borders, engage with our neighbour, help the Pakistani middle class grow. All this sabre rattling gets us nowhere. We need to put all the suspicion aside.'

'With all respect, sir, I think you are forgetting Pakistan is a fundamentalist state, founded on religion, only. Its military and intelligence community is suffering from total paranoia with regard to India. The Generals will never make peace. Nowadays they're having nuclear weapons pointing at us even as we speak.'

'We have a few pointing at them, too, Mr Puri.'

'As a deterrent, only.'

Bhatia smiled indulgently. 'Well I suppose we'll have to agree to disagree. But you know they're not as bad as you might think. Pakistanis, I mean. They're really no different than us – same language, same corruption, same love of cricket.'

'You said "guy", sir.'

Bhatia gave a quizzical look. 'Sorry, Mr Puri?'

The detective read from his notebook. '"Like the guy who spiked Khan's butter chicken." Your words a few minutes ago.'

'Just a figure of speech. A guy can be a girl, if you know what I mean. The word's not gender specific. You really shouldn't read anything into it. Guess I've spent too long in America.'

'I take it cricket and not baseball is to your taste, is it?'

'Guilty as charged.'

'Ever gamble on a game?'

'Not in this country; it's illegal. Something that should be changed, in my view.'

'Why is that exactly?'

'For one thing, the government's losing a hell of a lot of revenue. Thousands of crores a year. And the whole business breeds corruption.'

Puri made another entry in his notebook and Bhatia looked playfully over his desk to try to see what he was writing. 'What is that, my biography?'

The detective ignored the question. 'You grew up in Delhi, is it?' he asked.

'Born and bred, Mr Puri. I moved to the States when I was twenty-four, but all my schooling was here.'

'And your parents – Dilli also?'

'Dad's family hails from Amritsar. Mom came from what you'd call *enemy territory*. A village called Rawat in Pakistan.'

The detective wrote down the name while asking, 'She came over in 1947, is it?'

'That's right. But she's never really spoken of it.'

'Sir, my own mother lost her brother, actually, but not once in all my entire life has she talked about his death.'

One of Bhatia's phones rang.

'Excuse me a minute, will you?' he said as he picked up the receiver. He listened for a second before placing one hand over the mouthpiece and saying, 'Mr Puri, if there's nothing else I need to take this.'

'One thing is there, actually. I would be needing to speak with your mother.'

'Well, if you wanna hang on, she'll be here soon. I'm taking her to lunch.'

The detective, having indicated his willingness to wait, sat back listening to Bhatia talk more jargon for what seemed like an interminable period.

When Jasmeet Bhatia arrived, Puri recognised her immediately from the Durbar dinner. Despite her age — mid-seventies at a guess — she was wearing the same Chanel sunglasses with diamond-studded frames. A considerable amount of gold glistened on her fingers as well, and the manner in which she carried her bag in the crook of her arm with her hand held out as if she was presenting it to someone to be kissed made it hard to miss.

Beneath all the glam, however, stood a typical auntie type — at least that's how Puri would describe her later in his notes. Around five feet four inches tall with an unbalanced gait (she lurched from side to side like a boat caught in a storm, thanks to her worn-out hips), Jasmeet Bhatia had clearly come to wealth late in life. Her withered hands and pockmarked complexion betrayed a lifetime of work. Indeed there was an inherent toughness about her. Puri could picture her fighting to be first at the village well.

'Aaah, so you're the one,' she said in Hindi when Puri introduced himself. 'Satish said you'd be coming around.' The voice went with the face: forthright, strong.

'I was waiting to speak with you, actually, madam,' said Puri.

Her son was still speaking on the phone. Something about a ram.

'What is you want to know?' asked Jasmeet Bhatia. She hadn't taken off her sunglasses. Puri found it disconcerting not being able to see her eyes.

'During the dinner were you seated the entire time?' he asked in Hindi.

'Of course not,' came back the answer. 'I got up three or four times.'

'While Faheem Khan was away from the table?'

'I've no idea.' She gave a shrug. 'Look, I got up to talk to my friends – Harnam Talwar, Anita Bhangu. What's the big deal?' She gestured to her son to hurry up.

'Had you had any prior meetings with Faheem Khan?'

'I met him the night before.'

'You didn't know him or have any dealings with him in Pakistan?'

'I've not set foot in Pakistan since 1947!'

'You didn't know him when you were young?'

'Nothing like that,' Jasmeet Bhatia said with a wave of her hand.

Her son hung up the phone and shot the detective a playful smile. 'A handful, isn't she?' he said. 'But I'm pretty sure she didn't do it.' ·

Bhatia made it plain that the interview was at an end by walking round his desk and offering the detective his hand. 'Hey, listen, it's been fun,' he said. 'I'm going to have some complimentary tickets for the next ICT match sent over to you. I'd like for you to be my guest.'

Puri thanked him and left the office.

'*Pretty sure she didn't do it*,' he repeated to himself as he waited for the elevator. Had Bhatia been serious? Or was that American humour?

The inevitable call from the Chief's office came twenty minutes later as Puri was making his way back into south Delhi.

'He wants to see you in his office – no delay,' said his assistant.

'I've been suddenly taken ill, actually. High temperature is there. I'll pay Sir a visit day after. My sincerest apologies and greetings.'

The cat was out of the bag.

As for the dog, Dr Pathak's laboratory called at midday to say that the animal had indeed been poisoned with *Aconitem*. The technician was sure it had been ingested.

After eating a couple of kathi rolls at Khan Chacha's followed by a dessert of diet pills, the detective turned stalker. He'd learned that Mrs Anita Bhangu, who'd sat on the right of Faheem Khan, always went for a walk in Lodhi Gardens after lunch, and so he loitered in the Lodhi Road car park until she arrived in her modest Maruti hatchback.

Carrying a bulging plastic bag, she set off along the edge of the lake and the battlements surrounding Sikander Lodhi's tomb. For a lady in her mid-seventies, she walked at a sprightly pace, calling out occasionally to the *malis* busy tending the flower beds, all of whom recognised her.

A couple of mutts, both wearing warm winter jackets, came bounding towards her, tails wagging, and she greeted them by name – 'Indu! Kush!' Their yaps and whimpers attracted the attention of more hounds and soon she was surrounded by a pack, all jumping up excitedly.

'Yes, yes, coming, my lovelies,' said Mrs Bhangu. 'Hungry today, no?'

She stopped under a peepul tree and, from the bag,

took out four bowls. Placing them on the ground, she filled each to the brim with dry dog food. The animals immediately tucked in.

'Quite a feast,' commented Puri as he stopped on the path nearby. 'No wonder they're looking so healthy actually!'

'Pritika here got into a bad fight the other day. I had to bring the vet and he gave her injections. Seems to be recovering, thank God.'

Imported food, vets, winter coats – these dogs were better cared for than a lot of Delhi's servants, Puri reflected.

'You feed them every day, is it?' he asked.

'We take turns – myself and my husband. He comes early morning for his daily walk.'

'He's a dog lover, also?'

'Loves all animals. He's patron of many animal welfare societies in fact. A society should be judged on the way it looks after its animals – that's what he always says.'

'I could not agree more, madam,' said Puri, who in truth was all for rounding up Delhi's street dogs and putting them down on the grounds that one of them had once taken a chunk out of his right calf muscle. 'Such a shame about that dog at Kotla the other day!' he added.

'Oh I couldn't watch! I was actually there you know, in the stadium, attending the match. Imagine trying to shoot a poor defenceless animal! What were they thinking?'

The detective wished Mrs Bhangu a good day and walked on, mentally crossing her and her husband off his list of prime suspects.

He was down to eight suspects.

*   *   *

Puri soon had a brief, particularly unpleasant exchange over the phone with one of them: Neetika Sahini, the woman who described herself as a 'public relations' consultant but was in fact a lobbyist representing the interests of India's major corporate houses. She had sat five places away from Faheem Khan at the table.

'Is this some kind of stoopid joke or what?' she asked when Puri introduced himself. 'Mintoo, is that you?'

'Madam, allow me to assure you when it comes to such grave matters Vish Puri is always serious,' said the detective.

'Gaaaad! Who is this? Santa Claus? I've got nothing to say.'

'Five minutes total is required, only.'

'Bloody bullshit, yaar! I went through this yesterday with the police. I don't know anything.'

'I've come to know you sat next to the deceased at a cricket match in Dubai last year.'

This was fresh information supplied by Tubelight.

'So what, yaar! I was a guest at a lunch and I got stuck next to that lecherous creep. His eyes were practically glued to my cleavage! Got what he deserved if you ask me. Now read my lips, OK: I didn't kill that decrepit old Paki. I was talking to J.K. Shrivastav the whole time. He's confirmed that to the police.'

'During the meal you saw anyone put anything in Khan's food?'

'Are you stoopid or what? Think I'm going to tell you that?'

The line went dead.

No wonder she's thrice divorced, Puri thought.

Less than ten minutes later, Nariman Rathore, one of the most powerful lawyers in India, called.

'With regard to the tragic events at the Delhi Durbar Hotel this past Sunday evening, my client, Ms Neetika Sahini, has made a full statement to the police and has nothing further to add,' he said. 'Any effort on your part to contact her again will be regarded as an infringement of her privacy.'

Acting through an intermediary whom Puri had worked for in the past, the detective was able to arrange an appointment for five o'clock with multimillionaire Ram Dogra and his wife.

The Prince of Polyester, whose original fortune was made supplying dirt-cheap garments to the Indian masses, made no secret of the opulence to which he and his family had become accustomed. The entrance to his property, an enormous plot in the quiet, leafy and prohibitively exclusive area between Prithviraj Road and Lodhi Gardens, was not understated. Spotlights highlighted the brass plaques on the gateposts, the name DOGRA spelt out in an elaborate, calligraphic script, like a Fifth Avenue brand name. The grand front gates were made of dark Burmese teak. An illuminated fountain played on the strip of lawn along the front of the wall.

The contemporary bungalow and tropical gardens beyond could easily have been mistaken for a five star boutique hotel and spa. This was borne out by the sitting room to which Puri was led by a liveried servant. A perfect square of raw-silk-upholstered couches occupied the centre ground. Side tables held Venetian vases overflowing with an array of waxy, exotic lilies.

Ram Dogra's choice of double-breasted jacket, silk cravat and Italian loafers seemed no less affected to Puri. The eighty-year-old came from humble Ludhiana stock after all, his gnarled, pitted features suggestive of a life-time of battle.

'Mr Puri, your reputation precedes you,' he said, his voice deep, commanding, yet cordial. 'Swati speaks highly of you. Called you a man of great integrity.' Swati Saxena was the former client who'd arranged the interview.

'A great honour to meet you, sir,' responded the detective, markedly deferential in the presence of such a powerful individual. 'I'm most grateful to you for taking the time to see me, actually.'

Another man entered the sitting room. He was dressed in the badge of the male Indian assistant-cum-secretary: white open-collar shirt with breast pocket accommodating a row of pens. Without a word, he sat down on a chair next to the closed door, notebook and pen at the ready.

'Madam would be joining us, sir?' asked the detective.

'She's got a headache,' said Dogra as he sat on one of the couches and motioned for Puri to do the same. 'She should be along in a few minutes. We can start without her. Before we do, Mr Puri, I want you to know that I had a call this afternoon from the Delhi Chief of Police.'

'I see, sir.'

'He urged me not to speak with you. Called you a "meddler".'

'We two do not always see eye to eye exactly,' responded the detective, wondering where Dogra was going with this.

'Yes, well, I decided to ignore his advice for the simple reason that my wife and I have nothing to hide,' he stated.

'Most admirable of you, sir.'

Dogra checked his watch. 'Now, I can give you ten minutes,' he said.

'Ten minutes will be more than enough, sir,' responded Puri as if it was all a matter of mere routine. He took out notebook and pen. 'I wanted to ask you about the seating arrangement at the dinner, actually. Your good wife sat three places from the victim and you yourself to her right. Tell me: that was by choice, sir?'

'Not at all,' answered Dogra. 'We had no say in the matter.'

'You're part owner of the Delhi team, is it not so?'

'I'm the majority shareholder. I own fifty-one per cent. But I don't get involved with the catering arrangements.'

Puri made a note of this. Then he said, 'Please be good enough to tell me what all happened from the time you entered the banquet hall.'

Dogra described how he and his wife had spent fifteen, maybe twenty minutes talking with his 'old friend' Cabinet Secretary J.K. Shrivastav and then sat down at the table. One by one, the other guests had joined them. The food had been served straight away.

'You remember Faheem Khan leaving the table, sir?' asked Puri.

'Yes I do. I remember thinking his food was getting cold.'

'You saw any person standing there – behind his chair, that is?'

'I don't believe so, but then a few of us did get up from the table. I remember Kamran Khan excusing himself for a while. At one point, Mrs Talwar came and stood behind Mrs Bhangu and they talked. My wife paid a visit to the ladies' room after she'd finished eating. I went to the WC myself. I believe Satish Bhatia was gone for a short while as well.'

'During Faheem Khan's absence, sir?'

'Afterwards, I believe,' said Dogra, but he didn't sound sure and looked up at the ceiling again as if, somehow, the moulded plaster might hold the answer. 'To tell you the truth, Mr Puri, I can't remember.'

'Anyone else approached the table – aside from the waiters, that is?'

'Not while we were eating, no.'

'It is my understanding you spilt your drink, sir?'

'That's right. I knocked it over.'

'When exactly?'

'Oh that's hard to say.'

'When Faheem Khan was absent?'

'Yes, I suppose it was.'

'Must have distracted everyone.'

'I suppose so. Some of it spilled on Gunjan Bhangu, I'm embarrassed to say. But most got on to my trousers. That was when I visited the WC. To dry it off.'

The detective made a note of this and then followed up with, 'You'd been at the function the preceding evening, sir?'

'For the championship inauguration drinks? Yes, I was there for an hour or so.'

'And Madam?'

'She accompanied me, of course.'

'You met Faheem Khan, is it?'

'Briefly.'

'What did you talk about?'

'We welcomed him to India. Asked him if he'd had a good journey.' Dogra checked his Rolex. 'You've got another few minutes, Mr Puri.'

'Just I wanted to ask you about your business dealings with Pakistan.'

Dogra gave a gesture that suggested he'd anticipated the question. 'My company imports various commodities from there,' he answered.

'And you've visited Pakistan on no less than seven occasions.'

'You would not have found that information on my company's website,' answered the multimillionaire with a touch of pique.

'No, sir, I've other sources, actually.'

'Well, your *other sources* are correct, Mr Puri. But before you ask, I've no connection whatsoever with the Khans.'

'It is my understanding Madam was born in Pakistan, sir.'

Before Dogra could answer, the door opened and his wife appeared. She was petite and elegant. Her grey silk sari was immaculately tied, a diamond brooch pinned to one shoulder. Her hair, though white and thin enough to show the scalp beneath, was professionally coiffed.

'Aah, there you are.' Dogra sent her a sympathetic smile. 'How's your head?'

'Much better, thank you. The maid gave me *maalish*.'

She came and sat next to her husband, arranging the folds of her silk sari about her.

'Mr Puri here was just asking me where you were born,' explained Dogra as she sized him up.

'Oh, that's easy,' she said, her tone almost festive. 'My birthplace was Lahore. More years ago than I care to remember.'

'You came to India in 1947 is it, madam?' asked Puri.

'Along with my mother, yes. I'm afraid my other relatives were lost to us along the way.'

'There is any connection between your family and the Khans?'

'None. I believe they hail from Rawalpindi.'

The detective went back over much of the same ground he had covered with Ram Dogra and found her recollection of events tallied. There was one detail Mrs Dogra was able to add, however. Ten minutes before Faheem Khan died, she'd seen Kamran Khan heading towards the hotel's emergency exit. 'Why you didn't inform the police, madam?' asked Puri, sure that this detail had not appeared in the transcript of her police interview.

'It must have slipped my mind,' she answered.

• TEN •

There was no mistaking the change that had come over Puri's childhood neighbourhood of Punjabi Bagh in west Delhi since the late 1990s when the effects of 'liberalisation' – the loosening of the noose that had been strangling the Indian economy – had started to take effect.

In the 'good old bad old days,' as Puri referred to them, you had to wait years to get a telephone connection. And when, at long last, the engineers turned up and you could make a call from the luxury of your own living room (as opposed to a grubby PCO/STD booth), there was always a crossed line, or rather several crossed lines, and quite often a delayed echo too, so it sounded as if you were speaking into a wishing well along with a group of strangers.

Once, when Puri was fifteen, he'd overheard Asha Singh's mum at number twenty-five oblique three telling Mrs Bhullar about how her husband was having 'erectile dysfunctioning'. Believing that she might have been referring to some kind of DIY problem, he had asked his mother for clarification. On another occasion, Puri's father, Om Chander Puri, then still on the force, had overheard a known thief discussing plans with an accomplice to knock over Ambar Jewellery Emporium and, consequently, caught them in the act.

Buying a car had been a similarly laborious process. The waiting list was as long as the Ramayana. The choice of models had been limited – either an Ambassador or an Indian Fiat – and they came in any colour as long as it was white. Air conditioning was almost unheard of and most models came with fans fixed to the dashboard. Side mirrors were considered additional extras.

As for luxury goods, they were smuggled into the country in the bulging suitcases of Non-Resident Indian relatives from the US and the UK. Their arrival was always accompanied by a ritual unpacking. French make-up, diabetes medicine and the odd laptop computer would be shared out like rations during a time of war. The younger generation would then go and try on their blue jeans; their elders, meanwhile, would criticise Western cultural values while tucking into rare delicacies like KitKat bars.

How things had changed and in such a short period of time, reflected Puri as he walked along NW Avenue, feeling somewhat bewildered by it all. Now even the aunties had BlackBerrys, you couldn't throw a mango stone without hitting a BMW with a cool Punjabi dude in designer shades behind the wheel, and the black and white TVs that had stood in people's living rooms covered in knitted woollen cosies had been replaced by HD flat screens.

There was no mistaking the new enthusiasm in the air, either. For the educated, English-speaking middle classes, there were well-paid jobs in the private sector. 'India Inc.', as it was often referred to in the press, had bought British Steel and Jaguar. A guy from Chandigarh had co-invented Hotmail. PepsiCo was now run by a Tamil woman called Indra Krishnamurthy Nooyi.

The detective paused outside a café-cum-video-hall filled with teenagers dressed like the cast of an American high-school movie. They were eating plates of nachos coated in processed cheese, blasting aliens with laser pistols, addressing one another as 'dude' and 'bro' while catching up on Facebook on their Androids. Indipop spilled out on to the pavement. 'Just chill, chill. Just chill . . .'

This was the stuff of Mahatma Gandhi's nightmares. 'Waste of human mind space,' Puri muttered as he turned away. Was he witnessing a passing fad or the future? With half of India's population now under twenty-five, where was society headed? Did this *bindaas* brigade know anything of their own culture?

The thing that worried Puri most was the idea that the old extended family structure might break down. It was the glue that held Indian society together. And there were cracks showing in the system. Only last week, he'd come across a widower, a former engineer no less, living on his own at the age of seventy because his three children had taken up in other cities. Had they no shame?

He turned the corner and made his way into the Old Slum Quarters area, finding himself back in the *tamasha*. For all the tangles of wires hanging overhead and the treacherous uncovered manholes lying in wait like animal snares, he felt more comfortable here. There had always been many Indias, coexisting side by side – or perhaps one on top of the other – and there always would be, he reassured himself. Layer upon layer upon layer, like the very earth itself.

Puri found the door he was looking for and opened it. He was about to descend deep into the nether regions.

Concrete stairs and paan-stained walls led down into a faintly damp-smelling basement. Puri came to a heavy door. Behind it, he could hear voices, the sound of TV cricket commentary, male laughter. Its raucous nature caused him to hesitate.

Puri's relationship with his childhood friend Rinku was a complicated one. From the age of six or seven, they had roamed the streets of Punjabi Bagh together and got into every kind of trouble – spied on Swati Dhatarwal and seen her boobies, stolen the guavas off old Bunty's prized tree, even nailed old Titoo Lathwal with their water balloons on Holi. But as adults they'd chosen very different paths. Puri had gone into the army and then in the late 1980s set himself up as a private investigator. Rinku on the other hand had never been out of trouble.

The detective preferred not to know what his friend got up to. He was one of *them*, a part of the Nexus, the loose alliance of politicians, judges, bureaucrats, businessmen and mafias who were only getting richer and more powerful in the 'new' India. In the good old bad old days the likes of Rinku stuffed their black money under the mattress. Now he parked crores in remote rural branches of state banks and invested in agricultural land forcibly appropriated by the government at knockdown prices.

In truth, they were enemies, the two old friends, although neither of them had really faced up to the fact. On major holidays, they still dropped in on one another. Last year, Puri, Rumpi and Mummy had attended Rinku's son's wedding, a wildly extravagant affair at Pisces Garden. And now, against his better judgement, the detective was going to ask Rinku for help. He had no choice. Puri didn't know the world of illegal cricket gambling and he needed to get close to Full Moon. If anyone would know how to get into his satta party tomorrow night, it was Puri's childhood friend.

The door opened a crack and a man's grizzled face appeared, half hidden in shadow. He squinted and gave an upward, perfunctory nod. *'Kaun?'*

'I want to see Pappu.' Pappu was Rinku's nickname. 'Tell him it's Chubby.'

The door was banged shut. A minute later it was opened wide.

'Shit, yaar!' Rinku was moderately drunk, his eyes bloodshot. He put his arms around the detective. 'Long time, buddy,' he exclaimed, giving him a hug. 'What brings you round?'

Puri stared at Rinku's hair. He had dyed it: black with streaks of henna.

'What the hell you went and did, you bugger?' asked the detective, his tone suddenly different, almost loutish. It would not have gone down well in the hallowed corridors of the Gymkhana Club. 'What do you call this? Midlife crisis?'

'Crisis bollocks!' bawled Rinku. 'Fifty's the new twenty, Chubby! I tell you my dick is getting more workout than ever. From Russia with Love! I tell you these gori girls really know how to—'

'I need to talk,' interrupted Puri.

Rinku's face showed startled dismay. 'Wow, buddy. Forget the foreplay, haa. Just get straight down to business! OK fine, have it your way. You'd better come in, Chubby. I'll introduce you.'

He turned and addressed the other five men in the room. They were sitting in a haze of cigarette smoke watching the cricket on TV.

'Gentlemen, this is the great Vishwas Puri. Best private detective in all India and chaser of housewives.'

The others acknowledged him with sombre (but definitely not sober) nods before returning their attention to the game.

'Those bloody Jaipur jokers are forty-eight for four, yaar,' said Rinku as he led the way to the back of the room past stacks of cartons of unopened Japanese cigarettes. 'Can you believe, Chubby? Worse than useless. I've lost a bundle of moola.'

His office was nothing fancy: bare concrete walls, a couch, a desk and a gigantic fridge. On the desk sat a pile of cash. Wads of old notes, 500s mostly – more than Puri made in a year.

'Chubby, watch this,' he said. 'You're not going to believe.' He took a glass and inserted it into the fridge's ice dispenser. Cubes started dropping out, clink, clink, clink. Rinku beamed. 'Bloody mind-blowing!' he bawled. 'It does crushed ice, also. Can you believe? Used to be *only in America*. Now everything's available in India!'

He poured Puri a large Royal Challenge with soda and topped up his own.

'How's Mummy? I heard she's ailing,' said Rinku, who still knew about everything that went on in the neighbourhood.

'You know her, yaar. Fit as a horse. Yesterday a temperature. Today morning, only, she went gallivanting off to Haridwar with that Ritu Auntie.' Puri rolled his eyes.

Rinku did the same and muttered, 'Bloody pain in the nuts that woman.'

They spent a few more minutes catching up on family news and local gossip.

'We should do this more often, you bugger!' exclaimed Rinku when they had exhausted their stock. His words engendered an uncomfortable silence, the reality of their situation suddenly forced upon them.

'I'm investigating the murder of Faheem Khan,' said Puri eventually.

'Why bother, yaar? Who cares? His butter chicken didn't agree with him. Let it go.'

'Let it go is not in my vocabulary.'

'And getting yourself killed is?'

'What are you talking?'

Rinku let out a sharp, irritated sigh. 'I've got to teach you bloody ABC or what?'

'Not ABC. X, Y and Z, only.'

'Fine. X is for Ex. As in former, used to be, dearly departed – as in buss! Want that before your name in the newspaper? Take my advice. Go back to assisting virgins.

Didn't I read in the newspaper recently you rescued some doggie? Looked like a rat, no?'

Puri bristled. 'It was a chihuahua – a very rare breed actually.'

'Is that what it's come to, Chubby?'

Puri donned an expressionless mask. 'Faheem Khan was up to his neck in it – match fixing and all,' he stated.

The smile faded from Rinku's face. 'What? I have to spell it out for you, Chubby? Just like old times, haa?'

'Stop doing riddles, yaar. Tell me straight.'

'Look, Chubby, there's no prizes for guessing who killed the Paki. Everyone knows who controls the Syndicate. He might be a special guest of our neighbours but every bookie, from the guy on the street corner to the *khoka* punter, answers to him. Step out of line and you're *khatam*, history.'

'What's a khoka punter?' asked Puri.

'Where've you been, yaar? In some cave? Means a guy who deals directly with Dubai – twenty-five lakh spots and over. And before you ask, Chubby, a spot is a bet.'

Rinku picked up Puri's empty glass. 'Make it a single only,' said the detective.

'Don't talk shit, yaar,' he said, filling the glass to the brim.

'So tell me: how can I become a punter?'

'You? Mister Chihuahua?' Rinku guffawed again.

Puri had read recently that an economist called Galbraith had once called India a 'functioning anarchy'. He thought of this as Rinku outlined how the underground betting system operated. The Syndicate didn't maintain offices;

the vast majority of the betting public never met their bookie in person; and 90 per cent of the bookies themselves had no direct contact with the chief bookmakers, who were believed to be based in Dubai. On a big match day, bets amounting to an estimated 10,000 *crore* rupees were placed across the city. In Mumbai it was double that.

'The whole thing runs on trust, Chubby,' explained Rinku. 'Someone agrees to vouch for you, makes the introduction, you make a deposit and place your bet. All accounts are settled by day end – *latest*. Win and the boy makes delivery right to my door. Just like pizza.'

'What if you lose?'

'He collects.'

'And if you don't do payment?'

'Another guy comes round and gives you big kisses.'

'Doesn't sound like trust to me.'

Rinku pulled an exasperated face. 'What is it with you, Chubby? Always making judgement. Fact is the whole thing works. No need for any bloody oversight committee or regulatory board.'

'Or tax to pay. Most convenient.'

'Bloody right, yaar. And it should stay that way. Gambling's in our blood, Chubby. We Indians love to bet like no one else. It's in the Mahabharata, for God's sake. Pandava loses his kingdom and to gain his family's freedom has to play a game of dice, remember?'

'Only the dice are loaded,' said Puri.

'Right. That's India for you. Always count your cards.'

Puri asked him how someone went about making a bet. He wanted to understand the mechanics of the process.

'By phone, yaar. Used to be a separate line was required. But now any number will do.'

'And you provide a password.'

'These days it's computer generated. You get it over email.'

'These days?' repeated Puri. 'These changes came when exactly?'

'Six months back. Whole thing runs like clockwork, Chubby. Odds are updated by the second. Not like before.'

'Tell me about Mohib Alam.'

Rinku, who had his glass up to his mouth, hesitated.

'He's having a satta party tomorrow night,' continued Puri. 'At his farmhouse. During the Goa versus Mumbai match. I plan to attend. Have some fun.'

'Chubby, last time you had any fun you were still pissing in your *chuddies*. Look, I warned you before. Walk away. Think I'm a BC? This guy killed his own brother over an argument about a milkshake.'

'Milkshake?'

'He doesn't like chocolate.'

Puri stared at Rinku with granite-hard eyes. 'Listen, you bugger, when I asked for your help, ever, haa?' he asked, switching back to English. 'This is top priority. I need to get close to this fellow.'

'He'll see you coming, Chubby. You'll stand out like a white chick at a black orgy.'

'You can make the introduction.'

'What makes you so sure?'

Puri made a gesture. 'To use your words, Pappu, "Don't talk bullshit."'

'You'll need a lot of moola, buddy,' sighed Rinku. 'Where are you going to get it?'

The detective eyed the wads of notes on the table.

'What? Now you're wanting to borrow money, also?'

'Don't do tension. I'll pay you back, you bugger.'

Whoops of joy came from the other room. Rinku checked the match score.

'Shit, yaar,' he complained. 'Two lakhs down the bloody crapper.'

· ELEVEN ·

'Yes, yes, quite all right,' Mummy told Puri when he called her at around nine that evening. 'Air is so fresh and sweet here, na . . . Pardon? What you said, Chubby? I didn't get . . . Want to talk about what? Pakistan? Hello? Hello? Bad reception is there. Your voice is absent. Must be mountains and all. You're hearing me? Oh dear, so much disturbance. Should be I'll be reverting day after. Don't worry, na! Everything is totally fine.'

In fact things had not quite gone to plan. At five o'clock that morning, when Mummy went to pick up Ritu Auntie, her would-be travelling companion had announced that she didn't want to go to Haridwar because it was a Tuesday and it was inauspicious to start any new endeavour or venture on the second day of the week.

It had taken ten minutes to persuade her otherwise and then, before setting off, Ritu insisted on performing a puja for Ganesh, friend of travellers. A further delay came after they got downstairs and bundled themselves into the waiting car and Ritu realised that she'd forgotten to eat a pinch of sugar before leaving the house. Five more minutes were lost while she remedied this oversight.

Despite these delays, they might still have caught the train had it not been for Mummy's idiot driver, Majnu, who dropped them on the wrong side of New Delhi railway station. This meant they had to climb the steep stairs up to the pedestrian over-bridge, where they faced a tidal wave of pilgrims from Varanasi, all carrying bundles and big plastic containers of Ganga water.

By the time they reached platform 4, the 0530 Haridwar Express was pulling out of the station. The next train left an hour or so later – a local that reached their destination at six in the evening.

By the time they'd checked into the Good Luck Hotel, washed and eaten, it was almost nine o'clock.

Mummy's quest was going to have to start tomorrow. And she was fine with that. Ritu's idiosyncrasies were infuriating at times, but her husband's ashes had provided the perfect cover story. Besides, who was to say they weren't supposed to leave on the later train? Perhaps some terrible fate would have befallen them on the Haridwar Express.

Still, she would need to make an early start tomorrow – and find a way of splitting off from Ritu Auntie. There wasn't a lot of time: two days at the most. Bhuppi had already called three times to check up on her. And Chubby had sounded suspicious – wanting to talk about Pakistan.

He was obviously thinking along the right lines. Not my son for nothing, Mummy reflected.

Ritu had fallen asleep in front of the TV. Her mouth was wide open and she was snoring gently. The urn was on the side table next to her bed. Tomorrow evening they would need to find a priest to carry out the Asthi Visarjan scattering ceremony.

Wrapping her shawl around her, Mummy stepped out on to the balcony of their room. Below lay a lawn lit by lollipop lights. A family was sitting around a brazier, three generations in all, eating their dinner and warming their hands. At the end of the garden flowed the British-built canal that carried the crystal-clear waters of the Ganges to the lush farmland of Uttarakhand. The lights of the old city on the far bank coloured the water's surface in liquid gold. The sounds of clanging bells and chanting reached her from temples dotted amongst the dense profusion of narrow buildings. Flags fluttered above tapered roofs. Down on the far bank, some pilgrims were taking a dip, washing away their sins.

Mummy pulled up a chair and took a folded piece of paper from her handbag. There were three names written on it:

Megha Dogra (wife of Ram Dogra, the Prince of Polyester).
Harnam Talwar (wife of Sandeep Talwar, politician).
Jasmeet Bhatia (mother of Satish Bhatia, 'Call Centre King').

All three women looked to be in their late seventies to early eighties, roughly the same height and the same build. None of the three had any distinguishing marks, either.

Indian government records being unreliable and easily doctored, the only sure-fire way of checking their past was to consult the genealogical records kept by the thousands of Pandas living in the city.

That, though, was for tomorrow. There was still today's unfinished business to deal with.

Mummy took out her daily diary and began to write. This was a discipline she'd adhered to religiously since her sixteenth birthday.

'Ritu saw a gecko on the ceiling of our hotel and said it portends success,' wrote Mummy in Hindi using the elegant Perso-Arabic script she had been taught as a child. 'Let's hope she's right.'

Tubelight called Puri late at the office. He and his boys had spent the day doing background checking. When it came to Sandeep Talwar, they'd struck a rich seam. There was nothing 'Sahib' wasn't into. He controlled something in the region of 400 companies, many of them money-laundering fronts with pretend directors. Through these companies he owned thousands of acres of sugar-cane fields, numerous sugar-cane processing plants and at least four trucking companies. His illicit portfolio also included an IT park, a handful of hotels, a software development company in San Diego, an import–export business and a coal mine. Tubelight had it on good authority that he also got a 30 per cent cut from the petrol mafia in his home state of Madhya Pradesh.

Talwar was also a big gambler.

'One, two lakhs minimum. Goes to Dubai often.'

'Any direct connection with Aga?'

'Doubt it – fiercely patriotic.'

'Willing to screw India just as long as he's doing the screwing.'

'Exactly, Boss.'

'How about Talwar Madam?'

'First name Harnam. Comes from a village near Indore. Sixteen when she married. Numerous assets to her name. They've five children total.'

Tubelight had much less to say about Ram Dogra, the Prince of Polyester. He had his detractors, those who said he exploited his workers and had done all kinds of shady deals to secure land upon which to build his factories. But he gave generously to all the political parties and was on good terms with the country's major newspaper proprietors as well.

As for Satish Bhatia, the Call Centre King, he was a golden boy.

'Pays his income tax, gives to charity, campaigns for child literacy.'

'Keep checking. No one does business in India without getting stains on their kurta,' said Puri.

Satya Pal Bhalla, the former moustache raja, called ten minutes later. Puri held the phone away from his ear as he listened to his tirade, this time about how Gopal Ragi had been released without charge.

'I'm aware, sir,' said Puri, although he doubted his client heard him.

He put the phone down on his desk. It continued to crepitate for another few minutes until, finally, the detective picked it up again and delivered a string of platitudes, assuring his client that he was on the case and would contact him 'in coming days'.

He hung up and reread the fax that had been delivered earlier by his secretary. The message was typed on a blank piece of paper – no letter heading or signature. Just:

Dear Sir,

It has come to my attention that you are engaged in the investigation of the murder of the late Mr Faheem Khan. I am writing to inform you that I have in my possession important information regarding the case. For reasons of my own, I am only prepared to provide you with the aforementioned information in person.

Provided you are able, I suggest you travel to Pakistan this coming Friday so that we might meet and discuss the matter further. Please take a room at the Pearl Continental in Rawalpindi, where I will find you.

It was signed 'A Friend' and the sender ID in the top left-hand corner of the page was a London number. Puri tried it but got a disconnected message.

It was a trap, obviously. Aga had come to know that Puri was nosing around in his business and planned to lure him to Pakistan, where one of his henchmen would put a bullet through his head.

There: that was a good enough reason for *not* travelling to Pakistan. Final. Decided. Thank the God!

Puri locked the fax away in the top drawer of his desk

and decided to head home. It was getting late. Rumpi would be wondering where he was.

He got only halfway down the stairs when, suddenly, he stopped, shouted out at the top of his voice, 'Bugger it all!' and gave the wall a hard kick. Storming back up the stairs and into his office, he retrieved the fax and read it again. The language was polished, old-fashioned, written by an older man. This was not the work of Aga. Nor the Pakistani intelligence service. This 'friend' might well be able to provide vital information about the case.

Puri slumped back in his chair, defeated by his own conscience. He poured himself a drink and finished it quickly. Then, with grave reluctance, indeed with a sense of impending yet unavoidable doom, he called his client James Scott in London.

'I would be needing that visa we talked about in a jiffy,' he said.

It was 10 p.m. by the time Puri left the office. The Khan Market bhel puri vendor was still open for business. A few youngsters stood around his stand in the car park devouring plates of puffed rice laced with tamarind chutney. The detective tried to will himself to his waiting car, but the sight of all the crisp *papdis* and yoghurt proved too much for him.

'Usual, sahib?'

'Extra chutney and chilli.'

His order was soon ready and he joined the other customers, eating in silent solidarity. It was broken by the sound of an Ambassador pulling up. The car had government plates. A short, pudgy assistant-type got out.

'*Shri* Vish Puri?' he asked.

The detective answered with a mouth full of *sevpuri*. 'Present and correct.'

'Sahib sent me.' Puri was being summoned by politician and all-round crook Sandeep Talwar.

'It's a sin to waste good sevpuri,' said the detective, holding up his half-finished plate.

The PA looked unmoved. 'Sahib is waiting,' he insisted.

Puri crammed in a last mouthful, threw away the rest and got into the car.

Their destination was the Lakshmi, a hotel owned by the Ministry of Tourism and one that clung faithfully to its kitsch 1980s décor. The lobby, a vast expanse of grey marble as polished as an ice rink, was dotted with atolls of brown leather couches upon which the occupants sat, as if stranded. The reception desk was half the length of a football field, the dozen or so staff members standing behind it as dwarfed as Soviet leaders watching a military parade in the vastness of Moscow's Red Square.

Sandeep Talwar's suite was on the top floor.

Puri was led through a series of rooms, each occupied by businessmen, lawyers, junior ministers and bureaucrat clones in white shirts – all waiting patiently to meet the minister, many of them with stacks of papers on their laps. A final set of doors opened and disgorged over-fed, suited men with briefcases. The detective was shown into a sitting room where Sahib lounged in an armchair, drink in hand. A coffee table groaning with files stood in front of him.

Sandeep Talwar was almost eighty and obese, his grey suit trousers pulled halfway up his stomach like clown pants. His lower lip was weighed down by a crumpled chin scoured with lines. Drooping jowls obscured the edges of his mouth so that even when he smiled his whole face looked turned down. His sunken eyes completed the picture of a cunning, duplicitous individual racked by greed.

Puri could barely conceal his contempt. Talwar hadn't garnered power because of his ideas or inherent wisdom. Nor because he gave two damns about his constituents, most of whom lived on less than two dollars a day. No, Talwar had risen to power, prominence and wealth thanks to his abilities as a deal maker. He was a horse trader, nothing more.

'My PA says you came to my home this morning asking to see me,' he said, studying Puri through steel-rimmed glasses.

'I happened to be passing, sir.' Puri stood with hands held behind his back like a petulant schoolboy.

'*Happened to be passing*,' repeated Talwar, his tone mocking. 'You usually just drop in on ministers and request to meet their wives, also?'

The detective countered with flattery: 'You've a reputation for being an open individual, sir, accessible to the aam admi. No offence was intended, I assure you.'

Talwar's eyes blinked slowly like an iguana's. He looked half asleep. But it would be a mistake to underestimate him, Puri reflected. He could be dangerous, this man.

'What's your game exactly, Mr Puri? What is it you want?' asked Talwar, careful not to sound too concerned.

'I'm investigating the murder, sir – of Faheem Khan.'

'That's the job of the police.'

'I'm a private investigator.'

'And you're working for?'

'That I cannot say, sir.'

Talwar showed startled dismay. 'You're refusing me, Mr Puri?'

'Confidentiality is my watchword, sir.'

'I *see*,' said Talwar, as if he finally had the measure of the detective. 'You're one of these do-gooders, no? Like an NGO type? Think the system is not working properly so take matters into your own hand.'

'This is my job, sir,' answered Puri, putting it as bluntly as he could.

'And I suppose I'm on your list of suspects, am I?'

'You and Madam, also.'

'You're suggesting my wife murdered that man?' The politician's words were liquid indignation.

'Sir, she is a suspect, that is all.'

'Now you listen to me,' said Talwar, his tone controlled but menacing. 'I'm a politician and must therefore put up with a certain amount of scrutiny of my affairs. My wife on the other hand is a private person and she is not in good health these days. She's made a statement to the police and that's an end to the matter. Is that understood?'

'Most certainly, sir. Thank you, sir.'

Talwar dismissed him with a perfunctory gesture.

Puri left the room in no doubt that he had made a powerful enemy. The encounter had been worth it, however. Sahib was getting sloppy. He'd made the mistake of warning Puri away from his wife.

Mrs Harnam Talwar had something to hide – no doubt about it at all.

• TWELVE •

'We make the dream of having a loved one's cremated remains (cremains) scattered in the Holy Ganges a reality!' read the brochure for Sacred Rights, a travel agency that doubled as a kind of Hindu funeral home. 'Now even Non-Resident Indians can send us their cremains from any location in the world by secure shipment and we'll take care of the rest! You'll receive a custom-made DVD of the ceremony. Alternatively we offer our exclusive "Secure Air Express Brahman Priest Escort Service" from any country of your choice! That's right! A genuine Indian priest will fly out and collect your ashes and deliver them safely to the bosom of Mother India.'

Mummy handed the brochure back to Ritu. They were standing in the small foyer of their hotel.

'This is for NRI types, na,' said Mummy, confused.

'Not that part,' said Ritu, turning over the brochure. 'There. Where it talks about the boat. It says here they'll take us out into the middle of the Ganges to scatter the ashes.'

'A priest and helper will accompany you at sunset,' said the hotel manager, who was standing behind the front desk. 'It is experience of the lifetime, I can tell you.'

It had taken the manager all of three or four minutes, the time Mummy had used to visit the WC, to sell Ritu on the boat scheme. It was a nice idea but obviously flawed.

'You're doing seasickness,' pointed out Mummy.

'Madam, seasickness only comes at sea,' admonished the manager. 'On Ganges there is hardly a ripple. So smooth it is.'

'Honestly, I think it should be fine,' said Ritu.

'You were getting sickness in a paddle boat on Sukhna Lake in Chandigarh, even.'

'I had eaten so much of *barfi* beforehand, no?'

Mummy stood resolutely by her opinion. 'Listen, na,' she said. 'This evening, only, we'll take Bal's ashes to Har ki Pauri. That is the proper way.'

The manager could see his prospective customer (and presumably his commission) slipping away. 'Sacred Rights is offering ten per cent discount,' he said. 'One videographer first class is provided who will capture the ceremony for all eternity.'

Ritu's ears pricked up again. 'That does sound nice,' she said.

Mummy took her by the arm and led her away.

'Come,' she said as they stepped out of the hotel and hailed an auto. 'Better for all concerned persons we keep you here on land. Otherwise it would not only be Bal's ashes ending up in the holy Ganga, na?'

The three-wheeler squeezed up Haridwar's narrow lanes, straining against the mid-morning tide of pilgrims, ash-smeared sadhus and Western Hindu converts. Had Mummy reached out the side of the flimsy vehicle, she

could have scooped up handfuls of chunky black cardamoms from open gunny sacks sitting outside spice shops
or plucked plump marigold flowers from barrows stocked
with the paraphernalia required for Hindu ceremonies.

The walls of the narrow buildings closing in around
them had a waxy sheen, the grime that clung to the
brickwork and plaster having been buffed and polished
by generations of passing elbows and shoulders. Monastic
doorways revealed steep stairways winding up into rooms
that had been subdivided and then subdivided again. In
one window, two tailors sat stacked one on top of the
other like competitors in the game show *Hollywood Squares*,
false ceilings only inches above their heads.

The lane soon fell down the hill and the auto shuddered
over ruts and bumps, listing perilously when it sloshed
through an open drain, and came to a halt in a small
square. A banyan tree stood in the middle, gnarled and
ancient. The prop roots growing from its branches had
attached themselves to the façades of the surrounding
buildings like the tentacles of a giant squid. Three or
four cows grazed on freshly cut grass beneath the thick
trunk. Nearby, three women with dupattas covering their
heads, the ends between their teeth, were making patties
out of manure and leaving them to dry in the sun.

'Banyan tree and cows – so far so good, na,' said Mummy
as they dismounted from the auto.

'But I don't see a barber,' commented Ritu.

They were following directions that had been given to
them fifteen minutes earlier at the home of the Panda
responsible for keeping the records of the Ghatwal family,
Ghatwal being the declared maiden name of Mrs Megha

Dogra, wife of the Prince of Polyester and the first of Mummy's three suspects.

Mummy, who'd told Ritu that she was doing some research on behalf of a friend living in Canada, walked around the banyan and found the barber on the other side. His salon was arranged between the tree's roots with a mirror and washbasin attached to the trunk. Behind him lay the alley. It was too narrow for Ritu, given her girth, and she was unable to walk sideways thanks to her hips, so she elected to remain in the square.

'Pukka?' asked Mummy, hiding her relief.

'Don't worry about me. I'll be happy sitting here watching the cows. Such beautiful colours. Oooh, perhaps I'll buy some fresh milk! It's very good for you, no?'

The alley led into another smaller courtyard. From there Mummy was directed into a lopsided building. The floors sloped at a 15-degree angle and the doorways were all crooked like those in a fairground house of fun. The room in which she was asked to wait was bare save for a couple of dhurries and a bookstand.

Behind this sat the Panda – tall, lean, sixty plus, with a head of white hair pulled back into a ponytail. A red line ran from the edge of his scalp down to the bridge of his nose, an unusual *tilak* and one that somehow lent him a sinister air. His courteous greeting and pleasant demeanour immediately dispelled any sense of threat, however, and he called down into the courtyard for refreshments to be brought for his guest.

'Your family name is Ghatwal?' he asked.

'Actually not,' answered Mummy, who gave him the same story she'd told Ritu.

'You know which village your friend's paternal family originated from?' he asked. 'Without that information it will be very hard to help.'

Mummy got out her notes. Her friend Preeti, who worked in the National Archives, had done some research on her behalf and found Megha Ghatwal's 1947 refugee certificate. She'd been listed along with her mother, Harjot, a widow, who'd hailed from the village of Singhpuria in present-day Pakistan.

'That's north-west of Lahore,' said the Panda. 'Yes I believe I can help.'

He took a set of keys from his pocket, selected a large old brass one and opened a door at the side of the room. Beyond lay a chamber that looked like some secret monastic library full of forbidden gospels, the shelves packed with scrolls and parchments. The Panda spent a good fifteen minutes searching through them. When he emerged it was with an armful of dusty papers, which he proceeded to unravel on the floor before him.

Written on the brittle pages were the names and details of Ghatwals spanning back seven, eight generations. The newest writing belonged to his hand, but the earlier entries had been made by his father, grandfather, great-grandfather and so on.

'Anything earlier was put down on palm leaves but none have survived,' he explained.

It took him half an hour to find the right family lineage. The entry was written in the Perso-Arabic script.

'Here,' he said. 'Megha Ghatwal was born in 1927. Her father travelled to Haridwar in the month of Kartika in 1936 to scatter the remains of his own father. Look.

Here's the updated information he provided on his imme-
diate family and there's his thumbprint and those of the
witnesses.'

'Megha had brothers and sisters?' asked Mummy.

'Two brothers. But seems they were both killed along
with their father in 1947 – while the family was fleeing
to India.'

The Panda turned the page and found it empty. 'That's
strange,' he said. 'There are no more entries. The last was
made in 1949 when Megha Ghatwal's mother, Harjot,
visited Haridwar on pilgrimage and reported the death
of her husband and sons.'

'There's no record of Harjot's death?'

'None. Her daughter has never come.'

Mummy noted down the details and paid him a couple
of hundred rupees for his time.

It appeared that Megha Dogra was who she claimed to
be; her maiden name was Ghatwal and she'd arrived in
Delhi with her mother. Furthermore, her native place was
a good 150 miles from the village where Faheem Khan
lived in 1947. But why hadn't she recorded her own
mother's death?

'Did you find what you're looking for?' asked Ritu
Auntie, who was waiting in the square.

'Just I'm making progress,' she answered.

They climbed into their auto and started back up the
hill, passing a man whom Mummy had seen earlier outside
the hotel. Looking back, she watched as he mounted a
scooty and followed after them.

· THIRTEEN ·

The security guard approached the Mercedes Benz, clipboard at the ready, as it stopped at the front gate of Full Moon's Chattarpur farmhouse.

'Your good name, sir?' he said once the automatic window had slid down.

'Pujji. Mahinder C. Pujji,' answered Puri. 'Sagittarius.'

The security guard either didn't understand the reference to his assumed star sign or lacked a sense of humour. He ran his finger down the guest list with a straight face.

'I see your name here, sir. But there's no mention of Ma'am.'

He was referring to the woman seated next to the detective, his eyes lingering on the tantalising flash of thigh revealed by the slit of her tight black dress. She was Puri's junior by a good twenty years, and had long black hair, high cheekbones that punctuated her faultless caramel complexion and bewitching oriental eyes.

'This is Miss Nina,' said Puri, adding in an emphatic tone, 'a friend.'

His escort let out a childish giggle and squeezed his

left knee. 'Oh come on, Pujji wooji, I'm a *good* friend, yaar,' she said, her tone louche.

'Quite right, my lovely wovely.' Puri let out a hearty laugh that sounded especially sleazy. 'Better make that *good* friend, actually.'

The security guard apologised with heartfelt remorse. 'Unfortunately, sir, I cannot permit anyone to enter who is not here on the list,' he said.

'Come on, yaar,' insisted the detective. 'Just go check up, OK? No one told me anything of the sort.'

The guard agreed to do so, retreating to his sentry post, where, through the window, he could be seen talking on a phone.

All the while cameras mounted on the high walls surrounding the property peered into the interior of the car, their lenses opening and contracting like sea anemones.

'Full Moon takes his security most seriously,' murmured Puri. 'Wonder if he thinks he's the next target.'

The detective was taking no chances himself.

Mahinder C. Pujji was a persona he had developed and honed over the past couple of years for just such an operation. He was a Ludhiana resident with a successful machine tools manufacturing business, an account with the India National Bank, a driver's licence and, for good measure, membership of the All Punjab Rotary Club.

Mr Pujji was also armed with a number of handy gadgets. His mobile phone doubled as a voice-activated recorder. The gold medallion he was wearing as part of his disguise – he had gone for 'Indo Western', Western meaning cowboy – contained a pinhole TV camera and transmitter. And there was a location device secreted in the heel of his fake alligator boots.

The receivers for these devices were all in the back of a battered Bajaj three-wheeler van (one of thousands that plied the streets of Delhi and transported everything from chickens to schoolchildren) parked down the street. Flush, the young electronics and computer whizz, was secreted in the back. Tubelight was also on hand. And it was his mysterious Nepali operative Facecream who was playing the part of Puri's mistress.

No one else could have carried off the part quite as well as her, reflected Puri as they waited. The 'Pujji wooji' touch had been sheer genius.

'Ma'am may accompany you,' said the security guard when he returned. 'But before you can proceed I would need the password.'

'Most certainly,' said Puri. 'It's Humpty Dumpty.'

The automatic gates parted and the Merc purred up a driveway lined with giant dahlias. In front of the 'farmhouse', a mock Rajasthani-style palace with sandstone turrets, white marble balconies and a set of solid brass doors, stood a giant rockery with a bronze statue of Shiva mounted on the summit.

With Facecream hanging on his arm, her high heels making her the taller of the two by a couple of inches, Puri walked through a grand entrance hall and on into a galleried living-room-cum-hall. Stuffed animal heads stared down from the walls – as did the grinning likenesses of three generations of Full Moon's over-fed family. All of them had posed in their most garish finery for a professional photographer with a preference for soft lighting and smoky filters.

The match between the Goa Beachers and Mumbai
Bears was being projected on to a cinema screen at the
far end of the room. Some forty or so men, charged
tumblers of whisky in hand, were engrossed in the live
coverage. Amongst them Puri counted a minister, a couple
of senior bureaucrats, a music video VJ, a high-ranking
police officer and the Indian chief executive of an international bank. On the encircling chaise longues lounged
leggy women of various hues.

'You're Pujji?'

The voice belonged to Full Moon – a deep bass that
went with his black attire and ear stud. Standing face to
face with him – it was uncomfortably close – Puri realised
how apt the nickname he'd chosen for the bookie had
been. There was not a single hair on the man's head and
his scalp was riddled with squiggly bumps like those
made by sand worms on a beach. His forehead, however,
was smooth and shiny and sloped down to a prominent
hooked nose that bespoke Central Asian ancestry – and
not a little danger.

'Welcome to my home,' he said, his deep-set eyes
appraising Facecream's voluptuous figure. 'Help yourself
to liquor and food. The chef is Thai. I've brought in my
own paan wallah as well. You won't find better anywhere
in Delhi.'

'Wonderful,' said the detective, beaming. 'Rinku said
you were a man who liked to enjoy.'

But Full Moon's attention was still directed solely at
Facecream. 'We've not been introduced,' he said. 'You are?'

'Private property,' answered Puri, who promptly ordered
Facecream to go and fetch him a drink.

'Oh, Pujji wooji!' she said, objecting with a pout.

'Go!' he said firmly. 'I would be joining you. We two have business to discuss.'

He and Full Moon both watched her walk away.

'That is a first-class hussy,' said the bookie.

'Keeps me fit and fine.'

'I can imagine. Tell me: she's for sharing?'

Puri's mouth twitched into a smile. 'I've been here five minutes only and already you're wanting to steal my woman, you bugger!' he said. 'That takes balls, by God! But Miss Nina's not a library book for borrowing.'

'Everything can be bought for a price,' said Full Moon in a dark tone. He eyed the briefcase Puri was carrying. 'You brought the deposit?'

'Ten lakhs exactly.' Puri gave the briefcase a pat.

'Rajesh over there will keep a record of your shouts. *All* accounts to be settled by end of day. No exception.'

The bookie called over his number two, who took the cash.

'Let's make this interesting,' suggested Full Moon. 'Win and I'll double your takings. Lose and I'll hang on to Miss Nina for tonight.'

Puri shook his head. 'No deal.'

'Triple?'

'Not even ten times, bhai. She's a display item, only.'

Full Moon faced the detective square on. 'You're not understanding,' he said. 'I'm offering you excellent odds. You should take them.'

A voice broke in: 'Sunny! Good to see you, buddy!' It was Rinku. He walked over and gave Puri a playful punch. 'Seen all these women? Like Baskin Robbins, yaar!

Thirty-two flavours! I told you, Mohib bhai knows how to throw a party. Come! Let's get you a proper drink.'

Rinku led him away to the bar.

'You're welcome,' he said under his breath.

'Situation was totally under control,' said the detective.

'Like hell, Chubby. And what the hell are you wearing?'

'I'm in disguise.'

'Bloody joker! I could spot you a mile off. By the way, who's that girl, yaar – one with the amazing legs? Doesn't seem your type. Does Rumpi know?'

Puri was shocked by the sums being wagered by his fellow gamblers and the flippancy with which they indulged their habit. There was not, it seemed, an aspect of the game they were not prepared to bet on – from the outcome of the toss to the score of an individual over or the number of wickets a bowler was likely to take. Sums that most Indians only dreamed of earning during their lifetime were being thrown around like change.

The worst offender was a builder in a white linen suit. After just half an hour of play, he'd lost almost a crore and didn't seem remotely concerned. 'Easy come, easy go, yaar!' he boasted before making another shout, placing ten lakhs on the outcome of a single delivery and promptly losing. The minister, too, threw his wealth around with gay abandon. 'Without death there can be no heaven', he said in an indulgent, self-righteous manner after one of his bets paid off to the tune of two lakhs.

It was only while watching (and indeed participating in) this macho orgy that Puri really began to appreciate how much money was involved and how 'session' betting was driving the match-fixing industry.

For anyone with direct access to the teams – journalists, managers, umpires – there was a fortune to be made manipulating even the tiniest element of the game. And crucially such spot fixing was extremely hard to detect. Not just for the authorities but also for the spectators, fellow gamblers and fellow players. You no longer had to throw a match to make money. All you had to do was get one or two cricketers to co-operate.

What Rinku had said about gambling being in Indians' blood was true, Puri reflected as he sat on a couch next to a young Lithuanian prostitute (who'd told him that she liked Indian men because they were 'horny'). There was no prohibition against gambling in Hinduism. On Diwali, the biggest festival of the year, most families sat around gambling on cards. How much had Mummy taken him for last year? A thousand rupees at least?

But this was different: Full Moon's guests were addicts, their habit fuelled by a ballooning black economy. The amounts Puri wagered were tiny by comparison. He put 25,000 on the Goan number five batsman scoring nine in the ninth over and lost. He wagered 50,000 on number six losing his wicket on the twentieth ball. And he threw away another 40,000 on the Mumbai captain scoring a four off the last ball of the seventh over, only to watch a leg drive stop short of the boundary.

'*Arrey!*' Puri shouted each time he lost. He also made a show of calling a pretend astrologer to get his advice on where to place his money next.

Secretly, however, he was pleased with the outcome.

Rinku had offered him up to Full Moon as a prize sucker; it was the only way to get him in to the party at such short notice.

'Be sure to lose all your money, buddy,' he'd said. 'Should come easy to you.'

For good measure, the detective knocked back a few pegs and pretended to be plastered, reciting bawdy ditties to the Lithuanian prostitute, who seemed to appreciate them.

All the while, however, he was getting the lie of the land.

Full Moon's number two came and went from a room directly off the hall. At one point, he left the door open and Puri got a glimpse inside – a long table with a couple of laptop computers arranged on top; two men sitting in front of them wearing headsets, no doubt taking bets from punters across Delhi.

Full Moon himself spent a good deal of time in an adjacent room and Puri decided to try to get inside and plant a listening device. First he needed a diversion. So while Facecream kept their host occupied at the bar, he went to the toilet to call Flush and ask him to arrange a brief power cut.

Five minutes later, the lights and TV screen went off. Amid all the cries, jeers and confusion, Puri slipped unnoticed into Full Moon's room. Turning on the flashlight built into his Indian-manufactured mobile phone, he found himself in a study, furnished in keeping with the rest of the house – a desk with silver-plated legs, a chair that looked like a throne with red velvet covering. The books on the shelves were mostly about big game hunting and cricket.

The detective had brought along a few of Flush's ingeniously designed listening devices (these ones looked like ordinary car keys and were therefore easy to smuggle through the tightest security) and attached one to the bottom of the bookie's desk. Then he checked the drawers. The top one was locked, but the mechanism was simple and Puri opened it with ease.

Inside, on top of some pornographic magazines, he discovered a piece of paper with four rows of numbers written on it, three numbers to a row.

This he folded and slipped into the inside pocket of his jacket. Then he sent an SMS to Flush. A moment before the electricity came back on, Puri returned to the hall.

The match ended an hour later, a win for Mumbai. Puri had lost a grand total of 300,000 rupees, a little over $6,000. Facecream had also succeeded in keeping Full Moon distracted without having to compromise herself.

A few of the guests wandered upstairs, accompanied by the prostitutes; others carried on eating and drinking and took to the impromptu dance floor. A young man whom Puri recognised as the son of one of the country's richest industrialists sat down with a couple of friends and started to snort lines of cocaine.

By then, Puri had planted three bugs in various parts of the house; a signal from Facecream indicated that she had successfully placed her two as well.

Before leaving, Puri could not resist having a paan. He went over to the spot where the paan wallah was sitting behind a table and ordered a sweet one.

The man took a fresh lime leaf from his stock and began to open little stainless steel canisters full of ingredients. He scooped out a dollop of slaked lime paste and spread it on the leaf. Then came the areca nut, followed by dollops of fruit preserves and spices.

Full Moon came and stood next to the detective and ordered one for himself.

'You lost a lot of moola today,' he commented. 'Anyone would have thought you were throwing it away deliberately.'

'Just enjoying,' said Puri with a grin. 'Next match I'll make back my losses for sure – you can bet on it actually.'

The paan wallah wrapped the betel leaf and its contents into a snug but sticky little package and handed it to the detective. Puri inserted the paan into his mouth; his right cheek bulged outward as the juices began to fill his mouth.

'Thanks for the party,' he said, sounding like an Indian version of Marlon Brando in *The Godfather*. 'I had better get a move on. We would be driving directly back to Ludhiana this evening, only.'

'Don't you mean Khan Market?'

Puri looked down to find a pistol pointed at his belly. Over at the bar, Full Moon's number two had Facecream and Rinku covered as well. The other guests appeared oblivious to what was going on.

'What the hell is this, yaar?' the detective bawled, trying to bluff it out. 'You've got my deposit. Accounts are to be settled before midnight as agreed.'

The paan wallah, who couldn't see the pistol from where he was standing, handed Full Moon his order. The bookie took it with his free hand and motioned Puri towards his study.

'*Jao!*' he ordered.

The detective crossed the hall and opened the door. He could feel the muzzle of the pistol prodding into the back of his ribs as the bookie turned on the lights.

'Sit down,' he said, closing the door with his foot.

Puri did as he was told. Full Moon kept the pistol on him and placed the paan on his desk.

'Now give me what you stole from me . . . Slowly.'

The detective reached inside his jacket and took out the piece of paper with the code written on it. Full Moon snatched it away.

'Know what they used to do to thieves in my village when I was a kid?' he asked. 'Cover them in ghee and hang them upside down over an anthill. By the end they'd be begging for death.'

Then, without warning, Full Moon took a step forward and slapped Puri hard around the face, sending the paan flying out of his mouth. The detective felt stunned. For a moment he thought he might cry. But he managed to steel himself.

'How did you know?' he asked, nursing his cheek.

'I got a call from an old friend this morning. Said there was a certain low-life jasoos by the name of Vish Puri sniffing around, that he might come knocking. Didn't take much to figure out which buffoon he was talking about.'

Full Moon was sitting on the edge of his desk, looking pleased with himself. 'What puzzles me is what Rinku bhai is doing helping you,' he continued. 'We've had plenty of dealings together, he and I. Why this sudden betrayal?'

'We're childhood friends,' answered Puri. 'When I demanded his help, he couldn't refuse me.'

'Very touching. Childhood friends. Makes it all the more appropriate. You two grew up together. Now you'll die together.' He let his words hang in the air for a moment before adding, 'Maybe they'll have a joint cremation, save on the wood.'

Full Moon's number two entered the room. Facecream and Rinku were locked in the swimming pool pump house, he reported. He had also added up the total for the day's winnings: half a crore, around $110,000.

'Keep our remaining guests occupied,' said the bookie. 'I'll bring him out the back in a few minutes. We'll take the three of them to Provence Estate. They're pouring concrete today.'

The number two left the room and Full Moon made a phone call. His only words were, 'Amount is twenty-four lakhs.' And then he hung up and popped the paan into his mouth.

'That is Aga's cut, is it?' asked Puri.

'Shut up, yaar. I'll be asking the questions,' said Full Moon. 'Now tell me who you're working for.'

The detective didn't answer.

'Tell me, otherwise my associates will make a proper mess of your friend Miss Nina. All she'll be good for is begging at traffic lights.'

Puri held out a bit longer before appearing to give in. 'I was hired by Kamran Khan – to find out who killed his father,' he said.

Full Moon looked at him askance. 'Kamran Khan?' he repeated, sounding unconvinced. 'How did he hire you?'

'Through an intermediary – an Angrez.'

'Who?'

'He's with Scotland Yard. They know all about you.'

'What do they know?'

'That you and Faheem Khan had dealings – doing match fixing and all. Most probably you were falling out over winnings. That's why you killed him.'

'Brilliant work, Mister Sherlock, except I didn't do it. Faheem and I were partners. We were making a lot of money together.'

Puri regarded the bookie with puzzlement. 'But if you weren't the one . . .' he mused, his brow corrugated. A revelation suddenly came to him. 'Of course – it was Aga! He found out you and Khan were match fixing without his say-so.' There was an edge of triumph to Puri's voice as he added, 'No wonder you've got so much of security here today. He's put out a contract on you, isn't it?'

Full Moon cocked his pistol. 'Stand up,' he said. 'We're going to a building site. You, Rinku and Miss Nina are going to help strengthen the foundations.'

By now, the hall was empty, although the music was still playing. The lyrics to the latest Bollywood number blared out: 'I know you want it but you're never gonna get it . . . I'm too sexy for you.' As they passed the bar, Full Moon told Puri to stop and helped himself to a bottle of water.

'Keep moving,' he said, glugging down the contents. His voice sounded croaky. 'Through that door over there.'

Puri heard him clear his throat. He did it a couple more times before breaking into a cough. The water bottle fell to the floor.

'Stop!' he ordered.

The detective turned around slowly, hands in the air.

Full Moon was massaging his throat. An expression of almost ludicrous panic twisted his features.

'You've been poisoned,' said Puri. 'Aconite, most probably in the paan. Let me help you.'

Full Moon raised his pistol and with the words 'Bastard, I'll kill you!' pulled the trigger.

The bullet missed, hitting a stuffed bear standing in the corner, which keeled over. The detective moved to his right as fast as his body would allow, taking cover behind a column. Another bullet whistled past, then another.

Click, click, click. The pistol had either jammed or he was out of bullets. Puri risked a peek around the column. He saw Full Moon stumble towards the bar and grab another bottle of water. He poured the contents down his throat. Tottering backwards, he knocked over a candelabrum. A candle touched on a curtain and set it alight. The pistol clattered to the floor as Full Moon wrapped his arms around one of the columns, trying to keep upright. After a few seconds he slid down, his shoes squeaking on the polished marble.

Puri reached the dying man's side and managed to turn him over. Frothy red saliva oozed from the corner of his mouth.

'The code you and Faheem Khan were using. What's the cipher?' asked the detective. Behind him the curtains were alight, the flames licking at the wooden balcony above.

Full Moon gestured for him to come closer. Puri did so. And with his last breath, the bookie tried to spit in his face.

'Once a charmer, always charming,' said Puri as he took

the dead bookie's pockets and took his mobile phone. The he hurried back to the study to retrieve the piece of paper with the code on it.

He emerged, successful, to find the fire burning out of control. The alarm had gone off. Gamblers and prostitutes were running half dressed from the building. There was no time to search for his ten lakh deposit.

Puri made his way out through the back of the building in search of the others. He ran into them halfway across the garden. Facecream had their former captor in a half nelson.

'Full Moon's dead, poisoned by the paan wallah,' Puri told them.

'What about the money? There's got to be fifty, sixty lakhs in there,' said Rinku.

An explosion came from inside the mansion. Glass and flames burst from the ground-floor windows. Rinku stared, incredulous.

'It's only money, yaar,' said Puri.

'*Only* money! Chubby, you need your head examined!'

'No examination is necessary I can assure you. Now come. Let us get after that hit man. No delay.'

• FOURTEEN •

I nspector Surinder Thakur of the Laxmi Bai Nagar police station called while Puri and his team were in the middle of a high-speed chase after the paan wallah hit man.

The detective answered his phone, thinking it might be someone important.

'Vish Puri, sir. Hello? Your portable's been in power off mode these past hours.'

The detective had to raise his voice over the cacophony of car horns and screeching tyres: 'What all I can do for you, Inspector?'

The paan wallah hit man, who was obviously familiar with the roads (and pavements) of this part of Delhi, had a distinct advantage: he was on a motorbike, a Royal Enfield Bullet. But in Handbrake he had a formidable opponent. Puri's driver had been trained in the reckless art of Indian driving by the best of the best: Randy Singh of International B-Hinde Taxi and Limousine Services, who, as legend had it, once played chicken with a Bentley and won.

Puri usually kept his driver on a tight rein – 'Do lane driving!' he would admonish him from the back seat. The moment Handbrake was let loose, however, he could be relied upon to willingly and adeptly slalom through traffic at high speed, pull into oncoming lanes regardless of what was approaching in the opposite direction and, when necessary, tackle roundabouts anticlockwise.

While in pursuit of the paan wallah hit man, he showed no qualms about pulling through a petrol station fore-court, sending the pump attendants scattering. Nor did he hesitate when they reached Saket and he had to reverse down the Sri Aurobindo Marg ramp against the flow of the rush hour.

'You heard the news?' asked Inspector Thakur. Puri noted a distinct lack of confidence in his voice; evidently the moustache investigation was not going his way.

'What all happened?' asked the detective as he watched the paan wallah hit man speed up a mound of sand, jump over a drinking water wallah's cart and land squarely on the other side.

'Cow!' shouted Rinku as a large bullock stepped into the middle of the road.

Handbrake swerved, narrowly missing the animal, but knocked off one of the Merc's side mirrors.

'Doesn't matter!' the detective bawled. 'Go fast!'

'Better I call you later, sir?' asked Inspector Thakur.

'No, no, tell me,' replied the detective before shouting, 'There, there! Take next turn!'

Handbrake took a sharp left and Puri, Rinku and Facecream were thrown to one side of the car. A moment later, the vehicle hit a speed bump and they were all tossed upwards. This caused the detective to let out a baritone belch.

'You were saying, Inspector? Some development in the case?'

'Gopal Ragi was abducted today in broad daylight. From outside his home directly. And, sir, his moustache was taken – shaved clean off,' reported Inspector Thakur.

Puri digested this information as he watched the paan wallah hit man pass through a pedestrian gate and enter the Safdarjung Development Area.

Handbrake promptly threw the car into reverse. An SUV coming in the other direction gouged the Merc's right side.

'His fault, sir!' cried the driver.

'There's an access road up ahead,' Rinku contributed.

It crossed the detective's mind that the Gopal Ragi abduction might be a revenge shearing and that his client might have been behind it. This concern was quickly alleviated.

'A man was spotted at the scene who matches the description of the intruder at Shri Bhalla's residence on Saturday last,' explained Thakur.

'Ragi's moustache – it was clean shaven, is it?' asked Puri, having to repeat the question three times before he could make himself understood.

'Not a single hair left behind,' came back the answer.

The assassin was speeding down the backstreets of the colony, apparently lost. Finally, he turned into a dead end.

'We've got him,' declared Puri.

'Got who?' asked Thakur, confused.

'Apologies, Inspector! One minute hold.'

The car was doing a good 60 miles an hour now, flying past villas and parked cars. It would be only a minute or two before they caught up with their quarry. But then they ran into a perfect storm of servants and wallahs – a dog walker with five pugs, each on its own leash and straining in different directions; a *kabari* wallah peddling a rickety wooden cart piled high with old newspapers; and a *baraat* band on its way to a wedding.

Handbrake successfully negotiated this human and canine obstacle course with a minimum loss of speed. But a toy seller riding a bicycle while simultaneously blowing a kazoo and balancing a fifteen-foot-long bamboo pole festooned with inflatable ducks on his handlebars was one obstacle too many.

Puri's driver had to bank hard to avoid hitting him and found himself on a collision course with some school-children. Slamming on the brakes and swerving to the right, he ploughed into a parked, and thankfully unoc-cupied, Tata Nano, the cheapest car in the world, and as the impact conclusively proved, little more than a tin can on wheels.

'His fault, sir!' said the driver, his words muffled by the airbag now pinning him back against his seat.

Rinku started laughing – 'What a ride, yaar!' – as Puri exited the car.

The paan wallah was coming back down the road. He smiled at the detective as he raced past and gave him a military salute.

'Hello, hello? Sir, you're still on line?'

Puri lifted his handset to his ear as he watched the motorbike race out of sight.

'Yes, Inspector.'

'What was that noise? Sounded like an accident.'

'A minor one, only,' he said as he surveyed the damage.

The front of the Mercedes Benz was crumpled, there was a long tear down its right side and the side mirror was gone – tens of thousands of rupees' worth of damage, and none of it likely to be covered by the insurance. Puri just hoped that Scott had meant it when he'd talked about having deep pockets.

'Naturally you've located the owner of the next-longest moustache?' asked Puri.

'He's ninety-two years. Lives far off in some cave on the Nepal border,' said Thakur with despair.

After Puri had swapped insurance details with the owner of the wrecked Nano, reported the accident to the police and waited for the crowd of onlookers to disperse, he opened the boot of the Mercedes.

Inside lay Full Moon's number two. He'd been sick all over himself.

'Your boss made a *hawala* transfer. To who exactly?' demanded Puri.

A hawala transfer could be made between money brokers without the cash actually moving. This unofficial network handled the transfer of billions of dollars across South Asia and beyond every year.

'Saar-ji, please!' he begged. 'Let me out of here. I can't breathe.'

'First tell me the hawala broker's name.'

'Bhai never told me. My duties are organising the parties, getting girls, Buss!'

Puri slammed down the boot, listened to his captive's

entreaties for a minute or two and then popped the latch again.

'I . . . I can't. They'll kill me.'

'And if you don't, *we'll* kill you. My friend here owns a wheat thresher. He'll lower you into it feet first. Rest assured it would be most painful.'

'You don't understand, I . . .'

Puri started to close the boot again.

'Mihir Desai!' blurted the lackey.

'His location?'

'That I don't know, sir. I swear it! Bhai never told me. Believe me!'

But Flush had the answer. More or less.

'Full Moon's call was to a post-paid number,' he said when he caught up with the group in his Bajaj van. 'I called my batchmate at LBS and he was able to do a multi-lateration of the radio signals using the GPS system and—'

Puri cut him short. 'Tell me.'

'It was received in Surat, Boss.'

Puri turned to Tubelight. 'You've got any reliable person there?'

'That boy Sonal. From the Bollywood Bimbo case? One you called Chanel Number Five.'

'Get him to the location no delay. I want discreet surveillance. Meanwhile, you two' – he meant Tubelight and Flush – 'go directly to the airport. Be on the next plane.'

'You're not coming with us, Boss?'

'Gujarat is one place I am always happy to avoid.'

Full Moon's lackey was banging against the inside of the boot again, demanding to be let out.

'What about our guest, Boss?' asked Tubelight.

'I'll sit on him,' said Puri.

The detective had not made any progress with the moustache case, the trace of the goose and two snakes licence plate having come to nothing, and he had far better things to do than follow up on Inspector Thakur's phone call. Nevertheless he called Raju Pillai, Director General and Honorary Secretary of MOP, and asked him to arrange an interview with Gopal Ragi right away.

'Difficult,' said Pillai. 'These media persons are having a feeding frenzy. Dozens are camped outside his house. The story is running on every channel. "Moustache Massacre" they're calling it. They're treating the whole thing as a joke. I went on *Action News!* to put the record straight. This is a serious matter. Our members are getting attacked willy nilly.'

The detective arranged to enter Ragi's home through a back entrance and reached the place an hour later. He found the victim in his living room, distraught but calm, and in no doubt as to who had been behind his abduction and assault.

'Bhalla did this,' he said. 'He believed I had his moustache shaved off so he wanted revenge. He hired that goon.'

Puri was in no mood for conspiracy theories. 'Listen!' he said, his anger flaring. 'The description of your abductors match. Therefore it is safe to reason a third party is involved.'

'He made it look that way, to throw you off the trail.'

The detective sank his face into his hands. 'Just tell me what all happened,' he murmured through his fingers.

Ragi had left the house for the office at his usual hour, he explained. As he got into his car, someone came up behind him and grabbed him. A struggle ensued.

'He was wearing a ski mask but I noticed one thing: he had blotches on his hands,' said Ragi.

Puri wondered if the assailant might be a barber. Alum, which was used to heal nicks and cuts, causes blemishes to the skin.

'He held a rag over my face. Presently I passed out,' added Ragi who went on to explain how he regained consciousness lying on the back seat of his car, which was parked in the Pusa Hill Forest.

That made sense, Puri thought. It was a secluded spot where no one would have disturbed the thief while they removed the moustache. But why would anyone want to steal a moustache? Could the thief have some kind of fetish? Or was he indeed a collector of unusual curios, as Thakur had surmised? Perhaps Ragi's moustache was destined to be mounted above a mantelpiece like a prize stag?

There was one other possibility.

'Could be some individual or other wants you and Bhalla out of the way, so to speak. You were planning to make any appearances together?' asked Puri.

'We're not the best of friends – in case you hadn't noticed,' answered Ragi.

The detective left the house and called his client to bring him up to date. For once Bhalla had little to say. 'If it wasn't Ragi, then who?' he asked.

'Leave that question in my most capable hands, sir,' answered Puri.

· FIFTEEN ·

Chanel No. 5 pulled up in front of a mansion in the exclusive City Light Town District of Surat, about two hours after Tubelight had hired him to locate Full Moon's hawala agent. There were lights on inside – a man's silhouette was in a window on the first floor – and so the young operative went straight up to the gate and rang the bell. It was answered by a prim maidservant who behaved as if she owned the house. He knew the type.

'Pizza delivery!'

Chanel No. 5 held up a Domino's box that had been delivered to his place before he'd set off. He was wearing a uniform, stolen a few months ago from a genuine employee's washing line. He hadn't managed to get hold of one of those unflattering baseball caps, but then he probably wouldn't have worn it anyway. Hats interfered with his hairstyle. He wore it spiked and shaved on the sides. It went with the coloured strings and bands he wore on his left wrist, the birthstone stud in his left ear and his brazen manner.

'One peppy paneer with cheese-stuffed thick crust

and extra toppings of jalapenos, green peppers and pineapple, extra spicy,' he said in heavily accented English.

The maidservant scowled with contempt.

'No one ordered pizza,' she said, arms folded, head cocked to one side. 'This is number 22.' She pointed to the digits on the gate. 'Can't you read?'

'Hey, sister, no need to talk like that!' he replied. 'I'm just doing my job. Deliver in half an hour, they say. Get it to the customer hot and crispy. And that's what I do. It says here' – he read from the fake order slip he'd printed out – 'number 22, Mihir Desai. He called at exactly eight twenty-two. That's' – Chanel No. 5 checked his watch – 'twenty-nine minutes ago. See, you're holding me up, sister! The pizza will go soggy and then I'll get the blame! That could cost me my job!'

With a roll of her eyes, the maidservant told him to wait.

When she returned, triumph radiated from her snapping brown eyes. 'Like I told you, no one ordered pizza,' she said. 'Sir and Ma'am don't eat junk.'

'You checked with him yourself?'

'Who else? Now stop wasting my time or I'll call your office and make a complaint.'

'What am I supposed to do with the pizza?'

'Think I care?' she said with a toss of her head, slamming the gate shut in his face.

Chanel No. 5 thanked her under his breath. Desai was at home. He was the one in the window – had turned and talked to the maidservant when she'd gone to ask him about the pizza.

So far so good. He got back on his Vespa, rode to the end of the street and parked on an empty lot. Crouching down behind a bush, he took off the uniform and shoved it into his backpack; then he slipped on his favourite T-shirt, printed with a picture of the goddess Britney Spears.

He had already marked out a tree with plenty of foliage on the street from where he would be able to keep an eye on Desai. First he needed to take care of the street light that stood right next to it. For this he reached into his backpack and took out his catapult and a marble. The target was an easy one for someone who had grown up in the Bapunagar slum and routinely killed rats and pigeons and sometimes, for sport, took out the headlights of passing cars on the Bajipura Road.

The sound of the impact and subsequent shower of glass that rained down on the pavement and the parked SUV underneath brought the security guards posted outside the other houses running. They looked up at the shattered fixture, examined the shards of glass, discussed what could have caused the bulb to explode, looked up and down the street with bemused expressions, chatted for a while about this and that, and then, one by one, returned to their posts.

When the coast was clear, Chanel No. 5 emerged from his hiding place and clambered up the tree, taking his backpack and the pizza box with him.

Once he was settled on a sturdy branch, he sent Tubelight an SMS informing him that he was in position. He sent another to his new girlfriend, Padma, whom he had met at an illegal rave, and a third to his mother to

let her know he'd be out late. Then he stuck his headphones in his ears, selected Metallica's *Kill 'Em All* on his
MP3 player and tucked into a nice slice of peppy paneer.

While Tubelight and Flush were boarding the evening
flight to Ahmedabad, from where they planned to drive
to Surat, Mummy and Ritu were making their way down
to the water's edge at the Har ki Pauri ghat in Haridwar.
They'd avoided the crush of the. *aarti* ceremony when
thousands gathered to watch temple priests perform a
dramatic evening show complete with *thalis* of fire,
clanging bells and plenty of evocative chanting. But the
ancient steps were still busy with devotees washing themselves in the waters of Mother Ganga, the air perfumed
with incense, the atmosphere one of calm deference.

It was only a few degrees above freezing and the two
women were wearing bulky winter coats and thick-knit
sweaters over their white kurta pajamas. With their woolly
hats pulled down over their ears and dupattas draped over
their shoulders, they resembled Indian auntie versions of
the Teletubbies. Ritu had to tug off her mittens in order
to take from her purse the fee the pandit had quoted for
conducting the Asthi Visarjan ceremony. The three
100-rupee notes quickly vanished within the folds of his
saffron robes. The priest then set about arranging a few
stainless steel containers on one of the steps. These were
filled with the accoutrements of his trade – marigolds,
rose petals, brightly coloured powders – and the urn was
placed next to them.

The pandit began to recite the last rites, his nasal
delivery rising above the sound of the rushing water.

Mummy and Ritu saluted the Ganges with a namaste. They crouched down, holding their cupped hands before them, and these were filled with marigolds and rose petals. To this potpourri was added a few pinches of Bal Bawar's ashes, the timeless mantras flowing as freely as the river itself. *'Om brahm bakhtam samarpayamee.'*

The two women allowed the flowers and ash to cascade from their hands. The mixture floated on the surface for a moment and quickly dissipated amongst the eddies. The pandit then emptied the remaining contents of the urn into the river, where they began an epic, 1,500-mile journey across the great plains of India to the Bay of Bengal. Finally, Ritu crouched down on the last step and cast off a floral diya, a banana leaf boat filled with petals and an oil lamp made from clay. It was quickly captured by the current, which pulled the tiny vessel out into the middle of the river, the flame of its cotton wick soon a speck on the vast body of water.

The ceremony was over. Bal Bawar had departed . . . at least from this life.

Ritu stood on the steps for a while longer, tears running down her cheeks, saying a final, silent prayer for her late husband. Mummy remained by her side, one arm around her friend's shoulder, offering her words of comfort. She also kept one eye on the man who had been tailing them all day.

Trying to tail them, more like.

Shaking him off that afternoon had been simple. After lunch, while Ritu took some 'meter down' in their hotel room, Mummy crossed the busy pedestrian bridge that spanned the canal. Halfway across, she scattered a bagful of peanuts, attracting the attention of three or four of the city's bold and fearless monkeys, who started to fight over the pickings. With the way effectively blocked, Mummy proceeded to the other side of the bridge, where she got clean away in an auto.

The next few hours proved fruitful.

Mummy located the Panda who kept the records of the village in Madhya Pradesh where Mrs Harnam Talwar, wife of notorious politician Sandeep Talwar, maintained she'd been born. There was no record of either her or her parents. She was not who she claimed to be. This information might be all that Mummy needed to link Harnam Talwar to Faheem Khan. But she didn't want to jump to any conclusions. There was one last name to verify: Call Centre King Satish Bhatia's mother, Jasmeet, who had sat just two places away from the victim at that fateful dinner.

Mummy planned to go in search of her family's Panda tomorrow.

Of course she would have to shake off her tail first. He was working for Chubby — of that she was sure. Not an especially smart fellow, it had to be said. Once this was all over she would have to have a word with her son about the calibre of people he was using. He had underestimated her, imagined she was just some silly old lady who wouldn't spot him in the crowd. Ha! Just look at him now over on the steps, lighting a beedi and holding the match up to his face so it illuminated his features. A prize duffer if ever she'd seen one.

Still, he could easily ruin things for her. If he found out that she had been talking with the Pandas of Haridwar and researching the ancestry of some of the women who'd been present at the murder, the great Vish Puri would guess what she was up to.

Mummy gave Ritu's arm a light squeeze.

'Better revert, na,' she said. 'You've been fasting all day – should be eating something. Come.'

They mounted the steps and made their way along the riverbank. Ritu moved slowly, rocking from side to side like a Weeble toy, stopping periodically to give change to the beggars with crippled limbs pleading for alms.

They were nearing the footbridge, the one where Mummy had shaken off Chubby's man that afternoon, when a black cat ran across their path. Ritu recoiled automatically as if she'd come face to face with a king cobra, grabbing Mummy by the arm. She insisted they take three steps backwards before continuing. A moment later, four or five bricks came crashing down on to the path in front of them. Mummy looked up; they had fallen from the top of a half-constructed building to their right.

A crowd gathered, demanding the labourers on the scaffolding climb down and explain themselves. It was an accident, they insisted, apologising profusely and promising they would be more careful in the future.

Ritu was still shaking when they got back to the hotel. And Mummy felt jittery herself, although she was in no doubt that it had been an accident. Forgoing her supper and getting into bed to write her diary, she thanked God for Ritu Auntie. She'd saved their lives. Her and the cat.

It was five in the morning when hawala broker Mihir Desai's Range Rover pulled out of the gates of his Surat mansion. He drove himself, speeding through the empty residential streets of the City Light District, one of the city's wealthy new suburbs. A motorbike appeared behind him but, at the junction with Canal Road, peeled away to the left.

Desai headed east into the city, making short work of a route that during the day, in the gridlock of Surat's traffic, would have taken an hour or more. When he reached Chowk Bazaar, a Muslim-dominated area since the massacres of 2002, he pulled up outside one of the drab, narrow buildings that lined the claustrophobic lanes. A man carrying a satchel soon appeared from a doorway and climbed into the front passenger seat. Desai promptly made a U-turn, heading back the way he'd come, and joined the Dumas Road.

New shopping malls appeared on the outskirts of the city – 'Come Fill Up In Happiness!' Apartment complexes picketed the horizon. He passed the Grand Bhagwati, 'India's first five-star vegetarian hotel', and took the next right towards the shipyards. Cranes stood silent against the faint dawn sky. The hulk of a half-built ship loomed closer. At the end of a long line of corrugated iron shacks where labourers slept out in the open on charpais, Desai joined a muddy track that skirted the high fence encircling the shipyards. It led down to the banks of the Tapi River.

The Range Rover finally stopped near a coal barge anchored in the water. Desai flicked his high beams. Presently, three men appeared on deck. A long, narrow plank was extended to the bank. Two figures walked along it, balancing like trapeze artists, to reach the shore. They wore filthy clothes, their hands and faces also black with grime and soot. For this reason, perhaps, Desai failed to shake hands with them when he dismounted from his vehicle.

A few words were exchanged and then one of the men knelt down, reached up inside his trouser pocket and pulled out a small packet. This he handed to Desai, who in turn passed it to the short man sitting in the Range Rover.

A good ten minutes passed as the contents of the packet were examined.

Finally, Desai retrieved a bulging plastic bag from the back seat of his vehicle. This he handed it to the two men who promptly headed back to the barge.

'Dirty business,' whispered Chanel No. 5.

He and Tubelight had watched the whole transaction through binoculars from behind a rusty old goods container on the edge of the docks. The Range Rover, a magnetic homing device still attached to the back door, turned and pulled away.

'Our man Desai is buying blood diamonds,' he added.

'From Africa?' asked Tubelight, watching the barge as its engine puttered into life.

'First smuggled to Arab countries. Then by sea to India.'

· SIXTEEN ·

Puri stood on the flat roof of his mock-Spanish villa looking down, in more ways than one, at the new home on plot number 23/B. It had been built over the past seven months, a constant source of hammering, banging, and voices raised over the sound of loud machinery, but was now, mercifully, finished. The owners had spent lakhs of rupees on the facade, a cross between the White House and the Taj Mahal with reflective silver windows and a portico large enough to support a helicopter pad. The building's sides, however, were windowless and bare – just big, tall slabs of poured concrete. Given that the plots around were empty and there was no garden surrounding the property, it looked as if the house had been scooped up by a hurricane and randomly dropped by the side of the road.

The owner was a local Jat farmer who, by the looks of him, had spent most of his life in the baking sun dragging a wooden plough across mustard fields. That is until the local government, effectively working on behalf of a major property developer who wanted to build a mall or perhaps a new office block, had offered him several lakhs per acre for his ancestral land.

The fact that a Jat farmer could now live wherever he chose was progress of a sort, reflected Puri. Money now spoke louder than caste, at least in India's 'metros'. The new Indian suburbia was populated by people of different backgrounds, ethnicities and, to a lesser extent, religions.

Not that there was much of a sense of community. Few of Puri's neighbours knew one another. And even if they did, they rarely interacted. The high walls and gates of their mansions and villas were hardly conducive to neighbourly chats.

Puri certainly had no plans to welcome the family into the colony. They were not his type. Despite the luxurious pile they had built for themselves, the family (great-grandparents, grandparents, parents and a big brood of children) spent their evenings sitting on a couple of *charpais* outside the front gates of their home. They drank rot-gut *desi sharab*, told raucous jokes, sang bawdy songs and picked lice out of each other's hair.

'Delhi hillbillies,' Puri called them. Most definitely not his type at all.

He turned away from the edge of the roof and stepped into the small greenhouse where he kept his chilli plants during the winter. It was nice and humid inside, the perfect temperature, and his Naga Vipers were flourishing. Some of the fruit was already shiny and plump and he could hardly wait to pick them. The seeds had come from Cumbria in England, hardly chilli-growing country. However the friend who'd smuggled them into India on his behalf claimed they produced the hottest chillies in the world. An incredible 1,381,118 SHU!

The detective had yet to eat a chilli that was too hot for him; his taste buds were as anaesthetised as an Indian bureaucrat's conscience. The fact that these were Angrezi chillies made the challenge all the more appealing. Nothing short of national pride was at stake.

The same could be said with regard to the Faheem Khan murder case.

Former Deputy Commissioner Scott had called from London last night, concerned that another bookie had been murdered and wondering how he could have been poisoned while Puri was with him. The detective explained that the assassin was a professional – 'not your average five thousand rupee a pop goonda' – and had disguised himself as a paan seller.

'As in pots and pans or porn, Vish?'

'Paan, Sir Jaams. It's a kind of Indian snack with betel nut. We suck and chew on it, actually.'

'Right. And the killer was serving it.'

'Correct. The real paan wallah was himself found strangled few hours later.'

'Any leads?'

'Not as of yet, sir. That one I'm leaving in the hands of Inspector Jagat Prakash Singh. He's a most capable officer – that is, when it comes to straightforward tasks such as locating individuals.'

'Right. Well I'm sure you know what you're doing, Vish.'

He didn't sound convinced, however, and Puri hung up the phone feeling that sense of inferiority again – as if somehow the gora knew better, that as an Indian he was not to be altogether trusted.

Seven hours' sleep hadn't cured him of this lingering feeling. Nor had his morning cup of bed tea. And so he had come up on to the roof, the one place where he could be alone – with his chillies.

He spent a few minutes feeding his plants with his special blend of liquid feed, which was high in nitrogen and phosphorus with a few drops of the Indian elixir neem oil for good measure. Then he washed the leaves, spraying them with water and gently wiping off the thin layer of dust and pollution that had formed in the past twenty-four hours. Finally, Puri pollinated his Ghost Chilli plants, something he had to do manually during the winter because the local bees couldn't find their way into his greenhouse. It was but a few minutes' work rubbing the tip of a soft cotton bud inside one flower, then rubbing it inside another and so on.

Soon he felt better, ready to face the full day's work ahead of him, ready to prove his worth – and that of Indians in general.

That morning Rumpi had served pomegranate seeds yet again, so Puri decided to leave the house earlier than he'd intended, to get a proper breakfast. As the Ambassador was heading through the outskirts of south Delhi, Handbrake noticed they were being followed by a silver sedan. Despite its tinted windows, he could make out two occupants.

'Number plate has a missing digit,' the driver also reported in Hindi.

'Very good. Don't let him know you've spotted him,' instructed Puri.

Twenty minutes later, they reached their destination:
East Block Eight, Sector One, R.K. Puram, a government
administrative complex. Handbrake turned in through
the gate and found a vacant space in the car park. The
silver sedan, meanwhile, stopped on the main road.

Puri ignored it as he approached a banyan tree that
grew to one side of the building. Beneath the tentacled
roots hanging down from its branches, he found Lakshman,
who made some of the best aloo paranthas in Delhi. His
'kitchen' comprised a wooden platform mounted on the
back of a bicycle with a small gas cooker and iron skillet,
a little rolling pin and board, and a few stainless steel
containers for the dough, potato mix, flour and ghee.

The detective ordered three paranthas, watched
Lakshman prepare them with a swiftness and efficiency
that any five-star restaurant chef would find hard to match,
and ate the hot potato-stuffed bread with some home-
made garlic *aachar* while standing up.

His appetite fully sated, the detective ordered a cup of
chai, swallowed his diet pills and turned his mind to the
murder case. Something was now clear to him. In the
past six months, a dramatic change had come to the world
of illegal cricket gambling. New technology had been
introduced and two major bookies and a player's father
had been bumped off.

Had the new technology made them redundant? Or
was there a turf war raging among Aga's 'soldiers'?

He started to refer back to his notes from the past couple
of days, looking over the list of suspects. He was now
down to seven, having decided to cross off foul-mouthed
public relations woman Neetika Sahini (no fewer than

eight witnesses confirmed that she hadn't moved from her seat while Faheem Khan was away from the table).

The remaining suspects were:

Satish Bhatia – 'Call Centre King'
Jasmeet Bhatia – elderly mother of Satish Bhatia
Sandeep Talwar – politician, President of the ICB, crook
Mrs Harnam Talwar – elderly wife of above
Kamran Khan – son of murder victim
Ram Dogra – industrialist, known as the 'Prince of Polyester'
Mrs Megha Dogra – elderly wife of above

Puri had one lead to follow up: the piece of paper he'd taken from Full Moon's farmhouse, which he planned to drop off at Brigadier Mattu's later in the day. He'd also managed to arrange a viewing of the CCTV footage from the match day at Kotla Stadium.

What else? He was due to pick up his visa from the Pakistan High Commission. Not something he was looking forward to in the least.

Puri's phone rang. It was Aarish, the man in Haridwar he'd tasked with watching Mummy.

'Very, *very* good morning to you, saar!' he said.

'Tell me.'

'Your dear mummy-ji and auntie have been doing time-pass in the city. Last night they scattered ashes at Har ki Pauri. Later, they reverted to their hotel. A nice establishment next to—'

'You kept Mummy in your sights whole day, is it?' interrupted the detective.

Aarish hesitated. 'In the morning, sir. And evening, also.'
Another hesitation, then a clearing of the throat. 'See unfortunately after lunch your dear mummy . . . Well, sir, there were some monkeys and it was very much crowded . . .'

'Monkeys?'

'So many, sir. Very aggressive.'

'How long she was gone from your sight exactly?'

'One hour, sir.'

'No more?'

'Could be two maximum.'

More like three, Puri thought.

'After that I stuck to her like sticky toffee, saar!'

'Tell me: these monkeys, they came out of nowhere?' asked the detective.

'No, sir, normally they're hanging round the bridge making trouble and all. Yet somehow – how I cannot fathom or understand – one entire bag of peanuts got spilled and everything went for a toss.'

Aarish was only a tour guide and occasional messenger with no formal training in the ancient Indian art of spycraft. Still, Puri had thought him capable of keeping an eye on a little old lady. Apparently he'd been wrong.

'Sir, your dear mummy-ji and auntie – they've confirmed tickets for today. Train will be reaching Delhi at nine-fifteen p.m.'

Puri told him to stay on the job until they both left Haridwar, then headed back to the Ambassador. The silver sedan was still waiting on the main road. He couldn't be sure – yet whom the occupants were working for (there were at least four possibilities) and decided the best course of action was to string them along.

'Pull someone by the ears and the head will follow,' went the old saying.

No newcomer to Surat's frenetic Varachha Road could ever have imagined that it was home to most of the world's diamond cutting and polishing sweatshops – nor that these businesses each turned over tens of millions of dollars a year. The buildings were cheerless, their concrete facades marked with black stains as if the city itself was shedding self-pitying tears. The lack of signs above the entrances augmented the sense of anonymity.

Even Tubelight couldn't quite fathom it. 'There's no security,' he pointed out in Hindi as he and Chanel No. 5 followed hawala broker Mihir Desai's Range Rover down Varachha Road.

'No need,' explained the local boy. 'Everyone working in the diamond business comes from the same region – Saurashtra, on the coast. They all know one another. If an outsider tried to steal the diamonds, he'd be spotted before he got in through the front door.'

'And where do you fit?' asked Tubelight.

'Saurashtra's my native place,' Chanel said with a grin. 'My father's a pedi-worker. All my uncles and cousins are cutters and polishers.'

Desai, who'd returned home from the river for a few hours before setting off again, parked in front of one of the buildings and entered through the main door. Chanel No. 5 pulled over on the other side of the road, got out and followed him inside.

A staircase led past sweatshop floors where rows of barefoot men in sleeveless vests sat slaving at rudimentary machines. A repetitive whirr of drills, lathes and spinning brushes underscored the monotonous nature of the work, as did the bored expressions on the men's faces.

The sixth floor, however, was different. Here the employees wore smart shirts and trousers and sat at desks equipped with LED lamps. Little paper packets of diamonds lay in front of them. Like myopic pensioners they examined them through magnifying loupes.

The owner, Acharya Bakshi, also had his office on the sixth floor. Chanel No. 5 got a look through the glass door. Desai was seated in front of Bakshi's desk. The latter was examing a large rough stone.

'Who are you? What are you doing here?'

The question came from one of the factory managers who'd come up the stairs behind him.

'I'm looking for a job. Anything going?'

'First floor. Ask for Sanghavi.'

'Got it.'

Chanel No. 5 took the precaution of picking up an application form and then rejoined his colleague.

'What happens after Bakshi's people have cut and polished the diamonds?' asked Tubelight as they sat in the car discussing their next move.

'Smuggle them out of India and sell them on the world market.'

'How?'

'With the legitimate diamonds.'

Chanel No. 5 went on to explain how most of the world's raw diamonds, 92 per cent to be exact, were shipped legally from places like South Africa and Namibia to India. They arrived in Mumbai, where their total weight was recorded by customs. The stones were then transported to Surat for cutting and polishing. From there they were returned to Mumbai and on to Antwerp.

'The blood diamonds are mixed in with the other ones?' guessed Tubelight.

'They're untraceable.'

'And customs clears them.'

'Their counting skills can be weak.'

Tubelight smiled; the old thief in him couldn't help but admire the beauty of the system. 'A foolproof way of laundering black money,' he said.

'Everyone's in on it. The coastguard catches a few every once in a while to keep the media persons happy and our Chief Minister puts on his best *kedia* and denies India's involved in the trade.'

Desai was on the move again. 'How will they be transported from here to Mumbai?' asked Tubelight as they followed him.

'*Angadias* – special diamond couriers. They dress like ordinary people and carry the diamonds hidden on their persons – sewn into the inside of their trousers, down their crotch. Who knows? You won't be able to spot them and they won't be easy to follow. Believe me, they're good – as good as you, chief.'

The express train bound for Delhi was scheduled to depart from Haridwar at 12.55. Five minutes ahead of time, Mummy got up from her seat to go to the WC.

'I'll not be long,' she told Ritu.

She made her way to the end of the carriage. But instead

of entering the toilet, Mummy carried on into the next compartment . . . and then the next.

When she reached the front of the train, Mummy waited by an open door until the engine shuddered into action and the train began to edge forward. Then she stepped out on to the platform and waited behind a stack of cargo.

It was a couple of minutes before the train had pulled away. Puri's man soon left as well. With the coast clear, Mummy proceeded to the front of the station, hailed an auto and headed back to the old city. En route she called Ritu Auntie.

'Listen, na, just one small problem is there,' she said. 'See I alighted the train to buy one magazine and it took off without me . . . Yes, yes, quite all right . . . Don't do tension, ji. I've my purse. Just I'll purchase one ticket for the next train . . . No, no, pulling of emergency cord is not necessary. You've my *tachee*, na? Take it home. I'll pass by later. So sorry . . .'

Mummy was soon delving into the past of Jasmeet Bhatia, mother of Call Centre King Satish.

After hours of searching, she discovered that Jasmeet's maiden name was Chuggani.

'Her father's native place was Rawat in today's Pakistan,' a helpful Panda told her, reading from an old ledger. 'Rawat is close to—'

'Rawalpindi,' said Mummy.

She remembered the place, had passed through it many times. It was near the village of Bajal where Faheem Khan had been living during Partition.

The Panda turned the page, reading various entries

made by Jasmeet's father, brothers, cousins. Finally he found the details of her birth in 1932. The entry bore her father's signature, indicating he'd been educated. Details in earlier entries also suggested that the family had been wealthy.

Jasmeet Bhatia, née Chuggani, would have been seventeen in 1947, exactly the right age and from a good family.

It was time to return to Delhi, to do follow-up.

Puri had passed the Pakistan High Commission on Shanti Path in Delhi's diplomatic area countless times over the years, glimpsed the turquoise tiled dome and antenna array on the roof, and wondered what went on behind those high walls. Never had he imagined that he might one day enter inside – enter into enemy territory.

At three o'clock, however, Handbrake dropped him in front of the enormous walled compound and he approached the front gate. He found four men sitting on a wonky bench to one side of it. They looked bored, as if they'd been there for days. One of them directed Puri to the small window in the gatehouse with a gesture that suggested he was about to embark on a hopeless task.

'Yes? What is it?' asked an old man with chiselled cheeks, peering out of the window.

The detective explained that he had an appointment with a political officer by the name of Salim Afridi.

'You're from . . . ?'

Puri felt like answering 'India' but instead handed the gatekeeper a copy of his card.

'Wait there.'

Puri sat down on the end of the wonky bench, regis-tering the silver sedan parked down the road. The two occupants had been following him around town all day but were themselves now being shadowed by two of Tubelight's boys, who, naturally, remained out of sight.

Puri watched a wallah sweeping up leaves and a few labourers playing cards on the lawn that ran parallel to the road and wondered if they were with the India Intelligence Bureau – charged with keeping an eye on who came and went from the Pakistani mission.

'Visa?' said the man sitting next to him.

Puri gave a nod. 'You?'

The man was in the export business – 'Wheat to Pakistan,' he said, then gave a shrug. 'India bureaucracy, Pakistan bureaucracy, India corruption, Pakistan corrup-tion – no difference.'

The window opened again and the old man signalled to Puri to enter through the main gate.

Beyond stood a large concrete fountain that had evidently been dry for many years. A driveway encircled it, weeds growing in the cracks in the tarmac, leading to the embassy's main building. It looked just as lifeless. The main doors were closed; there were only a couple of lights on. But most striking of all was the absence of security. There wasn't a guard in sight.

It hadn't been that long since the two countries almost went to war again – a full-blown war with nuclear weapons, Puri reflected as he was asked to sign a register. And yet here were Islamabad's representatives living and working deep inside their enemy's territory, and feeling so secure that they didn't so much as check their visitors' pockets.

The only thing the old man in the gatehouse seemed concerned about was Puri's mobile phone. It could not be taken inside, he explained.

'This never leaves my sight,' said Puri.

'You switch off, don't worry, no one using.'

To make doubly sure, the detective took the device apart, retrieved the chip and the battery, and handed the Pakistani the casing.

The old man smiled. 'As you like, sir.'

A young man escorted Puri along the driveway to the side of the building. They entered a long, empty corridor. All the doors were closed except one. The sound of a ping-pong ball being hit back and forth came from inside. There was no other evidence of activity. At the end of the corridor, he was shown into an office with a big desk equipped with four phones lined up in a row. His eyes were drawn to the portrait of Jinnah, the founder of Pakistan, hanging on the wall. He couldn't help but stare at his drawn, gaunt face – one that he despised.

'Welcome, Mr Puri, it's an honour,' said Afridi. The depth of his desk would have made a handshake challenging and both men were satisfied not to try. 'Please sit, make yourself comfortable.'

Afridi was about Puri's age, Puri's height, Puri's weight, Puri's skin tone. He had a double chin and a tummy just like Puri's as well. They could have been brothers.

'You'll take some tea?' he asked.

'I brought my passport. Forms and photographs, also,' answered the detective. He placed his documentation on the desk and gave them a push in Afridi's direction. The

Pakistani picked up the passport and began to flick through the pages. Given that the detective hated to fly, was terrified of it, the pages contained few visas.

'You were in Yemen, I see?' stated Afridi with faint interest.

'Some years back.'

'A holiday?'

'Correct,' lied Puri, who'd gone there undercover in connection with an oil smuggling racket.

The Pakistani turned another page, where he came across one of the detective's Bangladesh visas, and paused. Puri could almost read the man's mind: he didn't want to have to say the name of the country out loud. Bangladesh had been one half of Pakistan after Partition, albeit separated by India. A revolt against West Pakistan's dominance had resulted in civil war. In 1971, with the help of Indian forces, the territory had established itself as a sovereign state. For Islamabad, for the army in particular, it had been a humiliation they would never forget.

Afridi closed the passport. 'You have the payment receipt?' he asked.

'Payment?'

'A payment of 4,000 rupees must be made at the Grimleys Bank.'

'I was not aware,' said Puri.

Afridi pursed his lips. 'Without payment I cannot process your visa. And the bank is closed this afternoon.'

Puri felt a sudden swell of relief and struggled to contain a smile. They weren't going to give him his visa after all! Then he remembered the fax, the series of numbers and the questions he wanted to put to Kamran Khan (particularly about his whereabouts while his father was eating the butter chicken), and decided not to give up without a fight.

'I would be travelling to Pakistan tomorrow. I suggest you check with your superiors,' he said.

Puri was asked to wait and was shown into a waiting room where the sole reading material was the latest edition of *Pakistan News*, a government propaganda newsletter. The Prime Minister had inaugurated a new literacy programme. The Chinese premier had visited the country and praised Pakistan's progress. The President had planted a tree . . .

An hour later Puri's passport was brought back to him. No explanation was given as to why the fee had been waived, but a single-entry 'business' visa valid as of tomorrow was stamped inside.

The same young man led the detective back to the gatehouse, where he retrieved his phone.

Outside, the same four men were sitting on the bench, waiting. Their eyes registered the passport in the detective's hand, the yellow sticky note protruding from one of the pages indicating that he had succeeded where they had so far failed. They knew as well as he did that someone had pulled strings on his behalf.

Puri wondered who that someone was. Why was that someone so keen to let him into Pakistan?

• SEVENTEEN •

'A wonderful spectacle! Such a river of life as nowhere else exists in the world.'

That was Kipling's description of the Grand Trunk Road, the 1,600-mile highway stretching across India and Pakistan into Afghanistan – or rather how Puri remembered it from English literature with Mrs Pawar.

Not a bad book, *Kim*, despite being far too long. Kipling Sahib might have been an outsider but he'd captured the spirit and flavour of India. All the details about spies, undercover operatives and secret identities were more or less accurate, even today. The 'wonderful spectacle' bit, though, didn't hold up at four-thirty in the morning. All the detective could see through the windscreen of his Ambassador were the blinding 'dippers' of angry trucks hurtling towards him through the darkness and, along the side of the road, trees with fat white bands painted around their trunks.

Puri could usually sleep through anything. Even the trucks' obnoxious klaxons, their three notes ascending and descending over and over again in a torturous key, were generally no match for the soporific motion of the

Ambassador. But since eleven o'clock, when he and Handbrake had set off from Gurgaon, the silver sedan trailing them all the way, the detective had hardly slept a wink.

Anxiety was keeping him awake. In just a few hours he would cross into Pakistan.

Pakistan! It felt as if he was hurtling through the darkness towards a precipice.

When they'd talked a few hours ago, however, Scott had assured Puri that the world did not end beyond the last Indian village of Atari. A car would be waiting for him on the Pakistan side and this would take him to Kamran Khan's house in Rawalpindi. The arrangements had been made by former Pakistan cricket captain and Clean Up Cricket member, Timur Baloch. A national hero who'd led his side to two World Cup victories, he was well connected and it was rumoured he was starting his own political party.

'You'll have a police escort so don't worry,' Scott had said. 'Nothing's going to happen to you. Pakistan's not as bad as you think. I've always found the people very friendly.'

Puri had managed to put down the phone before bawling, *'Not as bad as you think!'*

There were a whole slew of powerful characters in Pakistan who would still love to get their already bloodied hands on him – not least those within the country's intelligence service, ISI, whose plans he'd thwarted on a number of occasions. Major General Hamid Sharif for example, the man who'd masterminded the supply and training of insurgency groups in north-east India and sent agent Kashid Dar across the border straight into Puri's net (this during his time in Military Intelligence), would surely welcome the opportunity to even the score. Ditto the individual known in Indian intelligence circles as 'General Jihad'. A veteran of the Afghan and Kashmir conflicts, he'd planned and funded an operation to bomb a nightclub in Goa a few years back – except that a certain Vish Puri had unearthed the plot. Subsequently the terrorists had been captured and 'awarded' death by hanging (although the sentence was yet to be carried out).

Such Pakistani officers woke every morning with the word 'Hindustan' on their lips, convinced that the *kafirs* were plotting the destruction of their Islamic republic. So, too, did the Beardy Weirdy Muslim fundamentalists – the Taliban and such. Who was to say that they wouldn't decide to nab a nice plump Indian for their internet video execution collection?

And then there was Aga. He was probably sharpening his trademark ax as well.

A green sign appeared on the side of the road, lit up by the Ambassador's high beams: AMRITSAR 125 KM.

Assuming the road was good, they'd reach Atari in another couple of hours.

Better call that two and a half. Handbrake was yawning. He needed a break and a cup of chai. They both did. And maybe some tandoori chicken. This was Punjab, after all. Divided Punjab.

The road that skirted round Amritsar, home of the Golden Temple and now a city of some five million people, was lined with small 'resorts'. They offered water sliding, go-carting and paintballing, the weekend timepass of the new middle classes. Billboards appeared – one for package deals to Singapore; others encouraging voters to cast their ballot in upcoming state elections for grinning, fat-faced politicians, one barely distinguishable from another.

Soon the suburbs with their Greek-temple-like Punjabi mansions gave way to wheat fields crisscrossed with the irrigation canal system that had turned Punjab into the bread-basket of India. Brick kiln chimneys dotted the landscape, trails of black smoke billowing upward, the earth around them powdered with red dust like spilled cheek blush. Turbaned farmers could be seen heading out to tend their crops, red tractors trundling along narrow, muddy lanes.

The closer they came to the border, the greater the army presence grew. The road was soon busy with jeeps, fuel tankers and troop carriers filled with bored grunts staring out through open canopies. Puri passed a sprawling cantonment where some soldiers were exercising on a parade ground and others were hanging out their wet fatigues to dry on barbed-wire fences. There was no sign of heavy armaments – no artillery pieces or tanks. Still, the detective spotted a few concrete bunkers camouflaged by copses of trees. Ditches were etched across the land-scape, overgrown yet waiting to catch an invading tank unawares.

A long queue of trucks loaded with bags of grain announced the final approach. Then suddenly there was a barrier, closed, blocking the way. A soldier held up a hand for Handbrake to stop. It was only a few minutes past eight o'clock. The border wouldn't open for an hour. Puri would have to wait. He ordered Handbrake back to

Amritsar, watched the silver sedan follow after him and walked over to the dusty Bhale Bhale Dhaba on the side of the road. He ate a couple of paranthas and drank a cup of chai, harassed by flies and touts offering favourable rates for Pakistani rupees. Then he made some calls to Delhi.

Mummy had turned up at home late last night, a relieved Bhuppi reported. Tubelight and the team were making progress in Surat. And there had been a major development in the moustache case: Gopal Ragi, the latest victim, had received a phone call demanding three lakhs in exchange for the return of his former appendage.

'Looks like the motive's been money all along,' said Thakur as if moustache ransoming was a common crime in Delhi nowadays.

The detective felt strangely detached from these developments, however. Delhi, Haridwar, Surat: suddenly they seemed to belong to a different world. His mind was completely preoccupied with the thought that less than a mile beyond the barrier he would come to the point of no return. For all the bits of litter lying about, stray dogs, truck drivers pissing against a nearby wall, the Bhale Bhale Dhaba suddenly felt like a familiar and secure place to be. He could think of worse places to see out his days. At least here he was among his fellow countrymen – the sleazy-looking dhaba owner who employed child labour, the drunk slumped over one of the tables, the tout who was selling pornographic CDs. They all seemed like old friends.

Then he thought of Rumpi, secure and safe at home, and decided to call her.

She wanted to know where he was. He told her that

he was in Amritsar. She detected the apprehension in his voice.

'Everything's all right, Chubby?'

'Yes my dear. I'll be back in a few days – safe and sound. Not to worry.'

'What's that noise?' she asked.

An argument had broken out amongst some of the truck drivers. They were describing one another's mothers and sisters in less than complimentary terms.

'Nothing, my dear, just some fellow blowing off some steam,' he said. 'I had better get a move on. I . . .' He put his hand over the receiver. 'I love you actually,' he said.

His words were greeted with a moment's silence.

'You're sure everything's all right, Chubby? You don't sound yourself at all.'

Out of the corner of his eye, Puri saw the barrier go up. It was nine o'clock. The border was opening. 'Tell the girls I love them, my dear, and God bless, haa,' he said before hanging up.

A porter in a blue tunic and orange turban, his face as coarse as elephant skin, picked up the detective's bag for him and balanced it on his head.

Beyond the barrier stood the Plant Quarantine Station and the immigration and customs building. As he was the only person crossing the border that morning, Puri was through in a few minutes – 'Fast tracking,' joked one of the four officials who were sitting around with nothing to do – and emerged on the other side, where he found a small shrine to the goddess Durga. He stopped to say a prayer and then walked past India's only, and easily overlooked, memorial to Partition, a sculpture of two hands locked in a handshake, with an inscription chiselled into the black plinth beneath:*Dedicated to ten lakh Punjabis who lost their lives unsung.*

The last few hundred yards of Indian territory were lined with spectator stands where visitors gathered in the evening to watch the dramatic Beating of the Retreat ceremony and shouted patriotic slogans at the Pakistani spectators in the corresponding stands across the border: 'Hindustan! Hindustan!' Now, however, they were empty save for a couple of crows of indistinguishable nationality.

The detective's gaze was fixed on the set of double gates ahead. They were painted in the three colours of the Indian Republic, an Ashoka lion on each. Behind them stood the Pakistan gates emblazoned with a white crescent on a green background.

Both sets of gates were opened and an Indian soldier checked his passport for the last time.

A Pakistani Ranger stood only an arm's length away. He was tall, athletic. The butt of a Glock pistol protruded from his holster.

Puri looked down at the thick white line painted on the tarmac between them. It ran in both directions through no-man's-land, off between fences topped with barbed wire. Puri found himself wondering how long the line was. And who maintained it? Did the two sides take turns?

The passport was handed back to him, as was his bag. Puri watched the porter walk away, feeling as if he'd been abandoned. For the first time in his life, he was completely on his own.

'Sir?' prompted the Indian soldier.

Puri took one step forward. His back foot followed. He was in Pakistan.

The Ranger put out his hand for his passport.

Beyond the checkpoint stood a wall adorned with six-foot portraits of Pakistani generals dripping in medals.

'By God,' murmured the detective, a lump in his throat, wondering if he had just made the biggest mistake of his life.

• EIGHTEEN •

The power was off in Pakistan, at least on the border. 'A technical problem,' stated the immigration officer from behind his new but incapacitated computer. He looked embarrassed but added with optimism, 'The electricity should come on before long, insh'allah.'

Puri was shown to a waiting area, the only arrival from India that morning. He sat down on one of the moulded plastic chairs, striking a pose of dissatisfaction: arms crossed over his bulging belly, the only form of protest he felt he could display as a guest from an enemy state.

Seven officials all dressed in *salwar kameez*, which made it frustratingly impossible to tell their designation or seniority, sat nearby. They were smoking, apparently a pastime still permitted in public places in Pakistan, and chatting among themselves. The detective was able to eavesdrop on their conversation, hanging on every word as if they might start discussing some sinister ISI plot. But it was all pretty mundane stuff. A nephew was getting married . . . an uncle had been taken to hospital . . . sheep were being purchased and fattened for Ramadan . . .

Somehow Puri hadn't expected to fully understand the

language, despite the fact that spoken Urdu and Hindi are more or less the same. Perhaps this was because he'd grown so used to regarding Pakistan as a distant, disconnected entity shut off from the rest of the world. The common past the two countries shared – thousands of years of history in fact, their common language being a product of centuries of intermingling of cultures – had become an irrelevance. Mutual distrust, hatred even, defined the relationship between the two modern nations.

And yet hearing some of the turns of phrase and enunciation took the detective back to his childhood, when he used to roam the streets of Delhi's walled city where, after Partition, Urdu survived among a few old Dilli wallahs. In those days the bazaar storytellers used to gather on the steps of the Jama Masjid on Thursday evenings and the young detective would sit and listen to them recount the great epic the *Dastan-e Amir-Hamza*. Tales of dashing princes, cloaks of invisibility and evil djinns had held him transfixed for hours.

And the language!

The language had been pure nectar – long phrases linked like carriages to create a train of thought fraught with multiple meanings. A phrase as simple as 'the moon rose' would be rendered as 'the sorcerer of this world changed his robes'.

Modern Hindi, which had been systematically purged of most of its Persian and Arabic words since Partition, had lost this essence. Bollywood's lyrics were but a poor reflection of the genius of Mirza Ghalib and Mir Taqi Mir. On the rare occasion these days that Puri heard their prose, the richness sparked a longing in his heart. It was like recalling an early memory, something that stirred deep in his subconscious.

He looked up, suddenly aware that he had been daydreaming. The immigration officer had come and sat down near him.

'Sorry, sir! It won't be long, insh'allah,' he said, and smiled, offering the detective a cigarette.

'Not for me,' Puri replied, deliberately stand-offish.

The immigration officer fidgeted, evidently keen to engage.

'Sir, you're going where in Pakistan?' he asked.

'Rawalpindi.'

'You're on business?'

'Business.'

More silence, more fidgeting. Then, 'Where are you from in India?'

'Delhi.'

'That is where my family is from originally.'

The detective nodded and checked his watch again. He had been sitting there for half an hour.

'Sorry, sir,' repeated the immigration officer with an awkward smile, holding up his hands to heaven as if it was Allah who was responsible for running the electricity grid.

Just then, a young man wearing dirty overalls entered through the main door carrying a jerrycan. He called out to the immigration officer, 'I've got it!' and then exited again. This was the immigration officer's cue to return to his desk. Once he'd put on his glasses, he called to the detective to step forward.

Puri heard a generator hum to life outside the building. The lights flickered on. The computer beeped.

'You see! I told you it would not be long!' said the immigration officer.

The detective's passport was inspected and scanned. He was asked to look into the camera fixed to the counter and stared, unsmiling, at the lens, uncomfortable with the idea of the Pakistanis having his photograph in their system.

'Enjoy your stay, sir. Please proceed.'

As Puri stepped out through the exit, he heard the generator putter to a stop.

A smartly dressed chauffeur moved forward, the only individual waiting outside the building. He was holding up a piece of paper with Puri's name written on it in big, bold letters.

'Timur Baloch sent me,' he said, taking the detective's bag. 'I've been asked to take you to the airport.'

He led the way to a car. A police jeep was parked behind it. An officer and three jawans sat inside. They watched Puri closely as if he was a criminal whom they'd be chasing for years.

'Did you say airport?' asked the detective, when he was ensconced in the back seat of the car. He did his best not to sound alarmed.

'You've a flight to Rawalpindi, sir,' explained the driver.

To insist on going by road and thereby admit his terror of flying would be to lose face at the worst possible time. He would have to grin and bear it.

'Good,' he said, his tone officious. 'Flying is so much quicker, actually.'

*　　*　　*

The vistas along the side of the road to Lahore were patently familiar – wheat fields, brick kilns, boys playing cricket on dusty patches of open ground. But there was no mistaking the stamp of Islam on the landscape. The petrol stations all had mosques or prayer rooms attached. The women they passed, whether on foot or riding in bicycle rickshaws, were all, without exception, veiled. And although the fat-faced Punjabi politicians looked remarkably similar to their Indian counterparts, they nearly all wore prayer caps and pious beards.

All this went to affirm Puri's view of Pakistan as a deeply conservative state, and this in turn made him feel a good deal better about his own country. India was a secular democracy – tolerant and inclusive. It struggled with its corruption no doubt, but not once had it been ruled by the military; Pakistan on the other hand had remained under the thumb of the Generals for the best part of its existence.

He also took comfort from the fact that Pakistan (or at least the few miles of it he'd seen so far) looked down at heel compared to India. There were few new cars on the roads. On the outskirts of Lahore little construction was under way. And most of the petrol stations were closed, the government having imposed fuel rationing.

Perhaps that explained why there was so little traffic. Or did the locals know something he didn't? Had an ambush been laid up ahead?

Puri had rarely felt so tense, or so conspicuous. It seemed to him as if everyone outside his window – ordinary people carrying shopping along the road, that old man over there on the bicycle – knew he was an Indian and were all, potentially, a threat. Every time the car stopped at a light and a motorbike pulled up next to them, he imagined the driver was about to pull out a pistol and open fire. When the car hit a pothole in the road, he flinched. A truck backfiring almost gave him a heart attack.

He and the driver reached the edge of Lahore without incident, however, and proceeded along the elevated ring road. With no high-rises to block the panorama, the majestic sandstone minarets and white marble domes of the Badshahi Mosque, so similar to Delhi's Jamme Masjid, floated above the city's small houses.

'Sir, Lahore is a city of poets and Sufis,' said the driver, sounding as if he had been prepped. 'Perhaps you have heard of our Shalimar Gardens, most beautiful place in all the world?'

Puri had heard of the Shalimar Gardens of course. The Sikh ruler Ranjit Singh had enjoyed walking through them in the years after he had seized the city from the Mughals. Lahore was also legendary for its cuisine, particularly its kebabs. The one thing he had been looking forward to on the journey was sampling some of them. But that now seemed like a remote possibility. A sign on the ring road indicated they were approaching the airport.

The detective felt the palms of his hands growing increasingly sweaty and wiped them on the car seat.

He didn't know what he feared more: aeroplanes, Aga or beardy weirdies.

The flight went as well as could be expected. The twin-prop Fokker took off sharply, rattling and jostling like an old mixie. And the landing was no better, the plane coming down at an acute angle like a rollercoaster car. It was fortunate that Puri hadn't stuffed himself with kebabs and *kulfi* before boarding. The Bhale Bhale Dhaba paranthas caused problems enough. Puri had to make use of the paper bag in the pouch in front of him, as well as that of his neighbour, who changed seats soon after take-off.

He still looked off colour when, less than an hour after touching down, the car that had been sent to collect him from the airport reached Rawalpindi.

The Mohanpura district was not unlike the colonies of south Delhi: big cubist villas with high walls and elaborate gates standing on dusty streets. The Khans' mansion looked as if it had been modelled on a frosted wedding cake. There were eight or nine luxury cars and a couple of police jeeps parked outside. Puri sensed that he wasn't going to be meeting with Kamran Khan alone. This hardly came as a surprise; nor did it matter greatly. It would be enough to put a few questions to him, look him in the eye, make one hundred per cent sure that he had not been involved in the murder himself – and of course gauge his reaction to the death of Full Moon.

If possible, he also wanted to get a look at Faheem Khan's belongings, the possessions he had taken with him to Delhi and which, presumably, had been brought back by his son along with the body.

Look for any books, Brigadier Mattu had advised. *One of them could hold the cipher. It should show signs of having been especially well read – creased pages, bent corners, anything underlined obviously.*

A servant led Puri across a cavernous entrance hall with a sweeping marble staircase to a waiting room. He was invited to freshen up in the en suite bathroom. A tray of light snacks and tea was also provided.

The servant returned thirty minutes later and this time Puri was shown through a tall set of oak doors coated in shiny lacquer. The reception room beyond was arranged like a modern durbar with leather couches along the walls and a thirty-foot-long silk oriental carpet gracing the centre.

There were eight men in the room, standing in clusters of two or three, all holding delicate cups of tea. All eyes turned on the Indian as he entered. The conversation faded.

'Mr Puri, welcome,' said a voice in a polished Oxbridge accent.

The detective recognised the athletic, confident figure of former Pakistan captain Timur Baloch, who was striding towards him, hand extended.

'I trust you had a good journey?' he asked with a strong handshake and welcoming smile.

'No complaints, sir,' replied the detective. 'I've you to thank for the transport?'

'It's the least we could do.'

'And for sorting out the problem with the visa, it seems.'

'Your visa, Mr Puri? I wasn't aware there was a problem.'

'Never mind. Seems I've another guardian angel.'

'I think you'll find there are plenty of people here in Pakistan who want answers as much as you do. Now come, I'd like to introduce you to everyone.'

Puri shook hands with the deputy head of the Pakistan Cricket Board and his own deputy; the local representative of the International Cricket Federation; the Rawalpindi deputy Chief of Police; a senior lawyer (an advocate of the Supreme Court, no less); Kamran Khan's personal assistant, who'd been charged with recording the proceedings with a rudimentary tape recorder; and the local parliamentary representative, who claimed to have been 'a close, personal and above all *trusted* friend of Faheem Khan' and was 'assisting the family in their time of grief'.

'Kamran will be along in a minute,' explained Baloch. 'In the meantime, I think it would be useful if we clarified a few things.'

He motioned to an empty seat. It was a quarter of the way along the far wall. Puri sat down, feeling surrounded on all sides.

'First of all, and I know I speak for all of us, I'd like to welcome you here to Pakistan,' continued Baloch. 'I'm told that you are a man of integrity and that you are one hundred per cent committed to investigating the shameless murder of our dear friend Faheem Khan.'

Normally this sort of praise would have caused Puri to swell with pride, but he acknowledged the words with a sober nod, conscious that the other eight men in the room were scrutinising his every mannerism.

'On a personal note, I'd like to say that I joined the Clean Up Cricket organisation because I want to root out corruption in the sport. Cricket is bigger than any one nation and we must rid ourselves of any rotten apples before they spoil the crop. If there are any here on the Pakistan team then we should not hesitate in imposing the severest penalties.'

This statement was met with a general murmur of approval.

'That said, I'm in no doubt that the Khan family is innocent of any involvement in the match-fixing allegations doing the rounds in the press,' Baloch continued. 'The idea that Faheem Khan was in any way involved with bookies is preposterous. I can personally vouch for his character. He was above all an honest man – honest to a fault, in fact. And I'm quite sure that your investigation will help clear his name and that of his son of these baseless rumours.'

You'll make a fine politician, Puri felt like saying, wondering if Baloch's little speech was for the benefit of the audience or if he genuinely believed the Khans to be saints.

His reply was equally glib.

'Let me be the first to applaud you for your honesty and for taking the bold step of inviting me here in the interest of truth,' he began. 'And let me assure all the honourable gentlemen here present that Vish Puri never fails. By hook or crook I will most definitely get to the bottom of this crime. Allow me to assure you, also, that I have a personal interest in clearing up this matter – as a proud citizen of India. An honoured guest has been brutally killed on our soil and it is my duty to let no stone go unturned in doing positive identification of the person or persons responsible.'

This was met with a light round of applause.

'Thank you, Mr Puri,' said Baloch. 'Now if you're ready we'll send for Kamran. I'm sure you'll keep in mind that he has responsibilities to his family and that we don't want to keep him for any longer than is necessary.'

* * *

Khan's long frame was limp, like a sunflower in need of water. With a perfunctory salaam, he slumped down on to one of the couches, his giraffe-like legs protruding far into the room. He was wearing white, the colour of mourning, and a prayer cap.

'You've got some questions for me?' said Khan, his head cocked towards the ceiling in a gesture of total apathy.

'I'm endeavouring to solve your father's murder,' said Puri, who found the young man's lack of decorum highly insolent. 'You're interested in finding out who did it or not?'

Khan shifted in his seat, drawing his legs towards him.

'Yes, of course,' he answered with a frown. 'That's why I'm here.'

'Good. Then, yes, some questions are there.'

Silence fell over the room as everyone waited for Puri. He relished the expectation, the sense of finally being in the driver's seat. He took out his notebook and made a show of opening it to a new page and smoothing down the paper with the palm of his hand. Then he pulled a pen from the breast pocket of his shirt and asked Kamran Khan, almost as an aside, 'You remember we two met that night?'

The young man crinkled his forehead. He looked at Puri directly for the first time. 'You were there?'

'I'm Rohan's uncle. We two were introduced. You graciously invited me to Pakistan. As your guest, actually.'

There was a flash of recognition and a snap of the fingers.

'Right – of course. Sorry . . . um, *sir*. You were the one who kneeled by Baba, wasn't it?'

'Correct. I was by his side, only.'

Kamran Khan nodded, blinking repeatedly. 'He said anything to you, sir?' asked the young man. He sounded sad, at a loss.

'Nothing,' answered Puri. 'Too much pain was there actually. Why? You think he knew who poisoned him, is it?'

'No, sir. I've no idea.'

'He had enemies?'

Khan shrugged. 'None. Everyone loved Baba.'

'A man in his position, being a landowner and such, always has enemies no?'

'He was a much-loved man,' chimed in Baloch.

'Surely not by all and sundry,' said Puri. 'The person who killed him for example. He or she most definitely did *not* love him.'

Kamran Khan shifted his feet again as he said, 'I just can't think of who that would be, who would have done this thing, sir.'

The detective scrawled a couple of lines in his notebook before stating: 'You yourself were absent from the banqueting hall when your father was poisoned.'

'I went to make a phone call.'

'The receiver of that call was which person exactly?'

'My mother. She's been unwell. I wanted to check on her.'

This statement sounded rehearsed.

'You ate some butter chicken, also?'

'I didn't get a chance. By the time I came back . . . I found my father lying there.'

Puri asked how long he'd been absent.

'Fifteen minutes,' stated Khan. He placed the palms of his hands on his knees, the fingers gripping them.

'If at all possible, I would like to examine your phone records.'

Khan gave his lawyer a questioning look and the man replied in a laconic tone, 'My client's phone records contain confidential information.'

Including the numbers of half the bookies in India, Puri said to himself as he scrawled fiercely in his notebook like a teacher awarding a student an F grade. When he resumed his questioning, he focused on Khan's whereabouts the night his father died.

'There was another individual absent from the banqueting hall at the same time as your good self,' he said. 'One actress known as Dippy. You happened to see her?'

Khan's grip around his knees visibly tightened.

'I seem to remember passing her in the lobby,' he answered, his tone vague.

'Seem to?'

'Yes, I think so. In fact, I'm sure of it. Yes, she was there. Dressed in a sari, right?'

Dippy had been voted one of the most beautiful women in India recently by a lads' mag and looked especially ravishing that night. There hadn't been a man in the room whose eyes had not drunk her in. 'Seem to' didn't cut it.

'You've met her previously, is it? Before that fateful night?'

'Once or twice. In Dubai, London. I can't really remember.'

'Seems this Dippy lost one earring. Later it was discovered on the hotel emergency stairs. Must be she was there for some time.'

'Like I told you, I was on the phone in the lobby.'

'To your sick mother,' said Puri.

'Right.'

Puri paused for a moment, relishing the perceptible unease he had created in the room – the shared whispers, nervous coughs, crossing and uncrossing of legs. The fact that Khan had been on the emergency stairs with the actress had not been lost on any of the other gentlemen. But it meant a good deal more to Puri: Kamran Khan had played no part in his father's murder. Had he been aware of his father's rendezvous with Full Moon?

'What was your Papa doing out on the lawn of the hotel?' asked the detective.

The question caught Khan off guard. 'Sorry, sir?'

'He met someone there. I saw them talking with my own eyes.'

'Who?'

'A certain bald gentleman.'

'Bald gentleman?'

Puri flicked through the pages of his notebook. 'Name of Mohib Alam,' he read.

Khan blinked repeatedly and began to shake his head from side to side. 'Alam,' he repeated. 'No, never heard of him.'

'He was a bookie.' This revelation was met with pin-drop silence. Puri waited a beat before adding, 'He was · murdered actually. Two days back.'

'Murdered?' Kamran Khan looked suddenly alarmed. 'How?'

'Poisoned. With aconite. It was placed in his paan.'

The cricketer stared at the detective. 'Where did this happen?'

'He owned a farmhouse in Delhi. By coincidence I was present there also. A good deal of illegal betting was going on. Betting on an ICT match, in fact.'

Khan's face had gone blank. Puri detected fear in his eyes.

'You say you've never met Alam, have no idea who he was, have no idea why your father met with him minutes before he died?' he asked, pressing home his advantage.

The answer was a few seconds in coming. 'No,' he said. 'Like I told you, I've never heard of him.'

At this juncture, the lawyer intervened: 'My client has a pressing engagement . . . If there's nothing else?'

'Just one request is there,' he said.

Puri took a moment to think, addressing Khan. 'I wish to examine your father's personal belongings. Those he took with him to Delhi. That is at all possible?'

The young man was studying the design of the Persian rug, lost in thought. Puri had to repeat his question.

'Yes, yes, no problem,' said Khan, hearing him this time. 'His suitcase is still in the study.'

The detective asked to be taken to the study right away. Khan's assistant escorted him out of the room. Puri could hear the murmur of conversation break out as soon as the door closed behind them.

Faheem Khan's study was upstairs. In front of the window stood a desk messy with papers, notes, numerous pens. Next to this was his luggage.

Inside, Puri found a change of clothes, an extra pair of shoes, a shaving kit . . .

Beneath a pair of trousers, he also discovered a copy of the Koran.

He opened it and turned to page one. The first verse of the first sura was underlined and there were some numbers written in the margin. The detective started to take out his notebook to copy them, when Kamran Khan burst into the room.

'That was my father's most precious possession,' he said, snatching the Koran out of the detective's hands. 'I've been meaning to put it away.'

He placed it in the top drawer of the desk.

'Was there anything else you wanted, sir?' he asked.

'The truth if you please,' answered Puri.

'About what?'

'Your relationship with the bookie Mohib Alam.'

'I told you, I don't know who he is.'

'I think you do, young man. I think, also, that unless you make a full confession so to speak, the identity of your father's murderer will never come to light.'

Khan stared back at the detective.

'That is what you want, is it? Your father's murderer to go free?' continued Puri.

The cricketer answered with a shake of his head.

'Then you've anything more to tell me?'

Khan looked away. Ten, twenty seconds passed. 'I can't,' he said. 'You don't understand. They'll kill me as well.'

Footsteps approached on the marble floor outside. The door opened. It was Baloch.

'You found what you were looking for, Mr Puri?'

'Unfortunately not,' said the detective. 'My journey has been wasted, in fact. Now if it is at all convenient, I would prefer to go directly to my hotel. I have a reservation at the Pearl.'

Looking Kamran Khan in the eye, he added, 'If anyone would want to reach me later, I shall be there only.'

· NINETEEN ·

It was steak night at the Marco Polo restaurant in
Rawalpindi's Pearl Continental Hotel and promotional
posters of succulent cuts sizzling on flaming grills stared
down from the walls.

Puri couldn't help but stare back at them. He'd never
seen what slaughtered beef looked like and found the
appearance of the juicy red meat appetising. For a minute
or two, he actually considered ordering some. But the
thought of eating steak here felt . . . well, blasphemous.
It also crossed his mind that the Pakistanis might leak
his indiscretion to the press. HOLIER THAN THOU DETEC-
TIVE EATS COW was one headline he envisaged.

Besides, he wasn't sure he could live with the guilt.
He ordered the *chicken karahi* instead.

'And one peg whisky, also.'

The waiter frowned down at his pad of paper. The
hotel did not serve alcohol, he said apologetically. If the
detective wanted a drink he would have to consume it
in his room – that is, after first applying for a drinking
permit.

'A permit?'

228

'From the Department of Excise and Taxation. I should bring you an application form, sir?'

'Just bring one salty lassi,' he said with a dismissive wave of his hand.

The fact that he couldn't get a drink made him crave one all the more. 'Absence makes the liver grow stronger,' he told himself, and started to chuckle, almost guffawing the more he repeated the phrase in his head.

He wished he had company, someone with whom to share the joke; a priceless one, after all. He disliked being on his own. At home there was always someone around – family, servants, friends popping in.

He had to admit, however, that he'd been pleasantly surprised by the friendliness and courteousness of those he'd met in Pakistan so far. From the air hostess who'd assured him the plane wasn't going to crash, to the hotel concierge who'd talked about how much he'd enjoyed visiting India last year, Puri had been made to feel welcome.

The reception at Kamran Khan's had been perfectly civil as well, even if the detective felt as though *he'd* been the one on trial. By God, there were a lot of worried faces in the room. Did they know Faheem Khan and his son were involved with match fixing? Were they all involved themselves? Did any of them want the truth to come out?

Of one thing Puri was now certain: even if Kamran Khan had never met Full Moon in person, he'd undoubtedly heard of him.

The lassi arrived in a tall glass and proved delicious and creamy, with just the right blend of salt and ground cumin. Puri promptly ordered another, all craving for alcohol now banished from his mind, and then tucked into the karahi. It was nothing special – typical hotel food – and Puri found himself wondering if he would get the chance to sample some Lahori cuisine before he left. With any luck he'd be able to stop for lunch on his way back to the border. Nirala Butt's restaurant in Lakshmi Chowk was the place to eat, he'd been reliably informed. The house speciality was *kadai gosht*, a Mughali dish.

'Some dessert for you, sir?'

The waiter was back.

'That is what is generally called a redundant question,' said Puri to the waiter.

A bowl of kulfi was soon brought and this he followed up with a cup of milky tea.

When he stood to leave, he noticed a bored man in olive green salwar kameez and Peshawari sandals sitting in the lobby and looking completely out of place. His colleague was hanging around outside the main entrance. He was dressed in exactly the same get-up and wore an identical moustache. Perhaps they were government issue?

By the time he returned to his suite on the 'executive floor', it was dark outside. The front of the hotel was lit up and Puri watched the security guards manning the ring of concrete blast-proof slabs positioned in front of the entrance, checking all the cars entering the premises. Undercarriage mirrors, sniffer dogs, X-ray machines: as thorough as security at an international airport.

Puri assumed these precautions were in response to the recent targeting of a five star hotel in Islamabad. A suicide bomber had driven a truck straight into the lobby and detonated 1,400 pounds of explosive. But Pakistan's hotels were, clearly, not the only institutions under threat. To the left of the Pearl Continental lay the old British cantonment, headquarters of the Pakistan army. The entire sector was surrounded by walls, barbed wire, sand emplacements, slabs of concrete, lookout posts jammed with troops. All to protect the Generals from their own Frankenstein monsters. It was madness, sheer madness.

Puri withdrew into the room and lay down on the bed, staring up at the ceiling, wondering if the anonymous individual who had sent the fax from London would contact him — assuming of course that the message hadn't been a ruse.

'Travel to Pakistan this coming Friday. Please take a room at the Pearl Continental in Rawalpindi where I will find you,' the message had said.

Well it was Friday and here he was, waiting.

He paced up and down for a while, noticing a set of weighing scales under the sink in the bathroom. With nothing better to do, he decided to weigh himself to see if the diet pills were working — it had been four days since he'd started taking them, after all. He was relieved to find an improvement: a good half a kilo lighter. At this rate he'd lose a kilo in a week.

'Tip top.'

He turned on the TV and began to flick through the channels.

There had been another suicide bombing in Peshawar. A US drone attack in Waziristan. Fresh clashes in Karachi . . .

Something caught Puri's eye. Above the fridge, next

to the laundry bag and bottle opener, lay a book. It was a complimentary copy of the Koran, placed there by the hotel. He began to turn the pages, wishing he could remember the numbers he'd seen in Faheem Khan's edition.

At around one o'clock he finally decided to call it a day and changed into his VP monogrammed pajamas. He left the bathroom light on, checked that the door was locked and got into bed. He tossed and turned for half an hour, unable to sleep, spooked by any sound coming from the corridor. Eventually he got up and wedged a chair against the door. He slept fitfully.

The next morning, Puri lingered on in his room, still hoping that the anonymous fax sender might contact him or that Kamran Khan would come to his senses and confess his sins. But he was to be disappointed: by eleven-thirty, there was no word. He decided to leave (borrowing the copy of the Koran, which he would post back to the hotel once he'd shown it to Brigadier Mattu) and asked to be driven back to the border, willing to endure five hours on the road rather than another minute in the air.

A car promptly arrived and soon, free of a police escort, the driver was making good time along the Grand Trunk Road. Sitting on the back seat with the window down a crack, Puri felt relieved not to have to be flying again. He began to relax, watching the landscape through his window – a bleached, sandy terrain quarried by rain and seasonal rivulets with barren, reddish-brown hills floating above the haze. They passed a train of camels led by a group of wandering dervishes; brightly decorated trucks adorned with paintings, glassware and beads; villages with black flags flying over the roofs, indicating that they were home to Shia Muslims.

Beyond the great Jhelum River, the driver pulled into a petrol station and went to say his prayers in the mosque. Puri decided to stretch his legs while he waited. As he stepped out of the car, a Land Cruiser tore into the forecourt and screeched to a halt. A man wearing a ski mask and brandishing a Kalashnikov rifle jumped out. He grabbed the detective by the arm and shoved him into the vehicle.

The last thing Puri saw before a hood was drawn over his head and he was driven away was the helpless station attendant looking on in dismay.

· TWENTY ·

A charya Bakshi, diamond processing sweatshop owner,
ate his home-made lunch at his desk. Judging by
the amount of noise he made – molars chomping, lips
smacking together, fingers being sucked clean – he
relished every morsel. But for Flush, who was sitting with
Tubelight and Chanel No. 5 in a nearby hotel room, his
noshing made excruciating listening. The sticky induction
listening device attached to the outside of Bakshi's office
window (Chanel No. 5 had scored a direct hit with his
catapult) amplified every sound.

When he finished his meal and let out a loud and
protracted belch, the young operative pulled off his headphones and grimaced.

'Gaaaad!' he exclaimed. 'This is worse than having to
listen to Ram Yadav having sex.'

He was referring to a 320-pound seventy-three-year-old
whose wife had once hired Most Private Investigators to
gather proof of his infidelity.

'Nothing beats Boss's snoring,' commented Tubelight.

Flush nodded in agreement. 'True. Sounds like a preg-
nant water buffalo.'

He put his headphones back on. Hawala broker Mihir Desai, who'd brought Bakshi the blood diamonds, had arrived to pick up his 'parcel'.

Chanel No. 5 listened in on their conversation as well, translating from Gujarati to Hindi for the benefit of the others. The estimated value of the blood diamonds was US $ 223,000, Bakshi told his customer. In lieu of payment for cutting and polishing the stones, he was keeping two of them for himself. These he would sell in Mini Bazaar, Surat's wholesale diamond market, where jewellers from across India came to buy from the city's middlemen and no one asked questions about the origins of their wares.

'I've another shipment coming next week,' said Desai. 'Russian stones.'

They were due to arrive in Kathmandu by air, a route being used more frequently these days since the Nepali customs officials had started 'eating', or taking bribes, and could therefore be relied upon to turn a blind eye to illegal shipments. From there they would be brought in overland.

'Half a million dollars' worth.'

'Always welcome!' exclaimed Bakshi as his customer left.

From the cutting and polishing sweatshop, it was a short distance to the premises of the Angadia courier company that specialised in transporting diamonds: an unremarkable unit on the ground floor of an unremarkable building. A fat man with an oily face sat inside, a cast iron safe to his right.

Chanel No. 5 loitered outside the premises pretending to have a conversation on his mobile phone and witnessed the exchange through the window. First, Desai handed Oily Face the blood diamonds, now contained in a little paper packet wrapped in black tape. A form was then placed on the counter for Desai to sign. The *kachchi chitthi*, as the form was known, constituted a contract whereby the Angadia courier company agreed to deliver the diamonds to the address stipulated by the sender. It also guaranteed that, in the event of the diamonds being either lost or stolen, the total declared value would be paid to the sender. In return, the sender agreed to pay one per cent of the declared value of the goods for their transportation.

Desai paid the fee and left. Oily Face placed the diamonds in his safe and locked the door.

The hood Puri had been wearing for the past half an hour was removed. He squinted in the bright light, shielding his eyes with one hand. A man's voice said, 'Welcome, Mr Puri. I hope my men didn't frighten you. They can get a bit over-zealous at times. They're only young, after all.'

The detective's sight slowly returned. He found an elderly gentleman standing before him. There was no mistaking his military bearing – the straight posture, chin held up at 15 degrees, shoulders straight with hands held behind his back. Judging by the star and eagle emblem pinned to the lapel of his double-breasted suit, he had served in the Punjab regiment.

'I'm afraid certain precautions were necessary,' he continued. 'It wouldn't help either of our causes if we were found fraternising with one another.'

Puri looked around him. He was in a tastefully appointed sitting room – bookcases, Bokhara carpets, a pair of Jezail muskets with mother-of-pearl inlay mounted on the far wall.

'And what is your *position*, exactly?' he asked. He added the honorific 'sir' in deference to the man's age, but there was no mistaking his anger at having been abducted.

'At times I dare say you've regarded me as your enemy, Mr Puri. However, today I've the honour of being your host. There's no point in keeping my identity from you. You would discover it before long. My name is Major General Khalid Muhammad Aslam.'

Puri had heard of Aslam. He'd served in East Pakistan and helped supply and train certain Afghan mujahideen factions – the old guard 'Gucci Guerrillas', as they used to be known, former Afghan army officers loyal to the Royal Family. Retired generals like Aslam wielded considerable influence in Pakistan – certainly enough to ensure that a visa being issued at short notice and without the usual fee.

'You've an odd way of treating your guests, sir,' responded the detective. 'Why make it look like I was taken by militants?'

The question provoked a warm, almost familiar smile. 'I see you've inherited your mother's tenacity,' remarked Aslam.

'My mother?' said Puri with a frown. 'What all she has got to do with it?'

The General's eyes widened, surprise writ large across his face.

'I see!' he declared. 'Well, I seem to have you at a disadvantage, Mr Puri. I can't imagine that's a position you find yourself in very often.'

'I asked you what all my mother has to do with this.'

'That will become clear, I assure you.'

Aslam walked over to the French windows and pulled back the curtains. Sunshine streamed in.

'Would you like to join me in the garden? It's very pleasant at this time of year. My Damascene roses are in full bloom.'

'I want you to understand one thing before we proceed,' said Aslam as they sat on the veranda of his bungalow.

The garden was surrounded by a wall high enough to prevent Puri from seeing the terrain beyond. He could tell that he was deep in the countryside, however, apparently far from a main road. The air was fresh and the only sounds that reached them were of water buffalo bellowing and wheat being threshed by hand.

'I believe in my country,' the General continued. 'I have fought for its very survival all my life. I am a patriot. That's why I've brought you here. I believe the interests of Pakistan will be best served if the truth surrounding this Faheem Khan case comes to light. I believe that we can help one another in this endeavour.'

His abduction had stirred Puri's appetite, but he resisted the samosas that sat on the table before him. And he had yet to taste a drop of the General's tea. Despite his host's polite manner, and the punctilious care with which tea had been laid out, the detective wasn't about to accept his hospitality. This abstention was a form of protest, signalling his displeasure at the manner in which he had been brought to Aslam's house. All this talk of sharing information, of common interest, made him dubious as well.

Puri's obstinacy was not lost on his host.

'Come now, why not put aside this hostility?' asked the General. 'I freely admit there are elements within my country that are working against the betterment of the state. Some of them are hell bent on destroying it. These people are my enemies as much as they are yours. Can you honestly sit there and tell me that you're not pitted against your own set of adversaries in India? Elements that you would be happily rid of, that are an affront to the freedom you hold so dear?'

'There is one major difference, sir,' responded Puri. 'We in India have our problems, no doubt. But we're not in the business of training and abetting terrorists.'

General Aslam replied in a quiet, even tone, 'I'm not defending terrorism, Mr Puri. In the same way, I would hope you would not defend the human rights record of the Indian army in Kashmir or the slaughter of innocent Muslims in Gujarat. I am, however, offering you information – information crucial to solving Faheem Khan's murder. I indicated as much to you in the fax I sent to your office.'

Puri didn't react to the revelation. He brushed a piece of lint from his trousers and said in English, 'If it is information you're offering, sir, then answer me this: the man commonly known as Aga, who is wanted in my country for activities ranging from terrorism to narcotics smuggling . . . he has been living here in Pakistan. Correct?'

For years, despite all the intelligence to the contrary, Pakistan had strenuously denied that Aga was on its soil. An acknowledgement to the contrary would go some way to establishing Aslam's credibility.

The General was stony faced as he replied, 'I don't deny it.'

'In Karachi?'

'A guest of certain individuals within our security apparatus.'

Puri acknowledged his frankness by reaching for his tea. Aslam took a sip from his own, studying Puri over the edge of his cup.

'Do try the samosas as well,' he said. 'My wife made them herself.'

The detective helped himself to one to one of the snacks and bit into the crispy pastry. It was just the right consistency, the mixed vegetable filling nice and spicy.

'My compliments to Mrs Aslam,' he said with a full mouth.

'I'll be sure to tell her, Mr Puri; she'll be very glad to hear it.' The General, who'd eaten one of the samosas himself, wiped his lips with his napkin and then placed it back in his lap. 'Now, you were asking about Aga', he continued. 'There's something I should probably tell you before we get to the Faheem Khan case.'

Puri was all ears.

'Aga is no longer in Pakistan.'

The detective stopped chewing and surveyed Aslam with doubting eyes. 'Where, then?' he asked, putting his plate aside.

'That you would have to ask our common allies, the Americans. They took him seven months ago.'

'Why keep it secret?'

'Our people could hardly acknowledge that he'd been taken when we'd been denying he'd been here all along. Also, the operation to capture him was conducted by American special forces on Pakistani soil. Something of an embarrassment all round.'

'And the Americans have kept it hushed up also?' asked Puri. His voice was loaded with scepticism.

'They've their own reasons for doing so.'

'Aga is an Indian citizen, wanted on multiple counts. The Americans would be bound to hand him over to us.'

'Are you so sure your government would want him back?' asked Aslam. He paused to sip his tea. 'There are certain powerful individuals in Delhi who've done business with Aga in the past. Such men would do everything within their power to ensure that he never sets foot on Indian soil again. If the Americans are not making a song and dance of nabbing him, keeping him in cold storage so to speak, then so much the better.'

'And how about the betting syndicate? If Aga's no longer running the show, then who exactly?'

'Someone who knows that he's no longer in charge and has taken advantage of the vacuum. Someone under the radar.'

Puri didn't believe a word of it. Aslam was playing with him, trying to muddy the water.

'Sir, with respect, I don't see this conversation is getting us anywhere,' he said. 'I would ask you to have me driven back to my vehicle. My work lies elsewhere.'

'If that's your wish, Mr Puri . . . But first I'd ask that you indulge me for just five more minutes. I would like to show you something that will undoubtedly be of value to you.'

He picked up a box file from the side table. Inside he found an old black and white photograph of a young Punjabi girl in her late teens. Judging by the classic car in front of which she was posing, it had been taken in the 1940s. Aslam handed it to the detective.

'Her name is Kiran Singh,' he said. 'But your mother knows her as a young woman called "Saroya".'

'Sir, I would ask you again: what is this business about my mother?' demanded Puri.

Aslam handed him another photograph. It was of Mummy standing in front of an army tent.

'This one I took myself,' he said. 'I used to have a little Argoflex. There should be a date on the back.'

Puri turned it over. There was indeed a date, written in smudged fountain pen: 'March, 1948.'

'What all Mummy was doing in Pakistan at that time? She fled to Delhi in August '47 only.'

'That you had better ask her yourself,' said Aslam. 'She probably wouldn't appreciate my telling you – not if she's kept her involvement secret all these days. The two of us are friends, after all.'

A fit young man man appeared round the side of the bungalow. He approached, saluted, and then bent down to whisper something in the General's ear.

'Aaah, I'm afraid we've run out of time, Mr Puri,' said Aslam. 'Seems the police are looking for you. We'd better get you back before we spark an international incident.'

The General walked him to the Land Cruiser in the driveway.

'One last thing,' he said. 'Tell your mother that Kiran Singh came from Mandra, not far from Bajal, Faheem Khan's home village. She should remember the place. Her father's name was Manjit Singh. I'd have passed on this information when I came by it years ago. But I didn't have an address. Imagine my surprise when I was reading the file on you, in connection with this Faheem Khan business, and her name appeared!'

The detective climbed on to the passenger seat of the Land Cruiser, unsure whether to thank his host or not.

'Please give my salaams to your mother,' said Aslam like an uncle whom he'd known all his life. 'And don't judge her harshly. None of us like to speak of those times. They were . . . *complicated.*'

The hood was slipped back over Puri's head and he felt the vehicle pull out of the gates.

At eight o'clock, when Oily Face, the Angadia diamond courier agent, closed up shop for the night, the Most Private Investigators team in Surat were still watching him from the street.

'We've missed something,' said Tubelight as their mark got into his car and started the engine. 'He wouldn't take the diamonds with him.'

'What do we do?' asked Flush.

'Hold positions,' ordered Tubelight as he studied the building where the agent had his premises. All the businesses on the ground floor had closed for the night and the corridors that ran between them were empty. A couple of women sweepers, Biharis by the looks of them, were clearing the front steps of the day's detritus.

It was the action of their reed brooms that led the operative's eyes to the light coming from a vent at the foot of the building. Tubelight waited until Oily Face pulled away, then hurried across the street, got down on his knees and peered through the opening. He could make out two grey-haired men sitting on the floor playing cards. The small room in which they sat was sparsely furnished with a bed, sink, stove and fridge. There was something else about the room, something remarkable: a chute hung down from the ceiling and Tubelight realised that it originated beneath the safe in the agent's shop above. In other words, Desai's package of blood diamonds had slid down into the basement. But had it already been carried from the premises? He could only pray it had not.

'Go round the back. Must be another way out,' Tubelight ordered Chanel No. 5.

A few minutes later, the young Gujarati reported back that an alleyway ran behind the building and stairs leading down into the basement. By then Flush had placed a pinhole camera with a remote transmitter through the vent, providing a live picture of the room below.

At half past nine, 'A1' and 'A2', the handles Tubelight had given the two old men, put away their deck of cards and changed out of their clothes.

The disguises they donned were simple; brilliantly so, in Tubelight's view. A1, the taller of the two, wore an olive-coloured shirt with a sleeveless vest beneath, a pair of well-creased synthetic trousers that hung loose around his narrow waist, a pair of black shoes and a pair of glasses with thick plastic rims. The pens sticking out of the top pocket and chunky grey briefcase with a couple of tatty old airline security stickers stuck to the lid completed the picture of the Indian company *peon* or travelling salesman, droves of whom crisscrossed India every day.

A2, a short, wiry figure whose hair was parted down the middle so the top of his head looked like the open pages of a book, adopted the get-up of a Gandhian: topi and white *khadi* kurta pajama. He carried only a simple jute bag over one shoulder.

As Tubelight and Flush watched, riveted, A1 opened the safe, took out six small packets and placed them on the table. Desai's was among them, recognisable by the black tape he'd used.

A2 began to divide them into two piles. But just then, the picture suddenly went black. Flush spotted a rat scurrying away from the fan hole. 'Must have knocked into it,' he said.

By the time he had the camera back in position, A1 and A2 had left the room. Chanel No. 5, who was positioned on a fire escape behind the building, reported that they were making their way down the alley to Gandhi Marg.

'On our way!'

Tubelight and Flush soon caught up with their colleague and began to follow the two couriers. At the corner of Nehru Marg, however, they split up. A2 hailed an auto and Chanel No. 5 and Flush followed him into the old Muslim quarter, while Tubelight continued to shadow A1 on foot.

Puri's senior operative was soon left in no doubt that he was up against an extremely capable individual, one whom he would have happily employed himself. The courier varied his pace, paused now and again to look in shop windows and stopped to drink a banana smoothie at a juice stand with mirrors in which he could study the street behind him.

From there, A1 entered the crowded textile quarter, where Dickensian mills abutted the narrow streets. Amongst an army of porters carrying rolls of silk and linen like jousting knights armed with dummy lances, Tubelight lost sight of his mark. He scrambled up on to the back of a truck to search the crowd and eventually caught sight of him again. In doing so, there was good chance he was spotted. As a precaution he quickly donned a disguise he was carrying with him in his satchel – a wig, a Muslim prayer cap and a pair of glasses – and soon caught with A1.

The courier continued on to the train station and bought a third class ticket for the Vadodara Express. Its scheduled departure time was 11.37. He then went to the café and sat down with a cup of tea.

The station floor was littered with bodies huddled under blankets and coats, as cluttered as a battlefield. Victims of long delays on the network caused by Jat protestors squatting on the main lines further east (and demanding a quota of government jobs), they had been stranded in the station for the past twenty-four hours.

Tubelight befriended some Muslims who were on their way to the city of Ajmer to visit the shrine of the Sufi saint Moinuddin Chishti. Given his garb, they accepted him as one of them and insisted he share the food they had packed for the journey. He did so gratefully, all the while keeping an eye on the courier, who remained in the café.

A2 arrived forty-five minutes before the Vadodara Express was due to depart (with Flush and Chanel No. 5

not that far behind) and bought himself a ticket. Then he headed straight to the men's public toilets. A couple of minutes later, A1 got up from his table and followed his colleague inside.

Five minutes passed. Neither of them emerged. Tubelight grew anxious. He waited another minute. It was now 11.54 according to the station clock. Something didn't feel right.

He decided to investigate and found the toilets empty.

There was another door leading directly on to platform 1.

The Pune Express was pulling out of the station.

Tubelight made a split-second decision. He ran down the platform and leapt on to the step of the last door of the last carriage. Prising the door open, he clambered inside and fell to the floor.

'Wily old jackals,' he muttered to himself as he stopped to catch his breath.

• TWENTY-ONE •

At around the same time that Tubelight was picking himself up off the floor of the train, Gopal Ragi reached the first level of the multi-storey car park in Nehru Place, Delhi. As per the instructions he'd received over the phone, he was carrying a sports bag containing the two lakh rupee ransom demand for his moustache. The cryptic voice had insisted he come alone, if he ever wanted to see his 'precious pet' again. But he'd ignored the warning. Inspector Thakur and his men were hidden nearby, waiting to pounce.

A car came up the ramp, circled the parked vehicles in search of a space and then continued up to the next level. A security guard walked past, whistling a tune. A couple of pigeons began to flap around in a pool of dirty water.

The voice on the phone had said, 'eleven o'clock and don't be late'. Ragi checked his watch for the umpteenth time. It was almost half-past eleven. He could barely contain his frustration; he felt like going and kicking in the side of the nearest car. But he stayed put. He'd do almost anything to get his moustache back. It had been twenty years in the growing and he had every confidence that it would find a place in the National Museum. That way people would be able to continue to be inspired by his commitment and sacrifice.

More cars came and went. And then a motorbike pulled up the ramp. The driver was wearing a helmet with the visor down. He raced around the parked cars and pulled up next to Ragi, engine running.

'Give me the money!' he demanded.

'Where's my moustache?'

'Money first, bastard!'

'No moustache, no *rupiya*!'

Reluctantly the motorcyclist tugged a plastic bag from his jacket and held it up.

'I want to see it!' insisted Ragi.

Thakur and his men came running towards them, shouting, 'Stop! Police!'

The motorcylist managed to grab the sports bag and made a hasty getaway, evading the cops and racing down the ramp into the street beyond.

Ragi was left holding the plastic bag. He reached inside and took out the moustache. It was black, about six inches long, with a peel-away sticky back.

'*Maaaa-daaaar-chod!*' he shouted, the curse echoing off the concrete walls and ceiling of the car park.

Puri spent the night in Lahore, having arrived at the border after it closed. The setback came with some compensation. After checking into a hotel surrounded by more blast barriers and barbed wire than the American embassy in Saigon in 1975, he sent his driver to Nirala

Butt's restaurant in Lakshmi Chowk to fetch some of its famous kadai gosht.

Puri would never forget the meal as long as he lived. The marinated mutton was so tender, so succulent, that it melted in his mouth. The yoghurt-based gravy was a revelation: creamy with a perfect blend of coriander and chilli and just a hint of lemon. He lapped it all up with the crisp pieces of *roghini naan*, wiped the container clean with his finger and sucked every last bit of marrow from the mutton bones.

It actually crossed his mind that staying in Pakistan for another day might not be the end of the world. Not if it meant he could get his hands on some more of that Mughlai cuisine. Indeed, now that he was back at the border, with his homeland in sight, Puri felt a tinge of regret that his stay had been so brief.

One of Chanakya's sayings came to mind: 'Learning is like a cow of desire. It, like her, yields in all seasons. Like a mother it feeds you on your journey.'

The experience had certainly humanised Pakistan in Puri's mind. It was no longer an abstract entity, one that generated only bad news, but a country populated by ordinary people no different from ordinary Indians. They were labouring under many of the same difficult conditions, in fact. And no doubt the vast majority wanted nothing more than to live in peace.

Puri's distrust of the military, however, was unshakable. And he couldn't bring himself to trust Aslam. That story about Aga being taken by the Americans was pure fiction. 'Cock and bull,' he kept telling himself.

And yet as he waited for the border to open he found

himself reasoning the thing out. Could there be some truth to it? The Pakistanis would certainly be loath to admit that Aga had been found on their soil. As for the Americans, they could be equally duplicitous, one minute training Islamic militants, the next spending billions of dollars to hunt them down.

One thing was certain: if Aga was being waterboarded in a CIA interrogation cell (quite a pleasant thought, incidentally), then it helped explain the murder of the bookies and possibly the poisoning of Faheem Khan as well. Aga's deputies or a rival outfit were vying for control of the Syndicate.

Aslam had been adamant that it was someone in India and not Pakistan. *'Someone who knows that Aga is no longer in charge and has taken advantage of the vacuum. Someone under the radar.'*

But then he would say that, wouldn't he?

Puri removed his Aviator sunglasses and massaged his eyes. He had a strong aversion to this kind of conjecture. It always led to two things: the wrong conclusion and a headache. Cold, hard facts were the only antidote.

Thirty minutes to go before the border opened. Another fifteen to twenty before he'd be able to use his phone again. He hadn't dared contact any of his people from Pakistan, certain that his conversations would be recorded. But last night he'd called his elder brother and told him to put Mummy under 'house arrest'.

Bhuppi had informed him that their mother wasn't at home. She had been out all day, apparently, but not left word of her plans.

It was then the detective had lost his temper: 'Call her,

yaar! Tell her to revert! No delay! Enough of this bloody nonsense!'

The detective regretted having raised his voice; it was his mother with whom he was furious. She'd been playing detective again. Worse, she withheld information vital to the case from him.

As soon as he reached Delhi, he'd confront her and demand to know what she knew about Faheem Khan's past. Then *he* would get on with solving the case.

There could only be one detective in this family.

'I've met my match, Boss,' admitted Tubelight.

By now Puri was heading back down the GT Road towards Delhi, the silver sedan once again following behind.

'You lost the trail?' asked an incredulous Puri.

His operative took up the story again at the point where he had jumped on board the Pune Express.

In need of a new disguise in which to search the train and ascertain whether the diamond couriers were indeed onboard, Tubelight had reverted to his old trade: thievery. He waited until the lights in the carriages were switched off and most of the passengers were asleep, and then went in search of new clothes. From beneath a berth where a *sardar-ji* lay snoring, he helped himself to a change of clothes and a freshly laundered turban.

Tubelight then entered the toilet a Muslim and walked out a Sikh.

'What did you do for a beard?' asked Puri in Hindi.

'Beard net,' replied the operative. 'Cut a clump of hair off my head, stuffed it inside.'

He came across the Angadia couriers in one of the front carriages in confirmed berths. Tubelight managed to find a spare seat a few rows behind them and kept watch through the night.

By the time the train pulled in to Mumbai Central at 05.17, Flush and Chanel No. 5 had managed to reach the station by road, and Tubelight had called ahead for more help – four Mumbai boys with whom he'd worked in the past.

'You were seven in all?' asked Puri. He could count only a handful of occasions when he'd had cause to use such a large team.

'I tell you those old jackals were cunning,' said Tubelight.

But not cunning enough. After a pursuit across Mumbai on the city's busy local commuter trains, both couriers were followed successfully to their final destination: the city's Diamond Bourse, the largest exchange in the world. There Desai's blood diamonds were delivered to a firm called Shah and Partners.

'Couriers kept the packets well concealed. Even now I can't tell you where exactly.'

Tubelight's voice was thick with admiration as he continued: 'These Angadias carry nearly all the world's diamonds back and forth, but without any security. Could have been more of them on the train for all I know.'

'An unparalleled parallel system, one might say,' said Puri.

'Only in India, Boss,' replied Tubelight with a certain pride.

*　　*　　*

Satya Pal Bhalla had left no fewer than eleven messages while Puri had been in Pakistan, demanding to know what progress had been made and threatening to find himself another detective.

The detective felt inclined to wash his hands of the whole affair. He might have been the best detective in all India, but he wasn't a magician. A couple of Tubelight's boys were making enquiries around the city about a six-foot-tall Punjabi barber with white blotches on his hands and a scooter with a licence plate that ended in 288. For the time being there was nothing more to be done.

'Tell him I'm doing undercover work on the case,' he said. 'Anything else Madam Rani?'

'Another call from the chief's office – demanding you explain your involvement in the murder case?'

Puri just chuckled. 'Must be he's getting nowhere with the case,' he said.

Puri reached Delhi at lunchtime, made a quick stop at his father-in-law's house to drop off the copy of the Koran and then continued on to Punjabi Bagh, mentally preparing himself for battle.

Yet when he came face to face with the smiling, diminutive figure of his mother, he could muster none of the anger he'd felt since yesterday's encounter with Major General Aslam.

'Everything is quite all right, Chubby?' she asked. 'Looking so tired, na. Come, sit. You should take *chai vai*. Then rest. Such big eye bags are there. Black and blue. Must be sore, na. I'll bring some cucumber slice. And your favourite iron tonic, also.'

'No need, Mummy-ji. I'm fit and fine, believe me. Never better, actually . . .'

Mummy disappeared into the kitchen, to emerge a few minutes later bearing a tray groaning with cups of chai, a plate of macaroons, a plate of cucumber slices and a bottle of the iron tonic that she had fed him every day throughout his childhood and teenage years. The sight of it made him feel instantly nauseous.

'That Radhika didn't come today – can you imagine?' she complained as the detective cleared space on the dining table. Radhika was the maid. 'Some nonsense about ingrowing toenails. Such an idle one I tell you. Always taking offs. Just she's doing chit chat and ignoring her duties—'

'Mummy-ji, I've been in Pakistan these past days,' Puri interrupted, adding, pointedly, 'Rawalpindi.'

She was in the middle of pouring the tea. For a second, the pot in which she had boiled the leaves, milk, sugar and cardamoms hovered motionless above the tray.

'Oh,' she said. 'That explains it, na.'

'Explains what, exactly?'

'Those eye bags, Chubby. Tension is there, na.' Mummy sighed. 'Not to worry. Some iron tonic will do the trick.'

'I met an old friend of yours,' Puri continued. He gauged his mother's reaction as he said, 'Khalid Muhammad Aslam.'

Mummy finished pouring the tea and sat down, folding her hands in her lap. Her smile was full of tenderness as she asked, 'He's well, na?'

So it was true.

'Very much fine, Mummy-ji,' replied Puri, who thought it better not to mention how her so-called friend had arranged for him to be abducted at gunpoint.

'Aslam is retired, Mummy-ji, but being a former Major General he is one fellow who keeps his fingers firmly on the pulse.'

'Major General you say? In those days, he was Captain, na. So dedicated to his duty he was. A proper gentleman all round.'

A terrible thought suddenly struck Puri, something he could never have dreamed of considering before. Had she been in love with Aslam? Was this the reason why she had kept her time in Pakistan a secret all these years?

'Must be you're wondering why I never told you, na? About that time,' asked his mother, who had a canny way of knowing what he was thinking.

Puri didn't answer; he braced himself for the truth.

'In those days it was not done,' continued Mummy. 'Things I got up to, na? Not for young girls. Such different times.'

Puri felt like putting his hands over his ears to blot out her voice.

'See, so many women got left behind, Chubby. Thousands and thousands in fact. That is after the Britishers chopped up India. So much violence and chaos and all was there. Total one thousand lakh women could not be traced. Hindu and Sikh girls held back in Pakistan. Many Muslim girls grabbed here in India, also. Each and every one of them got abducted. Most were converted and married by force and all. Thus Premna Auntie said it was our duty to save our poor mothers and sisters, and invited me to join.'

The detective had heard his mother talk of Premna Auntie in the past, an aunt on Mummy's maternal side.

A former head teacher, she'd been a feisty, determined woman by all accounts.

'Mummy-ji, wait,' said Puri, holding up a hand. 'Allow me to understand one thing: you're telling me you reverted to Pakistan to rescue abducted women?'

'Hundreds of them, Chubby,' she said with a broad smile. 'I did volunteering, na. For Indian Recovery and Relief Operation. Premna Auntie said it was women's work. "Men cannot be relied upon. It is they who created such a mess in the first place," she said.'

The detective couldn't fathom what he was hearing.

'But why you kept it secret all these years, Mummy-ji?' he asked.

'We two agreed – that is, Premna Auntie and my good self – to keep it all hush hush. See, Chubby, people are always doing gossip and making utmost mischief, na. Had neighbours and all come to know I'd reverted to Pakistan, tongues would do so much of wagging. "That one's going round," and such. Then what? No marriage proposals would come.'

'Everyone must have wondered where you and Premna went off to, no?'

'Just we told them we were doing holiday in the hills, na. No one person offered objection. So much pain and anguish and all we'd suffered. Ma said rest was required. To forget all what I'd seen.'

Puri took this to be a reference to the murder of Mummy's brother, Anil. His next question was a few seconds in coming.

'Did Papa come to know – about your going to Pakistan, that is?' he asked.

'This was before marriage, na?'

'Yes but after did you tell him?'

Mummy shook her head. 'With marriage new life begins, na? After my *shaadi*, I packed away those times. My duty was to my husband – and my three boys, also. Past is past.'

'But it's never entirely forgotten, is it, Mummy-ji? It came back to haunt you when you met Kamran Khan at the durbar. You were totally thunderstruck, actually. He's his father's carbon copy.'

'Agreed,' said Mummy. 'But come, Chubby. Where's your appetite?' She picked up the plate of macaroons and offered it to him. 'It's your favourite, na?'

Puri took the plate and placed it back on the tray. 'Mummy-ji I want to know what all you know about Faheem Khan's past.'

'First thing is first, Chubby,' she replied. 'Must be Aslam found you and not the other way round. That means he told you something.'

'No more games, Mummy-ji,' replied Puri sternly. 'This is not some small matter like which servant stole the *daal*.'

The *pallu* of her sari had slipped forward. She pulled it back over her shoulder, her demeanour indignant. 'Why you shouldn't share what all Aslam told you first? It's my case after all,' she said.

'*Your* case, Mummy-ji! How exactly? I'm the detective, is it not!'

'Your voice is getting raised, na. Come. Take iron tonic. One spoon. Will make you calm.'

'I am very much calm!' he erupted.

The words penetrated into the next room where Bhuppi was watching TV. He put his head around the door. 'All OK, Chubby?'

Puri made a gesture as if to say 'as well as can be expected' and his brother gave a sympathetic nod before retreating.

'Mind telling me why all this is your case, exactly?' asked Puri. He was standing behind his chair now, hands gripping the top.

'It began in 1948, na. That is when she went missing.'

'Who?'

Mummy gave a tut. 'Saroya. Aslam didn't tell you?'

'He mentioned her but gave a different name, also.'

Mummy sat forward in her chair. Her face was alight with expectation. 'Tell me, Chubby.'

'You'll give me what I want, also?'

'It's my case, na. Since sixty years I've been waiting. It is only right and proper I be allowed to do conclusion.'

'Mummy-ji, how many times I've told you: detective work is for professionals, not mummies. Years of experience are required.'

'Case will not get solved without my know-how.'

The detective heaved a great sigh. 'Very well,' he said. 'Let us put our two heads together.'

He took out his notebook and read aloud the information Aslam had given him: 'Her name is Kiran Singh, daughter of Manjit Singh. Came from a village named Mandra. Aslam said you would remember it.'

Puri handed her the photograph Aslam had given him. Mummy gasped at the sight of it. 'So long I've been trying to picture her face, na,' she said. 'Yes, that is she.

259

No doubt about it. Aslam said how long ago he found out her real name?'

'Some years, I believe. He wanted to pass on the information but didn't know where to find you.'

Mummy was still staring at the picture. A tear fell and splashed on to it. She quickly wiped it away with a napkin, embarrassed.

'Clumsy of me, na.'

'Please, Mummy, no need to apologise.' Puri's tone was soft, understanding now. 'So many memories and all.'

He held her by the hand. 'This Kiran Singh, known as Saroya, also – she is who exactly?' he asked.

Mummy wiped her face, still clutching the photograph.

'Faheem Khan's wife.'

• TWENTY-TWO •

Mummy went upstairs to her room and returned with a small collection of tatty old notebooks: her diaries from 1948. She'd kept them hidden in a padlocked trunk all these years, something of an achievement in a busy Punjabi household in which personal space was an abstract concept.

'Here, Chubby,' she said, handing them to her son. 'You'll find what you want. All written down.'

'You're certain about this, Mummy-ji?' asked Puri. He had often seen his mother scribbling in her daily diary, but had never dared so much as peek inside. Their pages were the one place that had always been out of bounds, even to Papa.

'Hard for me, what with my eyes,' she answered. 'You go ahead. Just I'll take rest. Some tiredness is there.'

Puri stood as she left the room and headed upstairs.

'I'll be here only,' he called after her, staring down at the cover of the first notebook, marked in English in faded ink: 'February 1948'.

With a sense of guilt, as if he was trespassing, the detective turned back the cover.

Mummy had written in the Perso-Arabic script, which Puri had studied at the Military Intelligence Training School in Pune. But he was rusty and could only make sense of certain sentences by saying the words out loud.

The first entry was for February 8. It described the journey back to Pakistan, retracing the route Mummy and her family had taken in the opposite direction when they had fled to newly independent India only a few months earlier.

At Wazirabad, she had wept bitterly, reliving the scenes of men being dragged from the refugee train and vanishing beneath a ferment of bloody fists and weapons.

Reached Pindi at seven in the evening. As we decamped from the train I fainted – memory of those eleven terrifying hours when we were stuck in the station with a handful of jittery British soldiers holding back the mob too much to bear. Premna Auntie comforted me. But I felt embarrassed. God knows she has suffered more than me. Husband, son, father all gone.

Here Mummy reflected on how surreal it was being back in Rawalpindi, the city where she had grown up. This new country called Pakistan was her *watan*, her homeland, and yet she would never live there again.

At times she vented her anger: '*Strangers are living in Papa's house,*' she'd written.

Who are they? They have no right to be there! What have they done with our possessions? P said we should go and see. I can't. Not strong enough. Keep searching in the crowd, looking for the boys who came that night. I can picture every one of their faces.

She was referring to her brother's murderers, Puri concluded, and he read on:

How could people do such things? Slaughter their neighbours like cattle? Drive one another from their homes? P says there is only one explanation for such madness: Lord Shiva has danced the rudra tandava. *But no one has time to mourn. Everyone has started to put the past behind them – here and in India also. In this alone, in their common denial, are the people of our two countries now united.*

Puri reached the entry for February 21, 1948, where Mummy described her and Premna Auntie's modus operandi:

Dressed as poor Muslim peasants wearing tatty coloured salwar kameez, frilled dupattas, ta'wiz. Went barefoot and carried cloth bundles containing a few possessions on our heads. Had to hone our rural Punjabi accents.

Every day they would set off at dawn for villages in the Punjab hinterland, searching for abducted Hindu and Sikh girls and women being held against their will. When they received confirmation of one being held in a certain location, Mummy and Premna Auntie were bound to pass on the information to the local authorities. The governments of India and Pakistan had signed a pact to allow rescue teams to work in each other's countries and facilitate the search and release of the missing women. But the police often proved corrupt or uncooperative.

'*Some officers have abducted women themselves or bought them from others as wives,*' wrote Mummy.

On February 23, however, a certain Captain Aslam of the Pakistan army had been seconded to help them.

That morning he waited with his men on the Grand Trunk Road while Mummy and Premna Auntie set off to investigate a rumour that a young woman was being held in the village of Bajal.

While Puri read on, Mummy slept – and dreamed.

She was young Koomi Pabla again, nineteen years of age, walking with dear Premna Auntie . . .

It's dawn and the farmers working in the fields watch their approach. The fine layer of dust that coats the two women from head to toe, diligently acquired during a long, arduous walk along a rough track that leads to the village from the Grand Trunk Road, completes the picture of desperate refugees escaping the ongoing violence in the contested state of Jammu and Kashmir.

The only facet of their disguise that's not been improvised is the pain, anguish and sheer exhaustion that shows in their features. The memories of bloodshed and violence, the murder of loved ones, of being brutally uprooted from their homes in August of the previous year – all this is as fresh in their minds as it is for millions of others now living on either side of the new border.

'Amma! A-salaam-alai-kum,' calls out Premna, spotting a local, middle-aged woman returning from the fields

through the early-morning mist. 'Help us! Barely any food has touched our lips in days!'

'Wa-lai-kum-a-salaam!' the local woman greets them. Koomi judges her to be no older than forty despite the shock of pure white hair peeking from beneath her headscarf.

'Where are you coming from?' the woman says.

Premna answers, 'Jammu! My daughter and I have been walking for days. My husband is no more! And the kafirs drove us from our homes! May Shaitan stone them!'

Premna is weeping now, tears streaming down her face, her hands held up in supplication. 'What are we to do?' she implores the stranger. 'Amma! We have lost everything! May Allah protect us!'

The local woman approaches them with pitying eyes and asks, 'But, sisters, where are you going?'.

'To Rawalpindi! Word has reached us that my brother is there in a camp. Tell us: how far is it?'

'Two days.'

Koomi's eyes widen and then she, too, begins to cry. 'But Mother has not the strength in her,' she sobs. 'We were robbed on the road and have nothing left – only a few pots and no food to put in them.'

The local woman, whose name is Homaira, places a comforting arm around Koomi and says, 'Please don't cry, child. Come. You will have food and drink and you can take rest.'

She leads the women through the village, where the charred hulks of houses, scenes of unimaginable crimes that will go unpunished for ever, bear testament to the slaughter and pillaging that has accompanied the brutal division of India by the British and the creation of Pakistan. They pass a boarded-up well, a tomb for many of the village's Hindu and Sikh girls, who took their own lives rather than be seized by a Muslim mob. Further on lies a Muslim graveyard with freshly dug plots – more victims of the frenzy of killings that swept through cities, towns and villages where previously those of different faiths had lived side by side for generations.

Homaira's homestead has thick mud walls the colour of honey and a strong set of double doors. In the courtyard beyond, chickens peck in the dust and a carpet of bright red chillies lies drying in the sun. The visitors are taken into the women's quarters and then the kitchen – little more than a room with an earthen floor and a few blackened pots stacked in one corner. Coals glow beneath a tandoor where fresh naan is being prepared by one of their hostess's young daughters. Soon, Premna and Koomi are warming themselves in front of a fire, tearing off pieces of the soft, warm bread and hungrily stuffing their mouths. Sweet, milky chai is served, a rare luxury for these times, and they're joined by the other women of the household – more daughters; daughters-in-law; granddaughters; a mourning, ancient aunt; and a shy girl whom the family has taken in since her parents, their neighbours, were killed.

The Indians eat on in silence, watched by a bank of curious eyes. The murmur of male voices reaches them from one of the adjoining rooms. And then – hesitantly at first – the questions begin. What have they seen on the road? Is it true India is preparing to invade? Have all the Mussulmen been forced out of Jammu?

Premna and Koomi answer as truthfully as they can, accustomed to such questions. And when they sense their *hosts are at ease with their presence, Koomi begins the patter that has proven successful in many of the other villages they've visited across the length and breadth of Pakistani Punjab in recent weeks.*

'So many of our sisters were taken by the Hindus!' she says. 'They have been kidnapped and forced to convert and marry. Allah protect them.'

'They are saying Hindu and Sikh girls have also been taken by our brothers here in Pakistan,' says Premna. 'But I am sure that they are lying!'

Homaira's eyes are cast down as she answers in a lowered voice, 'It's true. But the government has declared that they should be returned to their families. Forced marriages are not being recognised.'

The aunt lets out a loud, angry grunt. 'Why should they be released when so many of our sisters are also being held?' she sneers. 'Many men have lost their wives. How are they to raise families? These women are Muslims now, bound by marriage.'

Homaira disagrees. 'No, Amina jaan, *it is not right what has been done.' Her voice is quiet yet seething with emotion. 'What about that poor girl being held by Faheem Khan? She must be barely eighteen years of age. Is she not as innocent in these affairs as any of us sitting here? And yet she has been passed from man to man. Sold like a farm animal. Then forced into marriage. That brute treats her cruelly. She has to work all day in the fields – and he is violent.'*

Beneath the tandoor, the coals are dying.

'She is Hindu, this girl?' asks Koomi eventually.

'Sikh – I overheard her repeating the Gurbani in the

fields.' The hostess lets out a frustrated tut. 'No, it's not right what is being done,' she repeats. 'But Faheem Khan's father is a powerful man.'

'Are there any others being held in the village?' asks Koomi.

'She is the only one.'

The aunt speaks up again: 'There's no point sending these women back to their families. They won't have them! They'll say they're unclean, polluted! That's what those Hindus have always said of us. Never would they allow us to eat in their homes or drink from their cups. Better these girls stay here where they have a future.'

Premna changes the subject, bemoaning the loss of her husband again and wondering if she will ever marry off her daughter. The women swap more stories.

Another half-hour passes and then the Indians announce their intention to continue with their journey.

'You need rest,' insists their hostess. 'Stay as our guests until tomorrow at the very least. I implore you.'

'Homaira jaan, we dare not,' says Premna. 'I feel my strength returning and we must reach Rawalpindi as quickly as we can. Who knows how long my brother will be there? If we don't find him then who will provide for us?'

Seeing that her mind is made up, their hostess wraps some provisions in a cloth and escorts them back outside. The Indians thank her, promising to return in happier times. Before they set off again, Koomi asks their benefactor to point out the homestead where the captive girl is being held.

She answers with a hint of suspicion in her voice: 'The house-fort over there, the one surrounded by tall walls.'

And as Premna and Koomi make their way north out of the village, Homaira watches them with a quizzical frown – as if there is something about the duo that she can't quite place.

It is later. She and Premna Auntie are returning to the village now with Aslam and his men. The place is deserted, doors and shutters all closed. The fields are empty.

'Someone sent word we were coming,' says the captain.

Undoing the clip on the holster of his pistol, he bangs on the heavy wooden door set in the high mud walls of the house-fort. It's opened by a tall young man with a fresh scar on his right cheek.

The Indians can't hear what Aslam says to him but it engenders a gruff response: 'I'm not hiding anyone!'

The captain asks him about the scar and he responds, almost mockingly, 'I fell in a thorn bush!'

The captain pushes past him. Two Pakistani women, brought along to help search the sections of homes where men are forbidden to go, follow Aslam in through the gate.

Faheem Khan glares at the Indians before returning inside.

They wait in the jeep with one of Aslam's men. Then something catches Koomi's eye. From the side of the house-fort, someone is signalling to her.

She gets out of the vehicle, making some excuse, and slips away to investigate. Behind a tree, she finds Homaira, a finger held to her lips. She watches over Koomi's shoulders to see if anyone has followed her. 'Come.' She leads the way along a sandy path.

Koomi notices some unusual tracks in the sandy soil. They've been made by a man walking backwards with his legs splayed and feet held well apart. A rut running between them indicates that he dragged something heavy. She and Homaira reach the edge of the field behind the house-fort. Homaira points out a few planks of wood lying on the ground with a millstone on top of them. Together they manage to move the millstone to one side. Fearing the worst, Koomi picks up the planks one by one.

Beneath lies a six-foot pit. And at the bottom lies a young woman. She's bound and gagged and her face is badly bruised. She turns her head and squints, the light hurting her eyes.

Koomi jumps down into the pit, unties the ropes around the woman's wrists and ankles and removes a piece of cloth that's been stuffed into her mouth. Together, she and Homaira help the woman out of the hole.

'Go! Before he comes!' whispers Homaira.

'Thank you, jaan!'

'Hurry!'

With that, Homaira disappears into the sugar-cane field.

Koomi helps the young woman back along the sandy path and hides her in the back of the jeep under a tarpaulin.

When Aslam and the two Pakistani women emerge from inside, Faheem Khan is not far behind, a grin stretched between his ears.

'What did I tell you? You've made a wasted journey, Captain,' he says.

Koomi looks back, watching him as the vehicle pulls

*away. The village of Bajal disappears behind a pall of
dust thrown up by the vehicle's wheels.*

Mummy's diary contained a description of how the woman
she'd rescued said nothing on the journey to the IRRO
camp. But there was no doubt her family was Sikh: she
was still wearing a *kara* on her right wrist. There was
every chance she could read and write as well. As for her
age – not a day over seventeen.

That evening the young woman sat in the mess tent
with an untouched plate of food on the table in front
of her.

'*Seemed like she could be suffering from memory loss*,' Mummy
had written.

There was nothing unusual about this. Many of the
women who were brought to the camp were suffering
from severe shock. Some had lost their mind entirely.

'Can you remember your real name, *didi?*' Mummy
asked.

No response.

'Can you tell us where you are from, child?' asked
Premna.

'What is going to happen to *him*,' said a voice – bitter,
hateful.

'I will not lie to you,' said Premna. 'An amnesty has
been offered to all Indian and Pakistani men who release
women they've taken by force.'

'He didn't give me up. I would still be in that hole if
you hadn't found me!'

'That may be so, child,' said Premna. 'But he won't

face justice – not in this lifetime at least. I wish I could tell you differently.'

The young woman was unable to accept what she was being told. 'He's a murderer,' she said. 'It's thanks to him that my sisters . . .' Her eyes filled with tears, but she fought them back. 'He should be punished,' she added, wiping her face.

Mummy reached out and rested a hand on the young woman's arm.

'All of us have lost loved ones,' she said. 'But now we must be thankful that we are safe, that we have a future. Now, please. At least tell us where you're from.'

Their guest was silent for a while and then asked, 'Is it true what they're saying? Women like me are being shunned by their families?'

Mummy hesitated. She and Premna had been directed by their superiors to answer no to this question, to dismiss it as Pakistani propaganda. But they well knew that many Hindu and Sikh women had been shunned by their own families and were now living in ashrams.

'Please understand, it's our duty to rescue you and arrange for you to be taken to India,' said Mummy. 'We'll provide you with every assistance once you are there. I promise you that, didi.'

'What if I want to stay here?' asked the young woman.

'Here?' asked Premna.

'Why not? I'm a Muslim now. I have a Muslim name – Saroya, he called me.'

'It's out of the question,' insisted Premna. 'The directive is very clear. Abducted women are to be reunited with their families.'

Resentment flashed in Saroya's narrowed eyes. 'So I'm a captive again,' she said.

'Didi, please don't say that,' implored Koomi. 'We're trying to help you. We brought you here for your own good. Better to go to India than stay in Pakistan. No one can guarantee your security here. Now please, co-operate and tell us your name.'

But Saroya refused to speak again.

Mummy was standing in the doorway of the living room.

'So late it is, Chubby. You've been sitting all this time, na?'

It was seven o'clock. Three hours had passed. 'I lost track, actually,' he answered.

'Must be hungry, na. Come. *Rajma chawal* is there.'

They sat at the dinner table eating the spicy kidney bean stew and rice with freshly made buttered rotis and curd. Puri had also helped himself to a generous portion of his mother's home-made mango aachar.

Neither of them spoke during the meal except to ask the other to pass this and that. Only when Mummy had cleared the plates and made tea and they were back in the living room did Puri put to her the question he had been itching to ask for the past hour:

'So must be this Saroya woman, Kiran Singh, she absconded from the camp, is it?'

'Everything is written there, na.'

'I failed to reach the end, Mummy-ji.' He picked up the last diary. 'I should carry on reading, is it?'

'No need, Chubby. I'll tell you. You are quite correct. She left in dead of night. Captain Sahib and we people searched here and there for three days, but not one trace we could find.'

'Could be she reverted to Faheem Khan's house in order to take revenge,' suggested the detective.

'Our thinking, also. Captain Sahib drove directly to the village in fact. But Saroya – sorry na, Kiran Singh – was totally absent.'

Still Mummy had not given up the search. In the coming days and weeks, she went through the ledgers containing the names of the thousands of women still listed as missing – many of whom would never be located, nor see their families again. Going by age, location and religion, she made a list of roughly 150 possible candidates. She then set about trawling through letters and photographs sent from families in India asking the IRRO for news of wives and daughters. This helped narrow the field down to twenty-seven.

By the time Mummy returned to India in April 1948, hundreds more abducted women had been located and the list stood at eleven.

'So now you understand, Chubby, na? It is my case. So many years I've been waiting. Just imagine my shock when Faheem Khan dropped dead here in Dilli. Before my very eyes!'

'Mind-blowing,' agreed Puri. 'But, it is by no means certain Kiran Singh murdered Khan. She may be dead also.'

His mother let out a loud tut. 'One of those ladies present is the one responsible. Just she changed her identity after coming to India,' she affirmed.

'You've proof?'

'Certain things you come to know in here,' she said, patting her heart.

Puri rolled his eyes. This was exactly why he never allowed her to get involved in his cases. 'Mummy-ji, I'm afraid we would be needing a little more than your say-so,' he said.

'Not just "say-so", thank you very much kindly, Chubby.'

'What then?'

She hesitated. 'Certain information came to me while staying in Haridwar, na.'

'You mean you went looking, most deliberately in fact, for certain information.'

Mummy glared at him defiantly and sat up straight in her chair. 'Correct,' she said.

Over the course of the next twenty minutes, Mummy divulged everything she'd discovered in Haridwar.

Harnam Talwar, wife of the infamous politician, was not who she claimed to be.

Jasmeet Bhatia, mother of the Call Centre King, had been born in Rawat, close to Faheem Khan's native place.

And Megha Dogra, wife of the Prince of Polyester, had grown up near Lahore, but strangely, there was no record of what had become of her relatives since.

'None of this is at all conclusive, Mummy-ji,' said Puri.

'It's a start, na,' she retorted. 'Now we can do follow-up.'

The mention of 'we' sat uncomfortably with him. She would drive him crazy with her so-called auntie's intuition and half-baked clues. And yet on this occasion, given everything she had revealed, he couldn't bring himself to shut her out.

'Fine, Mummy-ji, we'll do teamwork – but on this case *only*,' he stressed. 'How do you wish to proceed exactly?'

'Simple, na. Just I'll do checking in National Archives. Must be Kiran Singh's father, Manjit, got registered and all in 1947.'

'How will that help?'

'Obvious, na. His relatives can do identification of her.'

'Tip top,' said Puri, not in the least convinced that this line of investigation would work, but happy for Mummy to be safely tucked away in the archives while he tested Aslam's claim about Aga being in the hands of the Americans.

'You're certain you've told me everything?' he asked.

'Actually one thing is there, Chubby. Harnam Talwar, wife of that goonda politician, is not the one.'

'You mean you don't believe she killed Faheem Khan, Mummy-ji?'

'Correct.'

Puri asked her how she'd reached that conclusion.

'It's come to my attention Harnam is not her real name,' she said.

'What then, Mummy-ji?'

'She was born Fatima.'

'A Muslim? How you found out?'

'I came to know she's going to Old Delhi every Friday, Chubby, for prayers and all.'

'You followed her?'

'Just I happened to go to Old Delhi this past Friday also, na,' she said, all innocence.

Puri shook his head from side to side. His astonishment was derived as much from his mother's brazenness as the revelation about Sandeep Talwar's wife.

By God, no wonder Sahib had warned him off his wife. In all likelihood he'd abducted her in 1947 and forced her to become a Hindu – hence her continuing devotion to Islam. Most probably not even the Talwars' own children knew the truth.

'Anything else, Mummy-ji?' he asked, his tone a mix of exasperation and incredulousness.

'No, Chubby, that is all,' she answered. 'Just I was trying to do research on last remaining two suspects, Jasmeet Bhatia and Megha Dogra. But time was totally lacking. Energy also. No longer I'm twenty-one, na.'

• TWENTY-THREE •

Puri badly needed some meter down. The journey to Pakistan had been exhausting enough, but dealing with Mummy left him spent. His mind was still reeling from the revelations about her past. It was simply incredible to think that his mother, the woman who'd bathed him, fed him that bloody iron tonic all the time, had once worked as a satri, an undercover operative.

It wasn't only fatigue keeping him in bed that Monday morning, however. Before leaving for Pakistan, he'd forgotten to remove the peg from Rumpi's scales. It was only a question of time before she asked to check his weight, and with the scales stuck on 90 kilos the impressive progress he'd made thanks to the miraculous diet pills would be for nothing. He needed five minutes alone in the bedroom to undo his handiwork.

Unfortunately Rumpi was busy washing her hair in preparation for their grandson's mundan ceremony later that afternoon. It was a lengthy and complex process; she began by oiling her long mane and applying a 'herb tea' (a mix of warm water, *shikakai*, *aritha*, neem and sandalwood). This needed to sit for roughly fifteen minutes, after which her hair would be rinsed in cold water and then dried until damp. Finally coconut oil would be added as a conditioner and she'd spend ten minutes or so seated in front of the dressing table, brushing her shiny tresses.

In normal circumstances, Puri found the whole ritual powerfully alluring, a display of raw Indian femininity. The aroma of all the herbs and oils had been known to render him as giddy as a love-struck teenager. But not today. The detective lay in bed, willing his wife downstairs, groaning silently into his pillow when she decided to also treat her scalp to a little *amla* oil, to help strengthen the roots, and then attended to her eyebrows.

'Chubby?' she asked, talking to the reflection in her mirror in the vague, dreamy tone she adopted while engaged in her personal grooming. 'Before you go off today, we mustn't forget to weigh you. It's been over a week.'

He pretended to be half asleep. 'Yes, my dear,' he murmured, racking his brains for a way out of his dilemma. Perhaps if he just lay there long enough . . .

And then his prayers were answered: her mobile phone rang. It was her father. She had to pass Puri the phone.

'Good morning, young man,' said Brigadier Mattu, sounding fresh and alert. 'I woke you? Could you meet me at the club in one hour? I've got bridge at ten. There's something I need to show you beforehand. It's not good news, I'm afraid.'

'You're not able to solve the code, sir?'

'No, no, that was easy. This is something else. A grave

matter. It would be better if we didn't discuss it over the phone. Nine o'clock in the ballroom.'

Salvation.

'The answer's been staring me in the face all these days,' said Brigadier Mattu when the two sat down a little over an hour later. 'Someone with my experience should have seen it a mile off. I'm afraid old age is setting in.'

'Not at all, sir,' said the detective. 'You're a spring chicken, actually.'

'More like a headless chicken now that I'm retired,' joked the Brigadier. 'Too much time on my hands. My advice to you, young man, is never hang up your hat – or should I say cap in your case? Retirement is a kind of surrender. Life should be a fight to the death.'

They were tucked away in a corner of the ballroom, the heart of the Gymkhana's main building. During the day, it functioned as a lounge where tea, dry chicken sandwiches and oily samosas were served. The regulars were mostly elderly gentlemen killing time until the bar opened. Sometimes aunties in silk saris as crinkly as wrapping paper gathered there as well, but never alone.

'You cracked it then, sir?' asked Puri, barely able to contain his anticipation.

'Yes, yes, the *basmallah* was the key – a value of 786.'

He reached into the inside pocket of his tweed jacket and took out four or five pieces of crumpled paper. These he laid on the coffee table that sat between them and smoothed out the creases with the palm of his hand. They were covered in his workings, a jumble of numbers and letters, some Perso-Arabic, others Roman.

'Yes, it's quite simple, really,' said Mattu. 'Your cricket-betting friends have been using the Abjad System.'

'Abjad, sir?' asked the detective.

'Derived from *abjadiyyah*. It means "alphabet" in Arabic,' he added. 'Abjad's been around since the eighth century, since the time of the Prophet Muhammad. Urdu uses more or less the same script, so our Pakistani neighbours are naturally familiar with its intricacies.'

The Brigadier picked up one of the pieces of paper. 'See here,' he continued. 'The first letter, "ã", is given the value of one. The second, "b", equals two. The third, "j", is three – and so on. Yā is ten; "k" equals twenty; "i" makes thirty and so on. In standard Arabic there are twenty-eight letters. In Urdu there are thirty-eight but that's not relevant to the matter in hand.' Mattu listed the rest of the letters with their numerical equivalents. 'So let us take the word "Allah",' he continued. 'In the Arabic script it's written thus: ﻟﻠﻪ. So it has a value of one plus thirty plus thirty plus five. That equals sixty-six. Follow?'

Puri nodded repeatedly.

'Now,' said Mattu. 'Phrases can be assigned a numerical value, also. Let us take the *basmallah*, which is repeated in Muslim prayers and at the start of each sura in the Koran, apart from the ninth – "*b-ismi-llāhi r-rahmāni r-rahīmi*. It translates as, "In the name of God, most Gracious, most Merciful." Now let's look at how it breaks down mathematically.'

The total was 786.

'Now, where is the copy of the paper you took from Mr Faheem Khan?' asked Mattu. 'Aah yes, here it is. The first sequence reads 12, 11 and 6. So let us deduct 7, 8 and 6 and we get 5, 3 and 0.'

He took out his scorecard from the ICT match played the previous Sunday just hours before the murder.

'On the fifth ball of the third over, Kamran Khan bowled a no ball. See how it corresponds?'

'By God!' exclaimed Puri. He slapped the palms of his hands on his thighs in a playful manner. 'Sir, you've done it! Hearties congratulations!'

His words echoed around the ballroom. Newspapers were lowered. Necks turned and twisted.

'So the same formula can be applied to these other sequences?' asked the detective.

'Seems the third digit indicates what kind of ball is to be delivered,' he explained. 'Zero for a no ball. One equals a wide. Two stands for bouncer. Six for a full toss.'

'Mind-blowing,' muttered Puri. 'Sir, you're a genius, actually.'

'It's nothing, young man, really,' said Mattu with a shrug as the waiter finally brought their tea.

The liquid was dark and acidic, the milk separate, just as the Britishers liked it. Puri and countless others before him had tried to get the club's cooks to make it properly, 'ready-made' in other words. But for some sixty years they had failed. Club tea was supposed to be prepared this way, the kitchen always argued. It had been ordained. Anything else would be a break with tradition.

The little stainless steel pots, which invariably dribbled their contents all over the table as the tea was poured, were another part of that same system. Puri saw them as a metaphor for Partition: another British legacy still causing a mess on the subcontinent.

'Now there's something else,' said Mattu, a sudden gravitas to his voice. In his excitement, the detective had forgotten about the other matter. 'It has to do with the second set of numbers you provided me,' added his father-in-law.

He was referring to the paper Puri had taken from Full Moon's study.

'These relate to another match, the one played on the day your bookie was murdered: the Goa Beachers, Mumbai Bears showdown.'

Mattu moved closer to his son-in-law and said in little more than a whisper: 'There's another Pakistani bowler involved, Hamid Pathan. 'And' – he hesitated – 'an Indian batsman also.'

'Don't tell me.'

Mattu brought Puri's attention to his scorecard from Wednesday's match. One name was highlighted: star batsman Vikas Patil.

'Aaarey!' exclaimed Puri in disbelief, causing another flutter of newspapers across the ballroom. 'You're certain, sir?'

The Brigadier nodded gravely. 'I got hold of a recording of the match and watched it again,' he said. 'There's no doubt that he's in league with Hamid Pathan.'

'But why?' asked Puri. 'He's making so much of money from sponsorships and all.'

'I would hazard a guess at blackmail,' replied Mattu. 'He's married, as you well know. But I've heard it said he's very taken with the ladies. There are stories about him and some of these cheerleaders. At the after-match parties.'

'When he's due to play again, sir, you know?'

'Tomorrow. And there's something else. He'll be facing none other than Kamran Khan.'

'How so?'

'He's returning to India.'

'So soon?'

'Business is business I suppose,' said Mattu with a shrug.

The club's acidic tea worked its way swiftly though Puri's digestive system and before heading to the office to follow up on Mattu's revelations, he paid a visit to the men's changing room. There he spotted a set of electronic weighing scales and decided to check to see how his diet was coming along.

The LCD screen registered 91 kilos.

Confused, he stepped back off the pressure pad, looked to make sure the screen read zero and then tried again. Same result.

'Lohit!'

The 'boy' who worked in the changing rooms came running. He was at least sixty-five.

'Sir?'

'Scales are malfunctioning,' complained Puri.

'No, Sahib. Not possible.'

'I'm telling you. This thing has got my weight wrong certainly if not totally. See? Should read eighty-nine point five or less.'

Lohit scratched his head. 'Sir, it's a new one,' he replied.

Puri decided that all the tea he'd drunk had skewed the result and went and relieved himself.

'Bloody thing is wrong!' he cursed when he weighed himself again and got the same result.

Lohit suggested that perhaps Sahib might like to try the set of old-fashioned balance beam scales in the gymnasium. These confirmed Puri's worst nightmare. He hadn't shed a single gram.

'Bloody useless,' he cursed, throwing the last of his diet pills in the bin.

Tubelight called the moment Puri stepped into his office. The diamonds had been exported, complete with a bona fide certificate of origin stamped by Indian customs.

'What's the destination exactly?'

'Antwerp, Boss. A company called Patel and Patel. The stones will be put up for sale there.'

'Tip top,' said Puri, who promptly ordered Tubelight to return with Flush to Delhi, where he now needed them. He then called his client James Scott and asked him to find out everything he could about the Antwerp firm.

The detective's next call was to a sports journalist who owed him a favour. 'I'd be needing the mobile numbers of two ICT players,' he said, naming Kamran Khan and Vikas Patil.

'Saar, you should know media is not allowed direct access to players,' replied the journalist.

'Come on, yaar, don't talk nonsense!'

Ten minutes later Puri had both the numbers as well as the names of the five-star hotels where the players would be staying.

Finally he put in a call to a former batchmate working

for India's external intelligence agency, RAW. Had he any information about Aga's whereabouts?

'Nothing,' was the reply. 'We've not had a sighting of him in months in fact.'

It was all over in a few seconds. A flash; a series of sharp cracks like a string of Diwali firecrackers going off; the sound of breaking glass; people all around him screaming.

Puri felt himself collapse on to the pavement. He lay on his side, staring at one of the shiny hubcaps of the Ambassador, the reflection of his face grotesquely warped, as in a House of Fun mirror. The world was quiet for a moment, almost peaceful, and he found himself thinking how much he would love a nice plate of butter chicken right now, preferably without aconite. He became conscious of a throbbing pain in his shoulder and then a babble of voices crowded his thoughts. He rolled on to his back to find that a crowd had gathered around him. They were all staring down at him as if he'd washed up on a tide.

Puri sat up, non-responsive to the repeated enquiries as to his well-being. He began to run a kind of all-systems check to make sure there was no serious damage and found that the pain in his shoulder had been caused by his fall to the pavement, a bruise rather than a wound. Relieved, yet still dazed, he sat there for a moment or two longer, brushing away pieces of shattered glass from his clothes, and then accepted the offer of an outstretched hand.

It belonged to Handbrake.

'Boss, are you OK?' he asked in Hindi as the detective got to his feet, still shedding bits of glass like a skyscraper in an earthquake.

'It was that same bloody bastard on the motorbike – one from other day, the paan wallah assassin,' he said, suddenly remembering what had happened.

'He got away, Boss. Sorry, too much traffic.'

'Anyone else is wounded?'

'No, Boss. Just a scrape or two.'

'Thank the God,' murmured Puri in English.

'And the car. The bullets hit the side, Boss.'

'Don't tell me.'

Handbrake pointed out the holes.

'Bloody bastard,' cursed Puri. 'I'll get him if it's the last thing I do.'

One of the jawans who 'patrolled' Khan Market approached, dispersing the crowd with the tact and sensitivity for which the Delhi police are famed.

The detective suggested he might like to form a perimeter around the scene of the shooting before calling Inspector Singh and asking him to bring the ballistics boys over right away. Leaving Handbrake to guard the car, he returned upstairs to his office. He helped himself to a large Scotch and then opened the safe. Inside lay his .32 IOF revolver. This he loaded and slipped into one of the outside pockets of his safari suit.

Puri was an hour late in picking up his wife from home, arriving in a taxi without the flowers he'd promised to buy. He didn't want to have to tell her about the attempt on his life – she had a way of getting upset when people tried to kill him – so he said the Ambassador had broken down.

Thankfully, Rumpi let him off lightly and they spent the fifteen-minute journey to Lotus Gardens Phase Two reminiscing about their three daughters' mundans – how their second-eldest had cried and cried when her head had been shaved, and how Radhika, their youngest, had revelled in the attention and giggled uncontrollably as her locks had been shorn.

'Such a silly little *bachi*,' smiled detective with a fond smile.

The conversation set the tone for the afternoon. Puri and Rumpi entered their eldest daughter Lalita's apartment to find it heaving with members of both their families. Soon, the detective was able to put all thoughts of poison, match fixing, Antwerp and attempts on his life out of his mind – at least for an hour or so.

'Getting so big, beta, haa?' said Puri as he held up his grandson, Rohit, and gave him a hug.

The boy blew a loud raspberry.

'And naughty, haa?' he guffawed.

'Very naughty!' chorused everyone approvingly.

Rumpi disappeared into the kitchen where large amounts of *kheer* and *ladoos* were being prepared, and Puri's son-in-law Arun brought him a cold drink.

'All well, Papa-ji?' he asked, as formal as ever.

'First class.'

'You came from work?'

'Direct from office.'

'Heard there was some problem?'

'Where you heard that?'

'Mummy-ji said there had been some shooting?'

How the hell did Mummy find out these things so quickly? 'Just a small misunderstanding, that is all,' he told his son-in-law.

'Misunderstanding with a gunman?'

'Correct.'

Inevitably the conversation turned to cricket, with most of the men in the room gathered together discussing a recent controversial decision by an Australian umpire, which had almost certainly lost India an important international match.

It took Mummy to put an end to it. 'Cricket talk is getting over,' she said. 'Come. Challo!'

They all adjourned to the dining room where the family priest was sitting in the middle of the floor. After greeting the pandit and bending down to touch his feet, everyone found a spot on the Indian quilts that had been laid on the floor. Rohit, dressed in a smart kurta pajama, was brought forward by his mother.

The priest recited some mantras, sprinkled drops of Ganga water over the boy's head, and then, with a pair of scissors, snipped away a few strands of his hair. A local barber, hired especially for the event, then took over. Using a straight razor blade, he began to shave the head clean, shearing Rohit's mop like wool from the body of a lamb. The child began to wail and everyone tried to appease him – 'No need to cry, baby'; 'Not long now, *bacha*' – but the tears kept dripping down on to the floor along with his baby locks.

Puri found himself staring down at the hair, thinking back on the time when, as an adult, his head had been shaved. He'd been in his early twenties, stationed in southern India. While on leave, he visited the magnificent Vishnu temple at Tirupati.

Like all pilgrims, he was required to get his head

tonsured before entering the holy site. The shaving was carried out by one of the temple priests, a matter of a few minutes' work, his hair mixing with that of thousands of others carpeting the ground.

Puri only came to know later that Tirupati, the richest temple in the world, sold approximately a ton of hair every day to the international cosmetics industry. In other words, his youthful locks had ended up as part of a wig. In the years since then, he'd derived a good deal of amusement from the thought that someone was walking around wearing his hair.

The thought of hair and wigs recalled him to the moustache case. What if the thief intended to wear Gopal Ragi's moustache himself, perhaps as part of a disguise?

A chilling possibility came to mind. The moustache, once fixed to the thief's upper lip, could be used to strangle someone. Puri pictured the thief passing through tight security, getting close to, say, an unsuspecting dignitary who was under close guard, unravelling the tresses and . . .

He could think of another, less morbid possibility. And as the last of Rohit's hair fell away and the barber crafted a little tuft at the back of his head, Puri made a mental list of professions where a big, bushy moustache was required as part of the job description.

In regiments like the Rajputana Rifles, President's Bodyguard and Border Security Force, there was hardly a serving man to be found without facial hair. Those with the most outlandish of moustaches were always put on display during public ceremonies like the changing of the guard at Rashtrapati Bhavan or the Republic Day parade for example.

In some parts of India, like central Madhya Pradesh, officers were given financial incentives for nurturing growth on their upper lip. Male actors appearing in theatrical performances of the Hindu epics, during Dussera for example, were often well endowed in the facial hair department as well. Who else? Cadres of the martial Sikh Nihang order.

Puri could think of only one other profession: hotel doorman.

Many a five-star hotel employed Sikhs or Rajasthanis with dramatic moustaches to man their entrances. They wore colourful turbans and inauthentic uniforms – window dressing that bespoke romantic 'Indiaaaah'.

Puri was brought back to the present by a loud cheer as the last of Rohit's hair, deemed to be associated with his past life, dropped away.

The boy was still wailing as he was shown a reflection of himself in the mirror. The priest applied sandalwood to his forehead and blessed him. Envelopes of large rupee denominations (along with a traditional single rupee coin for luck) were laid before the child. And then everyone descended on the food.

Given the religious nature of the day, it was all vegetarian: gobi aloo, *pooris*, daal and *malai kofta*.

It was with a full stomach that Puri joined Rumpi and the rest of his family on the dance floor, where they strutted their stuff to the beat of Daler Mehndi.

• TWENTY-FOUR •

Puri was sleeping soundly on his office couch when the moustache thief entered through the window. Being a consummate professional and fancying himself as something of an artiste, he'd come well prepared – razor, can of shaving foam, even a little block of alum to treat nicks and cuts.

He began by kneeling down next to his victim and tying a towel around his neck so as to catch any wayward hairs. He inspected the perfectly formed handlebar moustache, appraising it as a sculptor might a block of virgin stone. There came a squirt from the can as a little foam was extracted and applied to the detective's upper lip. He opened a Sweeney-Todd-style razor and inserted a new blade. The steel glinted in the moonlight as it hovered a few inches above the detective's face. Then it began its descent. Slowly, as if in slow motion . . . closer. Puri felt the cold steel make contact with his skin.

With a cry, he sat up on the couch, his heart beating wildly.

He looked around him, convinced someone else was in the office with him, and putting a hand up to his face, felt his upper lip. His moustache seemed intact. Just to make sure, he made his way into his 'Executive WC'. His reflection in the mirror revealed everything in its proper place. Not a hair missing. It had all been a terrible dream.

'Thank the God,' he muttered before washing his hands and splashing cold water on his face.

He emerged to find that the mess in his office – pizza boxes, takeaway containers from Colonel's Kababz – was anything but imagined.

His operatives had all gathered at Most Private Investigators HQ late last night to plan the surveillance of the two ICT cricketers. Both Kamran Khan and Vikas Patil, the Indian batsman suspected of match fixing, were due to play on opposing teams at Kotla the next day and would be staying at the Maharajah Hotel.

It had been decided that Flush would work with a sidekick known as Gordon and shadow Kamran Khan. Facecream, with Tubelight as backup, would handle Vikas Patil. In the meantime, Flush was also working on hacking the players' email accounts and getting across their mobile phone lines.

Puri had reasoned that the same individual behind the killings of Full Moon, the Mumbai bookie and possibly Faheem Khan as well had now gained control of the match-fixing ring. It stood to reason, therefore, that this individual would now contact Kamran Khan and Vikas Patil and provide them with instructions for the forthcoming match. With any luck Most Private Investigators would be able to trace the messages to their source.

The attempt on his life had convinced Puri that Aga

was no longer in charge. Had he wanted the detective dead then surely he would have got the job done in Pakistan. This meant that Brigadier General Aslam had been telling the truth about the Americans grabbing him.

Someone else – an Indian living on Indian soil – had taken control of the illegal gambling business.

With the entire Most Private Investigators team engaged on the Khan case, Handbrake was assigned the task of visiting all the five-star hotels in Delhi to enquire if any mustachioed doormen had been hired in the last couple of days or if there were any job vacancies for which candidates were being sought.

Handbrake took the Ambassador, setting off at around ten; Puri meanwhile called for one of Randy Singh's taxis. His destination was the National Archives, where he wanted to check up on Mummy.

It wasn't that he didn't trust his mother. She'd made him a promise they would work as a team and could be counted on to share any information that came into her possession. There was every possibility, however, that she'd take her sweet time in doing so. Mummy had this tendency of interpreting things in her own particular way. She might decide that co-operating *actually* meant doing her own thing, at least temporarily, on the grounds that it was best for both of them. The fact that her phone had been switched off all morning didn't bode well for their partnership.

The taxi dropped him outside the National Archives at the intersection of Janpath and Rajpath, a stone's throw from India Gate, the heart of British New Delhi. He made his way along the front of the long colonial building with its grand red and brown sandstone facade and imperial columns, once emblematic of the Empire and suppression, but now much cherished in a city of architectural mediocrity.

Puri applied for a pass in the main reading room, where scholars were bent over Mughal parchments and rare Sanskrit manuscripts written on animal skin. From there a helpful librarian led him deep into the vaults. They passed through stacks groaning with great wedges of paper the colour of aged cheese and dusty box files bound in string. There wasn't a computer in sight, just the odd microfiche machine and blackboards with lists of categories and classifications chalked upon them – 'Foreign Deptt. Select (Secret) Committee 1756'; 'Persian Dispatches 1716–1881'; 'Deptt. of Ceded and Conquered Provinces 1803.'

Puri found Mummy sitting at a table surrounded by thick ledgers and piles of yellowing forms. Despite the daunting amount of paperwork, she was decidedly upbeat. 'Chubby, some progress is there!' she announced after explaining that her phone was out of range. 'See here.'

She'd been searching through the records pertaining to ration cards allocated to refugees in Delhi in 1947 and found a certain Manjit Singh listed.

'Manjit Singh was Saroya – sorry, Kiran Singh's father, na,' she reminded him.

'Yes, Mummy-ji,' said Puri, patiently.

'See, his native place is mentioned – Mandra. Here, also, it states he stayed in Purana Qila.'

Purana Qila, the walled ruins of the sixteenth-century

citadel of the Mughal Emperor Humayun, had become a refugee camp in 1947, housing thousands of the five million Sikhs and Hindus who arrived from West Pakistan.

'A forwarding address is listed there?' asked Puri.

'Unfortunately not. But all families got land, na. Thus Singh's address should be somewhere in here.'

She indicated the stack of seven or eight old box files lying next to her. They were all marked 'Gadgil Assurance Scheme'.

'I'll give you a hand, Mummy-ji.' Puri pulled up a chair. 'Shouldn't take too long, no,' he added.

'This is only part of an iceberg, Chubby. Rest is over there.'

Dozens more box files sat on the shelves. 'They're arranged in alphabetical order, is it?' asked the detective.

'Don't do joking, Chubby. It's all topsy and turvy. Nothing in the right order.'

'But this will take for ever, Mummy-ji,' he said, suddenly struck by the vastness of the task. The files, after all, contained paperwork pertaining to the allocation of land to some three million people.

'Do positivity, Chubby. Today I'm feeling very much lucky.'

At four o'clock Puri returned to ground level to check his messages and learned that James Scott had called from London. His enquiries into Patel and Patel, the company in Antwerp, had proven fruitful.

'They've been under investigation here in the UK,' he said when the detective called him back. 'As it happens, I know the officer in charge. Peter Kemp. Good man.'

Puri took 'good man' to mean that the colleague had been willing to share what he knew, albeit in confidence and most probably over a couple of pints of warm bitter.

'Seems the firm's been making regular payments to an account in Liechtenstein,' continued the ex Scotland Yard man. 'The account's owned by an Indian national. I can't give you a name; Peter doesn't have it himself. The authorities there won't release the details. Liechtenstein's a tax haven, as I'm sure you know. Very secretive. But he says the Government of India has the details.'

'How exactly?'

'Apparently your Finance Ministry petitioned the Liechtensteinians, or whatever you call them, for all accounts held by Indian citizens, citing tax evasion and money laundering.'

'When was that exactly?'

'Three years ago, Puri. All the details were handed over to New Delhi as part of a secret deal. Thirty or forty accounts in all, some allegedly containing hundreds of millions of dollars.'

Typical, thought the detective: the ruling party finds vast quantities of black money stashed away, knows exactly who's done the stashing and doesn't do a thing about it. Except perhaps use the information to elicit funding for their next election campaign.

'Most helpful of you, sir. I'll revert,' said the detective.

He wrote a quick note to Mummy, explaining that he had to return to the office, and left it at the front desk. He didn't expect to hear from her today. Nor tomorrow. Nor the day after that.

There were still dozens of files to search through – possibly more lurking yet undiscovered in the bowels of the National Archives.

By seven-thirty, with only half an hour remaining before closing time, Mummy had begun to wonder if perhaps her search might take many more days, perhaps even weeks. She sat back in her chair, rubbing her eyes: they had begun to sting after ten hours in the archives. She was hungry as well, having gone without her lunch. Time to call it a day.

Her friend Preeti passed by, reminding her that the archives would be closing in thirty minutes and that tomorrow was Maha Shivaratri, one of the biggest Hindu festivals of the year.

'Day after is an off as well,' she added. 'We're getting VVIP visit. That Maharani of Alwar is coming. She's donating all her family's private papers.'

'She'll be present all the day?'

'One hour maximum, but the DG uses any excuse to take a holiday.'

Mummy decided to make the best of the remaining half-hour and reached for yet another box file.

She was indeed very much lucky: Manjit Singh's land records lay at the bottom.

'Here it is, na!' she cried out, although by then there was no one else there to share her discovery.

The plot Manjit had been given was in the Karol Bagh area of west Delhi. She made a note of the number – 'T–5361, Block 7A' – and hurriedly gathered up her things.

Upstairs, Puri's note was waiting for her at the front desk. She slipped it into her pocket and then called her driver, Majnu.

'Pick me up right away, na.'

He started to whine about having to work late.

'*Chup!*' she interrupted. 'All day you're sitting idle, na! No duty is there. Now come! Hurry! No discussion.'

She disconnected the call and scrolled down the list of numbers on her phone until she came to 'Chubby Portable'. Her finger moved towards the dial button, but then she had second thoughts. Being a busy and successful private investigator, he'd probably been called away on important business, she reasoned. Surely, then, it made sense for her to go and search for the plot alone. Manjit Singh or his family might not be living there any longer, in which case Chubby would waste valuable time in coming to Karol Bagh.

Of course if she found that the Singhs were indeed still living at the same address, well, then, naturally, she would call him. Right away. Without fail.

Yes, that made perfect sense. This must be what Chubby meant by teamwork.

• TWENTY-FIVE •

Majnu, who had to be reminded no less than three times not to slouch behind the wheel, took the Upper Ridge Road, crossing the Delhi Ridge, a part of the ancient Aravalli Range and now a reserved forest. It was dark and where the road turned and undulated the headlights of the little Indica swept across rocky terrain thick with kair shrubs and babul trees. This was how most of the landscape surrounding Old and New Delhi had looked when Mummy arrived in the capital in 1947. In the winter, the banks of the Yamuna were carpeted pink with flocks of flamingos. Leopards sometimes strayed into the city. And it was not uncommon to find your path blocked by a king cobra. Once Mummy had even come across an enormous python with a head as big as a man's shoe, basking in the sun out in the garden.

She remembered Karol Bagh very differently as well: tents pitched on plots, their boundaries marked with lines of stones; the odd one-storey brick structure painted in whitewash; chickens clucking about on dusty roads. In the summer, the residents slept outside under a canopy of stars undimmed by smog. The cries of jackals sounded in the distance. At dawn, the call to prayer from Shah Jahan's Jamma Masjid reached them over the ramparts of the walled city.

Change had come gradually, sneaking up on Mummy street by street, building by building. Most of the *kothis* were replaced by three-, four-, even five-storey blocks. Gardens vanished beneath swathes of concrete. If you saw a cow these days it was wandering through traffic, chewing on a plastic bag.

As a member of the Punjabi Bagh Association, Mummy had always done what she could to help preserve public spaces and keep the colony clean. She was the first to criticise the lack of planning and the corruption of the local authorities. 'Moral fibre is totally lacking, na,' she often said of Delhi's elected representatives. Yet in her heart, Mummy was a city person, and the lack of aesthetics didn't bother her all that much. She thrived on the tamasha, on being in the middle of a crowd in the busy vibrant markets. The smell of *aloo tikki* frying in hot oil, the sight of dyers pulling cotton saris out of great vats of steaming liquid and twisting them dry, the haunting sound of *kirtan* spilling out from the gurdwara – all these things made her feel alive. Why Chubby had moved to Gurgaon was something she would never understand. The place had a manufactured quality about it – a kind of albino India. Mummy couldn't bear the idea of ending her days in such a place.

'Punjabi by birth, Punjabi by nature,' she often said with pride. 'We are big-hearted people, na?'

This was something Majnu, who was not Punjabi, would have done well to learn from, Mummy reflected as she watched him turn into West Extension Area, his face still long and sullen.

'What address, madam?' he asked with no enthusiasm.

'I told you, na! You're getting deafness or what? Block 7A. Straight, then left.'

She soon discovered that the plots allocated under the Gadgil Assurance Scheme no longer corresponded with today's house numbers. Mummy told Majnu to park – 'Don't sit idle, na! Do window washing!' – and then went and asked around the neighbourhood.

She knew more than a few locals and it took only half an hour to find the right address.

A square, three-storey block with narrow windows filled the plot. A nameplate on the door of the ground floor apartment bore Manjit Singh's name.

Mummy paused, a voice in her head reminding her that she should call Chubby and bring him up to date with her progress. At that moment, however, the door opened and an elderly man appeared. He looked frail, the bags under his eyes sagging like deflated balloons hanging from a light fitting the morning after a party.

'You're looking for someone, madam?' he asked in Punjabi.

'I'm searching for Shri Manjit Singh,' explained Mummy.

'He died two years back,' the man answered with a fatalistic air.

'I'm sorry to hear that. My condolences.'

'He was ninety-eight.' The man paused. 'Why are you looking for him?'

'I needed some information. Are you his son?'

'That's right: Hardeep Singh is my name.'

'I want to speak with you.'

'I was going for a walk. I always try to take a walk at this time.' He looked over her shoulder with a certain longing. The busy street held the promise of escape from domesticity.

'It's very important.'

Hardeep Singh sighed as if going to the front door and being prevented from getting any further was something he was used to. He opened it a little wider and invited Mummy inside.

'I'll tell Leela to make tea,' he said.

The living room was furnished with a couple of dowdy couches and armchairs, and a dining table finished in fake wood laminate. An almirah the green of tarnished brass contained a shrine stocked with images of the Sikh gurus. There were a few other personal belongings: a plaster ornament of a family of robin redbreasts perched on a snow-covered branch; a large teddy bear still wrapped in plastic and prominently displayed on a sideboard like a rare family heirloom. Bundles of old newspapers were piled up in one corner, ready to be sold at three rupees a kilo to the kabari wallah.

The Singhs were wealthy, Mummy reflected as her host went in search of his wife, the property alone being worth many crores. Thus their frugal existence was one of conditioning and habit. Every rupee that could be saved was put away, the number of light bulbs in the living room restricted to a total of one. The result was a murky twilight in which Mummy found herself struggling to make out the details of the family portraits hanging on the wall. The elderly man in the largest portrait was Manjit Singh, she decided. Judging by his style of clothes and the quality of the printing, he'd posed for the shot in a studio at some point in the early 1980s. Other pictures showed his offspring in more recent times – weddings, birthdays, the odd picnic. But of Mrs Manjit Singh, Kiran Singh and her two sisters there was no sign.

'That is my father, of course,' said Hardeep Singh when he returned to the living room and found Mummy still staring up at the wall.

'You came to Delhi in '47?' she asked, coming and seating herself on one of the couches.

'We arrived on a bullock cart, having lost everything,' said Hardeep. 'But my father knew printing. His father had owned a business in Rawalpindi. So he borrowed money and opened a press in Chandni Chowk. We printed newspapers, pamphlets, stationery. Then he got into boxes. He supplied all the sweet shops and packing houses. Things were very good for us in those days.'

'The business is still going?' asked Mummy.

'After my father retired, I took over. Then we started to face more and more competition. All the technology changed. It is all computerised today. Our shop is still there, but everything is lying idle.'

The story was not unfamiliar. Men like Manjit Singh struggled all their lives to improve the lot of their families, but their sons didn't prove as hard-working or resourceful. Mummy attributed this phenomenon to a flaw in the Punjabi family system. Sons were too pampered, in her opinion, and this made them lazy. If they inherited property from which they could derive a comfortable income, they simply sat around and did nothing. But of course their wives enjoyed no such privilege. It was their lot to keep the household ticking along. The sweeper-cum-toilet-cleaner and dishwashing *walli* required supervision; vegetables had to be purchased; meals prepared; children raised.

The preparation of chai was their remit, too, and soon Mrs Hardeep Singh appeared from the kitchen bearing a tray of steaming cups. A kindly looking woman with a gentle smile, she greeted Mummy politely before serving her. The two women then sat and talked for a while, exchanging social niceties and establishing their family credentials. They might have spent a pleasant hour or two in one another's company, but Hardeep Singh was growing impatient.

'Now tell me, madam,' he said, interrupting his wife mid-sentence. 'What's your interest in my father?'

'I'm trying to clear up a mystery – one that goes back to 1947,' explained Mummy.

'Oh?'

'Yes, you see in those days I was a volunteer for the Indian Recovery and Relief Operation.'

Mummy watched his reaction to see if her words had engendered any concern or suspicion. There was every possibility that he and his sister were in touch – that they had reconnected despite Kiran Singh's having adopted a new identity. But Hardeep Singh only frowned and asked, 'This was a government agency of some sort?'

'We were charged with rescuing Hindu and Sikh women from Pakistan,' she explained.

Hardeep Singh appeared to absorb this information and lapsed into silence over his tea. When he spoke again a moment or two later, it was on a different subject altogether. 'Delhi in those days was a very different place,' he said. 'You know, when we first came here there were only a few houses. There were some Madrasis around.' By Madrasi he meant South Indians: Tamils, Keralites, Kannadigas. 'We found their food very different. They ate *dosas* and *idlis* . . .'

Mummy listened patiently for a minute or two, used to the ramblings of Indian men, whose conversation often deviated with no warning – another consequence of male privilege. But then she spoke across him. Her tone was brutal. It was the only way.

'Now, I want to ask if you recognise this girl,' she said, handing him the photograph of Kiran Singh that Aslam had given Chubby.

It took a moment for Hardeep Singh to get his mind back to the present. 'Ah, yes, very good,' he said. 'But I can't see anything up close without my glasses.'

His wife suggested he might like to retrieve them from the breast pocket of his shirt. He did so, slipping them on, and then looked down at the photograph with marked indifference. The reaction, however, was instant. He squinted, furrowed his brow and stared intently at his guest.

'This is my youngest sister, Kiran,' he said. 'And that's our neighbour's car. This was taken in Mandra. Where did you get this?'

'From a former associate in Pakistan,' answered Mummy. 'The two of us found your sister in March 1948 in the village of Bajal and tried to help—'

'March 1948?' he interrupted. 'No, you're mistaken. Kiran died in August of the previous year.'

'You're sure?'

He gave a truculent nod. 'Yes, of course.'

'Were you there?' she asked.

Hardeep Singh didn't answer. His eyes met Mummy's and held them for a moment. She detected shame and guilt.

'I met the girl in that picture in March 1948,' she said, persevering. 'And I wasn't the only person to meet her. I received that photograph from a Pakistani military officer who was there with me that day. We brought Kiran to a camp. But she didn't want to stay and that night she ran away.'

'Impossible,' he insisted. 'You've got her mixed up with someone else.'

Hardeep Singh lapsed into silence again, staring intently at the photograph. Mummy felt a hand on her arm.

'Forgive me, but I can't see there's anything to be gained from raking up this past history,' said Mrs Singh. 'It all happened so long ago. What purpose is to be served by bringing up these painful memories?'

'Normally, I would agree,' replied Mummy. 'My family suffered losses as well. Those memories still cause me great pain. However, this is different. You see, I believe Kiran is alive. She's living here in Delhi.'

Hardeep Sing's eyes flashed with anger. 'That's enough,' he snapped. 'You've no business coming here and saying such things, madam. Now I want you to leave and don't come back.'

He was pointing towards the door. Mummy didn't budge. 'All I ask is that you look at these,' she said. 'I believe one of them is your sister Kiran.'

She held out two pictures, both cut from the social pages of Indian magazines. The first was of Megha Dogra, the second Jasmeet Bhatia.

'Please take a look, sir,' Mummy implored him. 'I need to know for sure myself.'

But Hardeep Singh was resolute in his decision. 'I told you to leave, madam,' he said, finger still extended towards the door.

Mummy could see it would do no good to argue with him. She began to gather up her things and apologised for having bothered them. And then Mrs Singh spoke up, addressing her husband in a soothing tone: 'At least look at them,' she said. 'Otherwise, you'll never know. What if Kiran is alive? How can you live without knowing?'

She took the pictures from Mummy and brought them over to him. 'Come now, what's the harm?' she asked. 'You've nothing to lose.'

Hardeep Singh gave a petulant shake of his head. 'I don't want to know – even if it's true, I don't want to know,' he said.

'Of course you do. Now come. This lady is only trying to help,' she said and laid the photographs in his lap.

He ignored them for a long while and then turned his eyes down.

The first picture drew a blank. But the sight of the second caused his lower lip to start trembling.

'That's her,' he said in a diminished tone. 'Even after all these years . . .' He looked up again. His face showed dismay. 'But it's impossible,' he continued. 'I . . . I heard the shots. Counted them. One, two, three, four . . .'

The picture dropped to the floor as he buried his face in his hands and began to sob. Mrs Singh put an arm around his shoulders.

'Mother begged him to do it, not to let her and my sisters fall into their hands,' he murmured through his tears. 'The mob was getting closer. We could hear them – like animals. Father knew what had to be done. He took them inside the house . . . My brother and I waited outside . . . I was only fourteen.'

Kiran Singh, her sisters and her mother had all been killed that night. But not at the hands of the Muslims.

Manjit Singh had made sure his womenfolk weren't seized by the mob.

Kiran, though, had survived. The bullet, *her* bullet, had missed its target and she had played dead.

No wonder she hadn't wanted to be reunited with her family, reflected Mummy, the tragedy of it all sweeping over her. It would have meant certain death.

'I'm so sorry,' she said in a faint voice.

Hardeep Singh didn't hear her. Nor did he seem to notice her collect up her things and steal from the room.

Mummy would have to return another day; it was her duty to do so as an officer of the Indian Recovery and Relief Operation.

Quietly, she closed the door behind her and stepped out into the evening air. She made her way to the front gate in a daze, her heart aching with grief.

It was only after she'd reached the car that it dawned on her that she now knew the identity of Faheem Khan's killer. Yet somehow, Mummy derived little satisfaction from her discovery.

• TWENTY-SIX •

At eight o'clock, as the rest of the Most Private Investigators team set off from Khan Market to target the Indian batsman suspected of match fixing, Flush checked into room 704 of the Maharajah Hotel.

It was as close to paradise as he'd ever come. The bed was enormous and very bouncy. There was a little fridge stocked with Angrezi liquor and imported chocolate bars. The TV was forty inches wide. And chicken nuggets were available from room service (which, incidentally, worked round the clock).

Not that he was there to partake of any of these luxuries, of course. Boss had been firm on this point. 'It is not a party,' he said.

Flush's assignment was to get a camera inside Kamran Khan's suite and the only way to do so was to send in Gordon. Hence the need for an adjacent room on the fourth floor.

'Sir, would be needing your bed turned down?' asked the bellboy who'd carried up Flush's cases – four heavy pieces in all, containing monitors, a couple of laptops, his (illegal) direct-to-satellite communications system and the latest edition of *CHIP* magazine, which featured a cover story on 'The Power of DLNA'.

'"Turned down" means?' asked Flush.

'The top sheet pulled back – so, um, well, you can get into bed.'

The operative frowned. He might have grown up in a village, but he'd lived in the city since he was fifteen.

'No need,' he said. 'I know how.'

Flush handed the bellboy a woefully inadequate tip, saw him to the door and then started to unpack. Once he had his direct-to-satellite system up and running and the jamming protocol operational, he checked that the scanning software he was using to monitor Khan and Vikas Patil's mobile phone signals was still active. Mrs Chadha in the communications rooms in the office was monitoring both lines and Tubelight was keeping abreast of the cricketers' emails on his smartphone.

Lastly, Flush opened the case that contained Gordon and gave him an affectionate pet. He was three inches long, remotely controlled (range: fifty feet) and equipped with night vision, a pinhole camera and a transmitter housed in his tail. The most ingenious thing about Gordon, however, was the suction system Flush had designed for his little feet. This allowed him to crawl up walls and ceilings and hang around – literally – pretending to be hunting insects. The fact that he was green with beady black eyes and a realistic little tongue meant that no one took much notice of him. Just like a real gecko.

'Happy hunting,' Flush told him as he placed his creation in the air conditioning vent. He returned to the desk, booted the remote control software and plugged in his joystick. Gordon the Gecko came to life and a green night vision image of the inside of the air conditioning duct appeared on his screen. Flush eased the joystick forward and his animatronic creation began to move. There were some thirty feet of duct to cover, the length of four rooms in all. Flush estimated it would take him three hours to reach his destination, assuming he didn't encounter any obstacles along the way. Then would come the most challenging part of the operation: manoeuvring Gordon down through the air conditioning outlet and into position on the ceiling.

Handbrake, who'd spent the day visiting most of Delhi's five-star hotels without coming across any newly appointed mustachioed doormen, drove Boss out of Khan Market at eight-thirty.

The silver sedan followed them down Lodhi Road towards the gardens and it was here that Puri suddenly ordered his driver to stop.

'You forgot something, Boss?'

'Not at all. I want a word with our friends back there. Better you keep this.' The detective wrapped his pistol in a handkerchief and handed it to the driver. 'Might be required later. I'm counting on you to follow behind.'

Puri exited the car and walked back down the road. When he came to the silver sedan, he knocked on the passenger window. It went down an inch and a pair of mirrored sunglasses surmounted by a thick pair of eyebrows appeared in the gap.

'Tell him I believe we can do business. Five minutes is required only.'

Puri had known for a couple of days now that these were Sandeep Talwar's men. They were there as a form of intimidation, a reminder that he shouldn't go poking around in Sahib's business.

The window closed again and the detective waited on the pavement, guessing that Talwar's goons were phoning for instructions. Presently, the back door swung open and he climbed on to the empty seat.

Neither of the two men up front uttered a single word as they drove north. Their abstention from speech coupled with their immutable expressions were rendered all the more forbidding by the surreal quality of streetlight that penetrated the car's tinted glass windows. The city's familiar landscape, too, looked distinctly spooky, the pedestrians on the pavements like zombies marching through a cloying Transylvanian mist.

Puri was expecting to be escorted to the Hotel Lakshmi again or perhaps Talwar's residence, but soon the sedan reached the deserted streets of Old Delhi. They turned on to Asaf Ali Road, where rats scurried through litter and blanketed figures lay on parked wooden carts. Puri caught glimpses of unloved *havelis* smothered in cobwebs of phone lines and power cables, and packs of battling street dogs.

And then, like a mirage, it appeared in a blaze of light: an art deco building lit up like a giant gumball machine. THE DELITE announced a neon sign above the grand entrance, and above this was a film poster for a remake of a remake.

The sedan pulled up in front of the entrance, one of the goons leaned back and opened the door, and Puri took his cue. He made his way up the steps, remembering all the times he'd come here as a boy to watch some of his favourite films – *Waqt, Aradhana* and the unforgettable curry western *Sholay*. The hall had been packed in those days for every show, but after TV and VCRs came along, the Delite, like so many of India's single-screen theatres, had fallen on hard times, condemned to Bollywood B movies for rickshaw wallahs – mostly semi-pornographic flicks about sexually perverted Indian werewolves.

Puri hadn't been back since the theatre had undergone a complete renovation and started screening mainstream Bollywood again. Beyond the glistening doors, he marvelled at the transformation – it was all Italian marble, teak wall panelling, polished brass handrails and art deco lights. The food counter looked like something out of a classic American diner, with an old-fashioned popcorn maker and soda machine manned by staff in vintage uniforms.

He found the ticket booth unmanned, a SOLD OUT sign hanging in the window. The usher in the foyer was expecting him, however, and led Puri to the auditorium.

It was deserted save for one occupied seat – a single figure sat near the front.

Puri made his way down the aisle and sat down next to him. Sandeep Talwar made it clear he did not want to be interrupted by keeping his eyes glued to the screen, his hand feeding his mouth with popcorn. The movie was not the one advertised on the programme outside; Sahib had apparently demanded an oldie, the old Dev Anand classic *Guide*. It was a favourite of the detective's too and he could not help but relax into his chair, enraptured by

Waheeda Rehman's beauty and the accompanying lyrics. 'Day recedes, oh, night remains. You won't come, but your memory haunts me!'

By the intermission, when the lights suddenly came on, Puri had become lost in the tragedy of the story.

'One of my favourites,' said Sandeep Talwar, finally acknowledging him. 'You know, it was in this very theatre that I watched it for the first time: 1965. God only knows how many times I've seen it since. Probably a world record. I should get my name in *Limca*.'

The usher appeared carrying a tray. On offer were some of the theatre's famous *maha* samosas.

'Heard you had some trouble,' said Talwar as he munched on the first of three.

'One comes to expect such things in my line of work,' said Puri, who'd restricted himself to just one samosa.

'Must be better ways of making a living. I understand you served in our armed forces, Puri. Then there was some trouble in Shimla, I'm told.'

Sahib had obviously been doing his homework, gathering what ammunition he could. It was what he excelled at – exploring people's weaknesses and exploiting them to his advantage. Not for nothing was it whispered that he retained a cabinet post because of his stockpile of smut.

That Puri (thanks to Mummy) had discovered Sandeep Talwar's greatest secret and could, with the dial of a number, send him into a tailspin provided the detective with a good deal of gratification, not to mention reassurance. But he hadn't come to make threats. He wanted a trade. The two of them had a mutual enemy, after all.

'I was present at Mohib Alam's satta party when his

paan was poisoned – as you are very much aware,' began Puri.

There was subtext to this statement: Talwar had been the one who'd tipped off Full Moon, warned him that he might get a visit from a certain jasoos. In doing so, he'd almost gotten Puri killed. But that hardly mattered now.

'There and then I assumed Alam was done away with on Aga's orders – one of those mafia vendettas over territory or some woman or whatnot. Normal thing. But then I came to know that Aga is out of commission, so to speak.'

Puri had Talwar's full attention now, even if the man maintained an air of detachment.

'Means he was murdered by someone here in India, only. And I've the key to finding out who exactly,' added Puri.

Sahib absorbed the information at his leisure. 'I take it you need some information,' he said eventually, before sinking his teeth into another samosa.

The detective explained about the Liechtenstein bank account held by a trust and how the name had been passed in secret to the Indian government.

'Seems you should be having it somewhere in your files,' said the detective.

The lights dimmed. The second half of the film was starting.

'I'll get you what you want,' said Talwar. 'But in return I'll expect a name. That is, before anyone else.'

Dev Anand's face appeared up on the screen – young, dashing, his dark quiff swept back. Puri was tempted to stay and watch but thought better of it.

* * *

Facecream brought two female colleagues, Lovejit and Mini, along to the MIRAGE, the hotel's nightclub. With their curvaceous figures, short skirts and long manes of dark hair, they turned heads while making their way to the bar. Their target, the Indian batsman Vikal Patil, was sitting over in one of the booths with a couple of his teammates and soon sent them a bottle of champagne. But then disaster struck: the Delhi Cowboys cheerleader troupe arrived. They were all blonde and blue-eyed with bared midriffs and flirtatious smiles. And the Indian men, including the players, couldn't keep their eyes off them.

'What's with our guys and these gori girls?' complained Lovejit, incensed at all the blatant gawping and wolf whistling.

'They're complete bimbos,' said Mini with a sneer. 'I overheard a couple of them talking in the ladies' room and one of them said, all excited, '"Did you realise, like, there's actually a place called Kashmir? I just thought it was a kind of wool!"'

The three women burst out laughing. However, things were not going to plan. Vikas Patil had taken to the dance floor with one of the cheerleaders.

After a couple of songs, he took her back to his table, where they started kissing.

Facecream decided to go to Plan B. She called Tubelight and then waited until her mark stepped back on to the dance floor with the cheerleader. Mini and Lovejit joined them, flailing their arms around and pretending to be drunk. The latter bumped into Vikas Patil, almost knocking him over.

'Oh my God so stoopid of me!' she screeched. 'I'm so, so sorreeee! I just can't believe it's you! Amaaazing! I'm like your biggest faaan. You wanna dance? No? OK, but later maybe? OK, but can I get your autograph? OK, well nice meeting you, gorgeous!'

Facecream made her way out of the club with the cricketer's room keycard in her possession.

Having updated Tubelight and taken the lift to the seventh floor. As she approached room 702. On cue, the hotel fire alarm went off. Within seconds, she had the door open.

It took her less than five minutes to install a pinhole camera and transmitter in the AC duct.

She called Flush to check if he was receiving a clear picture.

'Crystal,' he said.

Five minutes later, Facecream was sipping an 800-rupee mojito at the bar and the keycard was back in its rightful pocket.

Puri received the information he'd requested from Talwar shortly after midnight.

'Rawat Trust,' read the SMS.

The detective repeated 'Rawat' over and over again, sure there was something familiar about the name. He searched through his notebook and found it mentioned in his jottings from his interview with Satish Bhatia, the Call Centre King. His mother had been born there.

'By God!' exclaimed the detective. And without a moment's hesitation, he called his mother.

*　　*　　*

To elicit Rinku's help again, Puri had to sit up drinking Royal Challenge with him all night and exchange a lot of extremely bawdy *sardaar-ji* jokes.

At 6 a.m. he drove to the Maharajah Hotel where he found Flush eating his fifth plate of chicken nuggets.

'There's a problem with Gordon, Boss,' he reported.

'The gecko?'

'He dropped through the AC outlet on to the floor in Khan's room. He's still making his way up the wall. See there.'

Flush pointed to the 'Gordon Cam' window on his laptop screen. It showed a close-up of a wall with a ceiling beyond.

'He's about halfway up.'

'Where's Khan?'

'Just got out of the shower.'

'Turn that thing around.'

'He'll be spotted, Boss.'

'Do it!'

Flush pushed the joystick to the left. The camera turned accordingly and the room came into view. Khan was sitting on the edge of his bed clipping his toenails.

'How about Vikas Patil?' asked Puri.

'Still sleeping. He had company.' Flush looked flushed. 'It was, um, *lively*, Boss.'

Puri pulled up a chair and sat down.

'What's that you're eating?' he asked.

'Chicken nuggets.'

The detective reached over, took the last one and bit into it.

'Not at all bad,' he said.

*   *   *

Puri ordered two more portions for himself, as well as a pot of strong, black coffee, and sat back and watched.

It was a long couple of hours. Vikas Patil didn't rise until nine-thirty (the cheerleader having left in the middle of the night). He took a shower, ate a plate of pasta for breakfast, called an unidentified girl and talked dirty with her for a while, and then sat in his towel watching an American sitcom. Khan meanwhile said his prayers, called his mother in Pakistan and stood for a long while looking out the window.

Both men appeared to be biding their time; occasionally they both checked their watches. At ten-thirty, Khan's hotel phone rang. He answered it, listened for a few seconds and, without saying a word, replaced the receiver. Then he reached for the copy of *The Times of India* lying on the coffee table and opened the classifieds section. His back was now turned to the camera.

'Jaldi! Move the bloody thing across the wall!' ordered Puri.

The gecko started to crawl forward. By the time it had reached a position overlooking Khan's shoulder, the cricketer had found what he was looking for in the paper and, using his copy of the Koran, decoded the message. The detective could only watch him jot down some figures on a piece of paper, stuff it into his trouser pocket and leave the room.

Vikas Patil received no such call before changing into his match colours and heading down to the lobby to join the rest of the team.

Puri called Brigadier Mattu. 'Sir, one emergency is there,' he explained. 'By chance you've a copy of today's *Times* lying with you?'

• TWENTY-SEVEN •

Almost two hours later, Puri reached the top of the long flight of stairs leading to the Kotla Stadium VVIP stand. He was out of breath, beads of sweat trickling down his face. The usher on the door eyed him with concern. 'Do you need to sit down?' he asked in Hindi.

'I'm very much fine,' replied the detective. He took a big gulp of air before adding, 'Just my lunch actually – *golgappa.*'

The usher nodded sympathetically. It was common knowledge that once you started eating golgappas it was very hard to stop.

'Take a minute, sir. No hurry.'

The detective checked his watch. 'Match begins in five minutes, is it?'

The usher's answer was drowned out by the noise of a group of other guests coming up the stairs behind them. They flashed their invitations before entering the box.

'Match begins at twelve-thirty, sir,' replied the usher. 'Cowboys won the toss. They'll be batting first.'

Puri could feel the rhythm of his breathing slowing

down. His complexion was cooling as well. But the tension roiled unabated in his gut. Everything was now riding on Brigadier Mattu. If he couldn't establish which of the messages in the *Times* classifieds had been intended for Kamran Khan then everything, all the efforts of the past forty-eight hours, would be for nothing.

Worse, there might not be another opportunity to catch red-handed the mastermind who was running the gambling syndicate.

Puri waited another couple of minutes, checking his mobile phone repeatedly to make sure he was getting a signal. He debated whether or not to call his father-in-law to find out if he had made any progress and decided against it. Brigadier Mattu needed to concentrate. Every minute, every second, counted.

A roar rose from inside Kotla Stadium – the crowd welcomed the batsmen to the field.

'Match is about to begin, sir,' said the usher.

It was now or never. Puri took out his invitation card, the complimentary one Satish Bhatia the Call Centre King had sent to him after their meeting, and gave it to the usher. But as the doors swung open, a voice called out from down the stairs.

'Chubby, you wait, na!'

Puri turned around to find his mother making her way towards him. 'What are you doing here? I told you to wait in the car,' he said.

'But I saw her, na. She and her husband. They're very much present!'

'Doesn't matter. We agreed. Now go home. I'll call you later.'

'No, Chubby, you listen,' she insisted, reaching the top of the stairs. 'Visiting Hardeep Singh's house unaccompanied – it was my mistake no doubt about it. Your getting *so* angry was totally one hundred per cent justified, also. But I've every and all rights to be here. Without my assistance her identity would not be known. It is only proper we two do conclusion of the case together.'

Puri shook his head. There was too much at stake to risk having his mother coming inside with him: the resolution of three murders and, with any luck, the breaking up of the Syndicate.

'The invitation is for one and one *only*,' he said.

'Actually, sir, the invitation is for two,' interrupted the usher. 'See here . . . it says "for yourself and one guest".'

'See,' said Mummy with a smile, offering her son her arm. 'Now come.'

Puri didn't have time to argue with her. But he wasn't about to agree to her demand without driving home his advantage once and for all.

'Mummy-ji, I want your word that after today you will not get involved in any further investigation.'

She responded with a wounded expression. 'How you can say that, Chubby? I did solution of the case after all.'

'That's not the point, Mummy-ji.'

'You don't think I proceeded in a right and proper way?'

'You've done well – better than well, in fact.' His voice sounded sterner than he intended and he tried to soften his tone. 'But I've told you before, no? At your age and all you should not be running around. It is not a mummy's role, actually.'

Mummy folded her arms. 'Fine, na,' she said in an indignant tone. 'If that is your wish, Chubby. You've my word and such.'

Another roar came from the stadium. The first ball of the match had been bowled. Puri took his mother by the arm.

'Just one question is there, Chubby,' she said before they entered the box. 'If and when, that is after today, any small matter should arise . . . there's nothing stopping me bringing it to your attention, na?'

He eyed her wearily.

'What type of small matter, exactly?'

'Someone facing difficulty or requiring assistance, for example.'

'Wanting *professional* assistance, in other words.'

'Correct.'

'Then I'll do whatever is in my power to help, Mummy-ji. It's my duty, after all. Now come. We've a mystery to conclude.'

Inside the VVIP stand, they found themselves in distinguished company once again. Many of the great and the good who'd been at the Durbar dinner were present, most of them gathered around the bar. Puri spotted Sandeep Talwar and his wife, Harnam, chatting to that foulmouthed woman Neetika Sahini. Industrialist Ram Dogra was in attendance, as was his wife, Megha – both in conversation with Mrs Anita Bhangu, the pooch lover.

The detective found Satish Bhatia, the Call Centre King, relaxing in one of the armchairs in front of the floor-to-ceiling glass pane that overlooked the field.

'Hearties apologies for the interruption, sir,' said Puri as he greeted him. 'Just I wanted to extend my greetings – and thank you, actually. For the invitation, that is. Most kind of you.'

'The least I could do,' said Bhatia as he stood up to shake the detective's hand. 'I'm glad you could make it.'

'This is my Mummy-ji,' continued Puri. 'She's a number one fan of cricket, actually.'

Bhatia greeted her with a polite namaste. 'Pleased you could be here, Auntie-ji,' he said.

'Your own mother is present, also, na?' asked Mummy.

'She was.' Bhatia looked around the stand but couldn't find her. 'Must have gone to the ladies' room.'

There were two empty armchairs next to him.

'Don't mind if we join you?' asked Puri.

'Well, actually, I'm waiting—'

'So kind of you,' said the detective as he sat down and and took in the view. He could make out troupes of cheerleaders performing along the boundary. Ripples passed through swathes of fans like wind through a wheat field.

Somewhere down there was Rinku, waiting.

'This is the life, no?' added Puri as Mummy took the empty armchair to his left.

'It has its perks, Mr Puri,' said Bhatia, who had one eye on the match and the other on his BlackBerry. 'But sometimes I miss being in the stands surrounded by all the fans. You feel closer to the game down there, a part of it. Up here . . . well, you quickly lose touch.'

Puri watched one of the opening batsmen smack a delivery for six and the stadium's giant screen light up:

BAZOOKA! The euphoria sounded muffled through the glass. Bhatia was right: it wasn't the same up here in this ivory tower.

'Looks like Kamran Khan's next,' he commented as the Pakistani prepared to make his approach from the south end of the field.

Puri checked his mobile phone. Still nothing from his father-in-law.

'Any progress, Mr Puri?' asked Bhatia.

'With my investigation, sir?'

'What else?'

'Undoubtedly, sir. The pieces of the puzzle are coming together, actually. Just one or two remaining to be put in place.'

'You sound confident.'

'Always.'

Khan delivered his first ball, a perfect delivery that forced the batsman on to his back foot.

'Well bowled!' called out Bhatia with a clap of his hands that was somewhat hampered by his BlackBerry. 'He's in good form. Amazing that he's back in the game so quickly after what happened.'

'I believe he's returned out of fear for his life,' said Puri. 'Someone is threatening him. Making him believe he'll meet the same fate as his father if he doesn't play.'

'Why do you say that?' asked Bhatia.

'I was in Pakistan few days back and met with him.'

'You were in Pakistan, Mr Puri? Didn't you call it *enemy territory*? I'm amazed.'

'Sir, I do not mind admitting that I was full of apprehension. So long I've lived with hatred for that nation, actually.

Reality on the ground, though, was quite different. I found the people most accommodating and hospitable. No animosity was there. One distinguished gentleman provided me with a most important breakthrough in the case, also.'

'Well I'm glad to hear it.'

'Yes, sir. Whole thing – going there, crossing the border – was a life-changing experience we can say. Made me realise something, actually. We people carry around baggage we don't even realise we're carrying.'

'That's very profound, Mr Puri,' murmured Bhatia, eyes still fixed on his BlackBerry screen.

Mummy had turned in her chair and was surveying the company, searching for Kiran Singh. Puri placed one hand on her arm and gave it a pat as if to say, 'All in good time.'

Finally, his phone rang.

'Don't mind, haa?' he said to Bhatia, answering it as he stood up.

The detective began to pace up and down in front of the window. 'Haa . . . haa . . . haa,' he said, blocking his host's view.

Bhatia, visibly irritated, signalled for him to move out of the way.

'So sorry, sir, foolish of me,' Puri apologised, one hand over the receiver. He shifted to one side. 'Haa . . . haa . . . haa,' he repeated, adding in a loud voice, 'Very good, very good! Send me SMS with the details, sir . . . Good of you. I would be coming round later. We'll celebrate. Something stronger than your usual tomato soup.'

The text message came through a minute later. Puri forwarded it to Rinku and resumed his seat. The tension in his gut began to ease.

'Seems I've got hold of another piece of the puzzle,' said Puri, perfectly sanguine.

'Oh?'

'Yes, the identity of the killer is now known to me, in fact.'

'Someone at the dinner that evening?'

'Undoubtedly.'

'But why kill the old man?'

'Seems he did not.'

Bhatia sent Puri a puzzled look. 'I'm confused. Didn't you just say you know who killed Faheem Khan?'

'Actually, I was referring to the gentleman who ordered the death of the two bookies.'

'Bookies?'

'Yes, sir. See, they were involved in match fixing and all. Faheem Khan, also. The night he met his fate eating butter chicken, he had one meeting with a bald gentleman, name of Mohib Alam. It took place – the meeting, that is – on the lawn of the Durbar, directly outside the banquet hall. By chance I was witness to it. Another gentleman was, also. That gentleman put two and two together so to speak and thus realised Khan and Alam were engaged in match fixing.'

'And this individual poisoned Khan?'

'No, sir. Seems that murderous act was carried out by another individual.'

Bhatia's smile was coldly sceptical. 'Two murderers, Mr Puri?'

'Delhi bookie Mohib Alam was poisoned by a hit man posing as a paan wallah. He used aconite – a cunning ploy of the gentleman who hired his services. It was his idea to make it look as if Alam's murder and that of Faheem Khan were connected.'

'But they weren't?'

'Mummy-ji believes the motive for Faheem Khan's death was another one, totally unconnected to cricket in fact.'

Bhatia's mouth twitched into a smile. 'With all due respect, Mr Puri, is your Mummy-ji really in a position to know?'

'That we will know for sure within the hour.'

The ball was knocked deep into the stands again and everyone in the VVIP seats began to applaud.

'I'm still confused,' said Bhatia. Puri noticed his left foot tapping on the floor. 'You said there were *three* murders.'

'Correct. Another bookie was murdered in Mumbai, also. He was killed on orders of the same gentleman present on the terrace.' Puri paused for a beat. 'That individual in question is a most cunning and capable person – a topper,' he continued. 'In the past six months, only, he's taken over the running of the entire illegal gambling syndicate in India.'

'You've strayed into the realm of Bollywood,' said Bhatia, smiling indulgently. 'Everyone knows Aga controls the gambling business.'

'Used to, sir. Past tense. Seems our American friends grabbed hold of him. As of now he's rotting in some cell. The topper I mentioned came to know this. He's a computer genius, actually. Thus he was able to access the Pentagon system where he read certain top secret files.'

'Pentagon? Hacking? It all sounds pretty far-fetched to me.'

Down on the field, Khan was preparing to bowl his fourth over. Puri had timed his revelations perfectly.

'Allow me to prove it to you, sir. The second ball of this over will be a wide.'

'You couldn't possibly know that,' said Bhatia, with a dismissive, peremptory snort. But his eyes remained fixed on the field nonetheless. He watched Khan make his approach, as graceful as ever – watched as the delivery bounced a good two feet wide of the crease.

'You see, sir, I've a topper working for me, also. One hour back, only, he discovered the message in the *Times* classified pages.'

Bhatia didn't flinch. His gaze remained fixed on the field.

Puri continued: 'Most ingenious, sir – the whole operation, in fact,' he said. 'A call centre is the perfect cover for running a gambling operation. Rows of operators sitting at desks in front of computers and wearing headsets and all. Those on the top floor of your building are not selling life insurance or booking airline tickets, but taking bets directly from punters across India. Fact that you are offering more favourable odds means that most of Aga's bookies started passing on their risk to you. But one thing you would not tolerate was match fixing. Certainly not by others. Thus you hired a hit man. That left the field open, so to speak. You knew which players were involved. You cracked their encryption code, also. And thus earlier today you sent them coded messages – which I had the good fortune to intercept.'

'These are dangerous allegations you're making, Mr Puri,' said Bhatia, his tone distinctly menacing.

'I believe you are the one who should be more concerned.'

'You're threatening me, Mr Puri?'

'Not threatening, sir – *promising*. That is, unless you can pay your debts.'

'Debts?'

'Allow me to explain. See, I happen to know a certain individual who is most fond of betting on cricket. When he came to know I'd come by certain match-fixing information, he was naturally interested to know more. Unfortunately this individual is fond of Indian Made Foreign Liquor, also, and last night, only, he got to drinking a good deal. Thus his tongue started wagging and he passed on what was naturally confidential information to his buddies – and seems they in turn shared it around also. Right across India, in fact.'

Puri paused for a moment. 'You remember Khan's last wide ball – one I predicted earlier? That one proved my information is one hundred per cent correct. Therefore my friend and many of his buddies, also, will be placing large amounts on the next delivery, a full toss going for a sixer, I believe.'

Bhatia gave a sharp glance at the field, where Khan was about to make his approach. He pressed redial on his phone and held it to his ear. His foot was tapping at double the pace now. His glasses had slipped down his nose and he pushed the rims back up against the bridge, his Rolex jangling loose on his thin wrist. The ball went for a full toss. Vikas Patil knocked it clear over the boundary for six. Bhatia let his arms fall down on to the arms of his chair. A tinny-sounding voice came out of the BlackBerry.

'Hello, hello? Sir, are you there?' It went unanswered. Bhatia's finger pressed the disconnect button. He turned in his seat to face the detective and said, 'You don't know who you're dealing with, Mr Puri.'

'That is something of a stale line, no? And furthermore, it is one hundred and fifty per cent inaccurate. Even the existence of your Liechtenstein account is known to me. The name, Rawat Trust, gave you away actually. You told me yourself Rawat is your mother's native place.' Puri sounded triumphant as he added, 'No, sir, I regret to inform you it is over for you. I've taken the bails off your wickets, so to speak. Umpire's decision is most definitely "out".'

The Call Centre King leaned towards him. 'Believe me, Mr Puri, I'll get even with you if it's the last thing I do,' he said.

'Sir, I believe you have tried once before and failed. Better you look to your affairs, only.'

Bhatia stood up abruptly and stormed off through the throng of VVIPs, making for the exit without his mother.

'You're letting him get away, na,' said Mummy.

'Not to worry,' Puri answered, signalling the waiter to bring him a drink. 'With his identity out in the open, he's in hot water. The hottest, actually. I would not want to be in his chappals for one minute.'

'He'll make a full confession, na?'

'Most probably to the Americans, Mummy-ji. They want him for hacking their computers, after all. Here in India his life is not worth two *paisa*. Police, *netas*, corporators – entire Nexus will be after him, also Sandeep Talwe will want his head on a platter. Bhatia was his bag man,

Mohib Alam killed. All India is into gambling these days and no one likes a match fixer.'

The waiter returned with a large whisky and a fizzing *nimboo paani*.

Mummy now had a clear view of Kiran Singh.

She found it hard to believe that this was the same woman who'd been imprisoned in that foul hole by Faheem Khan sixty-odd years ago. Ageing was the best disguise of all and it had done its work effectively. All traces of her rural origins had been expunged. She had become a woman of refinement with a distinguished bearing. Watching her, Mummy could believe that her reputation as a caring individual who gave generously of her time and wealth to the less fortunate had been well earned. Certainly no one would ever have guessed the tragedy she'd endured – witnessing the execution of her mother and sisters at the hands of her own father; escaping death by what must have been a matter of millimetres; being abducted and violated by that animal.

It would have destroyed most women. But she was strong. Strong enough to smuggle herself into India. To build a new life for herself. To take revenge when the opportunity finally, unexpectedly, presented itself all these decades later.

Mummy guessed that it had probably been in Delhi that she'd met her adopted mother, Harjot Ghatwal. Bereft of her husband and children, the widow had mistaken Kiran Singh for her own daughter. Or perhaps the two women had adopted one another, come to a mutual under-standing. Either way, Kiran Singh had become Megha Ghatwal, later marrying businessman Ram Dogra.

But no one could ever fully escape their past.

'It's always there, na, like a ghost doing haunting,' said Mummy as she and Puri sat discussing how to proceed. 'Myself, I've tried to forget – memories of those terrible times and such. But it is hard. Just they're popping up from time to time. Sometimes in my dreams. Other times while going to buy milk.'

Mummy's throat had gone dry. She wetted it with a sip of her drink before continuing. 'Every time I can see clearly his face,' she said, referring to her brother, Anil. 'Just a boy he was, na. Never hurt a fly. So scared and terrified. Begging those boys to let him go. I can see their faces also. So much hatred is there. Then he is gone, dragged away. Just I hear his screaming – and . . . it's over.'

Puri closed his eyes. 'Mummy-ji, I'm sorry. What all you went through I cannot imagine in a thousand years,' he said.

'I was not alone, Chubby. Everyone did suffering, na. Hindu *and* Muslim. Our people were killing so many of their people, also. Children, babies, old women – no one was spared. Responsibility is on our heads also.'

'How can you say that, Mummy-ji? They murdered your brother,' said Puri, almost pleading with her.

'Those who did that thing were human beings, na. We should ask ourselves why human beings behave in such a way. Otherwise nothing can change.'

Puri frowned. 'You've forgiven Anil's killers, is it?' he asked.

'Not at all. I want justice, same as Kiran Singh. But doesn't mean I have hatred of all Pakistani or Muslim people, na.'

The match was still being played. Indifferent to the game, she watched the batsmen running up and down.

'Mummy-ji, one question is there,' asked Puri.

'Would I do revenge?'

He nodded.

'Answer is no, Chubby. Definitely. But for Kiran Singh it is different, na.'

'Why exactly?'

'To this very day, the names of Anil's murderers, they remain totally unknown to my good self. But she . . . she got abused by this man personally in the worst way. That is something different. Just imagine coming face to face with this man after so many of years.'

'They met at the drinks the night before the match,' added Puri. 'Faheem Khan came directly from the airport – his first time in India.'

'Then only she decided to do the needful. Next morning, na, she got hold some aconite.'

'Motive is there but rest is guesswork,' said Puri.

'Come now, Chubby. You know she did this thing.'

'A detective does not go by feelings, Mummy-ji. He goes by facts.'

'Fine. Then let us get them once and for all.'

Mummy stood and crossed the room with swift efficiency, reaching the table where Megha Dogra was now sitting on her own, her husband having gone up to the bar.

'Sorry for the interruption, na, but I would need a word,' said Mummy.

'Do we know one another?' replied Megha Dogra with a gentle, quizzical smile.

'We met long time back, na. It's been some sixty years

in fact.' Mummy switched to Punjabi. 'My name is Koomi Pabla,' she said. 'I was the one who rescued you. From that hole behind his house.'

A look of astonishment swept over Megha Dogra's face, swiftly followed by tender recognition. In an instant, however, this too gave way to perplexity. 'I . . . I . . . don't know what . . . what to say,' she stuttered. 'I think you must have me confused with someone else.'

'No mistake,' said Mummy. 'Now that I'm standing here, I'm sure. You were the one he called Saroya.'

Puri, who'd been caught off guard again by his mother's manoeuvre and had struggled to get up out of his armchair, reached the table. Megha Dogra's eyes moved between the two of them, making the connection. A shadow seemed to pass over her face.

'My son,' explained Mummy, the clarification redundant. 'We've been working together.'

'A most effective team we've made, I must say,' added Puri as he pulled up a chair. 'Indeed, Mummy-ji has been able to offer unique insight into the case. Having been part of events sixty years ago or more, she suspected the motive for Faheem Khan's murder might have to do with his past, not his present. Thus she searched for the woman he abducted in 1947. That trail has led to you, madam.'

'I see,' said Megha Dogra in a diminished tone. 'And you want to see justice done, I take it.'

'That is my duty, madam.'

'And what if I told you that justice has already been done, Mr Puri?' She was looking the detective in the eye, not a hint of remorse or compunction in her voice. 'It may seem cruel now, an old man poisoned in such a way,' she continued. 'But to his victims – and there were many – he was anything but helpless. His punishment was well deserved, let me assure you.'

Mummy and Puri exchanged a long, knowing look. They had their answer. And in that instant, without a word passing between them, they both came to the realisation that proving Megha Dogra's guilt would be impossible. There were no witnesses to her poisoning the butter chicken. No clues left at the scene of the crime. Even the link between the culprit and the victim couldn't be corroborated. It would be her word against theirs.

Still convention dictated – at least in Puri's book – that he should be the one to have the last word.

'Allow me to inform you, madam,' he began, sounding like a seasoned judge summing up in court, 'it is my belief that no one, under any circumstance, has the right to put the law into their own hands. Also, I would wish to state for the record that if the means and all were at my disposal, I would not hesitate for one minute or second, even, to pass the evidence to the proper authorities – in this case the Delhi police.'

Megha Dogra seemed to sense that she should allow him to continue with his homily uninterrupted. She sat with her hands folded in her lap, her chin held in perfect alignment with her straight shoulders, a portrait of calm composure.

'Furthermore,' continued the detective, 'I should like to add that it is my belief that ultimately we must all account for our actions to a high power. Therefore, madam, I leave it for the God to pass judgement at some later

337

date. It is Vish Puri's intention to take the matter no further.'

Megha Dogra acknowledged his words with a gracious nod.

They left her sitting at the table surrounded by celebrating Delhi fans who'd just seen their side add four more runs to the scoreboard.

Puri and Mummy walked solemnly towards the exit. They passed Ram Dogra along the way. 'I wanted to ask if you'd made any progress with the case,' he said.

'Unfortunately, sir, it is very much looking as if we have run into a dead end – too many stale clues and all.'

Puri had come to the conclusion that Ram Dogra was ignorant of his wife's actions and no doubt about her past as well.

'I'm sorry to hear that. You must feel very frustrated,' said the Prince of Polyester.

'Failure is not something I welcome or take lightly, sir. However in my case at least, it is a rare occurrence.' He paused. 'That said, sir, all is not lost.'

'Why's that?'

'No doubt our Delhi Chief of Police is hard at work, so we can all rest easy.'

Ram Dogra's laughter was still ringing in their ears as Mummy and Puri left the stand.

They were about halfway down the stairs when the doors behind them swung open with a bang.

'Koomi, just one minute, please,' pleaded a voice.

Megha Dogra hurried down towards them, her eyes moist with tears. She put her arms around Mummy and gave her a warm, lingering hug.

'I never got a chance to thank you,' she whispered. 'Bless you.' ·

And then she turned and headed back upstairs to her husband – to her life.

• TWENTY-EIGHT •

Puri hadn't slept in his bed for the past two nights and desperately wanted to return home to Rumpi. But there was no escaping work and he spent the next few hours tying up loose ends – most notably identifying Satish Bhatia's hit man, whom Inspector Singh had tracked down of his own volition.

It wasn't until nearly six that Bhatia himself was arrested at Delhi Airport where he'd been trying to board a flight to America, at which point Puri called his client to give him the good news.

'Well done you, Puri! Very well done indeed!' he said.

'Most kind of you, sir,' answered the detective, swelling with pride.

Now seemed like a good time to bring up the cost of the Mercedes Benz that had been written off and the ten lakhs Puri had lost to Full Moon.

'I can never quite get my head around all your lakhs and crores, Puri. How much is that in real money?' asked Scott in response.

The detective gave him an approximate figure in US dollars.

'Aaah . . . right . . . I see.'

'My sincerest apologies, former Deputy Commissioner,' Puri felt compelled to say.

'Yes, well, not to worry, Vish. Send me the bill and I'll get it sorted. Now back to the case. I still don't understand: did Bhatia have Faheem Khan killed or didn't he?'

'Sir, I believe you have what you and your associates wanted all along: the gambling syndicate is exposed for all to see.'

'Absolutely. And like I said, well done you. But you didn't answer my question.'

'Sir, I'd ask that you don't press me on this point. It was a matter of revenge – nothing to do with the world of cricket whatsoever.'

'Surely you're not going to just let it go?'

'Believe me sir, if evidence was to hand I'd not hesitate in pursuing the case. But nothing is there. It was a perfect murder – a perfect butter chicken murder we can say.'

Scott let out an uneasy sigh. 'Well I suppose you've got no argument from me. We'll just have to leave it at that. As far as the match fixing goes, the next step's to inform the IIC, obviously. You'll need to send me all the details. It's going to create a shit storm. Headlines for weeks.'

'Talking of which, sir . . . I regret to inform you that I don't wish my name to be associated with the case.'

'Oh come on, you can't be serious, Vish! You deserve the recognition!'

'Undoubtedly, sir. But it is often the way here in India. Better to remain in the shadows so to speak. Unfortunately this will hardly be the end of betting on cricket, sir. Other bookies and all will step in for sure. People are so obsessed with gambling, actually. And there is no way it can be legalised. Too many special interests involved. Better they don't become aware of my involvement.'

'Well, if that's how you want it . . .'

The detective hung up the phone as Elizabeth Rani entered his office bearing a cup of chai. From his disconsolate expression she guessed that, not for the first time, he wasn't going to be able to take credit for solving a major case. Knowing how much he hungered for recognition, and how much it would pain him not to be able to show up the Dehli police chief, she decided to try to perk him up.

'Sir, I don't know how you do it,' she said. 'There is not another detective in all of India who could have exposed the entire betting business.'

'Thank you, Madam Rani. As usual, you are quite correct. It was a considerable achievement, I must say. But let it not be forgotten that I received valuable assistance along the way. Had Major General Aslam not been good enough to provide me with certain information, then only the God knows where we would be. Just goes to show that in Pakistan, also, there are individuals striving for truth and justice. That is something we would all do well to remember, Madam Rani.'

'Yes, sir.'

Before Scott called, Puri had been in the process of dictating the details of the case to his secretary. This was something the detective always did at the conclusion of an investigation while events were fresh in his mind.

They now picked up where they had left off, with Puri recounting Megha Dogra's words in the VVIP stand.

'Sir, there's one thing you didn't mention,' said Elizabeth Rani when he was finished.

'Tell me.'

'Megha Dogra, the lady who poisoned Faheem Khan. How did she do it exactly?'

'If I was a betting man – and thank the God I am not – I would put money on one of her husband's syringes. He is diabetic. That is not common knowledge by the way. Being a man in his position, he keeps his disease top secret.'

'How did you come to know?'

'His complexion is waxy. That is a sure sign. Yet to be one hundred per cent sure, I got his manservant followed. Yesterday, only, he visited the chemist to pick up a supply – of insulin and syringes.'

'Aconite, also, is readily available,' added Puri. 'But she could not be sure of the dosage. Thus one pooch at Kotla got put out of his misery. And later, at dinner, she added something like double the amount to Faheem's Khan's butter chicken.'

'But how, sir?'

'It was easy, actually. Upon her return from the ladies' room, Megha Dogra found his seat unoccupied. She stopped to do chitchat with Mrs Anita Bhangu. She was wearing a shawl – it being cold outside. Thus when she leaned over the table to pick up something or other, the syringe could not be seen. Injecting the poison took seconds, only.'

Elizabeth Rani shook her head slowly from side to side.

'Personally I don't know whether to sympathise with her or not. She suffered so much . . . and yet to do such a thing . . .'

'It is impossible to fathom, Madam Rani. But that is the human mind, no? An eternal puzzle, we can say.'

Elizabeth Rani saved the case file on her laptop computer and closed the lid.

'I'm afraid there is one other matter for your attention,' she said. 'Your client, one who lost half his moustache, Satya Pal Bhalla . . . he called again today. He's demanding his payment be returned forthwith.'

'Seems I will have to give it to him,' said Puri with a sigh. 'The moustache case has hit a quagmire, actually.'

Handbrake had visited all the five star hotels in Delhi without coming across a newly hired doorman. Calls to the manager of the Palace on Wheels and the Maharaja Express, both luxury trains that employed mustachioed porters, waiters and bearers, had also proven fruitless.

'Thank you, Madam Rani, I would call Bhalla later, only,' said the detective. 'For now, some meter down is required.'

Puri could tell there was something on Handbrake's mind. However, it wasn't until they were halfway to Gurgaon and the detective had finished talking on the phone with Tubelight – and suggested he and the team take some well-earned offs – that the driver spoke up.

'Boss, one thing, I think, perhaps you should know,' he said in Hindi.

Puri's nod in the rearview mirror was encouragement for him to go on.

'You asked me to search for a doorman who'd been hired in the past few days.'

Another nod.

'At one hotel there was a doorman who'd been on leave
– sick leave. He'd come back to work only a few days
back. It's probably not important but—'

'He had a moustache?' demanded Puri, suddenly alert.

'Big one.'

'Which hotel?'

'The Durbar, Boss.'

Puri was struck by a terrible thought. On the night
Faheem Khan was murdered, Mummy had said something
about the Maharani of Alwar staying at the hotel.

'By God! Turn around! Jaldi!'

Handbrake couldn't turn around. By now they were on
the Expressway and there were barriers on either side of
the road. He had to drive three miles to the toll court
and make a U-turn. In the meantime, Puri called the
hotel. He asked for the manager and was put on hold.
For the next ten minutes he had to listen to the muzak
version of 'Greensleeves'. Finally with a frustrated 'Arrey!'
he hung up and called back, insisting the operator connect
him to the front desk.

The concierge who answered said that the manager was
on his break and offered to take a message.

'Tell him the Maharani of Alwar's Golkonda Diamond is
to be looted and he should revert urgently!' shouted Puri.

'Yes, sir, I'll pass it on,' replied the concierge,
nonchalant.

Half an hour later, they pulled up in front of the Durbar.
The front doors were unmanned. Puri found Mummy's
assistant manager friend, Rajneesh, on duty and asked
him about the whereabouts of the doorman.

'He's having his khana, sir. Something is wrong?'

'Could be his moustache is not his own,' explained the detective.

'Pardon?'

'He looted it.'

'Sorry, sir, I'm not sure I understand. You're saying he stole his moustache?'

'Could be.'

Rajneesh looked faintly amused. 'Sir, Shanti Balwa has worked here for some years. He's always had a moustache.'

'It is my understanding he took leaves not long back.'

'That's true, sir. He had some medical issues.'

'Cancer,' said Puri.

'I believe so.'

'He underwent chemotherapy. Thus his hair fell out, moustache included, and he required a new one. It explains the white blotches on his skin, also. At first I thought they had to do with being a barber. Then just this evening, only, I remembered one client from years back. He also underwent cancer treatment and came out in blotches.'

'Right, sir.'

'The Golkonda Diamond is quite secure?' asked Puri.

'Special security is in place. There's no risk.'

Puri thought for a moment. 'Let us clear up this matter once and for all,' he said.

It took Gopal Ragi forty minutes to reach the Durbar. As per Puri's instructions, he alighted from his car across the road from the hotel. Inspector Thakur was also on hand. They both listened to the detective's plan.

'We two, myself and you, sir' – he meant Ragi – 'will proceed to the front door, where I will ask this Shanti Balwa fellow for the honour of posing for a snap with his good self. You, sir' – he meant Ragi again – 'using your portable will play the role of photographer and thus be able to inspect his . . . sorry, the moustache in question. From there we'll proceed into the hotel in an orderly fashion. Assuming Balwa is the one, then, only, I will give one call to you, sir' – he meant Thakur this time – 'and you will make the arrest forthwith.'

'What if he recognises me?' asked Ragi.

'He won't – not without your moustache.'

'Agreed.'

'Tip top.'

Puri and Ragi climbed into the Ambassador and Handbrake drove in through the hotel's gates. Shanti Balwa was standing in front of the doors in his blazing uniform – tall and turbaned and sporting a fine bushy moustache.

It would have been a sharp-eyed aficionado indeed who could have spotted that the handlebar was not 'home-grown. He had shortened its length yet retained the muttonchops. They framed his beaming smile.

'Welcome to the Durbar,' he said, opening Puri's door and giving a courtly bow.

The detective got out and said, 'That's a wonderful moustache. Mind if my friend takes one snap?'

'A pleasure, sir.'

But the moment the Ambassador pulled away, the plan fell apart. Recognising his own facial hair, Ragi shouted, 'That's it! That's my moustache!' And before

Puri could stop him, he'd thrown himself at the doorman.

'Bastard! Give it back!'

Shanti Balwa was knocked to the ground and Ragi tried to tear the moustache from his face. Guests looked on aghast as the two fought and the doorman cursed in the choicest Punjabi. Hotel security came running. The managers came running. Inspector Thakur and his jawans came running.

Bloody and bruised, the two men were separated and the doorman was handcuffed and led away.

Puri caught up with Shanti Balwa a few minutes later. By then he was sitting in the back of Inspector Thakur's jeep weeping like a child. The moustache hung half off his upper lip.

'I wasn't after any jewels,' he protested in Hindi when Puri accused him of planning to rob the Maharani of Alwar. 'I just wanted to keep my job. Without a moustache I was finished. I've never stolen anything before in my life. I just thought those men could grow new ones, unlike me, so what was the harm?'

'And the ransom demand?'

'I had nothing to do with that! Someone else must have got the idea of making some money.'

An opportunist. It made sense.

'Please understand, sir. When I got cancer and had to have the treatment, all my hair fell out. If the hotel had found out, they wouldn't have taken me back. They don't care about us, sir. They don't give us any job security or insurance.'

He started to sob again. 'This job is everything to me, sir. I plan to pass it on to my son when he's old enough. He's growing his own moustache these days. Please help me, sir. Make the police understand.'

The detective left him sitting there and went and found Thakur. He'd impounded Balwa's scooter; the number plate ended in a goose and two snakes.

'This one is no arch-criminal,' Puri told him.

'He did breaking and entering – kidnapping and assault, also.'

'Correct, Inspector, and it is only right and proper he should face punishment. But some compassion should be there. This man underwent treatment for cancer. Then he lost his hair and his job, also. What with inflation and all, such people are getting desperate, no? Such jobs are few and far between. And what with inflation, the cost of living is on the up and up. I believe we would be seeing more crime not less in the coming days and years.'

'A thief is a thief whether he steals a diamond or a cucumber,' said Thakur. 'Now, I had better get this one to the station.'

Puri noticed a couple of TV crews racing towards them, microphones held at the ready. He groaned. 'Typical,' he said under his breath. 'The one case I don't wish to be associated with and . . .'

'Mr Vish Puri, saar!' called out a reporter. 'Is it true you tracked down the moustache thief?'

The detective straightened up, adjusted his Sandown cap and faced the lights.

'It is my honour to report the following only: this

evening Dilli citizens sporting long moustaches can rest easy thanks to Vish Puri,' he stated.

Rumpi had prepared *kadhi chawal*. As they ate together in the kitchen, he told her about his experiences in Pakistan and how he'd come to see the country and its people sympathetically; about the invaluable role her father, Brigadier Mattu, had played in solving the case; and about Mummy's extraordinary past and how, after all these years, she'd finally spoken about the death of her brother.

It was late and the food long gone by the time Rumpi broached the subject of a break. The weather was beginning to improve and soon the mountain passes would be open. They should make the pilgrimage to Vaishno Devi, she suggested.

'It's been so long since we went away, Chubby. And you're looking so tired. I worry about you.'

'You are right, my dear. So much work has been there, actually. The pilgrimage would be just the ticket.'

Rumpi made tea and they sat together in the living room for a while watching TV. The news was dominated by the arrest of Satish Bhatia. Graphics pulsated and flashed, excited newsreaders and reporters verbally climaxed, and pundits pontificated.

An *Action News!* anchorwoman said she could 'reveal' that two 'unidentified' players were facing 'possible' match-fixing charges. An umpire was also 'said' to be involved.

'An umpire?' asked Rumpi.

'Australian one,' answered Puri.

'Did Daddy figure that out?'

'That was my doing, actually. This Australian fellow was giving signals to the batsman with his feet. Right foot pointing out meant no ball and so forth. Seems he was on the payroll. Now you know what will happen to him, my dear?'

'No, Chubby, what?'

Puri smiled, raising both hands in the air simultaneously as he prepared to deliver his punchline. 'He will most definitely be going *down under*!'

Rumpi burst out laughing. 'Not g'day, mate, but *goodbye*, mate,' she added in a poor excuse for an Aussie accent.

They watched one of the many Indian soap operas for a while before turning in.

'By the way, Chubby, Dr Mohan called today checking on your progress,' she said as they reached the top of the stairs. 'We haven't weighed you in over a week. I'll get out the scales now.'

Puri felt his heart skip a beat. He'd meant to come upstairs and take care of the scales the moment he returned home, but the smell of the cooking had distracted him.

'Surely it can wait until tomorrow, my dear,' he said. 'So tired I am.'

'Knowing you, Chubby, you'll be off tomorrow on another case and I won't see you for days. Now come. Stand here so I can see.'

Puri looked down at the scales, hoping for the best. He put one foot on the pressure pad, then the other.

The needle reached 90 and held. Rumpi peered down at the dial.

'No change,' she said.

There came a creak, followed by a twang as the peg shot out of the mechanism across the floor.

She picked it up, examined it, and looked back down at the dial. It now registered 91.5 kilos.

Her eyes narrowed and then a shrill cry carried through the house and, no doubt, across half the neighbourhood.

'Chuuu-bbyyyyyyy!'